THE FIRST BODY

Goode's eyes followed the ivory feet up a pair of long legs to see it was not a mannequin, but the crumpled body of a raven-haired young woman, stunning even in death. Goode kneeled down to take a closer look. She didn't smell very fresh, but it was hard to tell with the heat. She was wearing a man's shirt, white with red pinstripes. And nothing else. Her lower abdomen was marked with purple blotches, as if two hands had grabbed her and squeezed. Her neck was bruised and patches of skin were ripped away, as if she'd been strangled. The red fingernails on one hand were ragged at the ends, like they'd been broken off during a struggle. But this was no skanky tweaker. He could tell by her hair, nails, and skin that she ate well and had recently had a manicure-pedicure. She was also well-toned, her hair looked highlighted and styled, and her shirt was a Ralph Lauren. It was clear she came from money and attracted men of the same ilk.

The kid suddenly reached out to touch the girl's shirt, but Goode grabbed his wrist before he could make contact.

"Don't touch anything," Goode said. "This is a crime scene now...."

CAITLIN ROTHER

NAKED ADDICTION

LEISURE BOOKS NEW YORK CITY

A LEISURE BOOK®

November 2007

Published by

Dorchester Publishing Co., Inc.
200 Madison Avenue
New York, NY 10016

ISBN 10: 0-8439-5995-9
ISBN 13: 978-0-8439-5995-6

Visit us on the web at www.dorchesterpub.com.

NAKED ADDICTION

Chapter One

Goode
Sunday

It was one of those hot September days when flies flock to the sweet scent of coconut-oiled skin and the rotting smell of death.

Santa Ana winds were spreading their evil dust and waves of heat were oozing from exhaust pipes, casting a blur over the gridlock of cars ahead of Detective Ken Goode. Santa Anas always made him feel a little off.

Sweat dripped into his tired eyes as he sat in his Volkswagen van, waiting for the light to change on Mission Boulevard in Pacific Beach. He'd stayed up too late the night before reading Camus' *An Absurd Reasoning*, pausing intermittently to deconstruct the state of his life. He needed a mind-bending career change. He felt it coming, any day in fact, just around the corner. But patience wasn't one of his strongest traits. He wanted out of undercover narcotics and into a permanent gig working homicides. Not just as a relief detective, as he'd been for the past three years, but the real thing. The only questions were how and when.

Goode always took stock at this time of year and he was rarely satisfied. After getting the green light, he drove a few blocks to a flower shop he'd passed a hundred times. He was constantly on the lookout for florists because he didn't want to go to the same one twice. He chose to keep his annual ritual to himself, even more private than the rest of his rather solitary existence.

Goode parked near the door and glanced at himself in the rearview mirror, running his fingers through his sun-bleached brown hair and wiping moisture from his forehead with a beach towel. His green eyes had been red around the edges since the Santa Ana kicked up and he hadn't been sleeping much either, although that wasn't unusual lately.

The cool air inside the shop chilled his overheated skin, making the hairs on his arms stand up. Inside the refrigerated case nearest the door, a few dozen long-stemmed red roses poked their heads out of a white bucket of water. He slid open the door and bent his tall, lean frame over to inspect them more closely. He wanted the most perfect one he could find, just starting to bloom. He selected one from the middle, sliding it carefully out of the bunch.

"How would you like a pretty bud vase for that?" the sales girl chirped. She was a teenager. Bright-eyed. Hopeful.

"No, thank you," Goode told her. He knew she meant well, but she had no idea. "That won't be necessary."

She looked a little disappointed. "Then how 'bout you let me wrap it up with some baby's breath?"

"Sure," he said, smiling weakly and nodding. He didn't want to have to tell her that wouldn't be necessary either. "That would be nice."

The cellophane crinkled as he walked back to the van and gingerly laid the rose on the passenger seat. He turned right on Grand Avenue and headed south on Interstate 5 toward Coronado.

He still remembered how green and sparkly the bay had looked that day thirty years ago. He'd just turned six. He, his mother, father and baby sister had finished a lunch of tuna sandwiches together at their small, rented house in La Jolla—all two high school teachers could afford—when his mother announced she was going for a drive. His father, Ken Sr., said he'd planned to take a nap while the baby took hers and asked if she'd take Kenny Jr. with her. She looked a little irritated and a little sad, so Kenny thought she didn't want him to come along. When she looked over at him and saw she'd upset him, she gave him that forced melancholy smile she'd been wearing of late and tousled his hair.

"Okay, then," she said quietly. "Let's go."

The two of them piled into the family's Honda Accord and she stopped at Baskin Robbins to buy him a Pralines-and-Cream cone and a strawberry shake for herself. She took a prescription vial of pink pills out of her purse and popped one of them into her mouth, chasing it with a long draw on her shake. She announced that she wanted to drive over the new bridge to Coronado.

"You can see forever up there," she said. "It feels like you can just fly off into the clouds. Don't you think?"

Kenny nodded happily, feeling privileged to have some one-on-one time with his mother. She'd been acting so down since Maureen was born. She hardly ever wanted to play with him. It felt nice when she talked to him like that.

They were about halfway across the bridge, where the two lanes turned into three, when she pulled over to the side and told him to wait. He watched her get out of the car in her black dress, the one with the bright red roses and green leaves all over it. She stepped out of her red pumps and reached through the driver's-side window to set them on the seat next to him, giving him that same droopy smile again. The skin around her eyes wrinkled softly, reflecting a sense of tragedy that made her seem older than her thirty-six years.

"It's dangerous out here, so stay buckled up, okay, pumpkin?" she said.

He'd watched her put on some red lipstick before they left the house, and he thought again how it set off the whiteness of her very straight teeth. She was so much more beautiful than any of his friends' mothers. It made him proud.

Kenny took her words as the law, never questioning why she'd parked where there was no shoulder. With his seat belt fastened as instructed, he watched the cars whizzing by and wondered where she'd gone. Strapped in and helpless, he couldn't see into the rearview mirror without undoing his belt. Surely she wouldn't be gone for long. Finally, he undid the buckle and twisted the mirror so he could see behind the car. There she was, gazing intently out into the distance. He carefully refastened the seat belt, feeling guilty as it clicked home.

Minutes later, he still couldn't shake the feeling of apprehension, so he looked into the mirror again. This time he saw her throw one leg over the railing, and then the other. What was she doing? Then, in one quick movement, she dropped herself over the edge.

For a while there, he was sure she'd climb right back over the top of the railing. When she didn't reappear, the ice cream began to curdle in his stomach and his heart began to pound.

It seemed like hours that he sat there, waiting for her, when a police cruiser pulled up behind the car. A young officer slowly approached, his hand on his gun, and stuck his head through the open window.

"Where are your parents, son?" he asked.

But all Kenny could do was stare straight ahead, his fists clenched so tightly his nails bit into his palms. He knew he would start crying if he met the officer's questioning gaze. He figured what the man really wanted to know was why he hadn't tried to stop his mother from jumping into the nothingness.

The officer went back to his cruiser for a minute to talk into his radio; then he got in the car with Kenny while they waited for a tow truck to arrive. He put his arm around the boy's shoulders and made Kenny feel safe enough to convey the bare facts of what had happened and to obediently recite his home address. The officer patiently walked Kenny back to the police cruiser and took him home to what was left of his family.

From that day on, Ken Goode knew he wanted to be a policeman.

Goode drove a little more than halfway over the bridge before he reached the spot where his mother had jumped. He pulled to the side, turned on his hazard lights and unwound the rubber band holding the cellophane together, easing the stem out of its casing. He brought the bud to his nose and breathed in its sweet fullness. He felt a stab of the old pain and his eyes teared up. He was feeling really tired and vulnerable for some reason. But that was okay. He'd allow himself that, for a few minutes at least. Maybe it was just the hot wind blowing the hair into his eyes.

He stood at the railing facing north. To his left was the small island city of Coronado and to his right were the blue steel towers of the bridge, curving around to the San Diego marina and downtown skyscape. He tried to push the hair out of his face so he could take in the view, but it was useless. He could only look down.

Goode began his ritual of tearing off the rose petals, one at a time, and watching them catch the breeze. It always amazed him what a long way down it was to the bay. He looked it up on the Internet once and learned it was a two-hundred-foot drop. Sometimes he'd start to wonder how much the fall would hurt from this height, but he'd immediately push the thought from his brain. He wouldn't go there. Couldn't go there.

"How are you, Mom?" he said into the wind. "Are you happy?"

A seagull swooped out of the sky, settled on the railing a few feet away, and looked right at him. Part of the bird's upper beak was chipped off. He found its proximity a little unnerving and he wondered for a second whether that could possibly be his mother. He wasn't a religious man, but he did get spiritual from time to time. It couldn't be, he thought. That's ridiculous. He turned away and watched the sun reflect off the ripples in the San Diego Bay.

"What's it like where you are?" he asked. "Do you have friends?"

A few moments later, a second seagull touched down on the railing, right next to the first. Goode really didn't believe in the whole New Age thing, but this seemed a little weird, even to him. He broke the stamen from the rose and tossed it over, watching it float down.

"Okay, if this is real," he said into the wind, "then show me one more sign."

One of the cars whipping past honked. He felt the wind pick up and blow his hair out of his eyes. It was a little cooler, there by the ocean. He closed his eyes and let the breeze kiss his face. But then, abruptly, it . . . just . . . stopped . . . blowing. The high-pitched traffic noise dulled and he felt a strange calm. Soon, beads of sweat began to form on his upper lip. He started feeling woozy.

He heard the crunch of tires on asphalt and turned to see a police cruiser park behind his van. Just like the first time. A young officer in his midtwenties approached with his hand on his gun. It could have been the son of the officer who'd stopped there thirty years ago.

Goode shivered. "No shit," he whispered. He smiled and shook his head.

"Everything okay here? You know you can't park your van on the bridge," the officer said, sticking his chest out with more than enough bravado. Bulletproof vests always made cops seem more macho than they really were.

Strangely enough, Goode hadn't had to deal with Coronado police much during his yearly ceremony, usually because he did it in the middle of the night when traffic was light to nonexistent. He figured he'd tell his fellow officer the truth.

Goode extended his hand to shake the officer's. "Ken Goode, San Diego PD," he said, retrieving his badge from his shorts pocket. "Just checking in with my mother. She jumped here thirty years ago today."

The officer gave him a firm shake, but his eyes softened and he relaxed into a less aggressive stance. "Joe Johnston, Coronado PD," he said. "Wow. That's rough." Johnston paused and shook his head as if he didn't know what else to say. "Well, I guess I'll . . . hang out here in my cruiser for a few minutes to make sure no one bothers you. Take your time."

Goode thanked him. He wasn't sure what it all meant, but he felt as if his mother was okay, wherever she was. Maybe she was a teacher there, too. Or maybe she'd become a painter like she'd always dreamed. He threw the rose stem over the side and watched it swing idly down to the water, coming to rest on the surface and bob along with the current. He wiped a tear from his cheek with his sleeve.

"See you next time," he whispered.

Goode waved thanks to the officer and drove the rest of the bridge to Coronado so he could make a U-turn and head back to a quiet surfing spot he liked in Bird Rock, the neighborhood between La Jolla proper and Pacific Beach. He longed to get out of his head and into the glassy tube of a six-footer, his surfboard cutting through the water as if he were Moses. He'd been so busy he hadn't been able to paddle out for the past week. Surfing was his primary stress outlet and going without it for long made him feel like he was coming out of his skin. A lack of positive ions or something.

He'd been ordered by the brass to do some weekend

catch-up work at the station, but he liked typing up reports about as much as scrubbing the bathtub. His talent for procrastination had been fully engaged that morning, most of which he'd spent at an outdoor café, enjoying the slow creep of heightened awareness that came with two café lattes and the Sunday *New York Times*. He felt twice as smart when he finished, although he knew enough to credit the fickle embrace of caffeine. He figured he'd do his personal business, get some surf time, and then run down to headquarters later in the afternoon. But first things first. He *was* feeling a little rundown. The Narcotics-Homicide double duty he'd been doing over the past few years was taking its toll. It was worth it, though, and a necessary step toward making the move. He really felt he belonged in Homicide; he had a calling for it. He'd paid his dues and he was ready, right on the brink. He could feel it.

Mission Boulevard was still gridlocked. To his right, a twenty-something brunette with long legs sauntered along the sidewalk, holding up her hair to cool her neck. The white nape beckoned to him. She recognized him, then smiled and waved, as if she had nothing but time to get to a destination unknown—with him, if he wanted. Goode grinned and waved back. They'd met at José's Cantina in La Jolla a few weeks back. Jennie was her name. She'd told him he was smart and sexy. Why didn't he have a girlfriend? He told her he liked being alone. He'd tried marriage and it didn't work out. He also recalled thinking he could really use some human contact. It had been too long, so long that he almost couldn't remember what it felt like to have a soft, warm body like hers curled around him in the middle of the night. But he'd resisted. This time, he almost gave in to the impulse, opened his door and asked if she wanted to join him for a beer.

That's when his rational mind took over. Even though she seemed like an innocent waif, he knew only too well that his picker was broken and that before long, she was sure to turn into another roller coaster ride. Then, as if to close the matter, he felt that queasy feeling come back and a stab of the old pain—the other old pain, that is.

"You've been doing so well," he said to himself in the rearview mirror, trying not to move his lips so people wouldn't see him talking to himself. "Don't blow it now."

Even after his divorce, he still seemed to attract the women with the most baggage: the neurotic and the narcissistic, the closet alcoholics and the prescription-drug abusers. He began dating to distract himself from the hurt he felt when his wife, Miranda, left him. Again. But one distraction led to another and his life became a bad game of dominos. So he developed the discipline he needed to stay celibate. At least it kept one part of his life simple. It kept his mind clear, which freed him up to focus on his career.

He'd had it with the traffic and was honking at the lowrider in front of him when he saw an opening. He cranked the wheel, hit the gas, and cut into an alley parallel to the beach, his tires squealing. It felt good to catch a little speed and the cool air that came with it.

He glanced at his watch to see how much time he could spare before he could expect a second call from his sergeant in Narcotics, telling him to get his lazy ass in gear on the paperwork. When he looked up again, something small and brown had come out of nowhere. His van was almost on top of it before he could tell what it was—one of those damned rat-dogs. He swerved to avoid it and practically put his foot through the floorboard trying to stop.

"Stupid dog," Goode yelled as his van careened toward a row of black trash bins and a young guy who was crouched down, examining something between the cans. Goode's brakes screeched as his van came to a halt just a few feet short of him. He was a stocky guy in his early twenties, a little heavyset and not all that tall, with short dark hair and big dark eyes, wearing a baseball cap backwards. Goode guessed he was probably of Italian or Greek origin. The kid's face conveyed a whole spectrum of emotions, only one of which was relief that he hadn't been flattened by a VW van.

Goode sat for a minute, took a deep breath, and let it out. He'd almost killed a guy, trying to avoid a dog. He was shaking his head when he noticed a pair of ivory feet with red toenails sticking out from between the bins next to the guy's checkerboard-patterned Vans skateboarding shoes. Was that a mannequin . . . or a body?

"Hey, sorry. Are you okay?" Goode asked as he hopped out of his van and walked toward him. The kid's eyes were dark brown, with long lashes, and he had a curiously inscrutable expression on his face.

"I thought you were going to run me over," the kid replied, smiling a little as he squinted up at Goode, who had the sun behind him. "My life flashed before my eyes, the whole deal. I was cruising down the alley when I found her," he said, nodding at his skateboard, lying wheels-up a few feet away.

Goode's eyes followed the ivory feet up a pair of long legs to see it was not a mannequin, but the crumpled body of a raven-haired young woman, stunning even in death. Goode kneeled down to take a closer look. She didn't smell very fresh, but it was hard to tell with the heat. She was wearing a man's shirt, white with red pinstripes. And nothing else. Her lower abdomen was marked with purple blotches, as if two hands had grabbed her and squeezed. Her neck was bruised and patches of skin were ripped away, as if she'd been strangled. The red fingernails on one hand were ragged at the ends, like they'd been broken off during a struggle. But this was no skanky tweaker. He could tell by her hair, nails, and skin that she ate well and had recently had a manicure-pedicure. She was also well toned, her hair looked highlighted and styled, and her shirt was a Ralph Lauren. It was clear she came from money and attracted men of the same ilk.

Goode sensed something familiar about this girl. He felt one of those jolts where a memory creased his consciousness and then dissipated like the trail of a firework. But he couldn't get it back. Something was blocking the image. The alley was quiet and still for a moment as time seemed to stop. The sun was beating down on his head. He felt dizzy again, like he had on the bridge.

The kid suddenly reached out to touch the girl's shirt, but Goode grabbed his wrist before he could make contact. His skin was all sweaty, and his face was flushed, too, which was not that surprising on such a hot day.

"Don't touch anything," Goode said. "This is a crime scene now."

A puzzled expression crossed the guy's face, as if the cylinders in his head were running but he didn't quite know what to say.

"What?" Goode asked. "You touched her already?"

The kid nodded, reluctantly. "Yeah, I don't know, I've never seen a dead person before. It was weird. Her cheek felt like a cold peach. Then I got freaked out by her eyes. They were this amazing turquoise blue, staring at nothing. So I closed them."

Goode stood up and pulled the guy to his feet, up and away from the body. "Let's talk over here," Goode said. "I'm a police detective."

The guy came willingly. When they reached the other side of the alley, about fifteen feet from the body, he still had that confused look on his face, but it looked a little more like fear than it had initially.

"I'm not in any trouble, am I?" he asked.

It was too soon to tell. Goode didn't get a killer vibe off him, but since he had been right there with the body, he was a natural suspect. And Goode had learned long ago that oftentimes a murderer came with no identifiable marks. You had to go deeper. Pretty much everyone he met for the next couple of days would be a suspect.

"You tell me," Goode said, staring into his eyes. The

guy had regained his composure and stared back. Then he started smiling again, which Goode found to be an odd response given the circumstances. "What's so amusing?"

"So, you're a cop?" he replied, shaking his head.

Goode noted that he answered his question with a question, a useful deflection technique if the other person doesn't notice.

"Yes, I am. Appearances can be deceiving."

"No joke," the kid retorted.

"What's your name?" Goode asked.

"Jake Lancaster."

"You have any ID on you, Jake Lancaster?"

Jake pulled a canvas wallet out of his back pocket and ripped open the Velcro flap to reveal his driver's license, which said he was twenty-three. Goode saw a student ID card in the wallet, from the University of California, San Diego. So he was no dummy. UCSD was a tough school. Goode had gone there a couple of semesters before transferring to UCLA.

"What are you studying up there?" Goode asked, hoping Jake would show his true colors.

Jake said he was in the biochemistry master's program. He'd applied to medical school but had been rejected, so he was going for a little "extra credit" to juice up his next round of applications.

"I know what you're thinking," Jake said, smiling mischievously and pointing at his shoes. "Appearances *can* be deceiving."

"You're Italian, aren't you?"

"Yeah, on my mother's side," Jake said, grinning. "How'd you know?"

"Just a feeling."

Goode was trying to make a subtle point that being a good detective meant he could sense things based on little or no information. He only hoped that Jake was as smart as he seemed, so that he would pick up on it. He told Jake to wait while he notified the Homicide unit.

Goode didn't want Jake disappearing while he was making the call, so he made sure to keep his tone suspicion-free.

"We're going to need to get a statement from you, Mr. Lancaster," Goode said as he started walking toward the van. Then he turned, paused, and said, "By the way, did you know her?"

Jake looked him straight in the eye, almost as if he knew he needed to show he was honest and sincere or he might end up as a case of wrong place, wrong time. Maybe he got Goode's point after all.

"Not really," Jake said. "I had just found her when you found me."

"Don't go anywhere," Goode said, as he got into his van and rolled up the window so Jake couldn't hear his conversation. Goode didn't want him to know that he was still a relief homicide detective, without a whole lot of pull. As Goode rummaged around on the passenger seat for his cell phone, he looked back over at those red toenails and flashed on the girl's beautiful face. She was so young. She couldn't have been more than twenty-four herself, about the same age as Jake. What a waste.

He found his cell phone and started punching in the numbers, glancing over his shoulder and around the alley as he waited for Sergeant Stone to pick up. He didn't want anyone or anything else to pollute the crime scene.

Rusty Stone was a surfing buddy who had been telling Goode for the past decade what a great homicide detective he'd make. He'd helped Goode land the prestigious relief job, and then tried to grease the way for him to get the experience he needed to get the transfer.

"It's showtime, buddy," Goode said when Stone answered. The sergeant had been napping in his backyard hammock and was still a little groggy. But the news perked him right up.

Stone told Goode to call the watch commander and report finding the body while he called the homicide lieutenant, Doug Wilson, to see if Goode could work with the team that was up in the rotation, especially since he'd already gotten a leg up on the investigation. In the meantime, Stone told him not to let Jake leave without giving a full statement. He also told Goode to ask dispatch to run a quick criminal check on the kid and make sure he didn't have any outstanding warrants.

"I'm on it," Goode said.

Goode called the watch commander and then dispatch. Jake came back clean. He tucked the cell phone into his pocket and watched Jake play with the rat-dog. Goode's body was flooded with so much adrenaline he could hardly think straight. He didn't want to do anything wrong. It was too important. He took another deep breath and let it out slowly. Down boy, he told himself. He had to show Stone and Wilson he could do this.

For months now he'd been thinking he couldn't take one more night of buying crystal meth undercover in Ocean Beach. So this was it. His big chance to get the hell out of Narcotics. But self-interest aside, he really did want to know what had driven someone to kill such a beautiful girl. Unless, of course, her beauty was reason enough.

Chapter Two

Goode

Goode told Jake to wait while he moved the van up the alley a ways.

"Just stay out of the way," Goode said. "We don't need you polluting the crime scene any further."

He wasn't out of undercover work yet and didn't want to be recognized or associated with his van by anyone else. So he parked it in an unobtrusive spot behind the apartment complex next door. He shook off his flip-flops and pulled on his Nike tennis shoes, without socks as usual.

During his seven years with the LAPD and his eight with the San Diego PD, Goode had certainly seen his share of the dead. Drug dealers sprawled on their apartment floors near the beach, track marks up and down their bruised arms. Homeless junkies, their skin so dirty he wondered if it would ever come clean. He found it curious that people thought the longer you're a cop, the easier it got to handle finding a dead body. Well, it didn't. Especially when it was hot out, accelerating decomposition. Even so, finding this young woman felt different. He couldn't figure out what it was about her that hit him so hard and so deep.

Goode was leaning against a garage door, running through the gamut of possible events that could have led to her being dumped in the alley, when the television news crews started pulling up in their vans with monster satellite dishes on top. The patrol cars rolled up as well, and officers began cordoning off the area with yellow tape.

Soon the alley was also swarming with reporters, cameramen and tripods as tall as people. Goode tried to duck behind a stairwell, but one of the reporters spotted him and asked him to do an on-camera interview. The guy said he'd heard from one of the patrolmen that Goode was the one who'd found the body, and that Goode was wearing shorts and a T-shirt that said SURFERS DO IT IN WAVES because he was off-duty.

"Not exactly," Goode said.

Following protocol, he told the reporter to talk to the sergeant, who had just shown up. Stone nodded at Goode to join him down the alley, where he told Goode that he was officially on the case.

"It's showtime, indeed," Stone said.

The stars must be aligned, he said, because virtually all the homicide teams were already busy working active cases. On top of that, three members on the team up in the rotation had gone camping together and had come down with some nasty virus and/or poison ivy, leaving only one healthy detective, Ted Byron. His wife was eight-and-a-half months pregnant, so he hadn't been able to go on the trip.

Stone and the lieutenant came to an agreement: The more experienced Byron would take the lead on the primary crime scene in the alley, while Goode, under Stone's close supervision, would have the unusual honor of taking the lead on the rest of the investigation, coordinating with two other relief detectives, Ray Slausson and Andy Fletcher.

This way, Stone said, Goode would get a chance to dig deeper and for longer than usual, really show what he could do and see if he was truly Homicide-worthy. One of the detectives was about to retire, so a spot would be opening up in a couple of months. Stone also said he would talk to Goode's sergeant in Narcotics and see if he could get him freed up from his regular duties for a week or so.

Goode was so excited it almost hurt. "I owe you about ten beers," he said.

"And don't think I won't be collecting them," Stone said, slapping him on the shoulder.

Goode knew the two other relief detectives by name and face only. They seemed like good guys, but he had never worked with them. Each was five to eight years younger than him, not to mention much newer to homicide relief duty. Previously, Stone had little to say about them, which either meant they hadn't screwed up any cases or he didn't know their work very well, so they, too, were in the proving stage. Slausson was a San Diego native, a graduate of San Diego State University and currently was working out of the Robbery division. Fletcher was originally from the Washington, D.C., area, where his father had worked some hush-hush intelligence job in the Department of Justice. His current post was in the Special Investigations unit, which coordinated with the FBI and other law enforcement agencies. Goode felt pretty lucky not to have been stuck with some of the other relief guys, who carried too much of the asshole gene.

Goode felt elbows in his back and side, and stepped back to make way for the television crews as they formed a circle around the sergeant, closing in like buzzards. He chuckled as Stone shuffled around, stepping over electrical cords and dodging his own share of elbows. Typically, the TV reporters would shout questions until the pack relinquished the floor to the reporter with the most personally intrusive or obtuse query. That afternoon was no different.

A hair-sprayed blond man with an open collar and no tie started the volley: "So, there was a murder here last night?"

"Ohhh, probing question," Goode whispered.

Goode scanned the scene and saw Rhona Chen from Channel 10, one of the more seasoned TV reporters. Talk about an oxymoron. But at least she got most of her facts straight. She was wearing a bright pink suit, a white silk blouse, and a string of pearls. Goode remembered the last time he saw her. Her legs were wrapped around a cop outside Denny's at about three a.m. a while back. He hadn't seen her in the flesh since, but he'd always had warm thoughts about her when he saw her on TV. Ready Rhona, he called her.

Stone made a very brief statement: "A young woman was found dead in this alley a few hours ago. As you can see, Homicide is investigating and we will issue a press release at some point today. That's all I can say for now."

Goode couldn't help but smirk. He knew damn well that the other homicide detectives hadn't arrived yet and there would be no press release until the lieutenant was good and ready. And that would be later. Much later.

Cops were usually careful around TV reporters, who were known among the ranks for going on the air without knowing what they're talking about, quoting sources who didn't know any better, and speculating a whole lot.

"You people are always jumping the gun," Goode muttered, louder than he'd intended. Unfortunately, Pretty Boy had heard him.

"So she was shot?" he piped up. Goode pictured him with a VACANCY sign hanging from his neck.

"Talk to the sergeant," Goode snapped.

"Didn't you just say she was jumped by a guy with a gun?" he asked.

Goode shook his head in disgust and walked away before he smacked the guy in his veneered teeth. Goode wouldn't be surprised to hear a teaser for the news that night as a result of his little quip: "Young woman shot in an alley in Pacific Beach. Story at eleven."

Goode had always liked newspaper reporters better than their TV competitors. The television infotainment crowd seemed to live only for blood, gore, and anything on fire. And they had bad manners to boot.

After Stone's briefing, the TV crews—pissed at the cops for withholding information—moved their tripods as close as they could to the yellow tape to do their live shots. By that time, the evidence tech had arrived. She was measuring the scene and taking photos, providing the perfect backdrop for the cameras.

Byron, Slausson, and Fletcher had arrived by then, too, so they all huddled up while Stone explained the team arrangement to everyone. He told Slausson and Fletcher to stay clear of the crime scene, while Byron looked around the alley to see if the girl's wallet or the rest of her clothes turned up anywhere. Once the Medical Examiner's Office showed up and moved the victim, Stone said, Byron and the evidence tech could go through the trash bins.

Goode told Stone he was going to fetch the building

manager to see if the victim had lived in the complex, and if not, if he or she could identify the body. Hopefully, the victim had been a tenant and they could start going through her apartment.

Goode said he needed a minute in the shade to cool off, but what he really wanted was a chance to pull his thoughts together. He pulled out a dog-eared, yellowed photo from his wallet. It was just as he'd suspected. Although the victim was at least a decade younger, she bore an uncanny resemblance to his mother. His father had taken the picture at his sixth birthday party, a week before she jumped off the bridge. Kenny Jr. was standing by her side as she held his newborn sister swaddled in a blanket. She'd named the baby Maureen, only she pronounced it "Marine." His mother had the same long, dark hair as the dead girl, so silky that everyone wanted to touch it. And from what Jake said, she apparently had the same bright blue eyes, too.

"Hey, Goode. Let's go," Stone yelled from down the alley. "Time's a wastin'."

Goode shook his head and sighed. This was no time for deep thinking and reliving his past. A rivulet of sweat ran down his spine. It was so damn hot out, yet he felt a chill. He tucked the photo back into its hiding place. He'd just turned thirty-six, the same age his mother had been when she died.

Mrs. Lacey, the manager, was a statuesque African-American woman, about forty years old. She looked annoyed when she opened her door, but she lightened up after Goode smiled and introduced himself.

She had a very soft and warm handshake and a nice way about her. She motioned for him to sit on the couch and said she would get him some coffee to freshen up the cold cup the patrol officers had handed him. The brew she poured was thick and strong, almost like espresso.

Mrs. Lacey seemed a little stiff, even formal, at first. Her head was wrapped in a loud, flowery silk scarf that teetered between tacky and trendy and matched the pattern on the loose-fitting housedress she was wearing. Her skin was so smooth and tight it looked like marble. She started making small talk in a throaty voice, and Goode's eyes glazed over as he fixated on what sounded like a Jamaican accent. Hypnotized by the cadence of her voice, he snapped to when she asked a question that ended with his name.

"Could I ask you to come outside and do a very difficult but very important job for us?" he replied, having no idea what she'd asked. He explained that he needed her to try to identify the body of the victim, and if she'd been a tenant, to tell the police which apartment was hers.

The woman lit a long brown cigarette she pulled from a pack on the kitchen counter. She took a powerful drag from it and that slogan, "You've come a long way, baby," popped into Goode's head.

Mrs. Lacey said she'd be happy to help. She let him guide her outside to the alley, where he motioned for Byron and Stone to come over to hear the possible ID. She took one look at the girl's face, gasped and grimaced, and ran across the alley, where she threw up into the bushes. She asked if they could go back into the courtyard to talk so she didn't have to look at the body.

For a moment, Goode felt like he was in Miami Beach, surrounded by salmon-colored stucco walls and doors painted teal. The complex was square and open in the center; the courtyard was broken up by a small Japanese fountain and a series of wooden planters filled with those hideous tropical plants with long pointy leaves and orange shoots that pass for flowers. If the tenants didn't shut their curtains, he was sure they could see into their neighbors' living rooms. It was an exhibitionist's dream and a recluse's nightmare.

By the looks of the economy cars in the parking lot

and the surfboards stacked against the walls in the courtyard, Goode figured most of the tenants were college students in their midtwenties. A couple of young blond girls wearing shorts and bikini tops were huddled outside one of the ground-floor apartments, speaking in low voices except for the occasional, "Oh, my God, I know."

He and Mrs. Lacey sat on a bench in front of the fountain, which was burbling and full of green algae.

"Her name was Tania Marcus. Apartment three-oh-four," she said finally. "She'd only just moved here from Los Angeles a little over a month ago. I can't believe it."

"What did you know about her?" Goode asked.

"I hardly knew her, and, well, I don't spy on my tenants. But now that you mention it, I did notice she had a lot of company. Mostly men, but a woman or two as well. The way she dressed, I could tell she was a party girl. She was very pretty, and very polite."

"Did you see anyone with her this weekend?" he asked.

Mrs. Lacey said she couldn't remember anyone in particular; she'd been a bit distracted by some personal issues she didn't want to talk about.

Goode asked for a key to the victim's apartment and a list of tenants, both of which she produced after disappearing into her apartment for a few minutes. He gave the key to Byron and then volunteered to talk to the third-floor tenants, including Tania's next-door neighbor, Paul Walters. The apartment on the other side was vacant. Fletcher agreed to canvass the first floor, while Slausson took the second.

"Are you Detective Goode?" a male voice with a New Jersey accent asked while Goode was scanning the tenant list to see if he recognized any names from his narcotics busts. He looked up to see a guy in his late twenties, wearing wire-rimmed glasses with black ink smudges on his face, presumably from where he'd tried to wipe the sweat off after reading the newspaper. He was holding a spiral notebook. Another reporter Goode couldn't trust.

Goode felt the urge to tweak him, see if he could take it. He gestured with the back of his hand at the guy's face and smiled. "You must be with the *Sun-Dispatch*. You've got those telltale ink smudges."

"Yeah," the reporter said, grinning sheepishly. He wiped his chin and cheek on the sleeve of his crumpled blue oxford shirt, and offered his hand for a shake. "Norman Klein. So, what's your first name?"

"Detective," Goode said.

"Oh, come on," Norman said, chuckling.

"You can't quote me so it doesn't matter. What took you so long, anyway? TV was here hours ago."

Norman shrugged off the jab, and then plowed ahead. "I heard you found the guy who found her."

So, despite his disheveled appearance, the cub reporter was already on the right track. Goode decided to cut him a break. Maybe this one would be different. Maybe he'd end up trusting him, at least as much as you could ever really trust a reporter. Goode thought he looked pretty young, though. Couldn't have much experience.

"Where's Sully?" Goode asked, referring to John Sullivan, the regular cops reporter, a white-haired guy who'd been on the beat for thirty-some years and drank beers with some of the older cops.

"He had to have emergency surgery," Norman said. "A hernia or something. I'm the night cops reporter. I'm kind of new."

"A cub reporter. Well, all right. Listen, I'll tell you some of what I know, but you didn't get it from me, okay?"

Norman nodded, his eyes lighting up and his mouth curling at the corners as he waited for details.

"It was her toes that stuck with me," Goode told him, the stark image coming to mind again.

"Her toes?"

Goode pulled himself out of it. "Yeah, they were perfectly shaped, like a mannequin's, and the nails were painted red. You could tell she was well cared-for. Follow me," he said, leading Norman out to the alley, where the body had been covered with a tarp until an investigator from the Medical Examiner's Office could get there. He wasn't sure if they were understaffed or just incompetent, but they often took a long time to show up. Not a good thing during a Santa Ana.

"See how they're sticking out from those trash cans?"

Norman grinned and jotted a few more lines in his notebook.

"Hey, now," Goode said. "I said this wasn't on the record, so don't go quoting me on any of this."

The last thing he needed was for the reporter to screw up his transfer. But he kind of liked the guy and the way he breathed in Goode's every word. Besides, Goode was excited about working this case, and he didn't mind sharing a few innocent details.

"Don't worry," Norman said. "I'm just taking down some color."

Goode didn't know what the hell "color" was, so he kept walking. "She lived on the third floor," he said quietly, so Byron and the evidence tech couldn't hear. "I'm thinking the murderer might have carried her down that iron stairway."

Norman turned to see where Goode was looking—a fire escape, which a blond man in his late twenties, dressed in khakis and a striped dress shirt, was creeping down, as if he could go unnoticed. He climbed into a red Mustang parked on the corner and drove away. Goode mentally recorded the license plate number, not wanting to raise Norman's suspicions by pulling out a notebook of his own. But when Norman scribbled something, Goode wondered if he was more experienced than he'd claimed.

"So, who was she?" Norman asked, his brow furrowed.

"You'll have to get her name from the ME. And they won't tell you that until they've notified next of kin."

The guy was starting to make him a tad nervous with all the questions, so Goode figured he'd better clam up. A little louder, he added, "I've got to get going now. The brass doesn't like me chalking up OT talking to reporters."

Norman looked panicked. "But wait," he hissed. "Where am I going to get this stuff on the record? No details, no story."

Goode told him what cops usually tell reporters: Not much. "Ask Sergeant Stone. If he won't talk to you, he'll issue a press release sometime soon. I've got to go."

He was heading back toward the stairs when Norman called after him. "But if you're the one who found the body, why can't I—"

"See you later, Inky," he said over his shoulder, chuckling. The guy had to pay his dues. Prove he was trustworthy. Maybe then Goode would think about giving him some of the good stuff.

He tried to imagine the girl walking down, or being carried down, those three flights of stairs unnoticed, wearing nothing but a man's shirt. It was highly unlikely; someone must have seen her. Maybe the blond guy in the Mustang killed her in the apartment and then carried her down. Or maybe she picked the wrong time to take out her trash, interrupted a drug buy and got herself raped. He wondered if anyone had heard her scream.

Goode wrote down Mustang Man's license number before he forgot it, and then called it in to dispatch. It came back belonging to Keith Warner of La Jolla, twenty-seven years old, no warrants. He copied the address underneath the license number and some notes about where and when he'd seen him. If nothing else, at least he was organized.

He joined Jake, who had been waiting for him on a bench in the courtyard, and took down a more detailed statement about finding the body. It didn't take long because Jake, who was fidgeting quite a bit, didn't have much more to say. He said he lived a few blocks away and did own some adult transportation—his mother's hand-me-down Saab, which he said he drove mostly to UCSD and back. The address on his driver's license was his mother's, but he said he'd since moved to his own place in Pacific Beach, a few blocks from the victim's. Goode jotted down both addresses along with Jake's home and cell phone numbers, just in case he decided to take an unauthorized trip somewhere. Goode let him go, but told him he might need to answer some more questions later.

Next Goode went up to the third floor and knocked on the next-door neighbor's door. He knocked again, harder, but still got no answer. It looked like no one was home on the third floor. They were probably all at the beach. It occurred to him that he'd missed his date with his surfboard again, but he quickly dismissed the thought as unimportant given the circumstances. As he was about to head back toward Tania's apartment, he saw Paul Walters pull back his curtain and try to drop out of sight. But it was too late.

Goode pounded on his door like a jackhammer, and this time Paul finally opened up. His hair was greasy and his eyes were glassy and bloodshot. He was lanky and looked to be in his late twenties. Dressed in a black T-shirt that said, NO DOUBT, and loose low-hanging jeans, he couldn't have weighed more than one hundred and fifty pounds.

"I'm trying to sleep in here. Are you trying to break down my door, dude?" Paul said. He looked like the type who watched a lot of MTV and rarely went outside. The skin under his eyes was purplish, as if he hadn't slept in a year or two.

"How well did you know Tania Marcus?" Goode asked in a no-nonsense tone.

"Did you say 'did'? As in past tense?" Paul asked, scowling.

"Yes, I did."

"Shit," he said, pausing. "Well, I know who she is, but I don't know her. I mean, I didn't know her. She hardly said two words to me." Paul went into a bout of coughing, a raspy smoker's hack.

Goode could tell a liar when he met one. He asked Paul a few more questions, but decided he was either uselessly unobservant or purposely evasive and headed for Tania's apartment.

Inside, the evidence tech was dusting the glass coffee table, doorjambs, and countertops, searching for the killer's fingerprints. Two opposite corners of the table had little piles of a white powdery substance, which he knew had to be cocaine or crystal methamphetamine. Meth was pretty popular in certain parts of San Diego County, but not so much with rich girls. They usually preferred coke or one of those designer drugs like X, otherwise known as Ecstasy. The tech was scraping the powder into a bag from one of the corners.

Byron was supposedly in charge, but Goode could see that he didn't have a clue about drugs.

"Hey, could you bag the stuff on those two corners separately?" Goode asked the tech. "The colors and consistency look a little different."

"Coke or meth, huh?" Stone said as he came out of the bedroom.

"Yup," Goode said.

Coke was often cut with meth, but meth was not cut with coke, and it might be important later to be able to differentiate between the piles and where they came from. Also, although they were both referred to as "white powder" in court, meth usually had a more yellowish tint than cocaine.

"Found her purse," Stone said, opening it up and showing him and Byron the contents. "She was twenty-four. Still has a Beverly Hills address on her driver's license."

Goode nodded. He'd had the age about right. Byron looked nonplussed.

"The kid's got more credit cards than I've had in my entire life," Stone said. "Car keys match to the black Porsche Carrera out in the lot. We'll have it dusted for prints as well. A guy from the Regional Computer Forensic Lab is on his way to pick up her computer so we can go through her e-mails, her Internet browser history and her BlackBerry. See what she was up to that might have gotten her killed. Goode, you'll want to hook up with the guy from RCFL and pursue those leads. I think his name is London. I'll call in the girl's name and address in Beverly Hills so we can get LAPD to notify the parents in person, then you'll want to follow up with a call later this afternoon to make contact since you were the one who found the body. *Capisce?*"

Goode nodded, jotting it all down in his notebook. Byron waited for his instructions.

"I'll have Slausson run a records check on the victim to see if she's been in any trouble before. Until then, Byron, why don't you look around and see if you can find anything useful."

"Will do," Byron said, heading off to the bedroom.

Goode was looking forward to perusing Tania Marcus's e-mails and Web browser information, which would answer many questions about her habits, lifestyle, and personal tastes. What he wasn't looking forward to was dealing with her grieving parents, but that task came with the job.

"Just our luck this girl will turn out to be the daughter of some filthy rich Hollywood producer and we'll have the national media breathing down our necks," Stone said. "Or worse yet, that it's a slow news day and those talking heads at CNN, MSNBC and FOX decide this is their latest dead-rich-white-girl-of-the-week story."

"Let's hope not," Goode said.

The sergeant gave Goode one of his trademark one-eyebrow raises as he nodded at the tech going through the trash bin in the kitchen. Apparently, Stone wanted

Goode to let Byron take the lead, but to keep his eyes peeled for clues as well.

Nothing beat the aroma of cigarette butts stuck to the slime on soda cans mixed with rotting fruit, Goode thought as he watched a dozen hairy flies the size of Texas circle and dive into the bin.

"Anybody find a pack of cigarettes?" he called out.

"Not so far," Stone said.

Since there were only two butts, Goode figured Tania wasn't a smoker, which could have meant that the murderer had brought his own. He asked the tech to put the two butts in separate bags for DNA testing, on the chance that different people had smoked them. They were both Camels.

Right on top, almost like a gift waiting for them, was a pair of cream-colored panties edged with lace. They appeared to be fairly new, but were ripped down one side. Goode figured they might have been torn off during a rape. A DNA test could help answer that question.

He held his breath as the tech dug a little deeper in the bin. Three half-eaten apples, brown between the jagged teeth marks. Droopy lettuce leaves. Carrot shavings. A *TV Guide* from two weeks ago. A container of cottage cheese—no need to lift that lid. Two steak bones and an empty bottle of Napa Valley Cabernet Sauvignon, vintage 1985. Not bad, he thought. She lived well and had expensive tastes for such a young woman. Unless she had a sugar daddy. Or maybe Daddy himself had come to dinner.

Goode gave a cursory look through the cupboards and drawers, but didn't find anything of note, so he moved on to the bedroom, which prompted Byron to head to the kitchen. Goode felt an air of competition and a little resentment coming from Bryon, so he decided to proceed with caution. Sort of.

Goode saw a stack of beauty school textbooks on the desk next to a stack of papers marked with a logo for Head Forward School of Hair Design on La Jolla Boulevard in Bird Rock. A glossy brochure on the dresser described it as a high-end beauty school for entrepreneurs, the first of its kind in the nation.

"No shit," Goode whispered.

This was some coincidence. His sister Maureen had just told him the week before that she was thinking of taking classes there after meeting a couple students at the Pumphouse, a bar in PB that she frequented. Goode whipped out his cell phone and called to see if she'd ever met Tania Marcus. He got no answer, which was nothing new, so he left a message saying he needed her help on something right away.

After a dumpy adolescence, Maureen had thinned down and turned attractive, but she still saw herself as an ugly duckling. She'd inherited their mother's nose and mouth, but they both got their father's brown hair and green eyes. She was never satisfied with her appearance, though. She was always messing with some new hair color, spray, goop, or cream. Sometimes Goode didn't even recognize her. He warned her about the short-short skirts and the leather boots, but she ignored him. He also got worried when she started hanging out in bars most nights, but she told him to butt out.

"You're not my father," she said.

Goode continued to look around Tania's bedroom, where Slausson was going through her drawers. Her shelves were lined with women's magazines and how-to books: how to start your own business, how not to love too much, how to improve yourself. Books by several supermodels on how to stay in shape and do makeup. Unauthorized biographies of Vidal Sassoon, John Lennon, and Howard Stern. On the desk there was a fax-phone, a computer, a DSL hookup, a CD burner, a printer and a flat-bed scanner. She was fully equipped. It looked like a business setup of some kind, which he thought was curious since she had just started school.

In the corner near the closet was quite a collection of

stuffed animals, including your basic teddy bear, a well-worn pink creature of undefined species and a three-foot-tall florescent green elephant. Goode wondered how many quarters some lovesick guy had thrown at a carnival game to win them for her.

On the dresser, Tania had staged a glass menagerie without walls. There were unicorns, cats, dogs, and swans arranged on a mirror as if they were gliding across water. One wall was hung with prints and posters framed under glass: Degas ballerinas and van Gogh sunflowers; wineglasses dripping with moisture on a shiny black table next to a block of Brie and a knife that picked up the glow of a candle. Typical girl stuff.

Then Goode saw three photos on the wall next to the bathroom door that didn't fit with the others. One was a self-portrait, with a soft light shining on her solemn face as she sat naked on a dining room chair that was turned around so that her arms grasped each other around its back and her legs dangled out the sides, her private parts hidden from view. Another featured an orchid, signed by Robert Mapplethorpe, which must have cost a fortune. The last was another nude portrait of her, only this time the fair-skinned Tania was in glorious full view: She sat on a dark floor, resting on her hands behind her, her back arched over a kitchen knife standing on its end, its point almost touching her. Her dark hair streamed down, nearly reaching the floor, and an expression of ecstasy played across her face.

Goode didn't quite know what to make of the photos, but they disturbed him almost as much as when he'd found her body. It was becoming clear that she was no ordinary young woman. And what was with the knife fetish? He saw a couple of photo albums on a shelf and looked through the pages until he found a recent and much more innocent head-and-shoulders snapshot to take for questioning witnesses. Tania, with her shapely

tanned legs, was posed in a crouch with a Springer
spaniel at the beach, looking up at the camera. She had
printed *Lucky and me at Malibu* in the white border. He
tucked it into his wallet next to the photo of his mother.

Her queen-sized bed sat in an ornate black iron frame,
with candleholder bedposts at each corner and covered
with designer sheets and a dark red satin spread. In the
nightstand next to her bed, Slausson had found her
"goodie drawer."

"You'll love this," he said to Goode, chuckling in a sor-
did kind of way.

Goode smiled to be polite, but he didn't really like his
tone. It wasn't very respectful, considering the girl was
dead, but he saw why Slausson was amused. She had a
whole collection of vibrators, gels, flavored body oils, a
couple pairs of handcuffs, some black satin ties, and a
strap-on dildo along with a short stack of girl-on-girl
magazines. Not what he'd been expecting, but definitely
a telling find. Nonetheless, he felt a need to protect her
honor. Goode doubted her mother would want to find
out that her baby had had such adventurous sexual
tastes. Was she a lesbian, a bisexual, or just bicurious?

He reached under the bed, just for drill, and felt a big
book of some kind. He stuck his head underneath and
found a red scrapbook with dated handwritten entries,
published articles and pieces of paper taped or pasted in,
almost like a collage of her life and interests. The lac-
quered cover was decorated with magazine cutouts—
women's breasts, red painted lips, and black spike heels.
The pages were thick from the paste-ins and dog-eared
from use. As Goode flipped through the pages, most of it
read like diary entries, but some of it read like creative
writing, so it was hard to tell what was reality and what
was art imitating life. One thing became clear, though. By
skimming it quickly, he saw far too many men's names in
that book for her to be gay. He almost felt relieved.

Goode took the book into the bathroom, locked the door and turned on the tap so his colleagues wouldn't hear him turning pages. He needed a little private time with the victim.

Chapter Three

Goode

Steam rose from the sink as Goode let the water run, fogging up the mirror. He switched off the knob marked cold, which obviously had been put on the wrong faucet by a dyslexic plumber, and turned on the one marked hot. He closed the toilet lid, sat down and opened the journal. He was only planning to skim it, but he soon lost track of the time.

The first entry was a double-spaced typed sheet that had been cut and glued onto the page. Scribbled in red throughout were comments like *Excellent phrase,* or *Very moving.* The top of the page was marked with an A. He assumed it was a creative writing assignment from college—UCLA from the looks of her other notebooks in the bookcase.

He stared at me and I stared back. But we weren't communicating. He was the artist and I was his subject. When we were in bed together, he called me his Little Conchita. I was eighteen. He was forty-five. Sometimes he wanted me to lie motionless like a statue so he could study every niche and curve. Other times, he'd sit me in a big red velvet armchair and tell me to sit very, very still while he drew me. If I moved, he'd rip a piece of paper off his pad, half-finished, and fling it to the floor. Mostly, they consisted of swirling masses of dots, lines, and cir-

*cles. I told him I didn't see why it mattered if I moved,
seeing how his drawings were abstract. He replied that
some were abstract, but all were precise. The last time he
threw a sheet of paper at me, the corner of it caught me
across the eyelid, slicing the skin. Luckily it wasn't my
eye. Had he cut my pupil, I would have taunted him sexually and then rejected him as many times as it took to
make him repent. But instead, I responded by crumpling
my beret into a ball and hurling it at him. Berets aren't
meant to be crumpled, I guess. By the time it reached
him, it had caught the air, stretched and extended itself,
and landed softly in his lap. I just laughed, which only
angered him more. "You're a silly old man," I told him.
"You'll never get a show." With that, he rose from his
wicker chair, which creaked when he breathed hard, and
headed for the cognac. It took me three snifters before I
could sit as still as he wanted. My eyes glazed over and
my face remained a blank so he could draw his silly little
picture. And when he finished, he showed it to me. It
looked just like him. He had drawn himself from looking
in the mirror behind me.*

Goode wondered if this was autobiographical and if
the "silly old man" had been one of her art professors at
UCLA. He pulled out his pocket notebook and jotted
down a note to himself: *Check out UCLA professors?*

Then he turned the page to a handwritten piece of
notebook paper that had been ripped out of a binder and
taped into the journal. Again, he wondered how much of
this was based in reality.

*Ex-stripper Finds Career is Taking Off. Sallie Mae
Johnson. Watch her sequins glitter. See them sparkle
under the bright lights. Watch the lustful stares of
bedraggled men with no place to go. They cast asper-
sions aside, the wife and the kids, they all fade into
oblivion along with the bills stacked up on the kitchen*

counter. All they see is Sallie Mae, the ambitious young girl who wrote to her mother last week: "Dear Mom," she said in a perfumed letter, stained with coffee. "My career is taking off. But not like before, Mom. I've cleaned up my act. No more whips and chains or spiked chokers. Today, I wear frilly lace, petticoats and pretty sheer pink stockings, the kind that end halfway up your thigh. My new job at the She-Shell Club pays me real good. I'm the Feature Girl this week. They picked me over the other girls who pose for Penthouse and Play-boy. They said I was the prettiest, the one with the most style. "You'll go far," they told me, "Just stay sweet and the tips will keep coming." It's like magic, Mom, just like you used to tell me. I wasn't really asleep all those times when you whispered to me in the middle of the night. I just kept my eyes closed and listened real good. I like the work, and the power that comes with it. I am what you always wanted to be before you quit the busi-ness: I'm a Feature Girl.

So, Goode wondered again, fact or fantasy? At the bot-tom of the page, he was pleased to see that Tania an-swered his question:

Of course stripping is just a fantasy for me, but I feel like this girl I wrote about for my creative writing class. Pretty and clean on the outside and dirty on the inside. Daddy would die if he knew some of my thoughts. Mom, too. Thank God she never found my magazines. If she only knew what kind of dreams I've been having lately. I feel so confused when I wake up. I don't know what they all mean. Maybe I'll never really figure it all out.

Tania seemed to be on a journey of discovery. Goode jumped ahead, and found another entry about sex. Either they were all like this, or he was merely getting lucky.

*I had another dream about Sheila the other night. But
it's never the Sheila of today. It's the Sheila I knew in
high school. She's so different now. She hardly seems
like the same person. And besides, she's married and
we're not even close. Her husband never shows up in
my dreams. It's always just the two of us, like it used to
be. I tell her about my sexual curiosity about her and she
acts shy. I caress and kiss her neck before she gives in,
but we always stop short of doing anything too intimate. It got me thinking, though, so yesterday I browsed
some lesbian porno sites on the Web. They're obviously
for men and not for real lesbians, so I didn't feel like I
was doing anything really wrong by looking at them.
There's something about watching two women together
that is so much more sensual than watching some gross
guy do things to a woman. It's funny, though, I can't see
meeting a woman who makes me want to put any of
those scenes into action. As long as it's on the computer,
it's all virtual reality anyway, so it's safe. Right?*

Goode flipped to a later chunk in the journal, where he
saw more references to San Diego, so he figured she'd
made the move by then.

*It's been a while since my creative writing teacher told
me that my stripper story lacked "verisimilitude"—yes,
that's the word she used—but I still remember thinking
that I can't write about strippers without actually meeting one. So, the other night, that cute guy, J. from
Pumphouse, asked me to go to Nude Nude Nude. I
thought it was kind of a strange place to take a girl on a
date, but I was up for it and that seemed to make him
happy. Like a naughty, excited little boy. We sat in the
front row and he bought us a couple of watered-down
vodka tonics. Then he started kissing me on the neck as
we were watching the girls onstage. It was hot. But then
this skank came over and told us to stop. "It bothers the*

girls," she said. "They think it's rude." In other words, we weren't paying them enough respect, which I found curiously ironic. J. was undeterred, though, and tried to buy me a lap dance. I said no thanks, so J. went for it instead. The whole time she was sliding all over him, I felt uncomfortably aroused. She had black hair in a pageboy cut, smooth skin, clean features, doe eyes, and an unbelievably tight body. I had to fight back the urge to run my hands all over her to see if she felt as good as she looked. When she was done, J. tucked forty bucks into her bikini top, but she leaned over and whispered in my ear. "You're really pretty," she said, and kissed me on the cheek. J. and I drove to the beach and made out some more. What I really wanted to do was have wild sex. Anything to get rid of all that weird energy. But he didn't have any condoms, so I decided we should stop.

Goode wondered who J. from Pumphouse was. Jake? Possibly. The handwriting in the next entry appeared hastily scribbled, with the letters all scrunched together, as if Tania had been under some stress. But this one seemed like an authentic diary entry.

I'm not sure if it's because I went to that strip club, or what, but I had a pretty explicit dream about Ms. X last night. Let's just say we did more than hold hands and kiss. I don't understand why I keep having these dreams and it seems like they're escalating. It's scaring me. I had all these butterflies when I saw her today, and that freaked me out even more. Really, all I want is to find a guy who's nice to me and loves me. I guess I still have a lot of years ahead of me to do that. At least that's what Mom keeps telling me. I hope she's right.

Goode was so embarrassed at the arousal he was feeling that he dropped his little notebook. But he couldn't put the damn diary down. Who was this Ms. X, he wondered. He figured he should read this stuff later, so he turned to the end to ensure he was doing real detective work. The last page was dated Saturday, the day before Jake found her in the alley. A drop of sweat fell from his face onto the page. He quickly removed the drop with his index finger, wiping his T-shirt sleeve across his forehead.

Last night at the Pumphouse was truly amazing. I saw this guy looking at me from across the bar, but I dismissed him as just another handsome playboy. When I refused to meet his gaze, he suddenly appeared at my side. Without saying a word, he took my hand and pulled me to the dance floor in an act of unadulterated confidence. It was the whole dominance-submission thing. Sexy, plain and simple. I like a man who can take me where I want to go without my having to give directions. When we were dancing, it was as if he could anticipate my every movement. Our eyes were locked as we moved in sync, side to side, hips swaying, drawn together but not quite touching, arms at our sides. The beat of the bass drum vibrated inside my chest as my head spun from the margaritas. He put his hands on my waist, guiding my body but still keeping me a few inches away from him. I could feel his breath on my face, the heat of his body seeping into mine. He moved a little closer, so that our chests were barely rubbing against each other. The heat, the tequila, and the endorphins made for quite a cocktail. I started to feel dizzy. I turned so my back was to him, and he lowered his hands to my hips, pulling my ass into him. I was hypnotized by the way we fit together as he moved us to the music. We stayed like that for what seemed like hours, his nose nuzzling my neck, his hardness pushing into my ass. I moved away from him, and turned around to look him in the eye. This time, I put my arms around his neck and

*pulled him to me. His mouth was less than an inch away
from mine as we danced. He brushed his lips against my
lips, then my cheeks, forehead, and nose. He came back
to my mouth, caressing me with his, slow and wet. It
was the most awesome first kiss I can ever remember. I
know I made a deal with myself to stop bringing home
men I just met because of all the heartbreak it's caused,
but I felt this intense connection with him. Plus, I
needed to get Ms. X out of my mind.*

There she was again, Goode thought. He jotted her
name down in his notebook, with three question marks.
This was a particularly long entry. Tania must have been
feeling the need to process a lot of confusion.

*I couldn't even admit it to myself by writing about it in
here last week, but Ms. X and I went out for drinks last
week and she started playing with my hair, kissing me
on the cheek, and pressing her breasts into my arm, stuff
like that. She wanted to come back to my apartment, so I
let her. We messed around for at least two hours, and it
got pretty intense. Finally, I said I wanted her to leave
so I could get some sleep. She seemed put off, but I
needed some space. I felt confused for days. I wanted—
needed—a man inside me, and so, last night at Pumphouse, Seth seemed like the perfect antidote. I thought
this could be the forever kind of connection I'd been hoping for, so I let him stay the night. Not surprisingly, the
sex was, in a word, magical. I have finally found Nir-
vana and his name is Seth.*

A loud rapping on the door startled him. "Goode,
what the hell are you doing in there? Taking a bath in the
sink? A few of us have some business to take care of."

"I'll be right out," Goode said, standing up and flush-
ing the toilet if, for nothing else, to stall for time while he

pulled himself together. It was going to be a long night. He ran his hands under the cold water and sloshed it over his face. He hadn't shaved for a couple of days, but he figured no one would notice since his beard wasn't very heavy. If he moved to Homicide, he knew he'd have to shave every day. But such is life. He wet the sides of his hair. It really bugged him when it got this long, but he'd been too lazy to get it cut.

When Goode came out of the bathroom, he told Stone about finding the journal and told him it would likely be a good source for leads on witnesses and suspects. Stone agreed, but said Goode needed to let the evidence tech log it in. Later in the day, he said, Goode could make copies back at the station if he wanted to study the journal outside the station. The idea was to try to match names with those in the address book Goode had picked up from the table by the phone, then divvy up the best leads with Fletcher and Slausson. Goode said he would study the journal more carefully later that night at home, where it was quiet. But truthfully, he wanted to be cloistered away from the other detectives' prying eyes.

For now, Tania's thoughts were all his.

Chapter Four

Helen

Helen Marcus was surprised when her doorbell rang at three o'clock on a Sunday afternoon. She wasn't expecting any visitors. Lucky, Tania's dog, was barking madly, so Helen opened the screen door to the backyard and put him outside.

"Just a minute!"

She padded across the carpet in her bare feet to the front door. When she opened it, she was surprised to see a Los Angeles police officer rubbing the brim of his cap back and forth across his palm. Helen figured he was there to investigate the burglary she'd reported a few days earlier. The CD player and speakers had been ripped out of her BMW in her own Beverly Hills driveway.

Helen hoped the handsome young man would come in and keep her company over a cup of coffee. She was feeling sluggish. She ran her hands through her hair, pulling it away from her face. She'd always wanted to be a blonde and now she was one. Besides, she had to do something to cover the white.

"Mrs. Marcus, I'm Officer Kelley from the LAPD. Can I talk to you and your husband for a minute?"

"Well, Tony is out playing golf," she said, smiling and gesturing for him to step into the foyer and then to follow her into the kitchen. "But you can talk to me. Is this about the robbery I reported?"

"No ma'am, 'fraid not. It's about your daughter," he said quietly.

A lump sprung up in her throat. Not again.

"Oh," she said with a forced nonchalance. "She's not in some kind of trouble, is she?" Yes, of course she is, she thought.

"I'm afraid I have some bad news," the officer said, dropping his voice. "I'm sorry to have to tell you this, Mrs. Marcus, but, well, your daughter was found dead this afternoon. Murdered."

A wave of heat flushed over her. She'd thought he was going to say Tania had gotten into another fender bender or something, maybe stolen a Gucci bag she'd been eyeing. "What?"

"I'm very sorry, Mrs. Marcus."

"Are you sure? She was just up here last weekend, telling us about her first month at that beauty school. It can't be. . . ."

Helen's mind went white.

"The apartment manager was able to give us a preliminary identification, but San Diego police were hoping you would come down there and make it official, ma'am."

Helen slumped against the refrigerator, covering her mouth and nose with her hands. "Oh, my God," she said, the linoleum floor tiles becoming a blur. She wanted to know more, but she didn't want to hear it.

"Ma'am? San Diego Homicide asked that you call them. As soon as you can handle it, that is."

She couldn't speak for a moment. "How?" Helen finally asked. "I mean, how did it happen?"

The officer struggled with the words. "I think it would be best if you talked with Detective Goode with San Diego PD, ma'am. He found her while he was off duty and he'll have all the latest details. We wanted to notify you personally right away, but we don't want to give you any misinformation."

Helen shuffled a couple of steps over to the sink and leaned her hip against it, looking out the window. She took a deep breath and then another. A hummingbird, perched on a branch of the bottlebrush tree, fluttered its wings and flew away. Helen was determined not to cry in front of a stranger.

"I'm really sorry, ma'am, but I've got to get going. If you want to speak with a crisis counselor this evening, just give us a call. I'll leave this card with the phone number right here on your table," he said, setting the card on the cherrywood antique in the foyer.

Helen felt a slight relief as she heard the front door click shut. But now that she was alone, she didn't know what to do with herself or all the thoughts racing through her brain. Was it one of those young men Tania was always running around with? Had she been in pain? Was she scared? Helen had never even considered this happening—her only child dying before her.

Helen's hands shook as she sloshed some Johnny

Walker Black into a crystal tumbler of ice. Her father used to call it his "courage in a bottle." Typically, she drank the cheaper stuff, but not today. Tony could go to hell. He was never there for her. The scotch was. And without an argument. She gulped down a couple fingers worth, then refilled the glass.

Helen grabbed the cordless phone from the kitchen counter and carried it to the sofa in the living room. She tried reaching Tony at the country club, but the man at the front desk said he hadn't seen him in about forty-five minutes, since he'd come in from the green.

"Damn," she whispered as she punched in the number for the San Diego police.

"Detective Goode is out at the crime scene, ma'am," said the woman who answered the phone. "I'll page him with a text message and your phone number so he can call you back."

Helen sipped methodically from the glass, feeling herself start to go to that warm and comforting, familiar place. As the tears came, the fine wood grain of the cabinet became a softer pattern of blotchy brown. The pain of it was too much. Her baby was dead. She grabbed at a chunk of her hair and pulled on it. She wanted to feel numb, have it envelop her like a fuzzy blanket, only it wasn't coming fast enough.

The scotch was helping, but what she really needed was a hot shower. That would speed things up, take her to the place she wanted to go. She'd grown quite attached to the soothing caress of the rushing water. It was certainly more fulfilling than the empty social hugs and air kisses from the women she played tennis with at the club. She and Tony hadn't had sex for three years. She had no interest in it. Especially after he'd started nagging her about her drinking. All she wanted was an escape from the boredom, the loneliness. The scotch consoled her, comforted her, took away the uncertainty and the fear. Lately, she'd started hiding bottles to keep

Tony off her back, but he'd been finding them and yelling at her. He didn't understand. She could stop whenever she wanted. She just didn't want to.

She carried her scotch into the bathroom, pulled back the shower curtain and turned the hot water all the way on. She got in, closed her eyes, and let the stream hit her face. The powerful jets hit the tight knots in her upper back and shoulders. It felt good, for a minute anyway. Anything to distract her from the pain she was feeling inside.

In her mind, she saw a much younger version of herself bathing two-year-old Tania at their old house in Encino. Helen remembered how much she'd hated the desperate summer heat of the San Fernando Valley. Yet Tania didn't seem to mind. She wouldn't sit still, though, jostling around and giggling as she splashed suds all over the terra-cotta floor. A few years later, her kindergarten teacher had called Helen several times at home, saying that Tania was touching herself inappropriately at school. So when Helen saw her doing it at home or in the bath, she would grab Tania's fingers and scold her.

"That's very dirty," she'd tell Tania as she scrubbed her hands thoroughly with soap and a brush.

Eventually, Helen stopped getting those horribly embarrassing reports.

She smiled at the bittersweet memory and turned the water a little colder. She poured too much shampoo into her palm and smeared it over her scalp. Tania had visited just last weekend, and combed Helen's hair in the living room. They talked about Tania's new apartment and the treacherous iron stairway she had to climb to bring in the groceries. Tania left in a huff after Helen chided her for wearing such a skimpy outfit, with her breasts hanging out. They hadn't talked since and now they never would. Helen would regret making that comment for as long as she lived.

Her daughter had always had a tough exterior, but underneath, Helen knew Tania was sensitive and insecure. Even though she was beautiful, she had some self-esteem issues. Helen blamed Tony, who had always wanted a son. He held her to such a high standard; nothing she did was ever good enough. He thought it would make her more successful, but Helen had her doubts. Tania wouldn't let Helen in, though, and often it was so hard to talk to her that Helen had given up trying. She wished now that she had worked harder at it. If she had known her daughter was in danger, she could have at least tried to protect her.

Helen squeezed her eyes shut even tighter. The soap was stinging, compounding the hurt. "Why didn't she take the money we sent her to get a nice apartment in La Jolla?" Helen said, her words garbled as her mouth filled with water. "Because she was stubborn and righteously independent, like her father. That's why."

Helen turned off the tap. She couldn't stop weeping. The mist in the bathroom seemed to coalesce with the fog in her head. Helen heard the phone ring. Wrapping the towel loosely around her, she moved into the hallway to listen to the voice on the answering machine.

"Hello. Mrs. Marcus? This is Detective Goode with the San Diego Police Department calling you back. I'd like to talk to you. . . ."

Helen hobbled over to the phone and picked up the receiver. Her tongue felt thick and furry. She could hear their conversation playing on the answering machine, but she couldn't remember how to turn off the recorder.

"I'm so sorry about your daughter," the detective said. "I know this must be a very hard time for you right now, and I want you to know we're doing everything we can to find out what happened."

"I appreciate that. Thank you," Helen mumbled, slurring her words.

"We'll need you to identify the body and, of course, we'll need your help to figure out what happened—who did this to your daughter. Do you think you and your husband can make it down here?"

"Make it down there?"

"Yes, ma'am. We'll be working on the case all night." The detective paused, waiting for her answer. "Mrs. Marcus, are you all right?"

"My husband . . . well, I don't know where he is. It'll have to wait until morning. Is that all right?"

"Yes, that's fine."

Helen felt paralyzed. She let out a long sigh. Her towel fell off as she reached for the scotch.

"Are you up to answering some questions for me in the meantime?" the detective asked gently.

"I'll try."

"Did Tania have a boyfriend in L.A.? Or was she seeing anyone here in San Diego?"

"She's always had lots of boyfriends. Too many."

"Okay. What about a girlfriend in San Diego? I understand she's been here for only a short time."

"Yes, she did mention someone. Let me think."

Helen's eyelids felt heavy, but if she closed her eyes, the room spun. Must've been the shower. All that steam. "El . . . Al . . . Alison," she sputtered.

"Alison Winslow?" Goode asked, offering a name from Tania's address book.

She spoke slowly. "Maybe. That might be right. She went to the beauty school, too." Helen felt her knees buckling. She needed to sit down. "I'm sorry. I've got to go now. My husband will have to call you back."

Helen poured herself another tumbler of scotch and walked naked over to the fireplace. The mantel was lined with photos. There was Tania with Mark the quarterback, with Craig the ASB president, and with Tommy, one of the Bad Boys, as Tania fondly referred to them, on his motorcycle.

Tony didn't like her dating so many boys. He told Helen he didn't like the way they looked at Tania or the way they touched her, even if it was just a quick good-bye kiss, because he knew what they wanted. Helen remembered the day after Tania's prom. Tania had stayed out all night, so she took a nap when she got home after breakfast, then went out again that afternoon. Tony came home from work, reeking of cigars, and headed straight for Tania's room. He threw one of her china dolls against the wall, and then ground the shards into the rug with his boot, which was still muddy from visiting a construction site that day. Daddy's little girl had forgotten to make her bed again. Helen had known deep down that it wasn't the unmade bed that made him angry. He was jealous. But Helen didn't even want to go there.

Helen was so scared of what Tony might do that she had never told him about the abortion Tania had when she was sixteen. Helen was angry with her daughter for being so irresponsible, but she dealt with Tania in her own way: She took away her allowance for the summer. Someone had to teach the girl that abortion was not a form of birth control.

Chapter Five

Tony

Tony Marcus came in from a pretty poor round of golf, a fried chicken dinner, and a few beers with his business partner, Jerry, who could talk of nothing but his sexually insatiable mistress. It was almost a relief to be home, even though he found his wife, Helen, passed out on the couch. No surprise there. Lucky was whimpering at the screen door to the backyard, so Tony let him in. The compact disc player was on and the plastic case for the Harry Connick, Jr. CD, which Tania had left during her visit the previous weekend, lay open on the table next to a half-empty bottle of the good scotch. A glass with two inches of yellowish water sat next to the bottle. Dammit Helen, he thought. Why can't you keep your hands off the good stuff? He'd told her time and time again to save it for guests. But she kept going through it as if it were wine in a box.

The fan whirred softly in the corner by the forty-two-inch high-definition television he'd bought Helen for her birthday. The digital clock on the DVD player read 8:30 P.M. Lucky was pushing his dish around on the kitchen floor, which was his call for food. Tony opened a can and dumped its contents into the dish. At least the dog was happy to see him.

He went into the bedroom and turned on the TV so as not to wake Helen, though he figured there was little chance of that happening.

"In other news, a twenty-six-year-old amateur boxer will spend his wedding night in the L.A. County jail tonight. Patrick Ortega was arrested in his tuxedo on suspicion of assaulting his forty-year-old bride at the Marriott Hotel in Encino this afternoon. Witnesses saw Ortega smack his wife so hard in the head he drew blood from her ear. Police said Ortega was the best-dressed prisoner in custody."

"The things people do to each other," Tony mumbled, clicking off the television with the remote.

He got up to get a glass of water and saw the red message light flashing on the answering machine. He had a love-hate relationship with the contraption. Impersonal, yes, but it saved him from having to talk to annoying salesmen. If they weren't real estate agents wanting to show his house (it was the nicest one on the block; he should know, he built it himself), it was someone selling something, or one of Helen's friends hoping to persuade her to donate his money to yet another charitable cause. Or even worse, it was another machine talking to his.

Tony hit the Play button. "Hello, Mrs. Marcus? This is Detective Goode with the San Diego Police Department calling you back. I'd like to talk to you. . . ."

Tony leaned closer to the machine, as if it were talking to him, and listened to the conversation the detective had had with Helen earlier that evening. He broke out in a sweat and felt incredibly nauseous. "My baby," he whispered. "My little baby."

The phone rang. It could be anyone, but he didn't want to answer it. He was likely to say anything. Anything at all. After four rings, the machine clicked on.

"Mrs. Marcus? If you're there, please pick up the phone. This is Detective Goode again. Sorry to bother you, but I have some more news about your daughter. . . ."

Tony held his hand on the receiver, trying to decide whether he could stand to hear anything more from Detective Goode. "Hello?" Tony said quietly.

"Is this Mr. Marcus?"

"Yes."

The officer paused. "I'm very sorry about your daughter, Mr. Marcus. This must be a very difficult time for you. I don't know if your wife mentioned it, but we'd like you both to come down and talk to us. We need your help, sir."

"What the hell happened?"

"We think she was killed sometime last night. She was found in the alley behind her apartment building this afternoon."

"But what happened? I mean, how?"

"We're not exactly sure, but it looks like someone strangled her. The medical examiner will do an autopsy tomorrow to determine the official cause of death."

The image of some man squeezing the life out of his daughter's neck flashed across his brain. It felt like someone had just punched him in the gut.

"Sir? Are you all right?" Goode asked.

"I'm okay. Go on," Tony said, his voice barely audible.

"So far, we don't have any eyewitnesses. We've talked to her neighbors, but most say they didn't know her since she had just moved here. We're going to try her classmates next."

"You'd better find her killer or I'll do it myself," Tony muttered.

"Excuse me, sir?"

"Nothing," Tony replied.

"We would have liked for you to come down tonight, but given how late it is, we hope to see you first thing in the morning. You'll want to ask for Sergeant Stone. He's my supervisor."

Tony hung up and pushed the answering machine off the table. It made a loud thud as it hit the carpet.

Helen stirred on the couch but didn't wake up. She snored like that only when she'd drunk herself into oblivion. He still loved her, but since she'd stopped wanting to have sex, they'd lived together like roommates. She kept saying she didn't feel sexy anymore, but he knew it was the alcohol. She was having an affair with the damn bottle and he couldn't compete with that. When he tried to talk to her about it, she'd blow up, say she didn't have a problem. He bought her *The Big Book* from Alcoholics Anonymous, but she refused to read it. Maybe she'd feel more like having sex later, she'd say, if he would just give her some time. She even gave him permission to do what he needed to satisfy himself as long as he didn't flaunt it in her face. He knew some men might enjoy the chance to explore other women. He'd done so recently, and it helped a little, but then she disappeared, so that only exacerbated his loneliness. He wished Helen would stop drinking so he could have his wife back. He missed her. And now Tania was gone as well.

Tony walked into the kitchen for a glass of ice so he could have some of the good scotch before it was all gone. The cubes clinked into the glass from the dispenser in the refrigerator door. The thing kept getting clogged lately. He fought back the urge to pick up the phone and call Tania's answering machine to listen to her voice. Maybe if he called, she would pick up and say there'd been some bizarre mix-up, a case of mistaken identity.

He walked into the living room and grabbed the scotch bottle by the neck, pouring until the glass was dangerously close to overflowing. He sucked in some of the liquid so as not to spill it. Then he picked up the glass, put the bottle under his arm and started for the door. He needed some air.

"Tony?" Helen's voice came croaking from the sofa.

"You awake?" he said.

"Will you come here?" she asked, her words slurring together. In the dim light from the moon, he saw she was lying naked on the couch. She held out a hand to him and he took it.

"Our baby is gone," she moaned.

Tony set the bottle and glass on the table and lay with her on the couch. It was the first real emotional contact they'd had in a long time. He'd missed her even more than he'd realized.

"I know, Helen. I heard all about it on the machine when I got home. Then the police called. Why didn't you call me at the club this afternoon?"

Helen rubbed his shoulder. "I tried, but you'd already gone. The police called and . . ." She disintegrated into tears.

"Shhhh," Tony said.

"What are we going to do?" Helen whispered.

"I'm going down there tonight," he said, starting to get up.

Helen pulled on his shirt. "No, it's too late. Let's get some sleep and go down in the morning."

"I guess you're right."

Tony settled back into her arms. It felt strange at first; it had been so long. Helen pressed her wet face into his neck. He felt her tears creep down his skin, seeking refuge in the deep wrinkles the sun had carved into him during the long hours he spent outside. He was touched that she had turned to him for comfort, but it was a bitter-sweet embrace. He knew it would be a fleeting moment.

The banter of crickets echoed throughout the room. The sound was so loud he thought there must be one or two under the sofa. He remembered sitting with Tania by the pool the previous Saturday night. Serenaded by the chirping, they discussed her plans to open a designer salon after she graduated from the high-end beauty school he was paying for in La Jolla. He'd promised to loan her all the start-up money she needed as long as she promised to work hard. She would have been a rich woman someday.

He turned his head away from Helen so she wouldn't feel his tears.

Then, he decided, to hell with it, and let them roll where they would.

Chapter Six

Norman

Norman Klein paced around the courtyard as he watched the detectives questioning residents. It was getting close to the point where he was going to have to leave to meet deadline and the sergeant still hadn't given him a decent set of facts about what had happened to the dead girl. This was Norman's first big story since getting promoted from editorial assistant to night cops reporter and he didn't want to fail as soon as the editors gave him a chance to prove himself.

He'd hoped he would get to see what a dead body looked like, but the police wouldn't let him near it. After chatting with Detective Goode, Norman spent a while trying to schmooze with the other cops, but he couldn't get any of them to talk on the record either. He also tried knocking on some doors, hoping to interview a neighbor who knew the girl, but that, too, proved fruitless.

Goode seemed like a pretty good guy, a little intense, but cool. Norman hoped he'd run into him again. He didn't even really look like a cop. More like a surfer. Muscular but not overly so, he had the kind of body Norman always wanted but knew he'd never achieve as long as he refused to join a gym and kept drinking beer after work.

Norman was sitting on a bench going over his thin set of notes when an officer came over, shoved a piece of paper at him, and walked away. It was a press release, if you could call it that, only two paragraphs long. Norman started to panic. He needed more on-the-record information, some good juicy details. He jumped up and made a beeline for the sergeant, who was standing next to a potted palm and talking to two young officers who seemed to be listening politely. The sergeant stopped midsentence and glared at him.

"Everything we know is in the release, son," he said before Norman could get a word out.

Norman didn't believe him for a minute. He slapped his thigh with the notebook as he walked back to his car. He looked at his watch again. It was six thirty P.M. and his head was pounding. He had two hours until deadline for the first edition. How was he going to make it as a reporter if he couldn't get anybody to talk on the record? Maybe he hadn't pushed hard enough. He wasn't good at confrontation. It made him uncomfortable. Nobody told him that getting people to answer simple questions could be so damn hard.

Norman tried to prepare himself for the grief the city editor would give him if he came back with nothing. He sped through two yellow lights, hoping they weren't the intersections with the red-light cameras. He couldn't afford a $350 ticket. He also hoped he'd have enough time to squeeze in a few phone calls to flesh out the press release and the few notes he'd taken. He had some decent quotes, but no attributions. He might just have to wing it. The other reporters said that if he turned in his story right on deadline Big Ed wouldn't have time to mess with it much. He felt his stomach eating itself as he turned into the office parking lot.

Big Ed, named for his large girth and his deep, resonating voice, didn't help matters by barking at him the minute he was within shouting distance. "It had better be good 'cause it's going A 1," Big Ed yelled, loud enough for the whole newsroom to hear.

A-1, Norman said to himself. That meant even more pressure than he'd planned for. At this rate, he'd lose his job faster than he'd gotten it. He had to come up with a lead, and quick. He didn't have a whole lot of time to make phone calls, but he didn't even have the victim's name.

Norman called the county Medical Examiner's Office and, after waiting on hold for five minutes, asked if the dead woman in P.B. had been identified. The investigator finally gave him the barest of information: Tania Marcus, twenty-four years old.

Norman managed to charm the woman into also giving him the names and phone number of Tania's parents, who lived in Beverly Hills. He called and talked to Helen Marcus, who sounded pretty drunk and quite upset, but she gave him a couple of quotes he was able to use. By the sounds of it, she probably wouldn't even remember talking to him.

With only an hour until deadline, Norman laid his fingers on the keyboard and stared at the computer screen. His brain was frozen. He had typed in his byline, hoping it would loosen him up, but he couldn't come up with a good lead. He typed a few phrases he thought sounded good. But then he decided they weren't, so he deleted them and tried again. All he could come up with were sentences that were not only too long, but loaded with clichés. With half an hour to go, he stopped trying to sound like he knew more than he did and wrote it straight. He put in every detail and quote he had in his notebook, using "sources close to the investigation" like he'd seen in the stories out of Washington, and hoped it would fly. The red toenails were so visual he had to mention them. He also said Goode found the body, despite his warning to leave him out of it. Norman couldn't believe that the detective would really mind getting credit for that.

Norman busted deadline by ten minutes, trying to ignore the string of e-mail messages from Big Ed saying, "Quickly, Klein, quickly." It was one of the most stressful nights of his life. Norman leaned back in his chair and tried to relax. He hoped Big Ed wouldn't have a whole bunch of questions on the story that he couldn't answer. Except for the deadline pressure that had almost melted his brain like candle wax, the whole day had been cool. Very cool. His career officially launched, he was on his way to fame and glory.

With four more hours till the end of his shift at 12:30 A.M., Norman got a message from Big Ed to keep calling the cops so they could put updated information into the later editions. With the big scoop under his belt, he felt entitled to leaf through his *Rolling Stone* magazine. If Big Ed asked him what he was doing, he'd say he was brainstorming for a follow-up story.

Norman was thirsting for a beer. He needed something to take the edge off all the stress. He figured he and a few of the editorial assistants and copy editors could head over to the Tavern to make last call after deadline and watch Lulu's butt wiggle as she toted cold brews around the bar. He loved that place. It was close to the airport, not far from the downtown jail, only a few blocks from a law school and a couple miles from all the high-rise office and condo buildings. So baggage handlers played pool with off-duty sheriff's deputies, biker dudes with law students, and secretaries with car rental clerks. There were always one or two attorneys sitting at the bar, their heads down and their ties loosened, finally able to decompress because no one they knew hung out there. And there were always baskets of cheese doodles and pretzels on every table.

Brooke, the county government reporter, had stopped by the night before with one of her buddies. She said hello to him, but spent most of the night talking to one of those guys with the loose ties. Norman hoped to get up the guts to ask her out one day, even though she was a good five years older than him. She could teach him a few things; he was sure of that. He planned to take her to that funky club where women with large breasts danced the hula in grass skirts while the patrons ate sweet-and-sour chicken and sticky rice. Just for something different. Other guys talked about Brooke, but no one ever asked her out. Bunch of wusses.

The phone at the city desk kept ringing and no one was answering it. Norman figured Big Ed had gone to the head, so he walked over to his phone and picked it up.

"Do you know how to get to that new water park?" a tinny woman's voice said to him over the speakerphone. "My niece and nephew are coming to visit and I want to take them there."

"What new water park?" Norman replied, trying to be pleasant.

"You know, that new water park, the one they just built."

Norman wondered why people thought they could
call the newsroom to get answers to any obscure question that occurred to them. "What's it called?"

"You know, the one near that big freeway."

"I'm sorry, I really don't know what park you're talking about."

"So, you're telling me that no one there knows about
this water park? What kind of newspaper are you?"

She waited for an answer.

"Have you checked the yellow pages?" he asked.

The woman slammed the phone in his ear.

Norman went back to his desk and reflected on the
events of the day. He figured it was a combination of
luck, talent, and sloth that got him The Story. He'd come
to work an hour early to clean up his desk and read
through the newspapers that had stacked up. As luck
would have it, Sully, the regular daytime cops reporter,
had to have emergency surgery and Charlie, the backup
daytime cops reporter, was out sick. Then Big Ed came
over and said, "This one's yours, kid. Don't screw it up."

Norman was rousted out of his nostalgic reverie by the
presence of Big Ed, who had a slightly crazed look in his
eyes. Not a good sign.

"Hey, kid. We don't use anonymous sources at this
newspaper unless we absolutely have to. I had to cut
most of that shit out of your story, but if I cut all of it out,
there'd have been nothing left to run. Next time get this
stuff on the record. We're not part of the Washington
press corps here. We're a local newspaper. We need people's names after their quotes."

Norman braced himself for the words "You're fired,"
but they didn't come.

"Anyway," Big Ed said, "I just heard something on the
scanner about a woman decapitated downtown at Fifth
and Broadway. Might be related to that P.B. murder.
Maybe it's the work of a serial killer. Who knows? Drive

down there and check it out. If the copy desk has any questions on your story, we'll call you on your cell."

Big Ed had some serious coffee breath with an undercurrent of something even nastier. Probably one of those hot dogs from the vending machines in the cafeteria upstairs. The ones that came with little plastic pouches of raw onions.

"Oh yeah, the deadline tonight for the last edition is eleven o'clock. That gives you some time to get down there and call in what you can get. Don't look at me like that. You're only as good as your last story. And that one wasn't very good."

Norman had never called in a story before. He needed a computer to formulate his thoughts because they weren't exactly linear. He thought that two big murder stories in one night was asking a lot of a new reporter, but he knew he had to get back out there and do a better job. He did not want to go back to making copies and sorting mail. He gathered up his notebook, pens, and the jumbo cup of soda he'd picked up on his way back to the newsroom, and waited for Big Ed to offer some kind of guidance.

Instead, Big Ed reached for the magazine on Norman's terminal. "So, uh, Klein," he said, pausing as he flipped through the pages, "what are you waiting for, a call from the Pulitzer committee?"

Norman turned and walked as briskly as he could without spilling his drink. He was only a few feet from the door to the stairwell when Big Ed shouted, "And don't stop for food on the way." He was one to talk. Norman tried to ignore the barb and decided to take it slow this time. Panicking wasn't going to help anything.

Norman could hardly see out of the windshield in his car. He turned on the wipers, which carved two half arcs out of a layer of grime. That was better. He really needed to stop procrastinating and get the car washed, especially if he wanted a woman like Brooke to get into it. He hoped she wasn't like the last girl he dated, a clerk named Kathleen who said she was allergic to just about everything and sneezed all the way to the movie theater. Sheba, his German shepherd, was a shedder. He let Kathleen pick Sheba's white hairs off his blue blazer because he thought it might get him somewhere later, but he was wrong. She refused to go out with him again. He didn't care, though, it was sloth that got him the Big Story.

As Norman drove toward the exit to the employee parking lot, he almost hit the executive editor, who was walking down the middle of the aisle. Norman wondered what he was doing in the parking lot for peons since managers got their own coveted spaces under the building. Norman waved politely at the balding Mr. Thompson, who tried to shield his eyes from the headlights.

Oh well, Norman thought, I'm just trying to do my job, Mr. Thompson, which is more than I can say for you, with your hand up your secretary's skirt the other night. It was a pretty disgusting little scene.

Traffic was pretty bad downtown and his windshield was still dirty on the inside. While he was waiting at a red light, he tried to clean it with a napkin, but that only made it worse. He didn't realize until too late that he'd wiped his cheeseburger hands on it after lunch. He could barely see in front of him through the glare of the streetlights on Broadway. Balancing the cup of soda between his legs, he spat on a clean napkin like his mother used to do, and tried to wipe the window again.

Up ahead, he saw the satellite dealie-bob on top of Channel 10's white van and knew he was in the right place. Rhona Chen was sure to be there, too. She was hot.

Norman put his foot on the brake as soon as he saw the starry reflection of another car's red rear lights in front of him. But it was too late. He heard the dull thump of his car hitting the fender in front of him and then his own gasp as a sudden chill rippled through his genitals. He'd spilled his drink—ice, cola, and all—into his lap.

He'd hit an old Plymouth Duster. A young guy with a pug nose stormed over to Norman's window. He gave Norman the hairy eyeball, but Norman was too busy to notice as he tried to wipe his pants at least semidry with what was left of his napkin.

"You going to get out or what?" Pig Boy snapped.

"Yeah, give me a minute here. I had a little accident."

"No kidding."

"I mean I spilled my drink."

"Drive much?"

"What?"

"Nothing."

Norman kept mopping until he realized he was spreading little white pills all over his pants. He got out of the car and walked over to Pig Boy's Duster. He saw that rubber had hit rubber. Cool. Very cool.

"I don't see any problem," Norman said nonchalantly.

"Yeah, well, I'm not so sure. It looks like you made that dent right there to me," Pig Boy said, pointing to a rusty area above his fender.

"No way," Norman said. He couldn't believe the guy's chutzpah. "That's been there for years. You think I'm an idiot? Besides, I don't have any insurance, so this is irrelevant."

"That's illegal."

He didn't need Pig Boy to tell him that. He needed to get to Fifth and Broadway. Fast. He'd have to make up something to get the guy off his back. "No, actually, under the law you have a choice. I chose not to get any."

Pig Boy was frowning and shaking his head, but since he didn't seem to know enough to object, Norman decided to leave as quickly as possible. If he waited around much longer, he figured he could lose his teeth. And his job.

"I'm a reporter at the *Sun-Dispatch* and I'm on deadline right now," he called over his shoulder. "Gotta go."

He truly did mean to get some insurance. He just couldn't afford it on his measly salary. They'd promoted him to reporter, but in name only until he could prove he could do the job better than the applicants whose resumes were stacked up in the Metro editor's office.

All the TV vans had already left, but a couple of traffic officers were still hanging around, drinking coffee and talking. He asked what was going on with the decapitated woman and they told him a city bus driver was in custody for vehicular manslaughter. He'd been drinking and hadn't seen the eighty-four-year-old crossing Broadway with a cane—in the crosswalk, no less. He'd hit her with the bus and knocked her down, then backed over her somehow. Great story. Piece of cake.

Norman figured the dayside reporters would fill in the details in a story the next day. The driver would undoubtedly lose his job, and the city would probably get sued for hiring a guy with a serious drinking problem. It was ripe for a multimillion-dollar personal injury lawsuit by the woman's family.

"It's not even safe to walk across the street anymore," an old man said as he surveyed the scene from his motorized wheelchair. "I should've stayed in Idaho. Can't get hit by a bus in a potato field, if you know what I mean."

Norman nodded. "Sure do," he said, copying the man's quote into his notebook. "Can I get your name?"

Chapter Seven

Alison

With the streetlight out, the full moon cast an unearthly glow over the cars parked on the street outside Alison Winslow's second-floor apartment. Alison sat on the cushioned seat in her living room's bay window, running her fingers through her kinky golden hair, trying to get the knots out. A bicyclist rode past with a white light strapped to each of his legs and a dog trailing behind, dragging its chain leash like a ghost in a low-budget horror movie.

Alison crossed her legs at the ankles and rested her socked feet on the coffee table Grandma Abigail had loaned her. She leaned back into the corner of the window seat, trying to get comfortable, when it hit her. What was she doing, sitting there in the dark? It was only exacerbating the emptiness inside her, making her one with the black night. She uncrossed her legs and reached over to pull open a drawer, from which she retrieved a box of wooden matches she'd picked up at the little Italian restaurant she and Tania had gone to Friday night. She struck the first one, producing a scraping sound but no spark. She had better luck with the second and managed to light three of the bayberry candles before the flame got so close to her finger that she had to drop the stick. She lit another one and finished the job, lighting the other two candles in the half circle she'd placed around her on the table, as the aromatherapy instructions advised.

The goal was to counteract the agitation that dusk brought down on her, along with the restlessness and anxiety that frequently came with it. She'd tried many remedies over the years and was always open to something new, even if it sounded hokey. The bad energy was tough to deal with because she often didn't understand the cause. Aromatherapy was the latest alternative to a glass of Chardonnay, a hot bath, rubbing her own shoulders, a chunk of chocolate, checking her e-mails, turning on the TV, watching a video, or any and all combinations. Anything, really, to distract herself from herself, to find a way to fill the gaping hole in her gut and make her feel whole. It wasn't a real hole; more of a deep emotional chasm. Escape was what she sought. Escape, of any sort, was the only solution she knew.

She'd thought it would be different in San Diego—a new city, a new apartment, working toward a new career, a geographical cure. She'd saved and saved for this beauty school, then was lucky enough to get a scholarship to close the gap. But only six weeks after leaving L.A., she still found herself haunted by the same feelings of sadness and loneliness, the same paralysis, and the fear that she would always feel this way.

Starting classes had certainly helped, and meeting Tania there was a healthy bonus. She had hope again, felt she was on the right track toward happiness. Finally. She dreamed of owning her own hair salon one day, earning enough money to dress like Tania—in diamond earrings, cashmere sweaters, silk shirts, leather jackets, and Italian suede pumps.

Alison went into the bathroom and turned on the vanity lights. At twenty-nine, she was afraid that turning thirty would make her hair go white. Overnight. It seemed so old. The way she was going, she might never find a guy who wanted to marry her, or vice versa. She opened the mirrored cabinet to try her new lipstick, thinking it might brighten her mood, and a tube of toothpaste fell into the sink and landed in a nest of her hair. She'd just removed a dozen strands from the drain the day before. Did she have some rare disease that made her hair fall out? No one would trust a bald female stylist. Relax, she told herself, it's probably just the stress of starting a new life.

One thing she didn't miss about L.A. was Grandma Abigail mocking her hair obsession. She said it made Alison seem trivial, shallow. Didn't she have better things to worry about? Alison tried to tell her that it was near impossible to avoid vanity and obsession having grown up so close to Hollywood, but she'd made an effort to widen her interests nonetheless. She'd bought a membership to the Museum of Contemporary Art and started listening to live music with coworkers from the

Nordstrom perfume counter. She also rented dozens of videos, spending more than she cared to admit. She read quite a bit, too, mostly murder mysteries and detective novels, but she worked in some of the classics and a bit of contemporary fiction, too. A good love story with a happy ending usually cheered her up.

She was feeling especially restless for a Sunday night. What she needed, she decided, was a combination approach. She carried the bayberry candles into the bathroom on a tray and set them down around the bathtub, turned on the hot water and dumped some lavender bath oil into the gushing stream. It smelled like she imagined paradise would. Then she went into the living room and put on the Billie Holiday CD that Tania had loaned her. She really liked her voice. It was so mournful, yet it lifted her spirits. Go figure.

That Tania. Alison wondered why she hadn't called the night before, at least to say she couldn't go out like they'd planned. They'd met only a month earlier, but Alison thought they were headed toward a promising friendship. Why did people have to be such flakes?

Tania was so much prettier, more confident, more everything than Alison, even though she was five years younger. She said she didn't see herself as being all that, but she knew people saw her that way. Over dinner, she told Alison she'd come to the beauty school to learn how to make other women more beautiful. She said her father had promised to help her launch a chain of designer hair salons like Vidal Sassoon's, where most of the beauticians were European or at least acted like it. When Alison explained that her own goals weren't as lofty, Tania encouraged her to set her sights higher.

Dropping her jeans and black ribbed turtleneck to the floor, Alison tested the water. Too hot. She let the cold water run for a bit, tested the bath again and, satisfied, she stepped in, one foot at a time. She twisted and pulled her hair into a knot, then sat back against the clam-shaped bath cushion she'd attached to the wall. She cupped her hands, pushing and pulling the water to make waves that caressed her stomach and breasts as she went over the events of Friday night.

She and Tania got dressed up, ate dinner at the Italian place and then walked to the Pumphouse, a dark bar near the beach that featured local blues bands. It wasn't long before Tania was dancing with this guy, Seth, and he and his friend, Keith, were sharing their table.

Alison was immediately attracted to Keith, whose sandy blond hair was just long enough to fall over his brown eyes. Seth was tall, well built, and had short dark brown hair and almost-black eyes that reflected an arrogance that rubbed Alison the wrong way.

While Tania and Seth were entwined on the dance floor, swaying just a little, as if everyone around them had disappeared, Alison tried to engage Keith in conversation. But he was so quiet and she was so shy, they barely spoke to each other. He seemed distracted by something or someone near the women's bathroom. A few minutes after Seth and Tania returned to the table at the end of a slow song, a woman named Clover stopped by. Alison had seen her and Tania whispering the other day after class at the beauty school.

"Hi, you guys," Clover said. She was standing behind Keith, with her hands on his shoulders. Her eyes flitted back and forth between Tania and Seth, who were sitting across the table.

Seth glanced at her long enough to say, "What's up?" then looked away.

Clover emanated sexuality, the adventurous kind, like anything goes. But it was obvious she came from money, so she didn't seem cheap. Alison had felt jealous when she saw Clover and Tania talking at school. Tania also seemed to be a favorite of the school's director, who never had a hair out of place, and was always touching Tania. It was almost like Tania was wearing pheromone perfume. It made no difference whether it was men or women. They never seemed to get enough of her.

Alison felt insecure around the beautiful women at the beauty school. She didn't want to get pushed aside if Tania felt she could get sexier guys with Clover than with her, but she couldn't really do anything about it, except be herself. Alison couldn't help but admire Clover's Scandinavian features, her lithe figure with those high, firm breasts, and the shapely arms of a weight-trainer. Her long blond hair hung down her back, silky and straight. Clover pressed her breasts into the back of Keith's head and, judging by the expression on his face, it made him uncomfortable. He chirped. Alison glanced at Seth for some kind of explanation, but he seemed oblivious. What was that noise Keith made?

As Clover headed for the bathroom, Seth shook his head and shrugged at Tania, who looked away. Alison couldn't read her friend's expression. Was it embarrassment? Jealousy? She couldn't tell. She wondered if Keith was hung up on Clover, because he certainly didn't seem interested in Alison. A few minutes after Clover left, Keith exchanged nods with Seth and headed out the front door. Alison tried to call good night to him over the music, but he either didn't hear or didn't much care. Seth got up a few minutes later, whispered something into Tania's ear that made her smile, winked at Alison, and left.

"They want to go out with us tomorrow night," Tania yelled at her over the music. She fingered the long thin strap of her black, sequined purse as if she was eager to leave, but Alison had just ordered a dirty martini with three olives and she wasn't going anywhere.

"Both of us?"

Tania came around the table next to her so she didn't have to shout. "Yeah. I wrote my number on a napkin and gave it to him. He said he'd call me. Don't you think he's gorgeous?"

"Tania, are you sure Seth said that they want both of us to come? Keith barely said two words to me all night."

"Yes. I'm sure Keith liked you. He's just shy. Why else would Seth say we should all do something tomorrow night?"

"I don't know. Keith was totally ignoring me."

"Don't worry about it, Ali," Tania said, putting her hand on Alison's shoulder. "It'll work out just fine. I'm going to go call a cab. I'll talk to you tomorrow, okay?"

She liked the nickname Tania had given her. She thought it made her sound exotic, like Ali McGraw in *Love Story*.

Alison sipped her martini for a while, watched two couples grope each other on the dance floor, and felt out of place. She had to get out of there. But she must have stood up too fast because her head started spinning, so she plopped back down. After a couple minutes, she got up again, this time slowly, and made it out of the bar. She was enjoying the fresh air, even though it was a little chilly, when a Yellow Cab pulled up.

"Are you Tania?" the driver asked.

"No," Alison replied. "She left a while ago."

"Well, she called for a cab," he said irritably. "You need a ride?"

Chapter Eight

Goode

After losing his private diary-reading spot, Goode went outside to the apartment balcony to finish writing his list of contacts that could be useful to the investigation. A woman named Alison had come up several times in the last few entries, so he cross-checked Tania's address book and found an Alison Winslow, 55 Jewell St. #216, in

Pacific Beach, which locals shorthanded as P.B. He didn't think she was Ms. X because he doubted Tania would use two different names for the same person. But he planned to keep his eyes open just in case. For all he knew, Tania could have been worried someone would read her diary, so she may have had her own rules for identifying people.

Goode told Stone he planned to interview Alison after he checked out Jake's story to make sure he really lived where he said he did and drove a Saab originally registered to his mother. In general, Goode just wanted to get a better feel for the guy. He'd been a little distracted when he took Jake's statement. Stone told Goode to focus first on following up leads from the diary, but suggested he review Jakes's story again later to look for any holes or discrepancies. Stone called in to run a quick criminal check on Alison before Goode went over there and she came up clean. He said Slausson had already done a check on Tania and the only thing he turned up was a shoplifting arrest when she was nineteen, though no charges were ever filed.

"Daddy must have gotten her a good lawyer," Stone said, suggesting that Goode call Tania's mother, Helen Marcus, to check in and get any new information now he'd gotten word that LAPD had finished the in-person notification.

Goode had gotten a text message on his cell phone that she'd called looking for him while he was in the bathroom, but he wanted to wait to return her call until he'd firmed up the game plan with Stone. When he called her from his van, the poor woman sounded drunk, but she confirmed his hunch that Alison was the right place to start.

He was cruising along Mission Boulevard when he looked in his rearview mirror and saw a red convertible with its nose to his fender. The driver was just asking to raise his insurance premium. Goode figured the guy had probably downed too many brews watching the Chargers game in a bar that afternoon and hadn't given them a chance to wear off. Goode pushed his foot harder on the gas. He didn't have time to waste dealing with a rear-ender, especially one involving a drunk driver. Alison Winslow might know something.

Alison's three-story complex appeared to have been built around the same time as Tania Marcus', as did most of the apartment buildings in P.B., a densely populated but laid-back beach community full of students and some of the more progressive people in San Diego. Some of the pastel-colored houses were more like cottages, packed along wide streets with jeweled names such as Diamond, Garnet, and Chalcedony. Framed by a couple of trees and some well-trimmed bushes, they often had a dog roaming about the yard. The only thing that bothered Goode about P.B. was the excessive number of stop signs. They were great for preventing hot-rod surfer types from speeding on the residential streets, but they made getting somewhere fast an impossibility. And Goode always seemed to be in a hurry.

The elevator in Alison's building rattled and jerked as it rose, very slowly, to the second floor. Goode felt relieved to step out of it.

When Alison opened her door, Goode was startled by her natural beauty. She had sparkling green eyes and a heart-shaped mouth, and her face was engulfed by wild, curly blond hair. Her skin was pale, but her cheeks were rosy, even without makeup. She looked like an angel from a Rubens painting, only thinner. As he introduced himself, he could see in her eyes that she had secrets, perhaps even from herself. He also couldn't help noticing that she had large breasts pressing against her white terry-cloth robe. He reminded himself that he had other, more pressing issues to think about.

"Alison Winslow?"

"Yes," she said, her smile fading as she glanced at the

badge he pulled from his jeans pocket. "Please tell me something hasn't happened to my grandmother."

"No, not that I know of. I'm here to talk to you about your friend, Tania Marcus."

"Oh," Alison said, frowning.

Goode didn't want to do this on the stoop. "Do you mind if I come in for a few minutes?" he asked.

Alison hesitated. "Okay. Sure." She ushered him in and motioned him toward a deep well-worn armchair next to the couch, which faced a bay window. "So, what's going on?"

Goode started to sit in the chair when it lurched backward. He jumped up and out of it, feeling his cheeks flush. He'd thought for a minute that he was heading over.

"Nice chair," he said, embarrassed by his own nervous laugh. He was acting really stupid. Not to mention inappropriate. Keep your head on business, he told himself.

"Sorry. You would have been okay, actually. It just feels like you're going over. Why don't you sit here on the couch next to me?" she said, patting the sofa cushion. She was looking a little more relaxed. "That chair was my grandfather's. My grandmother pulled it out of the garage and had it cleaned before I moved down from L.A., but I guess she never got that leg fixed."

Goode nodded. "So," he said, pausing to let her know he was going to change gears. "Tania Marcus. You two been friends long?"

Alison cocked her head with a lopsided grin. "No, not really. Just a few weeks. Why, did she rob a bank?"

"No. I'm afraid I have some bad news."

Her smile dropped from her lips. "Oh . . . What is it?"

Goode tried to say it as gently as he could, but that didn't change the truth. "Her body was found in the alley behind her apartment building this afternoon," he said.

Alison gasped. Her eyebrows shot up and her mouth fell open. "You mean she's dead? I can't believe that. We just went out Friday night. There's no way."

"She was murdered," Goode said, choosing his words carefully and watching for her reaction.

Alison turned away from him, shaking her head. Something about the way her shoulders folded into her neck made him want to comfort her. But he knew it wasn't a good idea, personally or professionally. She could turn out to be a suspect, or just as bad, a witness they needed to testify in court. If they got too close, the defense might find out and attack her credibility. Goode was not about to blow the case—or his future—by stepping over the line.

Alison's gaze was fixed on the coffee table as a single tear crept down her cheek. The room was still until a clock on the kitchen counter clicked over to 9:06. Goode could still taste the meatball sandwich he'd inhaled two hours earlier.

"Alison, are you okay?"

She nodded.

"I'd like to ask you some questions," he said gently.

She nodded again and wiped her eyes with the tie of her robe. His heart went out to her.

"Do you remember seeing her or anyone with her wearing a man's white shirt with red pin stripes?" he asked.

Alison watched a spider skim across the table's shiny finish.

"Alison?"

"God, this is such a shock," she said, squeezing her eyes closed. "I just can't believe it. Give me a minute."

"Take your time," Goode said. He paused to let the news sink in and give her some space to get her thoughts together. That also gave him a chance to study her reaction. She genuinely seemed to be taking the news pretty hard and it seemed to come as a surprise to her. That would fit regardless of whether she was Ms. X, but not if she had been involved somehow. He didn't get a lesbian vibe from her, although he picked up something unusual about her sexuality.

Scanning the room, he saw a framed photo of Alison, her arm around the shoulder of a woman with white hair. Her grandmother, he assumed. There was also a small, faded black-and-white shot of a young man in a military uniform. He looked so much like Alison that Goode guessed it must be her father. He saw no pictures of anyone who could have been her mother.

"It sounds familiar," Alison finally said. "But I've met lots of people in the past month. School just started. You know, I usually notice what everyone's wearing and I may have seen the shirt you're talking about, but I can't say for sure."

"We can come back to that later," he said. "Why don't you tell me about the last time you saw her."

She looked up at him intermittently as she recounted the events of that Friday night. "You know, now that you mention it, I think Seth was wearing a shirt like that." She paused for a minute, then almost jumped off the couch she got so excited.

"He had on this red tie with a little diamond pattern," she said. "He must have come straight from work. He was totally overdressed for a beach bar, but I was impressed that his tie matched his shirt. Most guys can't match reds."

Goode tried to appear calm, not wanting to spook her, but inside, he felt a shot of adrenaline spike through his veins.

"What was your impression of Seth?"

"What do you mean?"

"I mean, what was your gut feeling about him? What sticks in your mind?"

"Well, he seemed kind of arrogant. Probably because he's handsome. Like he's used to getting whatever he wants. I could tell he comes from money," she said.

"How's that?" he asked.

"He said his family's from La Jolla," she said, flicking the end of her nose to indicate he was snobby. "He said something about hanging out at the beach and tennis club. Plus, he wore a Rolex watch. And he talked about how he and Keith planned to make a buttload of cash in the real estate business. He also knew this other girl at Pumphouse that night. She goes to our beauty school, and she's from La Jolla, too. She and Tania were kind of friends, but not as close as we were."

"What's her name?" Goode said, his pen poised over his notebook.

"Clover," Alison said. "I don't know her last name."

Goode asked her a few more questions, including whether he could borrow a recent photo of her for questioning witnesses, and then decided that was enough for one evening. He tucked the photo into the same crowded slot in his wallet with the shots of Tania and his mother, got Alison's phone number and figured he could always call her if something else came up. Especially if he found some evidence linking her identity to Ms. X.

As he stood up to go, Alison still wouldn't meet his eyes for more than a moment. He figured it was shyness because he didn't sense anything sinister. But he'd been surprised before.

"Here's my card," he said hopefully. "If you remember anything else that might be important, call me, any time, day or night. . . . You going to be okay?"

She finally held his gaze and smiled a little. He could tell from her expression that she was used to dealing with disappointment. He felt a pang in his chest and squeezed her hand gently.

"Take care of yourself, Alison," he said, closing the door softly behind him.

He had a date with Seth.

Chapter Nine

Alison

Time became irrelevant after Ken Goode left. Alison could do nothing but stare at his business card and tap her bare feet on the carpet. She grabbed strands of her hair, twirled them around her fingers and pulled, repeating the motion again and again. She couldn't believe Tania was gone. Goode's last words played over in her mind.

"Take care of yourself, Alison," he'd said. Not in the usual brush-off tone she'd heard other guys use when they said that, but in a kind, caring way. Like he really meant it. She didn't want to jump to conclusions, but was he implying she might be next?

The more Alison pondered Tania's death, the more it fell into perspective. This was her destiny, to live through a series of losses that came in almost predictable intervals, generally not long after she thought she'd finally found the true path to happiness. The setbacks started when she was ten, the morning her mother, Lila, left for her secretarial job and didn't come back.

They'd been staying at Grandma Abigail and Grandpa Harold's two-bedroom house in the San Fernando Valley to save money. When her mother didn't return from the office that evening, Grandma Abigail kept saying Lila was going to walk through the front door and surprise them with some fancy chocolates. She said Lila always dealt with the bad times by buying expensive candy in gold boxes.

But Lila was gone for good. Night after night, Alison sat on the loveseat with her grandmother, watching sitcom reruns and waiting for her mother to return. Her father had disappeared, too, but she was too young to remember. Lila never talked about him, so the only image Alison had of him was the photo in her living room—dressed in an army uniform, with soft eyes that could've disarmed any woman. It sure worked on Lila.

Alison saw something similar in Goode when she'd opened her door and seen him standing there. She felt an immediate connection. He seemed to feel it too; he kept smiling at her even though she could tell he was trying to be serious. Under the circumstances, it felt wrong to even think about him that way. But she couldn't help it. Plus, the distraction lessened the impact of the news he'd delivered.

After he'd left, she stuck her face into the sofa cushion and breathed in the scent of his cologne, which had rubbed off on the cushion, until she couldn't smell it anymore. She knew it well. A big seller at Nordstrom, it came in a blue bottle and conveyed a strong but pleasant maleness. When she and Tania were at the mall the weekend before, Alison sprayed a tester on Tania's wrist. Tania's face went blank for a minute.

"Tom," she declared finally, and Alison knew exactly what she meant.

Alison knew it was selfish, but she couldn't help feeling angry about Tania. Why did she have to lose her so soon? She'd have to start looking for a friend all over again. She toyed with a series of what-ifs. What if she'd gone over to Tania's apartment Saturday night? What if she'd interrupted the murderer? What if she'd been killed, too? That's silly talk, she told herself. Think about something else. It left her feeling nauseated and strange.

Goode's voice echoed in her head: "Was Tania dating anyone? Had she broken up with someone recently? Did she mention any men from Los Angeles who'd been bothering her? Did she have any female friends in San Diego besides you?"

Alison wanted to know more about what had happened to Tania, but then again, she didn't. Who would have done such a thing? It couldn't have been Seth. He and Tania really seemed to like each other. And Keith? Quiet and not very friendly, but not the murderer type. Not that she'd ever met one. She wished that she'd pressed Tania for more details about her life in L.A. For all the talking Alison did about herself, Tania shared very little.

Alison's hair-pulling turned painful as her neck cramped up, but she couldn't stop herself. Dozens of hairs had fallen into the lap of her robe in swirled patterns, like silken threads of a tapestry. She jolted off the couch and grabbed a can of diet soda from the refrigerator. In her nervous haste, she poured it too quickly, watching helplessly as it foamed down the side of the glass. She swooped down to suck the river of beige suds before more of it could pop and sputter on the counter.

If Tania were still alive, Alison would've called to tell her about Goode. She figured he was a good six feet tall, a hundred and seventy-five pounds, with nice broad shoulders, a thin waist, a great jawline, and a sexy grin.

But Alison didn't trust her own instincts. She'd had pretty bad luck with men since her twelfth birthday, when Grandpa Harold had come into her bedroom to say good night, his head a silhouette against the moonlight, and pushed her hand inside his robe. His visits, which grew increasingly intimate, continued until she was seventeen. It was a heart attack that finally stopped him.

After that, she'd tried to date guys her own age, but few interested her. Sure, she'd had sex with a bunch of them. But every time, it felt as empty as the last. Eventually she just felt numb, so she stopped.

Then came Tony, an older married man she'd met at her perfume counter, where he bought one of her most expensive bottles. It was for his daughter, he said. She thought nothing of it—it was none of her business—but she did remember seeing him later that afternoon in the parking lot with a young woman with long dark hair. Alison never saw her face. He showed up again the next week and asked Alison to dinner. The dark-haired woman never came up in conversation and neither did his wife. Alison didn't ask. If he wanted to tell her, he would.

After that, Tony kept taking Alison to nice places. He treated her with respect, at least most of the time. But even that situation went bad. She'd seen the signs but had ignored most of them, including the nagging feeling in the pit of her stomach that the excitement she felt with him was wrong. He made her feel naked and vulnerable, even when she was fully clothed. She didn't trust him or her own instincts, so it was very confusing.

She and Tony agreed to meet at a hotel one Saturday night, and he was late. She put on the black teddy he'd sent her in the mail and stretched out on the purple velvet bedspread to read a magazine. When Tony walked in about an hour later, she asked him where he'd been. He slapped her face and pressed his fingers so hard into her shoulder that she cried out in pain.

"Don't ever talk to me with that tone again," he said in a low voice, his mouth a narrow slit.

He went outside to the balcony and lit a cigarette, then called room service for a bottle of Dom Perignon. He drew a bubble bath and guided her into it. He seemed to be trying to make peace, but never said he was sorry.

Tony was the first person she'd ever dated who smoked. He said it filled him up, made him feel whole. He was all nerves if he went too long without a cigarette. At least he chewed mints, which helped mask the dirty taste when they kissed.

Alison never told Tony she was leaving L.A. to go to beauty school in San Diego. She just stopped returning his calls and then had her phone disconnected without leaving a forwarding number. Alison wished she'd gotten Tania's input on the Tony situation.

Goode was quite a contrast to Tony. He made her feel

safe, and not just because of the gun and the badge. She thought he might make a good boyfriend.

She felt agitated, her mind suddenly spinning with images—Tony slapping her, then leaning against the balcony, smoking. Tania dancing with Seth. Goode leaning toward her as he asked his questions. She felt claustrophobic, like the room had no air. She wondered if there was something to what Tony said about smoking. It seemed counterintuitive, but she decided to go buy a pack anyway. She thought a walk in the cool night air would feel good, maybe even relax her a little.

She pulled on the jeans and turtleneck she'd been wearing before she took her bath and stepped into her ankle-high boots. To top off the outfit, she put on some "Burgundy Summer" lipstick.

The drugstore was about half a mile away. To avoid drunk skateboarders, she took a wide residential street parallel to Garnet, the main drag. The moon seemed even bigger from outside her apartment. She swore her hands were gleaming.

Chapter Ten

Goode

Goode reported the details of his conversation with Alison Winslow to Sergeant Stone as he was driving over to the Pumphouse bar in search of a Seth, Keith, J., or anyone else who'd seen Tania on Friday or Saturday night. Stone said he was pleased with Goode's progress so far.

Pumphouse was only a few minutes away from Tania's and Alison's apartments—not really far enough to take a cab. But then again, Goode could understand why a woman wouldn't want to walk the streets of Pacific Beach, which were crawling with young men teeming with testosterone. Goode certainly didn't like his sister living among them. He always worried that one would follow her home because she had let him buy her a drink.

Goode parked a few blocks away. By the time he got to the bar, it was about ten o'clock. The green neon sign cast a cartoonlike incandescence over the sidewalk. As he was opening the door, he heard the scratchy sound of small wheels on pavement and scooted out of the way just in time. He felt a breeze as a kamikaze skateboarder rode past him and jumped the curb onto the street. The surf rat skated away, his long, stringy golden hair flying behind him like the tail of a kite. Ah, he thought. Youth.

Inside, stools and round tables were clustered around the narrow dance floor, which skirted a stage that would comfortably fit a two-person band but likely would have to accommodate four and a drum set. The place had that fraternity house smell from so much stale beer seeping into the wooden floor that no amount of soap or wax could kill. No one was playing at the two pool tables in the adjoining room. The lights were low and Patsy Cline was playing on the jukebox. The music was a little loud but Goode didn't mind. He liked Patsy.

"I go out walking, after midnight, out in the moonlight, just hoping you may be somewhere a walking, after midnight, searching for me. . . ."

It seemed like an apt theme song for the night.

Apparently, Sunday nights were slow enough that the bartender could choose his own music, a marked contrast to the monotone bass-thumping noise emanating from bars along Garnet Avenue, where the Navy guys and the hip twenty-something crowd hung out. The bartender was polishing glasses with a towel, sliding them into an overhead rack and singing along with Patsy. There were only a few patrons, including a middle-aged man with a three-day beard, hunkered over the bar. He tossed back a shot of whiskey and a beer chaser, pounding the glasses so hard on the bar that Goode was surprised they didn't shatter. Goode couldn't picture Tania Marcus here. But then again, maybe he could.

"What can I get you?" the bartender asked without making eye contact. He was a big guy with a big beer belly, his T-shirt not quite big enough to cover the hairy roll. His sun-streaked blond hair was pulled back into a ponytail.

"Some information," Goode said, pulling his badge from the inside pocket of his windbreaker. "Detective Ken Goode, Homicide. And you are?"

"Jack O'Mallory." The bartender hung another glass in the rack and this time he looked at Goode for a moment. "What kind of information?"

The bartender had a lazy eye, so it was difficult to know where to focus when Goode talked to him. Goode settled on his nose. "There's been a murder," he said.

One-Eyed Jack shrugged. "Yeah?"

The guy probably played a good game of poker. Goode pulled the photos of Tania and Alison out of his wallet and laid them side by side on the bar as if he were doubling down in a game of twenty-one. One-Eyed Black Jack. He generally found humor in irony, but he didn't have time for that now.

"Remember these two women from Friday night?"

The bartender leaned over to examine them more closely, the towel still in his hand. "I remember that one, that's for sure," he said, pointing to Tania. He grinned, exposing a row of crooked teeth. His smile dissipated when he saw Goode's grim expression. "It's not her, is it?"

Goode nodded, monitoring Jack's face for signs of credibility.

"Oh," Jack said, grimacing. "That's too bad."

"Recognize the other one?"

"No. Well, I don't know. This place was jammed Friday night."

"So why do you remember the dark-haired one?"

The bartender cocked his head toward the dance floor. "She was dancing over there with one of the regulars. Pretty wild."

"Yeah? Who was that?"

"A young guy, Seth. He was here with another guy he usually comes with, Keith. She came over here and called for a taxi around midnight. I don't usually allow customers to use the phone, but she was hot, if you know what I mean. . . . It's a shame that she's dead. A real shame."

One-Eye seemed to be overdoing the mourning act a bit. "How well do you know these guys?" Goode asked.

"Not that good. Seth's got dark brown hair, and—"

Goode cut in. He needed more information than hair color and he didn't like this guy's evasive behavior. "What's his last name?" he said tersely.

"You got me."

Goode felt his blood pressure rising. "Thought you said he and his friend were regulars here."

The bartender pulled a pack of Camel cigarettes from under the bar and shook one out. "They are, but so are a lot of guys."

"Anyone who goes by the initial J?"

One-Eye gave Goode a "you've-got-to-be-kidding" look. "I'm sure there are at least three Jays, ten Mikes, and a few Daves. But like I said, I don't know them or any of the other guys you mentioned that good. Mind if I smoke?"

"Well, yes, I do, considering it's against the law," Goode said. He was losing patience. "So what do you know about Keith?"

One-Eye put his cigarette on the counter, probably waiting to smoke it after the law left. "Not much. The two of them have been coming here for about a year. This isn't really a support group where we bare our souls every night."

Goode felt a caffeine-tension headache coming on. He took a deep breath, which sometimes helped, and only half-pretended he was sighing with exasperation. "They work around here?"

"Yeah, over at the real estate office down the street. Something and Something. It's right on the corner." The bartender paused and gave Goode a funny look, bordering on concern. "You all right?"

"I'm fine," Goode snapped and turned for the door.

Outside, Goode leaned against the wall in the green neon glow and tried to will his temples to stop throbbing. He concentrated on listening to his breath going in and out. He was probably just dehydrated. He knew he shouldn't drink so much coffee, but he really wanted to stay on top of his game during this investigation. The drug dealers he usually dealt with never noticed if he got anxious like this, because they were always experiencing something similar, only their source was illegal.

Goode scanned the tacky business signs as he made his way down the block he called Neon Row. KATIE'S POODLE PUFF. WILLIAMS' OFFICE SUPPLIES. PACIFIC BEACH HARDWARE. LAZOWSKY & PUCCHI REAL ESTATE. He stopped, cupped his hand around his eyes to block the glare, and peered through the window of the dark office. All he could make out were a few desks, but they seemed pretty cush. The sign on the door said they'd be open for business at 8 A.M.

Goode walked back along the strip, stopping in front of Pumphouse again for a minute. He figured the bartender was probably lying when he said he didn't know Seth and Keith that well, probably to protect them, and himself as well. The question was why. He decided to go back in and see if he caught old One-Eye smoking, or doing something else he shouldn't, like calling one of Goode's potential suspects on the house phone. He also wanted to ask where he could find Clover. He figured he or one of the other detectives should call on her to see if she knew anything.

This time the jukebox was playing some hip-hop song he didn't recognize. The customers had either gone to the head or walked out the back door because the place was empty. Goode didn't see the bartender until he sat down at the bar in front of the swinging shutter-style doors that led to the kitchen. They looked like the ones in the old Western saloons, where you can see people's legs underneath, and if they're tall enough, their heads, too. From that vantage point Goode could see a very animated One-Eye arguing with someone who was out of eyeshot. He looked angry. Goode couldn't hear what they were saying over the music. When the doors pushed open, Goode saw a guy backing out, wearing a backward baseball cap. When he turned around, Goode was surprised to see the someone was Jake, especially since he had never mentioned working there. Jake's face froze when he saw Goode.

"Mr. Lancaster," Goode said calmly, with a little "gotcha" in his voice.

"Uhhh," Jake said. "Yeah . . . I just came in to pick up my paycheck. I work here part-time."

"How come you didn't tell me before that you worked here?" Goode asked.

"I didn't think it was relevant," he said. "It's not what I *do*, if you know what I mean."

Jake gave Goode a look like he was supposed to understand, smart guy to smart guy, that this job was beneath the would-be med student, Dr. Jake.

"Well, why don't you let me decide what's relevant and what's not," Goode said. "So were you here working Friday night?"

"Yeah," Jake said, "but I was in the kitchen a lot of the time, helping the cook, because he wasn't feeling too well."

"That's always a good thing—cooking for people when you're sick," Goode said. "Did you see Tania and Alison in here?"

"Who?"

Goode slapped the photos on the bar. One, two.

"That's the girl from the alley," Jake said.

"Yeah, smart guy. So, you had seen her before this afternoon, hadn't you?"

"I said I didn't really know her. I didn't say I'd never seen her before."

"You do go by the initial J, right?" Goode asked.

Jake looked puzzled, as if he didn't know how to answer, then gave him a strange smile. "Well, my mother calls me that sometimes, but I'm not sure that's what you're asking."

Goode raised his eyebrows as if to say *One false move and I'll have your ass*. "Okay. I'll see you guys. Later."

Goode casually sauntered out the front door, then turned and ran to his van. He figured Jake was sure to be hightailing it to his car, which probably parked in the back. Goode wanted to follow him and his Saab wherever he might be going now that he'd been rattled. Two encounters with the police in one day. That had to suck.

As he'd suspected, Goode saw an old red Saab driving down the alley at a good clip. Goode left his lights off so Jake wouldn't know he was following. He was worried about hanging back far enough that Jake didn't make his van, but close enough not to get trapped by a stop sign. Jake drove down the alley for several blocks until he had to turn onto a main street. Goode followed until the Saab pulled into the driveway of a small house a few blocks from where his sister, Maureen, lived.

Jake stood outside on the porch and took a few puffs off a cigarette before he stubbed it out in a planter; then he went inside and turned on the porch light. Goode could see the address matched the one Jake had given him that afternoon. So, he was telling the truth about that, at least.

Goode put on some latex gloves and quietly approached the house by crossing the lawn to collect the cigarette butt. He put it in an evidence bag and skulked back to his van. Back inside, he turned on the light and saw that it was a Camel. A popular brand, he had to admit, but he planned to have it tested just in case.

From there, he drove downtown to the station so he could drop off the butt at the crime lab and make some copies of the diary entries. He wanted to take them home for some uninterrupted reading in the privacy of his living room, this time with a beer in hand. He also wanted to finish getting his thoughts in order, figure out his plan for the next day and catch a few hours of sleep.

But since no one was in the lab that late, he put the bag with the butt in the top drawer of Stone's desk with a note to take it to the lab first thing. He got a big hassle over copying the diary pages from the guy in charge of the evidence lockers, so he got Stone on the phone and handed him over to the jerk, who grudgingly agreed to let Goode take the diary to a copy machine in another part of the station. They were all on the same team for Christ's sake. Why did some people have to be so damn anal about the rules?

Once he got home, he tossed his keys on the kitchen counter. There were no messages on his answering machine. He grabbed a Heineken and carried the diary pages and her address book to his black leather lounge chair. He eased into it, put his feet on the coffee table and popped open the beer, taking a long swig before resting it between his legs.

He flipped through Tania's address book, but found no Seth or Keith, no J., Jake or Jack, and no number for Pumphouse or Nude Nude Nude. Since Goode still didn't know Seth's last name, he'd have to assume the guy would show up for work in the morning that is, unless One-Eyed Jack advised him to take a quick trip south of the border. In that case, Goode could have himself a little Baja vacation. Hell, he thought, he could use one.

He pulled Tania's photo out of his wallet so he could really picture her while he was reading the diary, and soon became engrossed in the details of her love life. She was never very graphic, so he filled in a lot of the gaps himself. Given her appetite for sexual adventure and exploration, chances were that she could have easily died at the hands of a "Mr. Goodbar." Jake or Seth looked like good candidates, but then so did other men in her life. As he skimmed through the entries, he could see those with oddities, perversions, or wives were attracted to her, and vice versa. He turned to a page toward the end, an e-mail message she'd sent to a guy named Zlaviserciez.

"After disappearing the last time, you looked in my eyes, kissed me tenderly, touched my most private areas and told me you wouldn't disappear again. I said, "I really do like you, you know," and you said, "I really like you, too." I'd ask you to think about how I feel now that you refuse to return my calls. It makes me think of a story a wise old woman once told me about a man who chased the ghost of love: He meets a beautiful girl in a cafe. She's articulate and intriguing. She says she wonders if she will ever fall in love again. He has wondered that, too, and for the first time in years, he thinks maybe, just maybe, she will be the one. He only hopes she doesn't turn out to be another disappointment. For the next two days, he leaves messages at the number she gave him but he gets no response. So, he asks the café owner if he's seen the beautiful woman. "What woman?" the owner replies. "I saw you talking to yourself. Maybe you should go to a doctor." The man is confused, so he makes an appointment for the next day. He spends that afternoon and night feeling nauseated and listless. He lays awake, worrying. Could it be a brain tumor, or cancer? The next day, the doctor can find nothing physically wrong. Asked how he's been sleeping, the man tells the doctor of a dream about a woman he had broken up with. In the dream, she claims to have rejected him, and this angers him. The doctor suggests that the man see a psychiatrist and try to determine

*why he can neither sleep nor maintain relationships.
"Perhaps what you need is a paradigm shift in your
thinking and the way you interact with women," he
says. The man thanks the doctor and takes his receptionist out for a drink. She wants to take him home, but he
says no. He feels nothing for her. That night, he dreams
about the beautiful woman. The two of them have a sen-
suous session of lovemaking that surpasses any he has
ever experienced. He wakes up and calls her number
again. This time, a recording says the call cannot be
completed as dialed. He walks into the bathroom, feeling
numb, the phone still in his hand. He tries to repress his
disappointment, as he usually does, only it's not working. He stands naked in front of the bathroom mirror,
looks into his own eyes and asks, "Where have you gone
this time?"*

Goode shook his head with disbelief at how sophisti-
cated she was for such a young woman. What had happened to her as a child that would make her so, well,
cynical? He transferred Zlaviserciez's name and e-mail
address into his notebook two or three letters at a time to
make sure he spelled it correctly. It looked Polish, or
maybe Russian. Based on where it was in the journal, he
figured she must have known him from L.A., but he found
no match in the address book. He skipped ahead a bit.

*I had another weird dream last night. I was locked in-
side a walk-in closet. I tried to get out, but the door
wouldn't budge, so I started banging my head against
it. I became one with the sound and the rhythm of my
own sobbing. I realized that I was going to have to take
care of myself because no one else was going to. It was a
lonely realization, even in a dream, and it stuck with me
all day. Why wasn't anyone coming to rescue me from
the closet? Even in my dream, I kept telling myself that*

*everything was going to be okay, but I was so scared and
cold that my body wouldn't stop shaking. Then Christopher, the ad copywriter with the office next door, opened
the door with an angelic expression. He was holding
hands with a faceless woman. I knew who it was,
though—his wife. He'd been so nice when we first met.
Took me to nice restaurants, helped me put on my coat,
held my hand and kissed my neck until I was a puddle
on the sidewalk. I let him in and where did it get me?
Feeling used, humiliated. Why did he still love her? She
left him, treated him like dirt. Then he dropped me as
soon as she came back. Of course, now that I'm awake, I
can see what a jerk he's been to me. Why do I still care
about him? Probably because the sex was so good. It's
been six months now and I can't seem to stop rehashing
our time together. Maybe it's because I've just moved to
San Diego, and left all that's familiar behind me. I want
to meet someone new to get Christopher out of my head
for good.*

Goode added Christopher to his growing list of men's
names, and again found no match in the address book. So
he put a pink message slip in the journal to mark where
he'd left off and set the journal aside. He was beginning to
see a pattern. One man after another piqued her interest,
but eventually failed to make her happy, so they either got
the boot or left her, and never made it into the address
book. Since he felt himself drawn to her, too, Goode wondered what that said about him. As much as he didn't like
to admit it, he'd had plenty of time to think about this
tragic flaw of his. He'd always been attracted to slightly
crazed, addictive, or needy women. He seemed to be
drawn to their energy. He also got some fulfillment out of
feeling needed or helpful to them, but apparently what he
had to give couldn't satiate this type of girl. Yet, just like
his ex-wife Miranda, they always got his juices flowing.

Too bad he hadn't figured that out until it was too late. The only bright spot was that Miranda had finally stopped showing up in his dreams. He made a mental note to celebrate the small victories.

Goode felt a stiffness developing in his lower back, so he got up and walked around a bit to get the circulation going before he settled down with the journal again. He couldn't help wishing he had met Tania. Maybe he could've helped heal her, or better yet, vice versa.

Last night. What a nightmare. It was 4 A.M. and we'd just finished having sex. I guess I should call it fucking because Gregg didn't seem to care whether it was me or someone else. It was almost as if I were just a prop, a receptacle, to help him get off. He didn't kiss me the entire time. I faked an orgasm because I just wanted that thing out of me. After it was over, I lay facing away from him, my head hanging over the side of the pillow, and felt very sad. Below the waist, my body felt loose and relaxed, but my eyes and my fists were clenched with frustration. I wanted to cry, but I couldn't. So I locked myself in the bathroom, lay down on the floor, and silently brought myself to orgasm. I wouldn't have been able to sleep otherwise. I felt as if he'd stolen a part of me, just like the other times. I feel like I lose something every time I have sex with someone who doesn't care about me, but I do it anyway. I hate myself for needing it so much. I wonder if I would qualify as a sex addict. I probably shouldn't beat myself up about it so much, but I do want to stop giving in to short-term gratification. The ironic part is that, with guys like Gregg, there is very little gratification. I keep telling myself I should be more selective, but it's always, 'Next time I'll say no.' When I move to San Diego, this is all going to stop. No one is ever going to tell me again that I exude sex or that I flirt with every guy I meet. I need to rediscover my self-discipline. Still, how much of this esoteric stuff can be kept in a glass jar if the lid isn't screwed on tightly?

Goode had no idea what that last line meant. It was simply too esoteric. He jotted down Gregg's name, with an L.A. notation next to it. He felt empathy for Tania, unable to find someone to really satisfy her, physically or emotionally. Goode flipped through to an earlier section, written in the spring. The handwriting was cramped, as if she were feeling anxious. A man named Gary B. showed up in this entry and a few later ones.

I know Mom thinks I'm throwing away a good college education by going into this beauty school. I can see it in her eyes. I keep telling her it's important to learn the technical aspects of cosmetology, but also to get a business overview of the entire industry if I'm going to run a chain of salons. I've tried to explain how I see my future, but only Daddy seems to understand. I told him I would work at the ad agency through the summer, save some money, and start the program in San Diego this fall. After I finish, my plan is to take some hair styling seminars around Europe, then open a shop in Westwood. After that, I'll open another one on Melrose. I'm going to be very, very rich. I can feel it . . . Mark came up to me at his parents' anniversary party and whispered his usual, "Tania, you're beautiful, I love you." Mark is so nice, but I don't like being needed like that. It's suffocating. It's been three long months and I feel like I've given it a fair chance. There's a lot I want to do before I settle down. Like have an affair with Gary B. I don't care if he is married. He is the sexiest older man I've ever met, especially his graying temples. On Tuesday, he came up to me at the elevator and told me my bubble bath copy made him feel warm all over. I caught him looking down at my shirt and noticed afterward that the top button had come undone so that my black bra was showing. It made me feel sexy. I can tell he'll know exactly what to do. We're going to drive his little black Ferrari to that place in Malibu that's right on the water.

Goode turned to the next entry where Gary B. was mentioned and thought maybe he was on to something:

They stopped for a while, but I got more of those weird phone calls last week. The guy whispered. "I love you. I love you. I love you." The first one came Wednesday night about ten thirty. I was expecting Mom to call so I picked up rather than screen the call. I hung up on him, but he kept calling back. I replayed the messages, trying to figure out who it was and finally decided it was Gary B. Something about the intonation. He's been acting really strange since I told him I wanted to date guys my own age. At first, he was pretty good in bed, but then he started to do stuff I wasn't into. Like rip off my underwear, literally tearing it, even after I told him not to. But that only seemed to encourage him. The last straw was when he said he wanted me to slap him. Talk about a turnoff. What am I doing to attract these guys? I mean, I like sex, but not that kind. I think he was too much of a coward to ever hurt me. He just wanted to experience some pain. And I, being a sadist of sorts, refused to hurt him.

Goode made a mental connection between this entry and the ripped pair of panties he found in Tania's trash. In the address book, he found a Gary Bentwood of Dobson & Gray advertising in Los Angeles, and added the name to his L.A. list of contacts, with a star next to it. He'd definitely be paying that pervert a visit. He read on:

I got home after working late tonight, and I couldn't sit still, so I drank a couple glasses of Cabernet before making dinner. I worked my ass off all summer for this agency, only to find out that the copy for the five shampoo ads I've been working on for weeks were mysteriously deleted from my computer. No one knows where the file went. Well, I know it was there Tuesday because

*I slaved over the last one for three solid hours. Someone
is trying to sabotage me and I think it's Sandy. I'm sure
that dyed blond bitch has been sleeping with Gary since
we stopped seeing each other. She probably can't stand
the thought of me having been with him. Whatever. I
couldn't care less about the guy at this point. I have half
a mind to go talk to Mr. Benson about it and see if I can
cause her some grief. I'll probably just drop it, though,
in case I need a reference.*

After that, Goode decided to lie down on his bed and
try to shut down his overactive brain. He let his eyes
roam over the rows of tiny holes in the ceiling tiles, his
version of counting sheep. He pictured Tania, her black
bra showing. A man ripping her shirt off. Lying on the
bathroom floor, touching herself. Goode tried to push
the images away. He didn't want to feel aroused by the
words of a homicide victim. But he couldn't help it.

Chapter Eleven

Alison

Alison had walked three blocks east when she heard two
faint male voices half a block behind her. The voices fell
silent after she turned around to see where they were
coming from. She could see two figures in white T-shirts
against the night, but she couldn't make out their faces.
She jumped at the ratta-tat-tat sound, like a stick being
dragged along a ribbed metal fence. But it was the swag-
ger, the baseball caps, and the outline of baggy pants that
really frightened her. She thought she had escaped gang
violence by leaving the valley. She certainly hadn't expected gangs to roam the streets near the beach.

She heard that predators chose victims who smelled of fear and vulnerability, so she increased her pace and kept her head high to convey confidence. She turned right at the next corner and headed toward Garnet. People were walking under bright streetlights up there, but she hadn't realized it was a good three blocks away. As the young men got closer, their steps quickened and their stick banging grew more insistent.

For all she knew, Tania could've been taking a walk like this, on her way to the convenience store for a diet soda, when someone jumped her and dragged her into the bushes. They could've raped her, put her in a lowrider car and then dumped her in that alley.

Alison picked up the pace and fought the urge to face her assailants, even if it was just to see how close they were. She pounded the pavement with her boots, hoping to sound like a force to contend with and chanting to herself in time with her steps. *Don't be scared. Don't be scared.*

One of them, a short, scrawny kid about fifteen, caught up and fell in step next to her. She could hear his floppy pant legs rubbing against each other as he walked. She recoiled as his shoulder touched her bare arm. He was carrying a big can of cheap beer and who knew what else. She'd heard that San Diego County once had the world's largest market for methamphetamine, which provided a far less expensive and longer lasting high than cocaine.

"Hey, lady," he said in a singsong voice with a Latin accent.

A moment later, the second boy was on her other side, inserting his tall, string-bean body between her and the street. Her only chance to run away had been blocked. Out of the corner of her eye, she saw him swinging a baseball bat like a cane. Alison kept her eyes focused straight ahead. She didn't want to say something wrong, but she also didn't want to anger them by saying nothing.

"What, you think you're too good to talk to me, lady?" the first one said as he leaned into her. A strong waft of beer breath hit her as if she'd been sprayed by a skunk. She was so allergic to beer that she'd been hospitalized the last time she drank some.

"No," Alison said hoarsely. The inside of her mouth felt dry, as if someone had wiped it with a paper towel.

"I'm looking for a pretty lady to go party with. So's my homeboy, Frankie, here. You looking for a party?"

"No," Alison rasped. She could see the headlights of cars cruising down Garnet now. Only two more blocks before she would hit the well-lit street.

"Hey lady, why you walking so fast? My friend here is just trying to conversate with you," Frankie said in a nasal, slurry voice. The short one had fallen behind.

"I got to stop, Frankie. I'm going to barf," he whined.

"Shit, dog, I'm trying to get something going on here," Frankie said. He stopped in his tracks and pounding the end of his bat on the cement as if he were staking a claim.

Alison heard the short boy retching but didn't look back.

"Dog, you are disgusting," Frankie grunted.

Alison stepped off the curb and hustled across the street like a speed-walker straining to cross the finish line. She heard the two boys speaking Spanish in frustrated tones behind her. Their voices receded as she got farther away.

She was free.

When Alison finally reached Garnet, she was shaking. She squinted as her eyes adjusted to the bright lights of the Kentucky Fried Chicken on the corner. Safety was waiting up ahead in the drugstore, although the cigarette mission now seemed relatively unimportant.

Alison stood motionless in front of the magazine racks, staring at the shelves of airbrushed women as she tried to calm down. She would take a taxi home, smoke cigarettes on the balcony and paint her nails bright red to some more Billie Holiday, she decided. She picked out some polish and proceeded to the checkout counter, where she had to make a brand-name decision for cigarettes. She settled on Camel Lights, the kind Tony smoked.

Outside the store's double doors, she tried to light a match, but the wind promptly extinguished it. She turned her back on the breeze and wrapped her hands around the cigarette, like she'd seen Tony do. It worked. The smoke burned her throat and made her cough, but it got easier with each pull. Soon, the rhythm of her breathing had lulled her into a more comfortable realm of sanity. She smoked the cigarette down to the butt, then tossed it into the wet gutter, where it landed with a *pish* sound as the embers went out. She flagged down a taxi and ignored the driver's glare when she told him she was only going a few blocks.

Back at her apartment, Alison sat on her cold cement balcony and lit another cigarette. She still had not achieved that comfort, that fullness Tony had described. A dwarf evergreen, potted in a red clay tub on the balcony across the courtyard, caught her eye. Bathed in an ochre light from the lamp mounted on the wall above it, the tree and its setting resembled a Japanese painting, its strokes expressing the calculated precision of nature. It seemed so clear all of a sudden. Everything was going to be all right.

Detective Goode's face and deep, comforting voice popped into her mind. She'd gotten lost in it before, startled when he'd asked if she was okay. She'd said yes, but truthfully, she'd been feeling a bit overwhelmed. Her thoughts were racing so fast that she couldn't really focus on what he was saying, especially when his eyes seemed to see straight into her mind. They made her feel naked and vulnerable. But in a good way.

Alison could tell Goode was a passionate person, at least about his job. She pictured him rubbing a woman's back with massage oil like the detectives in the last video she rented. She particularly enjoyed the movies with plot descriptions that used words like "obsession," "seduction," and "betrayal." Typically, the main characters were the tough cop and the woman in trouble. He'd have a great body and a problem with relationships; she'd be scared after finding her husband murdered and would be forced into hiding from his killer. The cop usually ended up in bed with her, fell in love (or maybe just lust, it was so hard to tell), and then risked his job and his life trying to protect her. Of course, their coupling was forbidden because she was a witness, or worse yet, a suspect. But the tension would grow and, if it was a good movie, it would deliver a clever twist at the end. Things usually didn't work out between the cop and the woman. Too much baggage. Alison sighed. She wondered if Ken Goode would let her help solve Tania's murder.

She looked over at the tree again, and, as fast as it had come, the clarity disappeared and the little tree returned to its earthly state. It was most likely a stunted plant, starved of water and food by some junior executive with too few hours in the day. Alison stubbed out the half-smoked cigarette on the cement and threw it over the side into the courtyard below. She felt a little light-headed and her tongue was coated with a sticky film. She no longer felt the urge to paint her nails Red Red Red.

Chapter Twelve

Goode
Monday

Goode paddled his surfboard toward the horizon over the undulating waves at Black's Beach, a nude gay beach that was also frequented by surfers wearing full wet suits. The sun was rising, the sky was brightening, and the fish were chattering in an odd high-pitched sound as they retreated to the ocean's depths to hide from the light. A good swell was coming in.

Goode was riding a wave in when he hit something and the impact knocked him off his board. When he came up for air, he saw a body floating, alabaster white, its blue lips bobbing in and out of the water. He turned the head toward him to look at its face and saw it was Tania, her eyes open in a wide, blank stare. Goode hoisted her onto his board and towed her into shore with his bungee cord.

Three uniformed officers were waiting for him on the sand, leaning against a patrol car. He had no idea how they got the cruiser to the bottom of those steep cliffs without a driveway in sight. Before he could say anything, one of them handcuffed Goode's wrists. He tried to explain that he was a police officer, but they shook their heads and told him to hold the bullshit. One of them metamorphosed into the homicide lieutenant, Doug Wilson, who tried to push Goode into the back of the cruiser. Goode struggled to get out of his grip, but Wilson tied a dirty tube sock around his neck, so tight he couldn't breathe. Why didn't Wilson recognize him? As hard as he tried to scream, no sound would come out.

Goode woke up to find that he'd twisted himself up in the sheet until it had coiled itself around his neck. No wonder he couldn't breathe, he thought groggily. Coffee was evil. It made him sleep so fitfully. He really had to cut back. The alarm clock read 5:30. He'd slept for four hours, but it felt like a lot less. He popped a couple of extra-strength painkillers.

Sergeant Stone once told him that the department frowned on any homicide detective who went surfing during the first few days of a murder investigation because he was supposed to be working around the clock. But he also said that if a detective really needed to go surfing, he just shouldn't admit to having done so. Given the dream, though, Goode wasn't all that upset about going without.

He rolled out of bed feeling achy and disoriented. He cocked his neck to each side, trying to get the kinks out. The smell of freshly brewed coffee floated into his bedroom as he shuffled into the bathroom to turn on the shower and headed for the kitchen to get some. His resolve had lasted what, two minutes? Lighten up, he told himself, this is not the time to try to quit coffee. He'd forgotten that he'd set the timer on the coffee machine to 5:20 A.M. the night before. Goode vowed to drink only two cups. He poured himself a mug, with generous helpings of milk and large, brown grains of sugar.

The shower was just the right temperature. He hopped in and felt himself start to wake up. He rubbed the soap into his chest and wondered why the older he got, the hairier he got. Everywhere but his head. Goode took a long shower, letting the water stream into his face and massage the top of his head. When he'd had enough, he got out, rubbed himself off and wiped a hole in the steam on the mirror. He was in decent shape, worked out at the gym three times a week, and surfed as much as he could, but his body didn't look as good as it used to. He turned to the side and pinched a small roll of loose flesh on either side. How could you have love handles with no loving? He knew he needed to do more sit-ups on the incline bench, but he just hated doing them. Goode got closer to the mirror and pulled at the skin around his eyes. The wrinkles were getting deeper from being in the sun so much. He ran a comb through his hair and thought it was a little thinner on top than the last time he looked. He kept it long, below the collar, so he would fit in with the drug users, but he wouldn't be able to carry it off forever. God, he thought, he was as vain as a woman. Not good.

From reading Tania's journal, Goode got the impression that she liked older men. He could tell she particularly liked sexual guys with a dark side—like him. At least that's what Miranda used to tell him. Goode shook his head at his reflection.

"Get over yourself," he said. Sometimes he wondered who was steering the chariot he was riding in.

Goode slapped on a thick layer of antiperspirant in anticipation of a long day that likely would turn into two. He pulled on some sweat pants and a T-shirt, hoping a quick walk on the beach would help calm his stomach so he could choke down some steak and eggs. If he didn't have time to go surfing, at least he could check out the waves and mentally sort through his leads.

Goode left his place, a guest cottage behind a fairly large house near the beach, and headed west. He would talk to Seth and Keith at the real estate office and try to track down the cab driver who had taken Tania home. He'd ask Slausson and Fletcher to help him run down some of the names he'd jotted down from the diary. Also, the sooner the RCFL could print out Tania's recent e-mails and search her BlackBerry database, the better, so he'd ask Fletcher to get an ETA on that.

It was about a ten-minute walk to the beach, quiet except for the birds chirping. The homes in his neighborhood were owned by people with a lot more money than him, though that category included most homeowners in La Jolla. He knew it did him no good whining about how underpaid he was. He didn't go into police work to get rich. It was his calling.

Traffic was light so he was able to cross La Jolla Boulevard in the middle of the block. He jogged slowly down the hill until he reached the sidewalk overlooking Westbourne, the beach at the foot of the street by that name. About a dozen surfers were out at Windan'sea, the beach a block to the south. The palm trees were almost still, their fronds wavering only when the breeze picked up. Oddly enough, the sky looked like the one in his dream. It kind of creeped him out.

A little girl, about six years old, was playing at the water's edge. He watched her run out to meet the tide, squealing and giggling as the white foam washed over her feet. She scooped some of it into her hands and watched it ooze through her fingers. As she turned to look north, up the beach, one of her yellow bikini straps fell off her shoulder. She didn't seem to see Goode standing at the top of the hill behind her. What was she doing there at 6:30 A.M. without her mother? Goode tried to figure out what had captured her attention, but a couple of large boulders blocked his view. Then a beige mutt emerged, limping, from behind their jagged edges.

A set of eight-footers began to crest and lean toward the shore, but with her back to the water and her eyes on the dog, the little girl didn't even notice. As the first wave was about to hit, Goode figured he'd better do something.

"Hey, watch out! A big wave is coming!" he yelled.

But she didn't hear him. Goode knew he could never make it in time down the hillside, which was covered with hundreds of sharp stones, in time to save her. All he could do was try to warn her. He tried yelling again, but it was no use.

She jumped as the wave crashed on the sand right behind her. Goode felt paralyzed with helplessness as he watched the wall of whitewash bowl her over. She didn't even have time to scream before it swallowed her. The dog, which was far enough away from the ocean to escape the same fate, had stopped to lick his wounded paw. But as soon as he saw that the girl had disappeared, he took off, limping as fast as he could, to the foamy spot where she'd gone down.

The next wave was about to hit when suddenly something let go inside of Goode. He tore down the hill, slipping and almost falling as he clambered over the rocks. He tried to plow through the dry, sluggish sand to get to the wet hard stuff, but he was moving so slowly it felt like his dream had never ended. Goode barely missed sticking his foot in the middle of an illegal pile of smoldering coals, left over from the night before. He swerved around them and changed course. The girl's head had come up a ways down the beach. There must be some rip tide to drag her that far south so fast, he thought. She was struggling to stay afloat.

Two boys, about nine or ten, appeared from behind the boulders and sprinted toward her. They got to her first, dove in and pulled her out. She was wailing, but at least she was alive. Goode stopped running. He felt like a total failure, but he was relieved she was all right. He gulped in air as he stood there, hands on his hips.

He heard the wet dog before he saw him, panting at his feet. The dog sniffed the bottom of Goode's wet sweatpants and then shook himself, spraying Goode with saltwater. The mutt looked up at him with an expression that said he felt as bad as Goode did for letting the little girl down. Goode bent to stroke the dog's head as he watched the girl carefully place one foot in front of the other, shaking and clutching the boys' shorts as she went. They were about to pass Goode when he called out to them.

"Hey, good job, you guys. I couldn't get there in time. Is she all right?"

"Yeah, she's just scared," the older boy said.

As they headed for the stairs leading to the house with the giant palm tree, the younger boy called to the dog. "C'mere, boy."

The mutt limped after them and didn't give Goode another thought. Ah, the incredible lightness of being forgiven, he thought, playing off the title of one of his favorite novels. It was more than Goode could say for himself. He was just a little boy at the time, so he hadn't been able to save his mother. But today he was an adult, and he hadn't done any better with this little girl. Maybe he shouldn't even be a cop. Wasn't that his job, to save and protect? He kicked at a mound of dry sand, sending it into the air and back into his eyes. Frustrated as hell wasn't a good way to start the day.

Chapter Thirteen

Goode

Goode drove through the quiet streets of La Jolla to Harry's Coffee Shop, a family-owned restaurant and a cornerstone of the downtown area, which the locals called the Village. Growing up, he'd often eaten breakfast there or at the now-defunct John's Waffle Shop with his cohorts on the La Jolla High School tennis team before hitting the courts at 7 A.M.

Goode's parents were never rich—just a couple of teachers who got lucky and found a great deal on a house only a couple of blocks from work at the high school. They never had enough money to shop at the high-end boutiques in the Village, so they had to go to the malls.

After Goode's mother died, his father said he had too many bad memories in La Jolla and couldn't handle the stress of raising two little kids by himself. So he left Kenny Jr. and Maureen with his sister, Katherine, at her bungalow, and then took off to work on a ranch in Montana. Goode and Maureen used to visit him there during the summer, but he became more and more like a distant uncle. He never remarried and died of a heart attack at fifty-two. Goode figured it was more of a broken heart.

Aunt Katherine sold the bungalow after Maureen graduated high school and divvied up the money between the three of them. She moved into a nice condo until she met a rich retired guy whose gold-digger wife had run off with a younger and wealthier investment banker. After Katherine and her new husband moved to Hawaii, Maureen was really Goode's only family. He had always hoped to buy a house of his own in La Jolla, but even with the money from the bungalow, he knew he'd need two incomes to do it.

Goode often thought of his mother at odd times. Like that morning at the beach and now, as he opened the door to Harry's and was greeted by a new hostess. It struck him that she was old enough to be his mother, but nowhere near as beautiful as his mother would have been.

"Right this way," the hostess said, swaying her hips as she made her way between the counter stools and tables to the back of the restaurant. Her blond hair was pulled into a knot on the top of her head, exposing dark roots at the neck. He figured she'd been pretty once, especially if she'd ever let her hair be its natural shade of brown.

"If you need anything, my name is Dawn," she said, her face erupting into a smile of craggy wrinkles. She pointed him toward an empty booth. "It's my first day."

The skin under her eyes, which were rimmed with black liner, was a pale violet. Too much booze, a lack of sleep, or both, he thought. She had a sweet way about her, though.

Martha, his favorite waitress, seemed stressed, her red hair sticking out in tufts like Bozo the Clown. Still, she looked pretty good considering she'd gone to work at seventeen after having her second illegitimate child. And more importantly, she had more than her share of spunk. She looked like she could use a sit-down, but they were both too busy for that this morning. Her green eye shadow was smeared down the left side and her forehead shone with perspiration.

"The usual, honey?" Martha said as she slopped some coffee into Goode's cup.

Goode nodded and smiled. "Thanks, Martha. You're the best."

He'd grabbed a copy of the *Sun-Dispatch* out of the machine on the street after seeing Norman Klein's story at the top of the front page. He spread it out on the table and started to read it.

BEAUTY SCHOOL STUDENT SLAIN IN PACIFIC BEACH
by Norman Klein

PACIFIC BEACH—A beauty school student was found dead in the alley behind her apartment complex yesterday afternoon, wearing nothing but a man's pin-striped shirt, police said.

The body of Tania Marcus, 24, who moved to San Diego from Los Angeles about six weeks ago to attend a new school for entrepreneurial beauticians in Bird Rock, was found Sunday about 3 P.M.

"It was her red toenails that stuck with me," Detective Ken Goode said.

He pounded the table with his fist.

"That damn kid," Goode said louder than he'd meant to. He'd told him not to quote him. Didn't any reporter know what "off the record" meant? Getting quoted in the newspaper would only mean trouble from the brass. He'd have to give that kid a piece of his mind. He kept reading and saw the little bastard had even called Tania's mother. Apparently, she'd been distraught because she sounded quite incoherent.

Goode was about to call the paper and give Klein a piece of his mind when his cell phone rang. It was Sergeant Stone.

Goode tried to do a proactive strike, but Stone had already seen the article.

"File it under lessons learned," the sergeant said.

Stone told him that Byron would handle the autopsy duties that morning with the pathologist over at the county Medical Examiner's Office. He said Goode should

proceed with his other leads until he or Byron could call
him back with any results. It would be a few hours.

There had been some developments, which could be
positive or not, depending on your perspective. The
owner of Tania's apartment complex, who happened to
be president of the P.B. Town Council and a personal
friend of Police Chief Chuck Thompson, had called the
chief at home that morning, asking for the investigation
to be expedited. The owner was concerned about having
a murderer on the loose. Not just Tania's neighbors, but
other young women who lived in apartment complexes
he owned nearby could also be in danger.

Stone's biggest concern, though, was the chief himself.
Thompson had walked into his office first thing and told
him not to go home until his team had solved this case.

"He was only half-kidding," Stone said.

The good thing was that this got them a faster autopsy
and a put rush on their crime lab tests. The bad thing
was that it brought undue attention and pressure to the
investigative team.

But if that wasn't enough, a bunch of reporters and
producers from the national cable news shows had also
called headquarters that morning, asking for updates
from the story on the wires the night before. It was just
the team's luck—they had been hit with a slow news
day. The chief asked Stone to keep him updated constantly so that he wouldn't sound stupid when he was
interviewed on national television.

Goode finished his breakfast and then headed outside.
The sun was unusually bright for 7:30 A.M. It was going
to be another hot one. He remembered being a teenager
and feeling the excitement of a great beach day when the
sun was this bright so early in the day. He took it as a
good omen.

He started driving toward P.B., checking in with
Slausson and Fletcher on his cell phone to pass on
Stone's instructions about their duties for the day and to

arrange to compare notes later in the afternoon. In addition to the original tasks, Goode also told them to run a criminal background check on Keith Warner. He said he would call them with Seth's last name so they could check him out, too.

Goode parked down the street from the Lazowsky & Pucchi office, plenty early to watch Seth and Keith arrive at work, observe their moods and body language, and then head in as if he knew everything about them.

While he was waiting, he decided to call Yellow Cab. He got the manager on the phone and asked if his log showed a pickup at Pumphouse on Friday night.

"I've got it right here," the manager said proudly. "A short fare to Fifty-five Jewell Street in P.B."

"Wait, what was the address again?" Goode asked, surprised to hear an address that wasn't Tania's. The manager repeated it as Goode frantically flipped through his notebook, looking for a match. Damn, he thought. It was Alison's address.

"Can you see if you have another fare that night?"

There was a long pause while Goode heard the Yellow Cab guy pecking keys on his computer keyboard.

"Sorry. That's all I got."

Goode got the driver's name, his schedule for the next couple of days, and his cell phone number. He wanted to show photos of Tania and Alison to the guy and see if he might have taken Alison home first, and then Tania. The manager said the driver often didn't answer his cell phone because he taught karate during the day and didn't want to crush it in a fall.

Goode wondered if maybe the driver didn't want to leave any trace of Tania's address in the log for some reason, like maybe she refused his advances on the short ride to her apartment and so he came back the next night, raped and strangled her. It sounded a bit far-fetched, but knowing her background, anyone with a penis was a suspect.

He stood in front of the picture window at the real estate office and saw a red-haired woman near the back, holding a heart-shaped mirror up to her face. At the reception area, a blond woman wearing a low-cut red dress was bent over, moving papers around on a desk, her breasts practically falling out. Goode wondered if she knew she was giving passersby a cheap thrill. His guess was that yes, she did.

Two young men, one with dark hair and one with sandy blond hair, were talking near a row of antique wooden filing cabinets. He recognized the blond as Keith Warner, so he figured the other one had to be Seth. This was going to be like shooting fish in a barrel. When Goode opened the heavy glass door, Seth and Keith were so engrossed in conversation they didn't even notice him.

"What can we do for you today, sir?" asked the bubbly receptionist, a middle-aged woman who sadly appeared to be a *Playboy* centerfold wannabe has-been.

Goode flashed his badge, which shut down her enthusiasm. "I need to talk to those two gentlemen, actually," he said, nodding toward them.

"Oh, okay," she said, looking a little worried. "Go on back."

Seth and Keith still hadn't seen him. "Gentlemen?" Goode said as he approached.

Keith suddenly looked anxious, Seth unflappable, as he smiled and offered his hand.

"Seth Kennedy. What can we help you with?"

Goode shook his hand to be polite and showed him the badge. Seth didn't even blink. He looked like the type of guy who would sell a house infested with termites and not feel one ounce of guilt.

Goode looked at Keith, who was blinking rapidly. "Keith Warner," the blond mumbled, not offering his hand. Goode nodded, but didn't let on that he already knew his name.

"I'd like to ask you two a few questions about Tania Marcus," Goode said.

"Sure," Seth said, glancing over at the red-haired woman, whom Goode figured was his boss. Seth led them into a glass-walled conference room and closed the door behind them. It felt like they were fish in a bowl without any water, but that didn't bother Goode. He wasn't a potential suspect for murder being questioned at his office with his boss watching.

Seth reeked of a full Armani wallet, a red Mazarati with a black leather interior and two six-packs of imported beer on ice in the trunk, no different from the guys he'd gone to high school with. The snotty jerks whose fathers were neurosurgeons, corporate attorneys, and real estate developers, spent Christmas vacations skiing with their families in the Swiss Alps and went to dinner-dances every Friday night at the La Jolla Beach and Tennis Club. Goode had always resented the hell out of those guys.

Goode was curious what Seth would say about Tania's death. He could easily parrot what he'd read in the newspaper. Goode kicked himself for failing to swallow his anger and finish Norman's story so he'd know what was out on the street.

"So, how well did you know Tania?" he asked, not addressing the question specifically to either one of them. He just let it hang in the air, watching their faces closely. Keith's left eye twitched before he let out a small chirp. Goode looked at him for an explanation.

"Sorry," Keith said. "I've got Tourette's syndrome."

Seth, obviously used to the chirping, went on as if it weren't unusual or distracting, which it most certainly was. Seth settled back in his chair with his arms crossed, looking guarded.

"Not that well," Seth said. "I met her Friday night. We really clicked and I ended up staying at her place that night. She was supposed to meet up with us Saturday night but she never showed up. Then, last night, I saw the story on the news and was absolutely shocked. She seemed like a really nice girl. I figured you guys would want to talk to me sooner or later."

Keith chirped again as he moved around in his chair, crossing and uncrossing his legs.

"Yeah? Why's that?" Goode asked.

"Well, because I was with her until Saturday afternoon, and I'm sure my fingerprints are all over her apartment," he said matter-of-factly, his eye drawn to something going on in the outer office. Goode followed his gaze to the redhead, who grabbed her leather briefcase and said something to the receptionist as she headed out the front door. The receptionist swiveled her chair around to face the three human fish, continuing to file her nails as if she wasn't watching the interview. Goode figured the boss told her to practice her lip-reading skills.

"Seth," he said, trying to regain his attention. "Have you ever been fingerprinted?"

"Nope."

It occurred to Goode that he might have been arrested and released before he was booked, thanks to a well-connected family attorney. "Well then, how would we know they were your prints in the apartment?"

"I don't know. I just thought . . ." Seth trailed off and shook his head, looking away.

"You thought what?"

He stared right into Goode's eyes, probably the same way he did when he was closing a deal. "I was concerned you were going to think I did it. And I didn't."

Smart boy, Goode thought. "Well, that's not out of the realm of possibility," he said. "We aren't ruling anyone out as a suspect right now. So, when did you last see her?"

Seth leaned his arms on the table and glanced up at the wall clock as if it might help tell his story. "Well, I left her apartment around two thirty on Saturday afternoon. We'd stayed up all night," he said, pausing, "getting to know each other. And so we slept late and then just lounged around for a while. She said she wanted to take a long bath and do a few things before she and her friend met us at Pumphouse. She said she'd be there at eight or eight thirty. I got to the bar at eight fifteen and she wasn't there. Keith showed up at nine and we had a few beers. I called her around nine thirty and got her machine. I called one more time around ten, but there was still no answer."

"Did you leave a message?"

"No. We ended up leaving and went to a party out by San Diego State. It seemed a little strange considering we'd gotten along so well, but I just figured she freaked out at how fast things were going and blew me off. I mean, I met her in a bar, you know? I hardly knew her. There are a lot of flakes out there."

There definitely are, Goode silently agreed. "What about you, Keith?" he asked.

Keith, who was doodling on a lined yellow pad on the table, seemed startled by the question.

"What?" he said, letting out another chirp.

"Why were you at her apartment yesterday? I saw you coming down the fire escape."

Seth looked just as startled by the question as Keith and just as interested in his friend's answer. Everyone knows murderers often revisit the scene of the crime.

"I was . . ."

"You were what?" Goode interrupted. He stared at him. Hard. Waiting.

"I was looking for Seth and I thought he might be there," Keith said, his fingers tightening around the pen. "One of our clients was antsy to close a deal and Seth wasn't answering his cell phone."

"How would you know where Tania lived?"

"What do you mean?" Keith asked, chirping again.

"Well, unless you were both there Friday or Saturday night. Were you?"

Keith and Seth looked at each other, confused, both shaking their heads.

"Where did you get that idea?" Seth said, his brow furrowed.

Goode couldn't see why they'd hide a threesome thing if there was one. But then again, how else would Keith know where Tania lived?

Keith started to sound a little scared. "Seth was the one who hooked up with her. He just told you that."

"Okay. How about answering my first question?"

"Which one?" Keith said, visibly shaken. "He was with me at the Pumphouse Saturday night like he said, then we went to that party."

"Right. So maybe you both stopped over at her apartment on the way."

"No," they chorused.

"We're good friends, but we're not into that kind of action," Seth said.

"So maybe you went alone to her house after the party?" Goode said, hammering at Seth.

"No," Seth said in a very measured tone, as if he was trying not to get angry. "Keith and I left the party together around one thirty. I dropped him off at his house and then went home."

"Keith, I'm waiting. How did you know where Tania lived?"

Goode could tell that he had Keith in a precarious position, and he folded just as he'd expected. Only the answer wasn't what Goode had anticipated. "Well, this is going to sound like I was spying, but I wasn't. I saw Seth pick up Tania in his car outside the bar Friday night so I followed them, just to see what was going on. Sorry, dude. I know that sounds weird. But you have such a way with women, I was trying to learn something."

Goode decided to drop the issue, for the moment, anyway, and tucked away the details of this strange relationship for more thought later. "Okay. Seth, let's get back to the time you spent with Tania. Did you use a condom?"

"She said she was on the pill," Seth said.

Goode wondered if he was the only man on the planet who wasn't in denial about AIDS. Not that he had anything to worry about these days. He didn't have sex with anyone but himself. But unsafe sex was a good thing in this particular case.

"I think we'd better take a trip to the station and take some samples," Goode said, sighing, as if it were a big hassle.

"What kind of samples?" Seth asked quietly.

"Saliva. We'll need to rule you out as suspects," Goode said. "This appears to be a sexually-related crime."

"You seem to be referring to both of us here," Keith said.

"As a matter of fact, I am."

Keith scrunched up his face and let out a whine. "Aw, man."

"Why," Goode asked, "is that a problem?"

"No, I've just got a couple big prospects today and I don't have time for this," Keith said. "I also don't understand why you need a sample from me."

"Yeah. Me neither." Seth said. "I already told you I had sex with her. Of course you're going to find traces of me, you know, wherever."

"Standard procedure," Goode said.

He didn't tell them it was no such thing.

Chapter Fourteen

Sergeant Stone

"Why don't you two settle in and make yourselves comfortable here, and I'll get us some coffee," Sergeant Stone said as he led Tony and Helen Marcus from the lobby into his office. It was about 11 A.M. and Stone was expecting a call any minute from Byron to brief him on the autopsy results. He was going to do a conference call with Byron and Goode if he could remember how to do it on the phone system.

"Do you have anything yet on the bastard who killed my daughter?" Tony growled. "The memorial service is tomorrow in Beverly Hills and I'll bet you he shows up."

"No, sir, I'm sorry, we don't. But you might be right, so I'll be sure to have one of my men there," Stone said. "Detective Goode, whom I believe talked with both of you last night. We'll go over a few things as soon as I get us some coffee."

Stone went into the kitchenette across the hall, where he could watch without them knowing. They were trying to hang their jackets on the backs of two chairs in his office, but the slippery material kept sliding onto the floor. Tony finally gave up and draped his blazer over his knees. Helen left hers on the floor where it lay in a crumpled pile of cream-colored linen. Tony picked it up and put it in his lap.

Stone had seen many parents who'd lost a child. It was never pretty. The Marcuses both looked exhausted and hungover. Their eyes were red around the rims and bloodshot. Stone, who'd been sober for ten years now, thought he could detect that sweet smell of scotch on Helen. It could have been some bad perfume, but that seemed unlikely since she was carrying a Fendi purse. She sat stiffly in her chair and kept snapping and unsnapping the thing, while Tony kept rubbing his hands. It seemed they were doing everything possible to avoid breaking a composure that could crack at any minute like ice dropped into a cold drink. Stone wasn't all that eager to see what lay underneath the façade, unless, of course, they had something to do with their daughter's murder.

"How do you like your coffee?" Stone called from the hallway.

"Black," Tony said.

"Just cream for me," Helen said hoarsely. "With Sweet 'N Lo, if you have it."

"I'll check around, ma'am."

Those closest to the victim were always suspects, and although it was highly unusual for a parent to kill his or her own child, Tania's seemed awfully anxious. Before they'd arrived that morning, Stone had told Slausson and Fletcher to do background checks on them just in case. However, nothing came up but some speeding tickets. They also had been recent victims of a car burglary in their driveway.

Stone filled three Styrofoam cups with fresh brew from the coffeemaker, balanced them on his binder, and walked slowly and carefully into his office. He'd almost made it to the desk when one of the cups fell off and splashed its contents on the floor in front of Helen.

"Oh, God, I'm sorry," Stone said. "Did I get any on you?"

He looked up from the floor to see a tie-dyed pattern of brown stains on her linen suit. "Oh, geez, I'm so sorry," he said. "Let me run and get some napkins."

The sound of Helen cackling erupted into the hallway. Stone was frantically searching through the kitchen cupboards for paper towels, napkins, anything absorbent, when he heard it. She'd lost control.

Stone poured a new cup of coffee for Helen. When he returned to his office, she was dabbing at her eyes with a tissue. She'd been crying, not laughing. Apparently, his were not the only raw nerves in the room. He handed her some fresh tissues from the box on his desk.

"I'm so sorry about your suit. I couldn't find any napkins," he said, embarrassed.

"That's all right," she croaked. "It's par for the course, I guess."

The phone rang. It was Byron. "Yeah, hold on," Stone told him. "I've got to figure out this conference call thing in the office next door."

He excused himself, went into the neighboring office and closed the door. He didn't want them to hear any graphic details. He was also worried that the couple might tell the media something that could harm the investigation. Those goddamned reporters were always pushing that "right to know" crap on innocent people.

Stone fiddled with the phone until he had Byron and Goode patched in on the call. Stone filled Byron in on the new high-priority status of their case before he started his report.

"So, you guys aren't going to believe this," Byron said.

"Shoot," Goode said.

"It appears there were two areas of semen deposits."

"What do you mean?" Goode and Stone said simultaneously.

"Well, in and on her body, if you know what I'm saying."

"Not exactly," Goode said.

"Well, there was some crusty semen on her stomach and there also was some left in her vagina, so we took samples of both and we'll have them tested for DNA—ASAP," Byron said.

"Really?" Goode asked, his mind racing with possibilities, one of which was to outlaw all acronyms.

"So you know what that sounds like, right?"

"I'm not sure," Goode said, "What?"

"Sounds like a threesome to me. Unless it was one guy who missed the target the first time," said Byron.

"Could be," Stone said.

"Byron might be right," Goode said. "That fits with my line of thinking after interviewing my two witnesses this morning. They were acting suspiciously like suspects. Coincidentally, they both denied the ménage à trois theory, but I got them to give voluntary saliva samples down at the station anyway. Talk about dumb luck."

"Maybe not so dumb," Stone said. "Good work, Goode." He made use of the stupid pun on the detective's name as often as possible. He knew it was childish, but he figured what the hell.

"But wait. I'm not done. There's another weird thing," Byron said, pausing for effect.

"Well, don't keep us in suspense," Goode said.

"She wasn't strangled to death."

"What do you mean?" Goode asked. "Those were some nasty marks on her neck."

"Well, the pathologist said there were no pinpoint hemorrhages in the whites of her eyes and no internal bruising or bleeding under the ligature marks," Byron said.

"Dude, in English," Goode said.

"That means her heart had already stopped when someone tied something around her neck and pulled until they broke the skin."

"Really," Stone said.

"Yeah, so at this point, they can't say what killed her."

"You're kidding me," Goode said. "That's never good."

"No, it isn't. But hopefully, we'll know more when the tox results come back," Byron said, referring to the toxicology tests, which would show what, if any, drugs were in Tania's system when she was killed.

The last time Goode had asked why those tests always seemed to take days or even weeks too long to come back from the ME's office, his buddy, investigator Artie Hayes, explained that they took time, and with all the death going around, the lab could get pretty backed up. But now that their case had been put on the fast track, they would get a quicker turnaround.

"Wow. That's a lot to digest," Goode said. "Thanks. I think."

"So what was the time of death?" Stone said.

"Saturday between nine and ten thirty P.M."

Stone told the detectives he had to cut the small talk short because Tania's parents were waiting next door. Byron signed off after saying he was heading over to the

police department's crime lab with all the autopsy good-
ies. He planned to make personal contact with one of the
techs to explain what tests they would need—and how
fast. Stone said he'd already gone down there first thing
after the chief's visit, so they'd been forewarned.

"Goode, Tania's parents said the memorial service is tomorrow morning at ten in Beverly Hills, so you'll need to
drive up for that," Stone said. "You have anything to add?"

"I just had a thought."

"Don't hurt yourself," the sergeant said, chuckling.

"Now that we have this double-semen sample theory,
I'll be very curious to see those DNA results. I sent Seth
and Keith on their way and suggested they might want
to stay in town. I'll check out their timeline for Saturday
night with the bartender and we should have Slausson or
Fletcher talk to the kid who threw the party. For all I
know the bartender is playing CYA along with these
two. I think I ought to head up to L.A. to check out some
of her ex-boyfriends and other folks I found in the diary.
What do you think?"

"Sounds promising."

"You think the RCFL will have got those e-mails ready
for us yet?"

"You're feeling awfully optimistic today, Goode. You
know they don't get things done overnight."

"Yeah, well, I have a feeling there will be some juicy
stuff there. Especially after reading her diary. Maybe I'll
stop by their office right now and see if I can get them to
put a rush on this."

"Not a bad idea. But be nice, Goode. The forensic computer examiner assigned to the case is John London. I
heard he's new, just in from D.C. I don't know anything
about him."

"You know me chief. Charm's the word."

"So what's your gut so far?"

"Well, based on her lifestyle, it could easily be a case of
Mr. Goodbar. But it could just as easily be someone she

already knew. The short-term problem is that it's going to take some time to weed through the chaff before we can see who's important. I'm betting there's some drug tie-in, possibly through the beauty school, or maybe through the Pumphouse. Something hinky is definitely going on with Seth Kennedy and Keith Warner, but I'm not sure what their deal is yet. We'll have a better idea once we get the DNA tests. I'm guessing we'll have proof of the threesome. You sent the cigarette butts down for DNA tests, too, right?"

"Absolutely. George down at the crime lab is on top of all of that. Anything you're not telling me?"

"No, nothing solid, really. I'll fill you in as soon as I get a better handle on things. And don't worry. It's all good."

Chapter Fifteen

Goode

So Tania wasn't strangled to death, but she probably was gang-banged, Goode thought as he was driving east on the freeway. Not a pretty picture.

He arrived at his destination, the RCFL offices, which were in the same building as the FBI regional headquarters, just west of Interstate 15. John London came right out when the receptionist buzzed him. He was a young, stern-looking guy, with very closely cropped hair, and all business.

"Come on back," London said. "I've found some interesting stuff for you."

Goode was extremely pleased to hear that. He remembered thinking of the bright morning and his feeling of good fortune. "Well, that's a nice surprise, Mr. London," he said. "We're going to get along just fine."

London's serious expression gave way to a slight smile. This being his first case in San Diego, he explained, he wanted to make a good impression, so he had worked straight through the night. First he copied the contents of Tania's computer hard drive and Black-Berry database so as not to disturb the originals. Then he started searching her e-mails for any mention of cocaine, methamphetamine, or other recreational drug use. He, too, had seen the white powder on the tabletop when he had come to collect his hardware. Unfortunately, though, that was a dead end. So he printed out all the incoming and outgoing e-mails for the past year, punched holes in the paper and put them in a thick binder for Goode. He had just started searching her Internet browser history, and most of what had come up so far were porno sites. He hadn't gotten to her BlackBerry yet, which would contain her calendar and schedule, list of phone numbers, addresses and such.

"Damn, she sure knew a lot of men," London said. "I'm not sure how she had enough time to do everything she was doing professionally and still collect so many of them. You might be interested in the e-mails from the past couple of weeks, where she's talking about setting up an escort service with this other woman."

Escort service?

That would explain all the equipment in her bedroom—and Goode thought it also fit with his drug ring theory, because prostitution and stimulants often went hand in hand. Tania was a smart cookie. Why not make some profit from all of her contacts? Of course, it could be an aboveboard escort service, with no drugs and no sex, but that was unlikely. Goode wondered why, though, with all the new technology in her apartment, Tania would have a BlackBerry *and* a paper address book. The only thing he could figure was that the BlackBerry was new and she hadn't gotten around to transferring over all the information yet.

"What was the name of the woman she was discussing the escort service with?" Goode asked.

"The sign-on name was Ms. Monica," London said, smiling a little wider now. "I'm assuming it was a woman, although the messages she sent were rather suggestive in nature."

London said that professionally, but Goode wanted to cut that particular topic short before it got disrespectful to his victim. "'Nough said, Mr. London," Goode said. "I'll check it out."

London handed him the binder and said he'd call once he searched the other materials. He told Goode to call if he could suggest more keywords.

"Will do," Goode said. "Carry on."

He carried the binder back to his van and decided to read a few e-mails to get a flavor and see if they were any different from the diary entries. He scanned through the most recent ones, including those referring to the escort service. As he had suspected, Tania was bringing her long list of men to the negotiating table—and some girlfriends she thought would be eager and willing to make some good money. This was going to be a coed service, it seemed, where single rich women would be looking for arm candy as well. La Jolla was certainly a good place to find both genders. Ms. Monica said she would supply some of the Johns, but her main contribution was going to be her years of business experience, most of which came from selling real estate. The messages continued right up until Friday, the day before Tania was murdered.

All of this sounds good, Ms. Tania. Let's meet for dinner to talk more on Monday, Ms. Monica wrote in the last incoming message in Goode's binder. *I think we're going to have a very profitable future together, not to mention a little more fun on the side as well. Cheers.*

Goode felt a little overloaded with leads, but he was on a high like he hadn't felt in years. This case was really hitting his buttons, but in a good way. He decided to read more of the e-mails somewhere more private so he could concentrate, perhaps after he got to his hotel in L.A.

His immediate question was whether the drug ring and escort service could be tied back to the Head Forward School of Hair Design. Since it was also a business school, Goode thought it likely that Tania had met Ms. Monica there. His obvious next step would then be to head over to Nona's, his hairstylist, to get the scoop on the place from her because her shop was right down the street. He had nicknamed her Nona the Cat because she could be catty, but she was also wily, as cats can be.

Making the most of his visit, he asked for a trim while he was there, but not too much. He felt naked with his ears showing, but it would be good to have the hair out of his eyes. The subject of beauty school must've brought back some bad memories for Nona. Waving the scissors around as she talked, she told Goode everything she'd hated about the experience, particularly the lazy women who assumed they'd "do hair" for a living.

The idea seemed simple enough: Earn a certificate in a year and the money would flow in fast and easy after that. Wrong. What most students didn't know, she said, was that doing hair did not turn out to be such a lucrative career for most graduates, including her. She noted—as she did almost every time she gave him a haircut—that she needed to find a new job because this one sure didn't pay the bills. Still, she never quit. Goode figured this was her way of trying to get a bigger tip.

She said this new beauty school attracted a totally different crowd than your average cosmetology joint. These were career girls with ambitions, most with family money. The school taught students how to run a salon. Nona heard it was almost like getting a master's degree in business administration right along with the regular beauty stuff. As she was talking, Goode thought it sounded like the perfect front for an escort service, not to mention a sales operation for illicit stimulants.

Nona said she heard that the school gave out a few scholarships, but otherwise it was pretty expensive to go there. They had only just opened up, but she'd heard they were going to start practicing on people soon and she was pissed because she thought she'd probably have to move.

The school was in Bird Rock, a neighborhood on the southern outskirts of La Jolla. Some business owners there tried to claim they were in La Jolla proper so they could claim a more upscale niche. But they didn't fool the locals.

As Goode approached the front door, he watched himself in the facade of black tinted glass. It reminded him of the windows of a drug dealer's BMW. He felt an immediate sense of distrust, especially since he suspected criminal doings inside.

He'd half-expected to see what Nona described of her own school experience. The air a fog of aerosol toxins, women squealing with petty chit-chat about soap operas as they sat around pulling, brushing and spraying the nylon hair of doll heads, or, if they were daring or stupid, each other's. But instead, Goode saw that it was, as advertised, a different kind of beauty school. Once the heavy glass door had whooshed shut behind him, he was engulfed by an unexpected quiet. The air smacked of ambition and promise.

A few seconds later, a woman in a periwinkle silk suit and a string of pearls came out of an office at the end of the hall and started walking toward him. Her heels clicked on the green marble floor and she swung her hips provocatively, as if she were modeling high fashion on the runway, though she was a bit too old for that. Her blond hair was cut in that same calculatedly haphazard style as the actresses on nighttime TV, framing one of the most symmetrical faces Goode had ever seen. As she came closer, he could see that her skin was smooth and her tiny nose was a little too straight and pointy to be natural. He guessed she'd had some work done. Too much for his taste, in fact. Perfection was overrated. He liked women with a few flaws.

"Hello, I'm Samantha Williams, the CEO of Head Forward School of Hair Design," she purred in a voice like a late-night DJ. "We're closed."

"Detective Ken Goode, San Diego Homicide," he said, pulling out his badge.

Samantha seemed surprised for a second, but quickly regained her composure as she gave him a soft, feminine handshake that ended in a slow slide across his flesh. Her skin was cold, hard, and soft, all at the same time. Her long nails looked as if they could inflict pain, if you liked that sort of thing. Goode didn't.

He found it hard to keep a straight face as he connected the dots. This had to be Ms. Monica, or Mistress Monica, businesswoman extraordinaire. The question was, could she also be Ms. X in the diary? Is that what Ms. Monica meant by "a little more fun on the side"?

Samantha wasted no time taking him by the arm and leading him into her office. Before he could ask a question, she launched into an explanation of "the goals and purposes of the operation" while preparing two double cappuccinos with chocolate sprinkles. As she handed him a white cup and saucer with gilt edges, he thought he caught her looking at the opening of his shirt collar. She did it in a way that wasn't offensive, but he felt a bit like tuna tartarre on toast nonetheless. She was definitely comfortable with her sexuality.

"Here," she said, continuing her spiel, "ambitious men and women are taught how to launch designer salons. They not only learn the basics about cutting hair, setting perms and doing nails, but they study the economics of the industry and draft a complete business plan. The tuition is too high for students who aren't serious about their futures."

Samantha then led Goode on a brief tour of the facility,

starting with the foyer. Black marble walls with a high ceiling, softly lit by white track lights above and purple footlights below. Art prints and small bronze statuettes gave the place a feminine touch, not to mention a pretentiousness Goode's cottage would never know.

Back in Samantha's office, he sat on a suede lavender sofa to conduct his brief interview and found the cushion unusually hard. He much preferred his beat-up leather couch and his recliner with its lower-back massager to this hip furniture that would make his ass fall asleep in no time. But he wasn't planning to stay long. Mostly, he had come on a reconnaissance mission—to gather some info and to observe.

"So what was your impression of Tania Marcus?" Goode asked Samantha, who was pacing around her desk, nervously rearranging books and papers.

"Well," she said, "the program lasts for two years and we're only a month or so into it. I haven't really gotten to know the girls all that well yet."

"How about a general impression then?"

Samantha came around the desk to pat his forearm. Her touch was firm, not impersonal, yet not too personal either. Then she gave him a seductive smile. She's good, Goode thought, feeling himself respond a little. He also felt the flush of embarrassment from his body's apparent lack of self-control.

"Tania, Tania," she said.

The back of the sofa sloped down diagonally, so that Goode could only rest his head to one side or get whiplash as he tried to look up at her. He rubbed the back of his neck. What he really felt like doing was putting on a wetsuit and going surfing.

"Hmmm," she purred. "Let me see what I can remember off the top of my head." She let go of his arm and walked back behind the desk. "Oh, yes, she was the dark-haired beauty."

Goode nodded for her to continue. Her uncertainty

about Tania seemed feigned. Samantha sat down in a rather plush desk chair, facing him.

"Well, Detective Goode," she said, pausing and turning her head down slightly so that she could look up at him coyly. "My guess is that she had a lot of boyfriends. I think one of them killed her, don't you? Or is it too early to discuss that sort of thing?"

Samantha, the escort service entrepreneur pretending to be armchair-detective, was laying it on thick. Goode hated it when salespeople used his name in a sentence. As if that was really going to make him feel more like buying whatever it was they were selling. For now, he would play along with her, and wait to see if she would trip over herself.

"It's still early in the investigation, but yes, it may have been someone she had been intimate with," he said. "Do you remember seeing her acting edgy or upset lately?"

"No, now that I think about it, she seemed happy to be here. She was very focused, more so than most of the other girls. She told me on the first day that she wanted to make a lot of money. Her goal was to be first in her graduating class. She paid her fees up front for the entire year, and always looked exceptionally well put-together, which, as you might understand, is very important for those of us in this business."

"Did you ever see any men come to pick her up?" Goode asked. "Did she get any phone calls here?" He shifted around on the sofa, trying desperately to find a comfortable position.

"Her father came down once to take her to dinner, but no, she didn't get any phone calls here. She probably wouldn't though, with her cell phone and BlackBerry."

"How did you know she had a BlackBerry?"

"Oh, well, it's a requirement of enrollment. It's almost like a textbook, detective. It's a must-have."

Maybe, Goode thought. "What about drugs? Have you

ever caught any of your students with cocaine, meth, or any other substances?"

Samantha's eyes flashed with irritation. Her seductive act sank into her like a tropical flower closing at nightfall. "We don't attract that kind of girl here, detective. Does it look like that sort of place to you?"

The lady was getting a tad defensive. He pressed on. "Now why would that question offend you?" he asked.

Samantha, clearly uncomfortable, abruptly stood up and went back to shuffling papers on her desk.

"I'm not offended," she said, forcing a smile. "Why would you say that?"

"Well, we have a feeling that her death may have been drug-related."

Samantha raised her eyebrows, sighed, and sat down again. "I'm sorry. I guess I'm just upset that this could happen to one of my girls. I know this may sound selfish, but I really don't want this incident to reflect badly on my school. Appearances are so important in this town, and we only just opened."

"So I take it the answer is 'No' to drugs?"

"Yes, I mean, no, I haven't seen any around. We don't search the girls' purses, though, and I can't control what they do outside this building. I have to tell you, detective, I find the whole drug scenario highly unlikely and rather unseemly for one of my girls."

Goode smiled, noting her use of the phrase "my girls."

"These young women come from solid backgrounds," she continued, "and most have quite affluent parents, many of whom own their own businesses. This is the only school of its kind in the country, you know."

I'll bet it is, Goode thought as he sucked down the rest of his cappuccino and briefly revisited his vow to consume less caffeine.

"Have you crossed paths with a guy named Seth Kennedy?"

"No, that name isn't familiar," she said.

"How about Keith Warner or Jack O'Mallory?"

"Sorry, no."

"I understand you have a student named Clover here, is that correct?"

"Yes, that is true."

"Could you give me her last name, address, and phone number? We'd like to talk to her."

"It's Clover Ziegler," Samantha said, reciting her contact information off a list next to her phone. "Why, is she in any trouble?"

"Not that I know of," Goode said, although Samantha's curiosity about Clover only served to pique his. He stood up and started for the door. "I guess I'd better be going. Thanks for your time and I hope things get better around here, for both of our sakes."

"Thanks. Sorry if I was a little rough on you, but I'm sure you can understand how stressful this has been. Here," she said, handing him a business card embossed with gold letters: SAMANTHA M. WILLIAMS. "Let me know if you ever want a full-body scrub. We'll let one of the girls practice on you."

"What's your middle name?"

"Monica," she said, frowning. "Why do you ask?"

"Oh, I was just wondering," Goode said. "It looks nice in print and now that you mention it, it has such a nice ring to it, Samantha M. Williams. And you look far too young to have done so well."

Ms. Monica raised her eyebrows, shrugged, and smiled.

"Why, thank you, detective."

Her suspicions were apparently relieved. Her mistake, Goode thought, chuckling silently. "I'm guessing thirty-two," he said, purposely undercounting by five to seven years.

"Pretty close," she said.

He figured he was about right. As he walked to his

van, Goode saw her black Lexus convertible in the parking lot and called in the license plate to Fletcher. Goode gave him her approximate year of birth, so he could run her name, and get her address, social security number, and credit report to look for aliases and old addresses. Then Fletcher could run all that through the state and national crime computer systems. Goode was particularly interested to see if she had any previous prostitution or drug arrests.

He drove the few miles to his house, picked up an overnight bag with clothes for the memorial service the next morning, and made one quick stop before he hopped on the freeway toward L.A. As he went over the interview in his mind, he couldn't help but wonder what a full-body scrub would feel like.

Chapter Sixteen

Goode

Goode wanted to catch Gary B. before he left the office for happy hour, so he drove for three hours, the last of which he spent snarled in the stop-and-go traffic that only L.A. drivers were crazy enough to put up with.

He had been talking to Fletcher, Slausson, Byron, and Stone on a conference call on his cell phone most of the drive up, as they updated each other and brainstormed again about how to proceed. After his visit to Gary B., Goode was going to talk to a few of Tania's other L.A. contacts, whose names he'd cross-checked in the diary, the address book, and the more recent addresses Slausson and Fletcher had turned up. So far, none of Tania's friends had any serious criminal records, but Goode was keeping an eye out for potential escort candidates. If he couldn't identify any murder suspects, maybe he could make some narcotics and pandering busts.

Goode's instincts had been right about Samantha M. Williams. Fletcher found a couple of prostitution arrests for Samantha Williams, aka Monica Williams, fifteen years earlier in Detroit. It would have been too easy, he thought, for her to have drug or assault charges, too. Plus, the killer had to be a man, given the two semen deposits. Subsequent records checks found some old addresses for Samantha in Las Vegas. Prostitution is illegal there, but not in some nearby rural counties. More recently, she had lived in Los Angeles, primarily in the Hollywood Hills, so she probably had movie industry connections. She had moved to La Jolla a year ago and was living in a spacious house in the Muirlands neighborhood. About two miles from the ocean as the crow flies, some of the homes there had pretty nice views, along with healthy property values. Ms. Monica had done well for herself since she was a streetwalker in the Rust Belt. Goode asked Fletcher to go deeper and see if he could find any business or other connections, such as common addresses or previous employers, between Samantha M. Williams and Tania, Seth, and Keith.

Goode hadn't had time to check in with the taxi driver, so Slausson was going to visit the guy personally and ask if he had dropped off Alison and then Tania. Goode also gave Slausson the contact information for Clover he'd gotten from Samantha. He wanted to see if she had any useful information about Tania or her whereabouts Saturday night—the name of her cocaine dealer, in particular. Fletcher's job was to find the kid who threw the party that night, to see if Seth's and Keith's alibi held up. Even if it did, he and Slausson were going to trail Seth and Keith for a while, take notes on where they went and who they talked to. Normally another unit would do the surveillance, but since all the teams were so backed up, they would have to take on this duty themselves. If they had time, they were going to follow Jake around for a bit, too, to make sure he was in fact going to school, like a good boy, and not doing anything he shouldn't be.

They all agreed that if any one of them hit a lead that took precedence, they would reshuffle duties. Goode was eagerly awaiting the results from the toxicology tests, including a definitive answer from the crime lab on the white powder and its quality, which might help Goode determine its source. He was impatient for the DNA test results, too, but he knew those took longer even with a super-rush priority.

Everything in the waiting area at Dobson & Gray looked so clean and polished, he wondered if they bought new furniture every year.

"Hi, I'm here to see Gary Bentwood," Goode said to the receptionist.

"Do you have an appointment?" the receptionist asked in a bored tone, twirling her hair between her fingers.

"No," he said. "Tell him that Detective Ken Goode is here to see him."

The receptionist pushed a button on her console. "Mr. Bentwood," she said into the speaker, pushing the button again—twice. "Are you there?"

There was a long pause before a deep voice answered. "Just a sec, Babs. I'm right in the middle of something."

Goode heard a buzzing sound from the corner of the room. He looked up and spotted a camera mounted on the wall near the ceiling. It slowly turned until it pointed straight at him. He didn't like being watched, but he smiled and waved. A few more minutes passed before the deep voice spoke again. "Okay, Babs, what's up?"

"There's a police officer here to see you," she said.

Another long pause. "Send him in," the voice said with forced enthusiasm.

Babs opened the door into the main office and gestured for Goode to go inside. "It's all the way to the end and to the left," she said. "Now don't get lost, or I'll have to come find you."

Goode followed her directions and entered a spacious office with seafoam carpet. A man with graying temples sat in a cushy leather chair behind a massive cherry-wood desk, trying to appear relaxed.

"Hello," Goode said. "I'm Detective Ken Goode, San Diego PD."

"Nice to meet you," Gary said unconvincingly. "Did you say San Diego police?"

"Yes, I did. Why?"

"Oh, nothing."

Goode could tell he was lying already. The antique desk clock read 4:27. It reminded Goode of the receptionist: Tall, brassy, with a white face and long thin numbers. He spotted the TV monitor that showed the reception area. So, the freak had been watching him.

"Might I ask why you need a security camera in the reception area of an advertising agency?" he asked, unable to keep the sarcasm out of his voice.

Gary shrugged with embarrassment. "Oh, that, yes. Well, uh, the other partners and I worked out this system to warn us if someone we might not want to see is here. You know, freelancers, ad executives, and hungry copywriters who've lost their jobs through alcohol or substance abuse or, worse, a lack of talent," he said. "When I saw you out there, I thought, you know, he's a little on the lean side, but he's damn good-looking. He's probably an actor who wants to be in a commercial. Then Babs said you were a police officer and I didn't know what to think."

Goode let the silence hang in the air for a moment, knowing that Gary would fill it. He was curious to see just how.

"Ever thought about being in commercials?" Gary

blurted out. "I could hook you up with one of our casting agents. Big bucks in commercials, you know. Big bucks."

Gary seemed a little too ebullient, Goode thought. Guilty, in fact. But then, everyone seemed guilty to him right at the moment. Goode pretended to ponder the commercial idea for a moment. "No, thanks," he said. "I like what I'm doing. Long hours, lots of stress, and very little sleep."

Goode could see bruises on Gary's wrists, the kind you get from handcuffs. He flashed on the marks on Tania's neck. He already knew that Gary was into kinky sex, but was he sick enough to tie her up after she was already dead and have sex with her?

"So, what can I do for you, detective?" Gary asked, yanking his shirtsleeves down self-consciously after he saw Goode inspect his wrists.

Goode pulled out a photo and laid it on the desk. "Know this young woman, Mr. Bentwood?"

It was a shot of Tania, flashing her white teeth as she leaned against the driver's side of her Porsche. Goode imagined Gary's mind racing, trying to get his story straight. *Ah, yes, that sweet little thing from the beginning of the summer. She was a nice girl, but didn't like the spanking thing. She was over eighteen, right? Yes, of course, she was. I was trying to be a mentor to the girl. The agency was very impressed with her and didn't want to lose her. I was trying to convince her to continue working at Dobson and Gray before she started that beauty college. That's why I took her to dinner and . . .*

"Uh, yeah, I think her name was Toni, Teresa, something like that," Gary said. "She started working here after graduating from UCLA as an intern. Then we promoted her. She was a smart girl. I heard she moved to San Diego to learn parasailing or something. Couldn't understand why she'd leave us like that."

Good try, Goode thought. "Her name was Tania Marcus and she went to San Diego for beauty-business school, actually," he said. "Did you have any contact with her after she left?"

"No," Gary said. "I never really knew her very well."

"That's funny," Goode said, pausing. "She mentioned you quite intimately in her diary."

Gary's face turned white. He loosened his tie. "What's this all about, anyway?" he said, his voice rising.

"She's dead," Goode said. "Murdered."

"You're kidding," Gary said, his voice dropping.

"No, I'm not. So let's quit playing games here. Why don't you tell me what happened between the two of you. And where you were Saturday night. I know you slept together, because she described it pretty graphically in her journal. She said you liked to get a little rough."

"That's ridiculous. I never hurt her. I never hurt anyone that didn't want it. Besides, what would I want with such a young girl? I'm forty-five years old." Gary looked like he was having trouble swallowing. Goode enjoyed watching him squirm.

"And I was at dinner with a business associate on Saturday night. What exactly did Tania say in her diary?" he asked timidly.

Goode raised his eyebrows as if to say, *Cut the crap.* This guy was too much.

"Okay, okay," Gary said. "We dated a few times, but I broke it off with her after I met someone else." He grabbed a glass of diet soda and took a gulp. "Someone closer to my own age. She's an assistant creative director, works here in the office. Gave me this, in fact," he said, tapping his gold pen on the clock.

"You're married, though, right?"

"Yes, but we're, ah, separated."

"Uh-huh. So how many times were you and Tania together?" Goode asked.

"I don't know, two, three times," he said as Goode glared at him. "Okay, five or six times. No more than ten."

"Ever visit her in San Diego?"

"No, I told you, I broke it off and then she went to San Diego. I haven't seen or heard from her in at least a couple of months." Gary's eyes opened wide and his mouth dropped open. "I'm not a suspect, am I?"

Goode looked at him with a deep, searching gaze, hoping to pull out a confession if there was one to be had. But it didn't look likely.

"At this point, Mr. Bentwood, I wouldn't rule you out, especially given those marks on your wrists."

"Okay. Okay," Gary sputtered. "So I knew her pretty well. Liked her a lot, actually, lost my head a little, but she dropped me. She was looking for something, someone, I don't know. I tried to give it to her, but it obviously wasn't what she wanted. But I certainly didn't kill her, if that's what you think."

Goode actually believed him. He was just a pathetic kinky man approaching middle age, which in L.A. was nothing to be proud of. Goode decided to push a little harder.

"So, you were angry when she broke it off?"

"Angry? No, let's just say my ego was hurt. I would never do anything to hurt her, she's . . . she was a nice girl."

Gary pulled a DVD off the shelf behind him.

"Here," he said, thrusting it at Goode. "She had a way about her, if you know what I mean. We used her in one of our beer commercials. Watch it and you'll see for yourself. She was a nice girl, but a naughty one."

Goode knew exactly what he meant. He had his hand on the door when he decided he couldn't resist leaving the kinky sex man with a little anguish. "Don't leave town, my friend," Goode said.

Gary nodded obediently. "Listen," he said, conspiratorially. "I meant what I said about those commercials. You've got the look."

Chapter Seventeen

Seth

Seth Kennedy lay on his towel in the sand, his head facing the ocean. Detective Ken Goode had dragged him down to the station that morning to give a saliva sample, and Seth felt so annoyed by the experience that he decided to take the rest of the day off. He lifted his ear from the towel and pushed the sand aside to make a bigger hole for his face. He couldn't seem to get enough air.

The waves were coming in six- to eight-foot sets, powerful enough to send the teenage girls shrieking every time a breaker crashed on the shore. The sun felt so hot he thought it might burn a hole through his skin.

Jolene, a Texan divorcee who called him whenever she came to town on business, leaned over and pushed her finger into his shoulder. "Seth, hon, you're starting to burn," she cooed, reaching for her sunscreen. She squeezed a few blobs onto his back and rubbed it in, her long nails jabbing into him.

"Owww."

"Sweetheart, you are tighter than a virgin. You have got to quit workin' so many hours."

Jolene looked good even after raising two children, but Seth wished she'd let her daughter wear the red thong bikini. It was hard for a millionaire to do, but she'd made herself look cheap. He'd become bored with her the last time she visited, but she'd rekindled his interest a couple of weeks ago when she'd Fed-Exed him a Rolex watch. He hadn't wanted to be alone with his thoughts today, but he was starting to regret bringing her to the beach. The noise of her gold bracelets clinking together was really irritating him, though not as much as some kid's rap music.

"Take off those bracelets, will you, baby?" he said, raising himself up on to his elbows. "I need some quiet time today. In fact, why don't we move over to those rocks?"

"Sure, hon. I'm sorry," she said, pulling off the bracelets and smiling with perfect teeth. He'd never known a smoker with teeth that white.

Just after they resettled next to some rocks about twenty-five feet away, a breeze picked up, sending over a waft of Jolene's perfume, melded with her coconut oil. It was enough to make anyone nauseated. A month earlier, Seth would've been fine spending the day with Jolene, but this wasn't working out so well. He'd figured the police might label him a suspect in Tania's murder and now that they had, his life was going to be a living hell. He'd leave the country if it went much further. He'd never make it in prison with his looks.

His aunt Denise, his father's brother's wife, was always telling him how good he had it. As the CEO of a software company, it was her job to tell men what to do. She was the only one in the family who'd ever called him on his shit. In fact, she'd taken him aside the previous weekend during a cocktail party at his parents' house on Mount Soledad. They were standing on the deck, overlooking the homes that blanketed the coastline below and the palm trees that stood guard at measured distances along the shore.

"Seth, you know I care about you—I've known you since you were riding a tricycle, for Christ's sake," she said, cradling her glass of Chardonnay with a worried expression on her face. "Sure, you can make a lot of money in real estate, just like your uncle Richard, but that won't help you become a decent human being. It comes from growing up with money, I guess. How many other kids at your high school got a Porsche after graduation and then went to Stanford because their father went there? It's too bad you're so damned good-looking. You'll probably never have to work for anything a day in your life."

Denise took a sip and continued. "My advice is to start thinking about someone besides yourself for a change. Go serve a meal at the homeless shelter. You've got to do something before it's too late and you become as much of an asshole as your father. I will, of course, deny having said that. He bought us our house, after all."

Denise was right. Things did come easily to Seth. Especially the rich, older women like Jolene, the tanned and firm ones, the ones with enough cash for his Armani suits and the weekend trips to Cancun. Jolene mounted his lower back and massaged his shoulders. Maybe it hadn't been such a bad idea to bring her along after all. He wondered if he could convince her to buy another cottage in Bird Rock as a rental property.

"That feels great," he said. "You've got the touch."

Married women with husbands were the best, because they weren't looking for anything permanent. Plus, with homebuyers like Jolene, he got fat commissions as well.

Jolene was a friend of his mother's. She used to live in La Jolla until she met her second husband at a party and moved to Texas, where he was a big oil tycoon. She divorced him a few years later and took half his money. Many millions. Seth had met Jolene at one of his parents' cocktail parties last year. His mother made sure to introduce them.

"What are you, my pimp?" Seth whispered into his mother's ear after the introduction.

But it turned out to be a good idea. Seth ended up lying on the beach next to Jolene the next day and making a sale in the process.

His mother kept quite busy while his father cut open people's chests, inserted devices to keep their hearts beating, and kept the Kennedys in the lifestyle to which they were accustomed. She helped raise money for charities and political candidates with conservative Republican platforms, and was always attending some meeting to organize a ball or lavish party.

His parents still lived in the house where he grew up, a two-story mansion with neighbors like Ted Geisel, the author who wrote books under the name of Dr. Seuss. He'd died, but his widow, Audrey, still lived there. Seth was at his parents' house the previous weekend when the ground shook for a few moments and then stopped. His mother, her legs dangling in the hot tub, was munching on a chocolate-covered strawberry the size of a child's fist. She clutched onto his arm with her free hand until the shaking subsided.

"God, I hope we never have a real earthquake," she said, laughing. "Our property values would be shot."

Seth loved his mother and her dry wit. And women loved a man who loved his mother. His thoughts were interrupted as Jolene climbed off him and stood up. He felt the breeze on his sweaty lower back where she'd been sitting.

"I'm going to go for a walk down the beach. You want to come, hon?" she asked.

Seth rolled over and turned toward her. "No, thanks. You go ahead. I've got a lot on my mind right now."

Seth closed his eyes again. Detective Goode's face, with that cocky little smile of his, for one. He blinked away the image. He was determined not to think any more about him. Then an image of Clover undressing down to a black bra and panties popped up, her strawberry blond hair hanging bluntly across the middle of her back. Funny how the mind worked. Clover was beautiful in a California-girl kind of way, with smooth skin and a tight figure. Too bad she was so nutty, always crying and telling him he was going to leave her. They both knew it was true, but her saying it out loud only made it happen sooner. He wondered how far he had to

push her away, how badly he had to treat her, before she
would push back. He wished he felt strongly enough
about her to treat her better. But she only did it for him
sexually, not as a girlfriend.

Part of it was that something in Clover asked to be
victimized. In bed, they often played games. But even
when she was on top, he was in charge. He'd decided he
had to stop seeing her one weekend when the pros
stopped outweighing the cons. The cocaine, champagne,
and sex were flowing. It was 2 A.M. on a Saturday night
and, as usual, Clover had done everything he'd asked
her to do and a few things he hadn't. Then she suddenly
launched into him for making a complimentary reference to Tracy, an old girlfriend, and stalked out of the
room. When she returned, she was gripping an ice pick.
It was like a bad movie.

"Take it back," she said.

"What?"

"That comment you made about Tracy," she said with
a weird, determined look on her face. He was angry at
first, but then he began to feel the tiniest bit of respect for
her. Problem was, he couldn't really tell if she was kidding about using the ice pick or not. He decided not to
indulge her tantrum.

"You finished?" he asked calmly.

To him, they were playing the game they'd always
played, the one that put them both on the edge. She had
to know that game would end someday. She settled
down and they did some more coke. Then he made some
offhand comment about another old girlfriend and she
threatened to set fire to his swimsuit calendar. She
grabbed the champagne bottle and went into the bathroom. He heard glass breaking in the bathtub. When he
came in, she was sitting on the side of the tub, her hands
covered with blood. Shards of glass had scattered all
over the bathmat and the floor under the sink. In the tub,

they reflected the light from the ceiling, the bigger pieces sticking up sharply out of the drain like daggers.

He took a bandage out of the cabinet. When he turned around to sit down next to her, she had a blank look on her face. She obediently let him clean the wounds and wrap them. That's when he saw the scars on her wrists for the first time.

"What happened there?" he asked, wondering how he could have gotten this involved with such a sick girl without knowing.

"I was playing when I was little and got cut," she said quietly.

He knew she was lying and decided that was the last night they would spend together. On the edge was fine. Over the edge was not. He saw her at Pumphouse after that, and still sold her as much coke as she wanted, but there was no more playtime.

The sun went behind a cloud and Seth rolled onto his back. He put on his sunglasses to cut the glare and went over the night he met Tania. She was possibly the only woman he'd ever met who was worth remembering. And now she was dead. How was that for irony?

Seth had noticed her as soon as she came into the bar on Friday night. It was the way she moved, as if she knew she was being watched. He immediately imagined her naked. She was one of the most beautiful women he'd ever seen. He had to have her. He approached her table, and to his surprise, she seemed rather indifferent, yet at the same time, it was if she'd been expecting him.

"Hello," she said, extending her hand as if she wanted him to kiss it. He did, and she smiled knowingly. He'd never met a young woman so sure of herself. Seth felt a little turned around. His body hummed with an unfamiliar energy. Was he actually scared to ask her to dance in case she said no? But she didn't. She was an incredible dancer and when he put his lips to her neck, her skin smelled intoxicatingly sweet. It wasn't an artificial scent like perfume, but rather a human soap-and-water smell that would have been ruined by anything chemical. He couldn't get enough of it.

"Meet me outside and I'll take you home," he whispered to her. She didn't answer. When they finished dancing, he asked her again. She thanked him for the offer, but said she preferred to take a cab. He figured she was just playing hard to get, but that was fine. It only made him want her more. And he could play a game as well as anyone. So he left. He knew they weren't done yet.

Clover was outside waiting for him next to his car in the parking lot. "Why her, Seth?" she snapped. "I thought you only liked blondes."

He had zero interest in Clover at that point, not even as a way to relieve the sexual charge shooting through his veins. "Clover, don't be like this. You've got to let go."

"I don't want you seeing her again," she said, angrily. "She goes to that beauty school I told you about, and we've gotten to be friends." Clover flung her arms around his neck and started crying. "Let's go back to your place. I want to make you feel good."

Seth felt only pity for the woman and wanted her to get the hell away from him. He could see Tania standing on the curb at the other end of the lot and he was worried she would see them together. But when he tried to push Clover away from him, she slapped him.

"Fine. Fuck you," she said, charging off into the night.

Seth couldn't be sure Tania hadn't witnessed their little drama, so he decided to pretend nothing had happened and hope for the best. He cruised over to where she was standing and rolled down his window. She looked so sexy standing there in the moonlight, the curve of her back sloping down and around to that perfect ass. He could think of nothing but that smell of hers, how much he wanted to explore the rest of her body and kiss her some more.

"Seriously, why don't you let me give you a ride home?" he asked.

Tania smiled and shrugged and climbed into his car. Neither of them mentioned Clover.

Seth's daydream came to an abrupt end as a wave crashed, crept up the sand, and licked the bottom of his feet. He shot up, whipped his towel away before it got soaked, and moved to higher ground. He lay down, closed his eyes again, and tried to bring his mind back to Friday night. He ran his fingers through the sand and tried to remember how it felt to skim his fingertips over the unbelievably soft skin of her back, her breasts, her stomach. How she'd kissed him even more sensuously in her living room than she had in the bar, softly sucking away the wall of resistance he'd felt with other women. Until that block came down, he'd never even realized it was there. Until that night, he would've said it was an impossible scenario: Seth Kennedy, twenty-seven years old and in awe of a woman.

She took him by the hand and led him to the kitchen, where she gave him a choice between some very nice wines or a chilled bottle of Dom. He picked out a bottle of 1985 Cabernet Sauvignon from a vineyard he'd visited with his parents. She opened it like an expert, poured them each a glass and they toasted—to new friends. Then she kissed him again, teasing him with her lips and barely touching his chest with her breasts. He could feel her nipples harden against him. He was on fire. They spent the entire night, the next morning and into the early afternoon, alternating between making love and sleeping.

As his mind went over the images that followed, the cloud moved away from the sun and Seth saw only red. He realized that he'd never used the phrase "making love" before, even in his own head. For a few moments, his body trembled with the memory of her touch.

Chapter Eighteen

Goode

Goode punched the pillow, but it barely bounced back. It just sat there, flat and lumpy. He felt mildly pissed, first at the motel and then at himself. Why would he check into a cheesy motel and then expect the pillow to bounce back? Not only that, but the room smelled of stale smoke. He'd specifically asked for a no-smoking room.

Goode felt a spring poke into his butt, so he moved over a bit and felt himself slide slowly into the valley that was the middle of the mattress. If he continued to dwell on the lack of amenities, he'd never get to sleep. The red numbers on the clock read 11:45 P.M.

Just as he was dozing off, a car alarm ripped through the damp night air. Goode leapt up and pulled back the orange and green plaid curtains. They felt thin, a little slimy and were coated with little rubber nubbins. The streetlights cast a glow over a beat-up red truck, a yellow Honda Civic the size of a six-pack, and a dark blue Camaro. They'd all seen better days.

The noise seemed to be coming from the Camaro, which was parked under a pepper tree in the back corner of the lot. Every fifteen seconds, the sounds switched from a high-pitched siren to a low staccato beep, an even louder siren, and then back to the beep. Goode wanted it to stop. Now. Or somebody was going to get hurt.

Stone had told him not to go crazy at an expensive hotel, so he thought it best to go on the cheap. But he promised himself he'd do things differently the next time—spend his nightly travel allowance and then pay the difference so he could get a decent room. In the meantime, he had to kill that alarm. He called the front desk and sputtered into the phone: "Can't you do something?"

The night clerk said something in a Middle Eastern accent and then hung up. A few minutes later, he came to the door in his slippers, offered a lightbulb to Goode, and mumbled something unintelligible. Goode slammed the door, sighed, and shook his head. Then he felt bad that he'd yelled at the poor guy, who was still standing there when Goode opened the door to apologize. Goode pointed down to the Camaro and put his hands over his ears. The man looked hurt as he shrugged, said something incoherent, and shuffled back downstairs to the front office.

Goode figured it would be at least an hour of hell before the car battery went dead, and by then, he'd be ready to shed his own skin. Searching the room for a distraction, he tried picking up the TV remote, but it was glued to the bedside table. It was David Letterman time, and he couldn't get the damn thing to work. The battery was probably dead. How ironic was that?

Goode was really exhausted. It felt good to lie down, even on a crummy bed. He'd spent the afternoon cruising around the Beverly Hills neighborhood where Tania had gone to high school; he had interviewed several witnesses, many of whom were still living with their parents. The homes were like fortresses—expansive estates with high walls, coniferous trees, and tall iron gates. One of them had a beautiful Japanese garden with decorative rocks and a black marble fountain, circled by bonsai trees.

Goode didn't learn anything that he hadn't already gleaned from the diary. His picture of her was becoming more three-dimensional, although not a whole lot less focused on her sexuality. Her friends said she was a well-liked, beautiful girl, but on the edge of the popular crowd because she was in smarter classes than the rest of them. Nonetheless, she was still voted Homecoming Queen, probably because she exuded sexuality, but also because she was very friendly. In the end, he didn't find any of her friends to be likely escort candidates, but vice wasn't his area of expertise.

He was curious to put a face on Tania's mother after having talked to her by phone. He wondered if she knew how complicated her daughter had been and whether Tania had taken after her. But since Tony and Helen had already talked to Stone that morning at headquarters, he decided to let them grieve in peace and leave his prurient curiosity unsatiated.

He knew the saliva samples from Seth and Keith would be analyzed by the time the memorial service started the next morning, so he decided to withhold judgment until he had the results, but he would keep his eyes open for clues that could be helpful later.

Goode still had no cause of death and no motive. He told himself that the more he read of the diary and the e-mails, the better chance he had of connecting the multitude of dots he was gathering. But for the moment, he was feeling a little scattered—overwhelmed, in fact. Maybe it was the caffeine, or maybe not enough sleep. He was looking forward to the moment when he could say, *Aha!* Perhaps he felt he needed to go over the reading materials more carefully so he could start seeing those connections.

He was embarrassed to admit, even to himself, that he'd been in a more or less constant state of arousal since he started reading Tania's writings. He hadn't been able to stop imagining how she'd moved, the scent of her hair and the taste of her lips. He told himself it was only natural for him to picture what she'd been like. Plus, he had to really *know* her to find her killer. Didn't he?

He pulled the binder of e-mails out of his overnight bag and opened it to a page two-thirds of the way through, from the previous summer. It was addressed to felicity@girls.com. He seemed to remember *Girls* being the name on one of the magazines in the stack under her bed.

I could describe it as a craving. A sexual craving is not all that different from a physical hunger, because starving myself sexually can produce a hunger all its own— a longing and an emptiness that I feel compelled to quiet and fulfill. It usually hits me on a Friday morning and distracts me from work until I plan a night on the town that promises some interaction. I've tried fantasizing instead, but it's only good in a pinch. I've come so close to the real thing in my head as I'm lying in bed, touching myself, that I can actually feel my body tense and my breathing speed up. I imagine tangled limbs, soft strokes alternating with firm squeezes. Being engulfed by a man's muscled arms or held inside the bend of his leg. Him kissing me up the back of the neck and rubbing my ass. Bending me over the arm of the sofa and pulling my skirt up. The problem is, no matter how much I fantasize, or even how much a man actually touches me, I always want more. You know what I mean?

Totally, Felicity wrote back. *You have a way with words. Send me some more of your writing and maybe we can publish it in the next issue.*

Wow. Published at the age of twenty-four? What an interesting mind this young woman had. He wished he'd known her, even if only for one night. He skipped ahead and found another note to Felicity, but this one sounded full of more angst than fantasy.

You know how some days you wake up in someone else's bed and you wonder, "What am I doing here? Do I really need to be held that badly? Do I really want someone I don't know all that well to touch my most private parts, even when I know those hands were touching someone else the night before?" I had one of those interludes last night and now I feel so detached and alone. My body feels like it doesn't even belong to me. I guess I'm in transition mode, getting ready to move from L.A. to San Diego, and then who knows where. Maybe that's why I'm just jumping from one guy to the next. A med student to a doctor, a law student, a screenwriter, an actor . . . What's next? I've always wanted to date an architect so he could help me design my life. Like Jason, the art director I worked with this summer, told me, "Just keep thinking white space. You don't always need to fill it with something." That's easy for him to say.

How could this woman be only twenty-four? Goode allowed himself one last e-mail before he put the binder away. Maybe he'd have more pleasant dreams than usual.

Sometimes I don't even know who I am. Like last weekend, I wore knee-high boots, tight black jeans, and a low-cut black sweater, kind of trashy, really, but it worked. I caught the eye of that cute bass player at the Spritz Club. He took me back to his place and showed me his pierced nipple. It was such a turn-on I almost melted. Last Thursday, I wore a flowered dress with a high-necked collar and a string of pearls, and I felt virginal. Ha. That's pretty funny. I don't think I'll ever be able to let a man get too close to me 'cause I don't want anybody trying to figure me out, asking me questions like that therapist did last year. He was so gross, so old and so wrinkled, not to mention lecherous. I'm still pissed my Mom made me go see him. Like she couldn't find someone other than Dad's golf partner to send me to. Well, I guess my friends are pretty bizarre, too. Rachel told me yesterday that she only sleeps with black guys. And Joanne likes men in uniform. She's been out with security guards, police officers, firefighters, even with that guy who runs the elevator at the Hyatt. I don't get that at all. I'm just looking for a guy who can hold my interest.

Goode fell asleep imagining what she looked like in those knee-high boots.

Chapter Nineteen

Goode

The alarm on Goode's watch roused him out of a dream in which he was being chased by a man with a pierced nipple. His T-shirt was clammy.

"Show time," he whispered as he pulled back the covers. He'd slept as well as could be expected, given the alarm mishap, the bad pillow, and the valley in the mattress.

The cold bathroom tiles felt good on his feet after sleeping in Santa Ana heat. He took a deep breath and felt a stinging in his nose. That evil dust was still in the air. He'd definitely had enough of the stifling hot, dry winds, and he'd forgotten to bring his allergy medication. He hopped into the shower, expecting a nice soothing wake-up, but the water kept going from hot to cold, hot to cold.

Goode was shaving when he heard his cell phone go off on the sink. It was Stone, calling from home, and he sounded pissed. Said he was just getting ready to go play catch with his son in Balboa Park when the lieutenant called. Another beauty school student was dead in P.B., a redhead named Sharona Glass.

"So now we know there's some connection to the beauty school," Stone said.

"Shit," Goode said.

"What, did you know her?"

"No. Maureen told me a couple of weeks ago that she'd met a few women from a new beauty school in La Jolla. I didn't think anything of it until I found Tania Marcus. I called and went by Maureen's house in P.B. before I hit the road yesterday, but no one was home. I should have gone in. . . ."

"Simmer down now," the sergeant interrupted. "You go to the memorial service and I'll send a unit over to Maureen's to see if she's all right. I haven't seen her around for months. What's the address?"

"It's on Turquoise Street, near Cass. The address fell off the house but it's white with yellow shutters. Her roommates are two surf bum pool cleaners. Call me when you get a chance and let me know if you hear anything, okay?"

"Will do. You just concentrate on the funeral and see if you can figure out what that connection is. I'll have Byron process the new murder scene. So, when you're done there, head over there ASAP and he'll bring you up to speed. It's one of those apartment complexes right near the beach on Chalcedony. By the way, Slausson and Fletcher said they trailed Seth, Keith, and Jake for a while, and the three of them didn't meet for a giant drug pow-wow or do anything else suspicious. Seth and Keith mostly went separately to real estate appointments and Jake got up early—really early—to drive up to UCSD. Fletcher hung out in the parking lot for a while until he saw another student, who said the building Jake had gone into was for biochemistry majors. So it sounds like he told us the truth about being in the master's program up there. Looks like a dead end to me."

"What about those cross-checks between Tania, Samantha Williams, Seth, and Keith? Anything there?"

"Sorry, no. Dead end. No connections at all, at least with the names we've got for them."

"What about the taxi driver? Did Slausson catch up with him?"

"Yeah, the guy swears he dropped off Alison and never met anyone named Tania Marcus. He grumbled about the short fare but said she gave him a nice tip so it all worked out."

Goode jotted down notes as Stone rattled off the information, and then hung up. He was late but he decided to try Maureen's number one last time and got the rambling answering machine message again. He left a message in that fatherly tone she hated. He couldn't help it when he was this worried.

"Wherever you are, whatever you're doing, stop it immediately and call me on my cell. There've been two murders at that beauty school you were telling me about. I hope you were smart enough not to waste your time with that, but I can't seem to find you anywhere and I'm worried about—"

Damn thing cut him off with a beep. Where was she? Goode had wanted to move to P.B. from his cottage in La Jolla to be closer to her, but she'd said no. She liked having him close, but not that close. Goode told her he needed to save money so he could buy a house, but she didn't believe him. He didn't tell her he was still paying off credit card bills his ex-wife had racked up.

Sometimes it was tough, but he usually tried to cut Maureen some slack, considering how the two of them grew up. She'd always wished that their father had stuck around, and so had Goode. He didn't mind looking out for his little sister, but he could have used a male role model himself. Maureen had grown up quite a bit in the last few years, but he still worried about her. For one thing, he didn't trust her roommates, Chris and Mitch. Goode had known them since junior high school, and frankly, he'd rather she live with strangers than let those guys see her getting out of the shower. She said she could take care of herself, especially after all those Tai Kwon

Do classes. When Goode tried to encourage her to move in with female roommates, she told him to "Get a wife."

Goode smacked his hand on the steering wheel. He'd forgotten to ask Stone one very important question, so he called him back. "Hey, one more thing. How are we doing on the analysis of that white powder from Tania's coffee table?"

"Funny you should mention that. I got the paperwork right after we hung up, but the lieutenant walked in and wanted a full report first. You know how that goes. There was pretty high-quality cocaine on one corner and some of the purest methamphetamine the lab has ever seen on the other. Looks like the little lady was connected to some people who could supply her with a smorgasbord of high-end stimulants."

"That is very interesting," Goode said.

"I've gotta run," Stone said. "That's the chief on the other line. Call me after the service."

The test results were helpful, but Goode still had no clear motive and still no direction to follow other than the drugs. The problem was, people don't act rationally when they're high on stimulants, so that always made it difficult to find reason in their behavior. He figured Seth brought the drugs to Tania's, but it was also possible that Tania had her own stash, or even that Keith was her supplier and that's how he knew where she lived.

Goode quickly packed his bag and drove away from the pathetic excuse for a hotel. He'd planned to leave earlier, grab some breakfast and show up at the funeral half an hour early so he could watch people arrive. But with all the phone calls, it was too late to stop for anything other than a donut.

His stomach started gurgling around nine thirty as he was pulling into Beverly Hills, where he couldn't afford to buy any food anyway. What he really wanted was a meatball sandwich with hot peppers and mozzarella cheese, doused with oil and vinegar. After he parked near the church, he leaned over and opened the glove box, just in case he'd left something to eat in there.

"C'mon," he said, riffling through maps, wadded-up papers and empty gum wrappers. He found a flashlight, a dead battery, some breath mints and a half-eaten package of tropical fruit LifeSavers.

"Excellent," he said, popping one of the mints into his mouth. It was soggy, but he was so hungry it almost tasted good.

He leaned back and propped his feet up on the dashboard, alternating between LifeSavers and mints until he'd finished them all. A tall guy in a black shirt and pants walked past the car, but Goode couldn't see his face. The guy had a very determined gait even though he had a slight limp. This was L.A. and a funeral to boot, so it was unlikely this guy would be the only one wearing black. Goode made a mental note to ask Alison if she knew which of Tania's friends had a limp.

A few minutes later, the street was full of Mercedes, competing with the BMWs and Jaguars for parking spaces. Goode wondered how all these people were going to fit into the church. There were more men than women, walking solo, or in twos and threes. A black Ferrari almost mowed down Seth and Keith as they crossed the street. Turned out the driver was Gary Bentwood. Goode saw him park illegally down the block.

Goode wandered over to the church to find Alison, and picked her out of the crowd pretty easily. She was standing alone on the front steps, pulling on the skirt of a dark purple velvet dress. She smiled as he got closer. But before she could say anything, he put his finger to his lips and shook his head. He didn't want her calling him by name or talking about the investigation. He wanted to remain incognito. The scent of gardenias greeted them as they entered the church.

"Gardenias were Tania's favorite flower," Alison whispered, pointing to the glass bowls of them that were placed around the spacious room.

"Follow me and we'll stand together in the back," he whispered as they joined the throng of mourners filing in. The way people were dressed and chatting each other up, they could have been at a Hollywood party or an art gallery opening. He headed for an open spot along the back wall.

"I recognize some of these guys from photo albums Tania showed me," Alison whispered. "She sure had a lot of old boyfriends. She said she stayed pretty good friends with a lot of them."

"Any of them stick in your mind?"

"She was seeing some married guy at the ad agency where she used to work, but that ended at the beginning of the summer. I didn't meet her until orientation, which was about a week before school started, so I'm sure there were others."

"Did she date anyone once she moved to San Diego?"

"She may have, but Seth is the only one I saw her with. Her next-door neighbor, Paul, tried to date her, but he wasn't her type. We'd see him trying to hide in the parking lot, taking pictures of her. Kind of creepy, don't you think?"

"Yeah," Goode said. "Did anything happen between them?"

"He asked Tania out a few times, but she always said no. Then he started getting weird. You know. He knocked on her door late at night without being invited and asked if he could come in. The usual stuff guys in love do."

"So how did Tania handle that?"

"She tried to be nice, but firm. She didn't want any conflict with a next-door neighbor. I guess he didn't really get the message."

"When was this?"

"She told me it started as soon as she moved in."

"Anything else unusual about him?"

"Ummm . . . yeah. He walks with a limp. A bad motor-cycle accident or something."

Goode perked up.

A couple of bruisers pushed past them, jostling Alison. "Hey. That's weird. That's him right there," she said, pointing to a guy at the front of the line of people who were waiting to pay their respects at the casket. "I can't believe he'd drive all the way up here. Well, yeah, I guess I can."

Goode hadn't noticed Paul limping the day he'd inter-viewed him. But then again, he hadn't seen Paul walk anywhere. He remembered that the kid had barely stepped outside his apartment to talk to Goode, when he'd curled around the front door like a cat.

Goode and Alison watched Paul look up at the huge white cross on the wall. Then, as if the sight of it pained him, Paul dropped his eyes to the casket. He touched the coffin for a moment, but pulled his hand away quickly, as if it had burned his hand. He tried again, tentatively, then rubbed his fingertips along its edges. Finally, he kneeled and laid his head on the wood.

Chapter Twenty

Helen

The morning of her daughter's funeral, Helen awoke from a dream in which she was wearing the same pink suit that Jackie Onassis had worn the day JFK was shot. Helen walked into her everyday closet and scanned the tightly packed rows of blouses, skirts, and dresses, each encased in its own clear plastic bag. The gowns were in a separate closet. She loved to buy pretty outfits, but she'd had fewer and fewer occasions to show them off in the past couple of years. Today, she didn't care much about looking pretty. She just wanted to wear something black that wasn't too short or too tight.

She finally decided on the modest dress that she'd bought as a way to get herself back to church. She'd never worn it. She wrapped her head in a black silk scarf and applied some opalescent lipstick. The sunglasses weren't just for show. Her eyes were bloodshot and the bright light streaming through the bedroom curtains burned something fierce.

Helen knew she should try to eat, but she couldn't even get a piece of wheat toast down with her coffee. Her head felt like a block of lead. Tony didn't do much better. He ate a couple bites of English muffin and pushed the plate aside. They didn't have much to say to each other. Helen had a Bloody Mary while Tony was in the shower. She knew he wouldn't approve.

The air was heavy in the kitchen. She and Tania had always gabbed away before a big party at the house, preparing hors d'oeuvres and drinking white wine. Tania would arrange cold cuts on the glass platter, moving from deep red salami to rose-colored ham. But a wake was not your ordinary party and Helen didn't have her daughter to keep her company. Her throat tightened and the tears came again.

Helen wiped her eyes with a tissue and looked over her cold-cut plate in the refrigerator. She just didn't have Tania's touch. She envisioned her daughter's ivory hands with their red fingernails, making up the dessert plate. She'd bake muffins, slice pound cake, and then lay the slabs like fallen dominos. Helen didn't feel like sweet stuff this time so she didn't bake anything.

Helen bought two cases of Zinfandel for the guests. She saw her daughter as a sacrificial lamb and the wine she would serve as a symbol of Tania's blood. Just like Jesus. Just like communion. Not that her daughter was a saint or anything, but she was so young. Her murder seemed so senseless, so random and so wrong. Her death had to have a purpose, didn't it? Maybe she died so others could live. That's how Helen wanted to see it, anyway. She would toast to Tania's spirit and goodness at the wake. Helen could feel it in the air around her.

She had planned to talk to her minister about Tania's death, but she hadn't had a chance. She wanted to tell him about the lamb and the wine and the sacrifice, but she wasn't sure he would understand, comparing her daughter to Jesus and all. Maybe she would take him aside while her guests drank their wine and ate their pate de fois gras on French bread and ask how she could ease the pain that wracked her soul and made every joint ache. He would have an answer to that, wouldn't he?

As she and Tony drove up to the church in the black Mercedes, Helen couldn't believe how many people had come to the funeral. They were milling around on the lawn and filing slowly into the building. She felt feverish, as if she had the flu. She wished she'd had another Bloody Mary before they left.

"Tony. For God's sake, look at them. They're all dressed to the hilt, like this was a damn cocktail party. I don't know if I can face this."

Helen had been dreading the ceremony. She wasn't ready to say good-bye to Tania. And if that wasn't enough, she had to face a long afternoon at the wake with her relatives, who had insisted on flying out from Iowa. Thank God they had the courtesy to stay at hotels.

Tony circled the block several times and still couldn't find a parking spot on the street. The neighborhood was so crammed with cars he had to create his own space between garage doors in an alley. He offered her his arm, and, after considering the possibility of how it would look if she didn't take it, she held onto the crook of his elbow. They walked slowly together, each being careful of the other as they stepped from the curb into the street. Tony seemed so beaten down that she felt she needed to try and overcome the usual distance between them. But with her frayed nerves, it was going to be difficult. Then she remembered the flask she'd put in her purse that morning. She squeezed his arm and he smiled down at her.

Helen sighed as they approached the church and all those people. As the two of them pushed their way through the crowd, people kept touching Helen on the arm and saying how awful it was that Tania had died so young. She felt somewhat shielded by her sunglasses and managed to nod stiffly at them. Please, she thought, please don't ask me a question.

Helen did not want to break down in front of strangers. Not before the ceremony, at least. They'd all be watching for her reaction. Helen had heard from a friend at the club that she'd frustrated many women who had tried to invite her to dinners and parties with the girls. After three rejections, the friend told her, they wrote her off as a bitch. Helen hadn't felt like socializing much the past few years, making pathetic small talk with women who knew their husbands were running around on them. Most of the time, she wanted to be left alone to watch movies and read her magazines in peace. Occasionally, she'd venture out to play some tennis or have a drink at the club, but she never really enjoyed it much.

Now, just like before Tania was born, Helen would have to deal with these women alone. As she and Tony crossed the threshold, Helen could hear her Aunt Martha's voice behind her. "It's such a shame," Martha was saying. "She was just getting started."

Once they stepped inside the church, Helen needed to stop a moment so her eyes could adjust to the dim lighting. They slowly made their way to their reserved seats at the front, nodding at a few friends from the club. Within a few minutes, though, Helen felt so claustrophobic she thought she was going to explode. It was another one of those damn panic attacks.

Helen's throat was so dry she couldn't swallow. And that made the panic worse. What if she couldn't swallow again?

"I can't swallow," she whispered.

Tony rubbed her upper arm. "Try and relax," he said.

But it didn't work. Her throat was constricting. She had to get something to drink. "I'm going to find a bathroom," she said.

"You want me to come with you?" he said, starting to follow her.

"No, I'll be fine," she said. "Why don't you find our seats?"

Helen turned sideways and pushed through the people as she searched for the bathroom. It had to be deserted. It just had to be.

People turned to see who was shoving them, but she didn't stop to apologize. She was on a mission. She tried again to swallow, but the walls of her throat would not meet.

She couldn't stand having so many people pushing up against her.

Finally, she was alone in a hallway, but none of the doors was marked. She looked side to side for the bathroom, but couldn't remember where it was. She tried to turn a doorknob, then another. She still couldn't swallow. She tried to gather some saliva in her mouth so she'd have something to wet the back of her throat. But nothing would go down. She spotted the door she was looking for and, almost without effort, she swallowed. It was such a relief. After pushing the door open, she practically dove into one of the stalls. Her chest heaved for breath.

Safely inside, she quickly pulled out the antique silver flask, dropping the purse in her haste. Helen took a couple of long slugs of scotch. They went down as if she'd never had a problem. They coated her throat as heat swept through her chest. She breathed in deeply and exhaled. Her heartbeat began to slow and she felt herself begin to relax.

The flask was engraved with a monogram, GTL. She'd come across it at an estate sale and fantasized about its former owner. It had to be a man. She'd originally bought it for Tony, but she liked it so much that she kept it for herself. She took another big sip. That familiar warmth crept over her, like a lover's embrace. She sighed.

Helen stayed in the stall for a while longer, not really knowing how much time had passed, only that a number of other women had found the bathroom, too. She heard one of them say the line outside trailed all the way down the hall.

"It's almost as bad as a concert," one of them said as she primped at the sink.

Helen pulled her hair away from her face, straightened her dress, and pushed open the stall, staring straight ahead. The girls smiled awkwardly at her and gave her their condolences as she washed her hands. Helen thanked them politely. She forced herself into the hallway, wobbling a little, and found her way back to the pews. The sharp staccato voices had quieted into a more comfortable allegro, or at least it seemed that way to her. The rough edges of the crowd had ebbed away. Her mind felt numb again. Thank God, she thought.

The pews had filled up and there was standing room only along the back and side walls. She knew her daughter was popular, but she had no idea that Tania had this many friends. As Helen approached Tony in the center of the front row, she saw him looking at a young woman wearing a purple velvet dress that hugged her rather large breasts. What kind of dress was that to wear to a funeral?

"Who is that?" Helen asked. She sat down next to

him and placed her purse on the floor underneath the bench.

"Who is who?"

"That girl you're staring at."

"I don't know. Must be one of Tania's friends."

Helen settled back as much as she could and re-arranged her dress so it didn't bunch up on one side. She watched a young man dressed in a black shirt and pants limp past her. He was staring straight ahead, his face tight and pale. He had hollowed eyes. She nudged Tony.

"Look at that strange boy," she whispered. "Isn't that Linda Henry's son?"

Tony shook his head and shrugged, then shifted his attention to the white cross in front of them. He seemed pretty distracted. Agitated even. A few minutes later, Helen saw a single tear trickle down his face. She took his hand and squeezed. Her eyes went from the coffin, to the flowers, to the collage of family photographs the two of them had made the night before. Then everything went blurry, as if she were underwater. That's how it had been when they were putting the collage together. They'd spent hours going through envelopes of photos, searching for the right ones. Neither of them could stop crying for long. Helen reached into her purse and pulled out a tissue, wiped her eyes and blew her nose until she could see clearly and breathe normally again.

If it wasn't one thing, it was another. The strap of her dress kept falling off her shoulder under her blazer. She'd forgotten that she'd lost ten pounds since she'd bought the thing, five in the last two days alone. Even though she'd been cooking for the wake, she hadn't eaten much of anything. The thought of food sickened her. Scotch went down much easier.

Helen felt guilty she hadn't asked Tania more about her life in San Diego that last weekend she'd come home. Helen had been living in a fog of depression for so long she hadn't known how to find her way out of it, let alone how to focus on her daughter's well-being. Now she wished she'd felt stronger and tried harder. Maybe if she'd shown more interest in her daughter, Tania would've told her that some new boyfriend had been giving her problems, or that an old boyfriend was stalking her. Maybe then Helen could've stopped this whole nightmare from happening.

But Tania was never one to confide in her mother. Ever since the pregnancy, it had become increasingly obvious that Tania kept many things from her. Helen now knew that her worries had been warranted. Only this time it didn't feel good to be right.

Chapter Twenty-one

Alison

Alison gathered up her courage to brave the crowd and pay her last respects to Tania. A little unsteady on her black high-heeled shoes, she teetered up the red-carpeted aisle to the front of the church. She could feel people looking at her, wondering, *Who is that under-dressed nobody?*

Only a few minutes before, she'd been standing next to Ken Goode at the back of the church, feeling assured that she could make it through the service without getting too upset. But now, as she approached Tania's polished oak coffin alone, she felt a shawl of emotions drape itself around her shoulders. She'd only met Tania a month ago, but she'd gotten very attached to her. She really missed her.

Alison joined the line of people waiting to touch the coffin or say a few silent words. She gazed at the yellow poster board that was covered with photos of Tania, her

family, and friends. Alison leaned in for a better look at a
blurry picture of a young Tania and two adults, probably
her parents, standing together in front of a two-story
house surrounded by trees. Most of the other photos
were larger and clearer. In one of them, Tania had her
arm around an attractive older woman who was blond
but otherwise looked just like her. Alison figured she was
Tania's mother. They were together in a relatively recent
shot, too, taken at Tania's college graduation. A glowing
Tania stood with her mother, and an older man standing
between the two. Tania was looking up and smiling co-
quettishly at the man as she held on to his arm. He looked
very familiar. Something about that wide-mouthed grin,
the laughing eyes, and the cowlick that puffed over to
the left. Alison felt the wind go out of her.

That older man was Tony.

Tania's father. She had slept with Tania's father.

Alison's eyes stung and then glazed over with tears.
She tried desperately to hold them back, but they began
to spill down her cheeks as she remembered being with
Tony in the hotel room, how he slapped her and made
her face sting. She touched her cheek where he'd hit her
and it felt hot. She remembered him guiding her into the
bathtub afterward, as if a glass of champagne could
make the horror of it all go away. She remembered his
hands rubbing her breasts as she lay, emotionally paralyzed, on the bedspread.

When her eyes were able to focus again on his face in
the photo, she felt herself shudder as if someone else was
controlling her body. Part of her wanted to run out of the
church, but she also didn't want to turn toward the front
row, even a little, because she knew he'd be sitting there,
watching her from only a few feet away, with his wife,
Tania's mother, by his side. Alison took a deep breath
and tried to calm down, but it was no use. She took in the
familiar scent of Chanel for Men and her shoulders and
spine went stiff. How could she have missed that smell?

Alison tried to rationalize it away. You didn't know, she told herself. And besides, you'd already stopped seeing him by the time you met her.

Somber music swelled throughout the hall as the organist began to play, signaling that the service was about to begin. She heard Tony clear his throat behind her and that was it. She had to go before he came over to her. She pushed out of line for the coffin, walked briskly toward the center aisle, turned, and followed it to the back, where Goode was standing. Out of the corner of her eye, she could see people turning their heads and watching her as she flew past. *There goes that underdressed nobody again.*

A man in his sixties standing with a girl, probably about twelve, caught her eye. He was near the door, craning his neck in search of a seat, clutching the girl's hand as if she were his lifeline. Alison saw a familiar look of discomfort on the girl's face. She felt her throat go tight and her eyes glazed over again.

She'd been that girl's age when Grandpa Joe started coming into her room at night. Alison looked at the old man, clutching that girl's hand, and remembered the way her grandfather's penis had felt in her own hand, his rough fingers tightly wrapped around hers as he stood next to her bed. He would tell her to be quiet, get under the covers with her and rub his hands inside her flannel nightgown. He'd press his thing into her thigh like a stick, and then push it inside her, grunting. Her only escape was to let her mind go numb, try to ignore the pain and pretend it was happening to someone else. After he'd finished, he'd kiss her cheek and say, "Good night and sweet dreams." Alison would cry and rock herself to sleep, fantasizing about the next time when she would yank so hard on his dick that Grandma Abigail would hear him cry out. Alison felt like running over and whispering in the little girl's ear, urging her to do what Alison had never had the guts to do.

She finally reached where Goode was standing and pushed in between him and a snotty twenty-something woman who looked like she had spent two hours in the bathroom getting ready that morning.

Goode must have read the distress on Alison's face. "You okay?" he asked softly.

Alison nodded as nonchalantly as she could, adding a weak smile for good measure. Now that she'd realized Tony was Tania's father, she wanted to tell Goode—about his bad temper, anyway. She doubted that he had anything to do with Tania's murder, but what if he had?

The snotty woman pushed over to let someone in next to her, pushing Alison's shoulder even closer to Goode's muscular right arm. He didn't seem to mind the sudden intimacy and neither did Alison.

The morning sunlight sent streams of color through the stained glass windows, illuminating the scenes of Christ on the cross. It was a vast contrast to the dark-paneled Baptist church Grandma Abigail used to drag Alison to on Sundays, dressed in a white lace dress from K-mart and shiny, white vinyl shoes. Alison's grandparents never could afford clothes like the other kids wore, so as she grew older and more aware of fashion, she had to find creative ways to buy them herself. It wasn't like she stole them. She merely switched price tags, careful not to tear the fabric when she removed the plastic tab from a cheap garment and inserted it into the threads of the one she wanted.

Alison picked up a fold of her new dress. The material was so soft and comforting, nicer than anything she'd owned before, yet so inexpensive. It was almost free. She felt Goode's large, warm hand envelope hers and give it a squeeze before he let it go.

"You sure you're all right?" he whispered.

Alison nodded. His calm seeped up her arm as if it were coursing through her veins, and spread throughout her body.

Chapter Twenty-two

Tony

Tony's ass was already sore from sitting on the wooden pew and he had a headache to boot. It felt as if two cruel hands were gripping his temples and jabbing sharply every few seconds. He wished he'd brought some ibuprofen from the bottle he kept in the Mercedes' glove compartment.

Tony turned around and watched some of Tania's high school classmates whispering and giggling as they entered the church. How could they be so disrespectful? They should be silent and solemn. Where were their manners, their senses of decency? At least his teenage nephews were behaving properly. He was glad his and Helen's relatives had come, but he was equally pleased that they were sitting back a few rows to let him and his wife grieve with some semblance of privacy.

Tommy, the cocky quarterback Tania had dated in high school, came over to offer his sympathy. He looked a lot heavier than Tony remembered. Tony did his best to be gracious, but he didn't much feel like being polite to Tania's old boyfriends, especially that one. He had never liked the expression of lust in that boy's eyes when he had looked at Tania. After Tommy walked away, Tony looked down at his stomach and tried to pull up his pants, but they wouldn't go past his protruding belly. Well, he thought, at least he was old enough to have one. He'd earned it.

All the bourbon he'd consumed in the past couple of nights hadn't helped. He felt bloated and the heartburn was killing him. That was part of the reason why he hadn't taken any ibuprofen. His stomach was upset enough already. Tony didn't know how Helen did it night after night. Come to think of it, she'd been in the church bathroom an awfully long time. He was starting to get worried about her. He wished she would do something about her drinking. It seemed to be getting worse and worse, with no end in sight. But he knew that this was not the time to bring it up again. She'd slapped him the last time he told her she needed to get some help. Please, God, he thought, don't let her fall in front of everyone.

Tony hated funerals. This was the third one he'd been to in a year, but of course this was unlike any other. There was something very wrong with outliving your only child. The first funeral was for a man who'd lost his footing on a high-rise job downtown, forty stories up. Some of the guys thought he jumped because his wife had just left him for a truck driver. Tony had been at the site that day. It looked like the guy was flying when he swooped down from those steel beams. For months, he'd had a recurrent dream about the guy arching up through the air and flying off into the clouds. The dreams stopped after Tony's liability insurance premiums went up.

Then, last fall, his mother died of cancer. When he learned she was finally gone, he felt sadness and relief. He'd put her in a fancy nursing home that cost half as much as his mortgage payment, but he couldn't bring himself to visit her more than once every few months. He just couldn't take more than an occasional afternoon of that smell. And he couldn't stand to watch his mother turn into a pathetic stranger. He wanted to remember her the way she was before she got sick.

First his mother and now his daughter. Gone. He felt a tugging in his chest and his eyes welled up with tears. He closed them and hoped no one would notice.

He'd been cheated out of watching his daughter grow

up. What had he done to deserve this? He kept trying to think about the good times he'd had with her, but he couldn't seem to quell the anger he felt at God for taking her so early. What purpose could her death serve? He wanted the police to find the scumbag who'd killed her and give him the death penalty. An eye for an eye.

Since Tony had formed his own development company nine years earlier, he and Helen had been able to move to Beverly Hills, send Tania to a private high school and buy her the dog she'd always wanted. She loved taking Lucky for sunset runs on the wet sand in Malibu. He and Helen decided to take the photo of Tania and Lucky and make it the central focus of the collage they'd put together the night before. They'd gotten so involved in the project that they forgot to eat dinner. Drank scotch instead. By the time they'd finished, they'd left teary blotches all over the poster board.

They decided to set the collage on the easel Tania had used for oil painting. One of Helen's sisters set it next to Tania's casket, only a few feet in front of the pew reserved for Helen and Tony. Helen said they shouldn't try to remove the paint chips from the easel because they represented a part of Tania—her choices, her moods. They were an expression all their own. Tony's favorite of Tania's paintings, a soft portrait of Lucky on the beach, hung on a wall in his office.

Everything seemed to trigger a memory of her. Like when he'd called home from the store the night before to ask Helen if she needed anything. He got the answering machine, so he punched in the code to check for messages. Neither of them had erased the last one from Tania: "Just calling to say hi. Hey, did you see that beautiful sunset today? Tell Lucky I said hi, too. Bye now."

Tania used to call when she knew they'd be out so they'd have a personal greeting waiting for them when they got home. The messages never really varied, but Helen's mood always perked up when she heard them.

Tony hadn't realized how much he'd counted on hearing them, too, until now.

Tony opened his eyes and wiped the wetness from his cheeks. When he was able to see clearly again, he saw the back of a young woman only a few feet in front of him. She was leaning over, looking at the collage. As she turned to the side for a moment, he recognized her profile.

It was Alison.

His heart started racing. What was she doing there? How could she even know Tania existed when he'd made sure to never even mention her name? He hadn't wanted Alison to know he had a daughter her age. It was embarrassing.

Out the corner of his eye, he saw a somewhat more composed Helen walking toward him, wobbling a little and watching him watch Alison. He pulled at his tie. It felt too tight around his neck.

"Who's that?" Helen asked a little too loudly as she sat down. She reeked of scotch.

"Shhhhh," he whispered. "Who is who?"

"That girl you were staring at," she said, her words slurred.

"I don't know. Must be one of Tania's friends," he said, patting her knee. He realized after he did it that he'd patted her too hard and too fast. Helen was smart. She might figure out what was going on. But then he remembered the liquor and knew his secret was safe.

"Why were you gone for so long?" he said, trying to deflect her attention. "I was worried."

"I was in the bathroom, trying to pull myself together," she said.

Tony tried not to look at Alison, but he couldn't help it. Her cute little figure, the curly hair she could never tame, and that silky white skin. She had disappeared after that night a couple of months ago in Malibu and he'd thought he would never see her again. Now here she was, looking at Tania's collage. She straightened, turned, and walked quickly toward the back of the church, her face flushed and her lips pursed. He assumed she had recognized him from the photos and panicked. He was relieved they'd both been saved a scene.

Tony turned around and saw the row of people standing against the back wall move aside to make room for Alison. She squeezed in next to a tall, handsome guy who looked like he spent a lot of time at the beach.

Tony wondered if Alison could possibly have met Tania at the Nordstrom perfume counter in the valley. It was so bizarre to see her there. It made him a little queasy. He pulled out his pocketknife and began to clean his fingernails.

Chapter Twenty-three

Goode

As Alison leaned against Goode during the ceremony, he felt a warm, magnetic feeling, part sexual attraction, part something more tender. He knew it wasn't the smartest emotion to have, but he couldn't deny it was there. When he bent down to whisper in her ear, her hair smelled good. A soft and flowery scent, not too overbearing. Like her.

Really, the only memorial services Goode attended these days were those required for his job. They always prompted powerful reminders of his mother's death. Although the most painful memories had faded over time, something unexpected could trigger a fleeting but poignant surge of emotion. Like the red roses displayed artfully across Tania's casket. But when he remembered the seagulls from Sunday morning on the bridge, he felt better again.

Alison tugged at his sleeve and brought him back. The service was over and it was time to go. Other than Paul Walters, no one had really raised his suspicions. Paul had left the church rather suddenly, his face streaked with tears and his skin the color of dried milk. Goode couldn't see how Paul could have any connection to the beauty school or the escort service, but his eyes showed he was a druggie. He wondered if he had a Pumphouse connection.

The crowd filed out of the church and into the sun like lemmings. Goode felt his irritation level rise as one person elbowed him in the side and another stepped on the back of his shoe. He whispered good-bye to Alison and stepped away to call Maureen on his cell phone. Still no answer. Where the hell could she have disappeared to? He'd blame himself if she turned up dead. He struggled to think of innocent possibilities. She'd seemed sort of sullen lately. Maybe she'd gone to Baja for a change of scenery. Maybe she was staying with that girlfriend of hers in San Francisco. Or maybe she was at home. An image of her lying dead in a bathtub full of red water flashed across his mind. He shook his head and pushed it away.

He called Stone to see if he had any updates on Maureen, or anything else for that matter.

"Well, like you said, she wasn't home. But I heard from the beat cop that one of her roommates is some shaggy guy with hair down his back and a serious attitude. Asleep in the middle of the day. Didn't even know what time it was."

"Did they ask him where she was? Did they search the house?"

"No, they didn't search the house. There was no probable cause. They asked him where she was—said you wanted to know—but Shaggy had no clue. Said he wouldn't tell the cops if he did. Real cooperative. I wouldn't let her go back there if I were you."

"Yeah, well, you're assuming that she listens to me, Chief. Thanks for sending those guys over there anyways."

"Sure. No problem. Turn up anything new at the service?"

Goode told Stone about his new Paul Walters angle and said he was going to get Keith to ride back to San Diego with him so he could needle Keith a bit about that and other things.

Goode strolled over to Seth and Keith, who were standing on the lawn talking to a couple of attractive young women. The detective stood behind a tree while he watched them exchange business cards with the women. He waited for the women to leave before he approached.

"Nice ceremony, don't you think?"

Seth gave Goode a forced smile and Keith nodded, sticking close to Seth like steel to a magnet. Hoping to get away from Goode, by the looks of it. They were an odd pair. Keith was obviously the weak link, and Goode hoped he could push Keith to slip up and lead Goode to a possible motive, a link to the beauty school, drugs, the escort service, or Paul. Anything.

"Which one of you drove?" Goode asked.

"I did," Seth said.

Keith chirped. It was like a hiccup, only louder.

"Good," the detective said, looking directly into Keith's eyes without blinking, an intimidation tactic that usually proved effective. "Keith, why don't you ride back to San Diego with me?"

"Um, okay," Keith said, dumbfounded. He glanced over at Seth, whose mouth had set in a grim straight line. Keith chirped again.

"Let's go," Goode said. He motioned for Keith to walk in front of him, and then fell in beside him.

Goode could feel Seth's eyes drilling into his back. He

turned and saw him standing there, his arms folded across his chest, watching them walk away. When Goode looked a few minutes later, Seth was climbing into his Porsche down the street.

Goode hated driving in L.A. People were so rude. You could count on three cars to turn left after every yellow light turned red. It was an unwritten rule. He purposely waited until he'd been driving for fifteen minutes on the 405 freeway before he broached his first question. He wanted Keith to sweat a little.

The silence hung heavily in the car like L.A. smog hugs the horizon on a hot day.

"Keith, are you aware that if Seth did commit murder and you had anything to do with it, that you could be looking at prison time for being an accomplice? Same thing if you tried to help him cover it up, which would make you an accessory after the fact."

Keith's shoulders drooped and he bowed his head, staring at the floor. He let out a long sigh and shook his head.

"So?" Goode said, waiting.

When Keith finally looked at him, he could see fear in his eyes. "What do you want me to say?"

"I get the feeling that you're not telling me everything you know," Goode said. "Are you trying to protect Seth?"

"No," he said. "And I don't need to. You don't know Seth like I do. He would never kill anyone. . . . The only thing he needs protection from is this incredibly jealous woman he used to go out with, 'cause he always did more coke when she was around. He always lets the little head think for the big head, if you know what I mean."

Keith looked at Goode as if he would understand. It was hard, but Goode managed not to laugh and focused on the road so Keith would keep talking. If Goode got lucky, Keith would give him enough information to charge Seth with a crime before they reached Irvine.

"She did a lot of blow—you know, cocaine. For all I know, she was dealing it, too. He used to do it with her at

Pumphouse, but I finally got him to stop. I didn't want him to get busted. He finally got a clue and blew her off. Anyway, she was at Pumphouse the night he met Tania."

"Who is this jealous woman we're talking about?"

"Her name is Clover."

"So, what are you saying? That I should pick her up for dealing drugs?"

This time, Keith answered a little too quickly. "No, I mean, I don't know if she's a dealer, but she's definitely got a personal habit."

Goode wondered who Keith was truly trying to protect. So what if Clover had a coke problem? Keith had offered him a possible source for the drugs on Tania's table, but something didn't ring true about his story. Why would he volunteer all this information about Seth doing drugs and his relationship with Clover? Maybe he was trying to distract Goode or throw him off the trail of something more important. And where had the meth come from? Most users picked either coke or meth and stuck with their drug of choice.

"Is Seth selling drugs at Pumphouse? Or are you?"

"No, man, I told you. Recreational use only," Keith said. "Shit, you're not going to arrest me, are you?"

"I've got bigger fish to fry right now, pal. . . . So, what about Saturday night?" Goode asked. "Where were you between nine and ten thirty P.M.?"

"We already told you—at Pumphouse with Seth, waiting for the chicks to show up, and then we went to that party. You can ask the bartender, man. He knows us. Or ask Richard, the guy who threw the party."

"Oh, don't you worry, we will," Goode said.

Goode drove on for a while, letting Van Morrison sing and the conversation sink in. He finally turned down the stereo where Interstate 405 turned into the 5. They'd passed Irvine and Goode still didn't have enough to arrest anybody for anything. But they were still an hour away from home. Keith looked uncomfortable, claustrophobic even, as he shifted around in his seat.

"Does the name Sharona Glass ring a bell?" Goode asked.

"Yeah, she's Clover's friend. Why?" Keith sounded sincere.

"She's dead, too," Goode said.

"What?" Keith said. He looked startled. "How?"

"Strangled."

"Shit. This is getting weird."

"That's one word for it," Goode said. "Do you know Paul Walters?"

"Who?" Keith asked, frowning.

"Paul Walters. He was Tania's next-door neighbor."

"No. Why do you ask?"

"Just doing my job, pal."

Keith kept pulling the seat belt away from his neck, as if it was too constrictive, as if he'd rather be anywhere else. Goode sped up to pass a Buick that was going way too slow. Left him in the dust.

"Tell me more about Clover," Goode said.

"I don't know. She goes to some beauty school during the day and gets blasted at Pumphouse most nights."

Goode pulled a pen and a notebook from his inside coat pocket, rested the pad on the steering wheel, and wrote her name under Paul's, with the notation, "Jealousy?" He swerved suddenly to avoid a blue vintage Corvette that shot in front of him, sending the pen onto the floor at Keith's feet.

"Shit," Goode exclaimed. You have to keep your eyes on the road at all times when driving in Southern California or you'll end up dead.

"Asshole," Keith said to the Corvette driver for Goode's benefit. He reached down and handed the pen to Goode. "She's a pain in the ass, you know, neurotic as hell. I don't know why Seth kept seeing her, apart from the obvious."

"You know Tania Marcus went to that beauty school, right?"

"Yeah," Keith said. "She was talking about it that night we all met. Hey, maybe Clover knew Tania from there."

Or maybe she knew Maureen. "What about a woman named Maureen? You know her from around P.B. at all?"

"Yeah, maybe," Keith answered a little too quickly. "Why?"

"Just wondering if you knew her."

"That's right," Keith said, turning to Goode with a trace of a smirk. "You guys have the same last name. She your wife?"

That threw him. No one had put Goode and that word in the same sentence for quite some time. "Not that it's any of your business, but no, she's my sister, smart ass. So?"

"Yeah, we went out a couple times."

Keith wasn't a good liar. Goode figured it was more intimate than that, but this guy didn't seem like his sister's type. He seemed like a decent guy, but as he kept reminding himself, everyone was a suspect at this point. Goode decided to drive the rest of the way and let Van Morrison do the talking.

Chapter Twenty-four

Norman

Norman knew P.B. pretty well, so he didn't have much trouble finding the murder scene. He took a little longer than he should have to get to the dead woman's apartment building because he stopped to get a slice of pizza at Bronx Pizza in Hillcrest. He missed the pies from home.

Al, the dayside editor, had called him at home and

told him to start his shift early so he could see if there was any follow-up story to do on the Tania Marcus murder. By the time he got to work, Al had already heard a bunch of talk on the scanner about a second dead girl in P.B. Sully, the regular cops reporter, was still out on medical leave and Charlie was still sick. It was another lucky day for Norman Klein.

"Let's see if you can improve on the other night, kid. Or we'll fire your ass," said Al, chortling.

Al was a wiry, no-nonsense guy who ate rocks for breakfast; Norman was sure of it. He felt very intimidated by Al and Big Ed, but didn't know what to do about it other than dig in and hope for the best.

Norman scanned the crime scene for Detective Goode, but there was no sign of him. Most of the cops were the short-haired, uptight ones who hated talking to reporters. Goode was way cooler. Norman figured he got a lot of women. The good kind.

"Are you the officer in charge?" Norman asked a uniformed cop who had stripes on his sleeve and a no-nonsense attitude.

"Sergeant."

"Oh, sorry. Sergeant. What's going on?"

"Dead girl."

"What happened to her?"

The sergeant was apparently too busy standing with his arms folded over his potbelly to answer. Norman struggled to remember all the questions Al told him to ask. "Any connection between this murder and the Tania Marcus case?"

That got the cop's attention. He turned and looked at Norman. "Could be. Who are you with?"

"The *Sun-Dispatch*."

The sergeant grimaced. "Are you the jerk who got my name wrong on that armed robbery last week?"

"Uh, no, I don't think so," Norman said, knowing full well that it was his story, only he didn't know what he'd done wrong. "But while we're at it, why don't you spell it for me so it doesn't happen this time."

"It's Love. That's L-O-V-E, not L-I-V-E."

Shit, Norman thought. A stupid typo spell-check couldn't catch. "What's your first name?"

"Sergeant."

What was the deal with cops and these dumb stone-walling tactics? Norman wondered. It must be in the manual. Norman had a lot riding on this story and he wasn't going to let some jerk-off dick him around. But he had to stay cool. Use the charm like Al told him.

"Come on. I have a police department roster back at the newsroom. I can just look it up. How 'bout helping me out a little here?"

Sergeant Love looked Norman up and down. "All right, all right. It's Mike. Screw it up and this is our last conversation."

The two of them stared at each other for a good thirty seconds until the sergeant finally cracked a smile. "So, what else you want to know, kid? She was a beauty school student just like that other girl. I saw you there the other day. I was on crowd control. A little late, weren't you?"

"Yeah, yeah, yeah."

The sergeant looked at his watch. "Speaking of the time, I've got to get going." He turned and started to walk away.

"Wait," Norman called after him. "I have a few more questions."

Sergeant Love stopped, turned partway around and then spoke so fast Norman could hardly write fast enough to keep up. "You know, you're lucky I'm in a good mood. Look, here it is, kid. We found a twenty-three-year-old white female dead in the apartment. Cause of death is pending. Could be a drug-related homicide. But don't quote me. You've got to talk to Sergeant Stone from Homicide. I'm just helping to keep the lookie-loos like you out of the way. It's Stone's case and he's not here yet. So no quotes. Got that?"

"Yeah, yeah, right. Autopsy today?"

"You'll have to call the ME's office."

"What's her name?"

"Can't release that. Family hasn't been notified. And by the way, kid, you'd better wipe that newsprint off your face. You look like you got in a fight with a bag of charcoal briquettes. And lost."

Al's voice echoed in his head: *Push the envelope.* "Can I see the body?" Norman asked.

The sergeant shook his head. "You're really getting to be a pain in the ass, you know that?"

Norman just smiled.

"Sorry, kid. As much as I'd like to watch you lose your breakfast, we don't want anyone contaminating the crime scene."

Norman didn't really want to see the body anyway. He was just trying to test the boundaries. It was time to head back to the office and start making some calls, anyway.

He walked to his car and started back. As he careened around corners, the newspapers slid around in the backseat. He really needed to do something about those papers this weekend, he thought, especially if he planned to ask out that tasty waitress, Lulu.

It was ironic. By murdering young women, some sick bastard was creating an opportunity for Norman to get on the front page. He felt bad for thinking something so cold, but it was the truth. And he was all about the truth.

Norman hoped he would have as much luck reaching this girl's parents as he had reaching Tania Marcus'. He'd felt like he might have taken advantage of Helen Marcus a bit in her intoxicated state, but he also knew he had to be tough or he'd never get assigned another big story. So he kept going. She had sounded like she wanted someone to talk to, so it couldn't have been all that wrong. Right?

As he approached the freeway exit in Mission Valley that led to the office, Norman changed his mind and decided to reverse course. If he went to the beauty school, maybe he could get the name of the dead girl without having to wait a day for the ME to release it. Besides, he was still looking for ways to follow up on the first murder, because he was convinced that the two cases were related.

Norman sang along to the radio, letting the wind whip through his hair. This was what Southern California was all about. Warm breezes and hot babes in dental floss bikinis, their long hair flowing down their backs and their tight abs glistening with oil as they flounced down the beach. It was a far cry from New Jersey, where he grew up. Norman drove back to the beach on Grand Avenue, the same way he'd come, but this time, he hit one red light after another. If he'd thought of this an hour ago, he'd be back at the paper writing already. He turned right onto Mission Boulevard when his car began to sputter, even with the accelerator to the floor. Then he noticed that the gas gauge was on the big red E. He'd forgotten to fill her up that morning.

"Dammit," he yelled. "Why didn't I stop last night?"

Luckily, there were no cars coming the other way and he was able to guide his car across the street into a supermarket parking lot. He'd seen the yellow and red of a Shell station sign about five blocks back. He may have been stupid enough not to fill the tank, but at least he had that empty gas can in the trunk.

Norman eased the car into a parking space and came to a stop. He sat there for a few seconds and shook his head. "Get over yourself," he said. "Everything will work out."

Then Norman opened the trunk, saw there was no gas can.

"Shit!" he said, accentuating the t for emphasis. He'd forgotten that he'd loaned the can to Lulu the other night at the Tavern when her car wouldn't start. He'd offered to take her to the gas station, but then Big Ed beeped him and told him to run on that armed robbery, so he left the can with Lulu and she got some prison guard to take her to a station nearby.

He took off on foot, hoping that the Shell attendant would loan him some kind of container. He was not going to lose this story—no way, no how. He hadn't gotten this far without knowing the meaning of intrepid. He was determined to get a page one story and a date with the fabulous Lulu, all in one day.

Ten minutes later, as he approached the yellow and red sign, he saw that a chain-link fence had been erected around the perimeter of a vacant lot, which was piled high with chunks of torn-up asphalt. There were deep holes in the earth where the underground tanks had been removed. A cardboard sign said a Fresh-Mex restaurant would be opening soon.

Norman began to panic. What should he do now? He needed to clear his head and come up with a game plan. This, he decided, called for a cheeseburger, a chocolate shake, fries, and a bottomless cup of coffee. He retraced his steps and headed for Denny's.

Chapter Twenty-five

Goode

Goode was really worried about his sister, especially now that he'd learned she had dated Keith and hung out in the same bar as this group of friends who were doing drugs and getting murdered. He knew he needed to get over to the new murder scene, but he felt compelled to check Maureen's house one more time.

As he drove up Turquoise Street, he visualized her Red Honda CRV in her driveway. Be home, be home, he chanted silently as he approached. But her driveway was empty. Neither of her roommates' trucks was there either, although their pool cleaning supplies were scattered all over the lawn. The neighbors couldn't be too happy about that.

Goode parked down the street, walked to Maureen's, and went into stealth mode. Going from one open window to another, a burglar's fantasy, he peered inside for signs of life. But he saw no shadows moving, heard no music playing or water running, and smelled no food cooking.

Goode snuck around back and saw the surfboard he'd bought for her birthday a few years back leaning against the wall. Custom-made by a friend in Cardiff, the board was silk-screened with a dark-haired woman coming out of an aquamarine tube. This was not a good sign because it ruled out the possibility that Maureen was surfing in Baja. Goode walked sullenly back to his van and gunned the engine hard, just to hear it roar. Where the hell could she be?

Sharona Glass lived less than a mile from Maureen. As much as he wished he could dismiss his big-brother worries as needless, he couldn't ignore the fact that these murders seemed to be the work of one killer still loose in his sister's neighborhood.

By the time he got to Sharona's apartment, Stone and Byron were huddled up outside and the ME's investigator was preparing her body for transport to the morgue. Since Byron was the lead on the crime scene investigation, Stone told Goode not to go inside until Byron and the evidence tech had cleared it. Goode peeked in and saw Sharona's body lying on the living room carpet, just short of the bar counter that bordered the kitchen. Her arms were sprawled out as if she had fallen backward unexpectedly or was pulled down from behind. The tech was dusting the bar counter and stools for fingerprints. Goode looked around for Norman Klein, but didn't see him around. He still needed to talk to him about that "off the record" problem.

Goode said he hoped they'd get lucky again and find a journal, and Byron came back a minute later with a calendar that had been tacked on the refrigerator with a magnet. It featured the ass of a different male college student each month. Goode could barely read the numbers on the days because of all the red pen marks: Most were men's names with notations such as "Dinner," "A movie," and sometimes, just "Wow." He wondered if she, too, was a potential escort service babe since the only male name he recognized from the case was Seth's. The two of them apparently had a lunch date in between two nights when Sharona had dinner and then drinks with Clover. This was no coincidence; they were all in this together somehow.

Goode watched the tech go through the kitchen cabinets and drawers, which were filled mostly with diet food like canned tuna in water, though she did find a stash of chocolate bars. In the end, however, there was nothing more inflammatory than a box of birthday candles.

"We found a mirror on the bar counter next to her, with some white powder and a rolled-up dollar bill," Byron said, handing the mirror to him in an evidence bag. "Looks like coke to me."

"Aha," Goode said, reveling in the fact that he'd finally been able to say it. "Could be meth, though. We'll have to test it to find out."

Now all he had to figure out was who was supplying Sharona, Tania, Clover, and Seth.

If Goode had to guess, Seth was not just a recreational user, as Keith had claimed, but a dealer, maybe even a successful one. And despite Keith's innocent act, Goode thought he was probably involved as well. It was possible that Keith had been trying to frame Clover as the mastermind behind their drug operation. If that was the case, it wasn't going to work.

"How's it going?" Lieutenant Wilson said, suddenly appearing at his side.

This was starting to look like a serial killer case, so the stakes were getting higher. Wilson didn't often come to crime scenes unless they were big. Goode figured the chief told Wilson to get over there to put some pressure on the investigative team and put up a good face for the cameras.

After Byron finally cleared the scene, Goode made his way into the bedroom and studied the magazine cutouts of supermodels that consumed an entire wall over the bed. But he was more interested in the framed photos on top of her bureau. The blonde fit the description of Clover Ziegler. She was definitely attractive, but he picked up some of the personality traits on her face that Keith had described. He took one of the photos and put it in his pocket to show Alison.

Slausson showed up, headed straight for Sharona's bureau, and wasted no time before fingering her silk panties. He practically dove into her nightstand, looking for another "goodie" drawer.

"That's her, the redhead," he said, pointing at a photo of Sharona in a bikini. "You know about redheads, right?"

"A little respect here, okay?" Goode said. Slausson was definitely a pervert with too much of the asshole gene. And Goode had been really hoping he wasn't.

In several of the photos, taken at various ages, Sharona had her arm around Clover. Both women were tall and athletic looking.

"Hey, did you ever get an interview with Clover Ziegler?" Goode asked.

"No, I went by her house at that address you gave me, but no one answered the door," Slausson said.

Goode sorted through the piles of envelopes and other

papers on Sharona's desk. They were mostly junk mail and unpaid bills, some several months old. He also didn't see the same expensive clothing, furniture, and other household items he'd seen in Tania's apartment, so joining the escort service would have seemed an attractive opportunity for her. There was an address book in the top drawer underneath some old letters. He looked in the G section and found a Patricia, a Jason, and a Melissa Glass. Goode wrote down the phone numbers and addresses before handing it over to the tech. He knew he was going to have to start asking Alison some hard questions about the escort service. He could only hope she wasn't involved.

By the time he was done at the crime scene it was too late to go talk to her, so he went home, where he reread the diary entries and tried to reach his sister again.

Chapter Twenty-six

Goode
Wednesday

The next morning, Goode tried to avoid the stop signs by driving the back way to Alison's and inadvertently found himself in the same alley where he'd found Tania. It was chilling to say the least. As he headed toward the trash cans, he pictured Tania's body, but not the way he'd found her. This time, her long black hair was streaming out from between the black trash bins.

He knocked on Alison's front door, heard a faint "Wait a minute," and then waited for what seemed like five minutes before she opened up. Dressed in a white terry-cloth bathrobe, her hair up in a towel turban, she had green goop around her hairline. She looked a little embarrassed.

"You're not dying your hair, I hope," he said.

"No, it's just henna."

Goode must have looked puzzled because Alison felt compelled to explain further. "It's this stuff you put on your hair to make it thicker and shinier. Plus, it gives it a nice, warm glow. It has to stay on for an hour and I only just put it on. Sorry."

Green goop or not, she still looked pretty. It was something in her eyes and the way the corners of her mouth curled up into a coy, shy smile. He tried not to think about how the tie on her robe looked so loose that it might fall open at any moment and expose her rather ample breasts.

"No problem," he said. "Can I come in for a minute?"

"Sure," she said, gesturing him toward the couch. "But you'll have to promise to ignore the mess. I haven't been in a tidying-up kind of mood." Alison pulled the tie tighter on her robe before sitting in her grandfather's chair.

"I really miss her," she said. "I can't get her out of my mind."

Neither could he. "Well, unfortunately, I have some more bad news," he said.

"What now?" she asked.

"Did you know Sharona Glass?"

"The name sounds familiar," she said. "Why?"

"Another girl at your beauty school."

This time, it was Alison who seemed puzzled. "What does she look like?"

"Pretty, red hair. She's dead, Alison."

"Yes, I know who she is," she said, turning her head away. "I can't believe this is happening."

Goode got off the sofa and stood next to her chair. He wanted to be comforting. But when he put his hand on her shoulder she jumped a little. He sighed. He never knew what to do in these situations.

"It's okay. We're going to find this killer. I'm starting

to worry about your safety, though. Maybe you should go home and stay with your parents for a while."

Alison shook her head. "No, I can't," she said, her lips pursed tight.

"Why not?" he asked.

"I just can't."

Obviously, troubles at home had sent Alison farther south. She would tell him if and when she was ready. An awkward silence fell over the room. He wondered whether she was too upset for him to pull out photos for a Q&A session, but he didn't have a whole lot of time to wait for her to get comfortable.

"Ken," she said suddenly, sitting up straighter and meeting his gaze. "I have to tell you what happened at the funeral."

"What do you mean? I was there, standing right next to you."

Alison pulled at a loose thread on her robe. "Well, I saw Tania's father in the front row, and it turns out he was the older guy I was dating before I moved to San Diego."

Goode was pretty tough to shock, but that one floored even him.

"Wow," he said. "How bizarre is that?"

Alison's voice shook as she spoke. "I know. First I find out Tania is dead and then I find out I slept with her father. It's so creepy."

The cogs in Goode's head started clicking as he tried to determine whether this meant anything to the case. He kneeled in front of her, and this time she let him take her hand. To hell with ethics and police procedure. It was a long shot, but Goode's curiosity was piqued.

"Did he ever hurt you in any way?" he asked, searching her eyes for the truth.

Alison nodded, wiping her cheek with the back of her other hand. "He hit me one time," she said so softly he almost couldn't hear her. "How did you know that?"

Goode squeezed Alison's hand. "I sensed it somehow. I don't even know why. . . . Tell me what happened."

Alison looked vulnerable and scared. Something about this damaged young woman really touched him. He wanted to make her feel safe.

"Well, it happened the last time we were together," she said. "It was right before I moved to San Diego. We were in this hotel room and he grabbed my shoulder and slapped me. Never said he was sorry. After that, I decided to stop seeing him. Especially after what my grandfather did. . . ."

Alison pulled her hand away and he wondered whether she now regretted telling him. He didn't know where she was going with all this and he didn't know how he was supposed to react.

"Your grandfather hurt you, too?" he asked carefully.

She nodded. "He used to come into my room at night and make me touch him."

"You mean . . . ?"

"Yes. Down there." She nodded down at Goode's crotch and then looked away, her eyes and nose crinkling up with distaste. She put her hands over her face and started to cry. Goode felt like taking her in his arms and holding her, but he couldn't tell what she wanted him to do. Alison let her hands fall into her lap and stared at the carpet.

"When I first met Tony, he was so nice to me. He took care of me, spent lots of money on me, treated me like I was worth something. One time, he bought me a pair of sapphire and diamond earrings. But then, after he hit me, I felt bad inside, just like when I was growing up. . . . I haven't told anyone else about my grandfather but Tania. I trusted her and felt some kind of bond with her. But it's funny. I never told her about Tony for some reason. Pretty ironic, huh?"

Goode nodded, not wanting to say the wrong thing. His thoughts were flying every which way.

Alison frowned. "Why are you looking at me like that? Are you grossed out that I dated a man who was old enough to be my father? Or is it because I let my grand-father touch me?"

"No, no, that's not it at all. You were a child, Alison. You're not to blame for what he did," he said, putting his hand on her knee. "I was just wondering whether Tony ever did anything like that to Tania, or had anything to do with her death."

What he didn't say was that he was trying to figure Al-ison out, too. Things were making a bit more sense now—her vulnerability, the way she disappeared into herself.

"I'm sorry you had to go through all that," he said. "You're a very sweet, beautiful young woman. You should never let your bad memories make you feel any less than that. Have you ever talked to a counselor about this?"

Alison shook her head. Goode decided it was now or never and leaned in to give her a hug. She let him, and pulled him closer still. The two of them stayed like that for a few minutes, with their faces buried in each other's necks. It felt nice. A little too nice.

He started feeling a rush of heat sweep across his face, neck, and chest. Then she started lightly rubbing her nose back and forth under his jawline. He felt her warm breath on him, the friction of her skin, rubbing against him, her lips on his neck. What was she doing? Goode was breathing heavier now. He could feel the flush spread downward. Alison was leading him somewhere he knew they shouldn't be going. She slowly brushed her lips across his ear, over his cheek and down to his lips.

Then she kissed him. Softly at first, her wet mouth barely touching his. But soon, she was pressing harder and, by that point, Goode didn't care about what he should or shouldn't be doing about the case, about any-thing. He lost sight of protocol, of where he was. All he knew was that he was kissing her, his head awash with white heat. She put her tongue in his mouth gently and then a little deeper. He pulled her closer and felt her breasts pressing against his chest. It had been so long since he'd allowed himself to feel like this. He wanted her. He moved his hand up her robe and started to loosen the tie.

But as if she had turned off a switch, she suddenly went cold. "We shouldn't be doing this," she whispered.

Alison moved away from him and he let his hands fall to his side as she ran into the bathroom. He sat on the floor, feeling stupid and a little bit angry. Why had he let himself lose control like that? She was a pretty messed-up girl. She needed help, not sex. Goode heard her turn on the tap. She was probably trying to wash off the mess he'd made of the situation. He wandered over to the kitchen area and saw a pack of Camel Lights lying on the counter.

"No shit," he said. He looked around for an ashtray so he could quickly grab a butt. He saw one on the balcony, so he grabbed it and quickly put it in his jacket pocket.

When Alison came out a few minutes later, her eyes were red, but they were dry. She sat in the armchair, and he sat on the couch. He didn't know what to say. He'd wanted her, even though he'd known it could be disastrous. Hadn't he learned anything? What was the point of waiting all this time to do things right and then let this happen?

"I'm really sorry," she said.

She didn't have to say it. He could see it in her eyes. "You didn't do anything wrong," he said. "I shouldn't have hugged you."

"No, it's not your fault."

"I thought you wanted—"

"Don't."

Goode wondered if he was trying to sabotage his first big chance at getting that transfer. He still needed Alison's help with the case. What if she turned out to be a whack job and reported him? What if his hormones had blown the opportunity he'd wanted so badly? Or worse, what if her DNA on the Camel cigarette matched the ones in Tania's trash?

"So, where were we?" she asked, forcing a weak smile. "I mean, you know, with the case?"

He felt relieved. "Are you mad at me?"

"No," she said, shaking her head, "just embarrassed. I'm not usually aggressive like that."

Goode didn't know who she was, or who he was, or where they were supposed to go from there. All he wanted to do was get up and leave. But he told himself he had a job to do and it was time to get down to it.

"Let's pretend it never happened," she said.

Goode took a deep breath and ran his hands through his hair. "Okay. If you're up to it, I've got some questions for you. But first I want you to look at these photos."

Alison nodded and blew her nose. He laid a couple photos on the coffee table, and as she leaned over to look at them, her robe opened up to reveal the top of her breasts. It was hard not to look after they'd been pushed up against him.

"That's Clover," she said right away, pointing to the blond girl next to Sharona.

"Right. The girl who does a lot of coke and is the bane of Seth's existence. But that's Keith's story, and, as the saying goes, he doth protest too much. Do you think Keith is involved with her somehow or just Seth?"

"Neither one, actually," Alison said. "Seemed like she was a pain in both of their butts. But Tania seemed to like her. I saw them talking at school. Sharona and Clover hung out a lot, too. I got the feeling they were longtime friends."

"Well, Sharona had red marks on her neck, just like Tania."

Alison gasped.

"Yup, but there was no sign of sexual activity this time, so now I'm even more confused. I've been thinking there might be a drug-dealing operation at Pumphouse or at the beauty school—high-quality cocaine and methamphetamine. What do you think?"

"Well, I don't know. I don't do drugs."

Goode believed her. "What about Tania?"

"I don't know. She never did them when I was around. How do you tell if someone's doing coke?"

"They look nervous, agitated. They grind their teeth, talk fast, sniffle and wipe their noses a lot."

Alison shook her head. "In that case, then no. Not that I could tell. She always looked totally put together, and I didn't notice any of that."

"Well, we found coke *and* meth in Tania's apartment, and some white powder in Sharona's apartment. We don't know for sure yet, but I'm guessing it's coke."

Alison's eyes widened. "Wow. I guess Tania had me fooled. . . . But why would she get involved in drug dealing? It's not like she needed the money."

"Yeah, that's one flaw in my theory," he said. "But then, how do you explain the drugs on her living room table? Maybe she only did it when you weren't around. Plus, the manager says she had quite a few visitors. Anyway, it's something I'm exploring. You could end up being right, my little detective."

That got a smile out of her, which relieved Goode.

"One more thing. Did Tania smoke?" he asked.

"No, why?"

"I just noticed that you did, so I thought maybe she did, too."

"Oh, I don't really smoke. I was just trying something."

Goode nodded as though he understood, even though he really didn't.

"Did Tania ever mention that she was trying to set up an escort service?"

"An escort service?" Alison asked. She looked sincerely shocked, so Goode got the validation he was seeking. "No. Are you serious?"

"Sure am."

"You know what? I didn't know that girl at all," Alison said, blowing her nose again. "See? Now that my nose is running you're going to think I'm doing coke, too."

Goode chuckled. "Don't worry about that. You seem like a good girl to me."

He didn't exactly know how to exit gracefully, so he offered his hand, and she took it. She held it for a minute and looked at him with those sad, soulful eyes of hers. Goode was totally confused about what was going on between them. He just knew he had to leave before he grabbed her again and really went for it.

Chapter Twenty-seven

Goode

Goode felt complete culture shock as he left P.B. and drove to a tiny suburban community in the eastern part of the county known as Lemon Grove, where Sharona Glass' parents had moved from La Jolla some years earlier. All Goode needed to know before making up his mind about the place was that its proud fathers built a giant lemon statue on a grassy median downtown. He tried to avoid East County whenever possible. It made him feel like he was in a small town in the Bible Belt, surrounded by white men driving trucks with gun racks. He was curious to meet Sharona's mother, though, so he could see if there was a connection between Sharona's and Tania's deaths other than the obvious—the beauty school, Pumphouse, and drugs.

Goode met with Patricia Glass for a couple hours,

gathering quite a bit of background information about the family and their long connection to Clover Ziegler's. However, when he read over his notes in his van afterward, he realized that most of it was generally irrelevant to solving the case. Sharona and Clover had been childhood friends, and because Clover was also a beauty school student, Goode knew a visit with her was long overdue.

Patricia Glass said Clover lived with her mother and stepfather in a large house on Mount Soledad, in La Jolla. He was feeling a little frustrated that he had wasted two hours that morning, so it didn't help when he rang Clover's doorbell and no one answered. He left his card in the crack next to the front door, marked urgent, with a message asking her to call him right away.

After that, he sat in a coffee shop and reviewed Tania's e-mails again. He still couldn't find any new ties between the two murders. His mind ran through the variables once more: the escort service, drugs, the beauty school, Pumphouse, Ms. X, Ms. Monica, Seth, Keith, Paul, Clover, and One-Eye. Alison? Tony? Goode made a mental note to swing by the station and drop off Alison's cigarette butt at the lab.

Once again, Byron was handling autopsy duties, so Goode felt a little out of the loop, especially with the two murders occurring so close together. Stone had been coordinating all the logistics and tests, but by late morning the cable news networks had descended on them in full force and the chief had developed a sudden fear of cameras. After a few flubs, Thompson decided Stone should be the public face for the case, leaving the sergeant little or no room to refuse. So Stone had to run around the city, doing satellite interviews the department's public information officer had arranged. Stone said it was a little unnerving to sit in a small, dark empty room with a backdrop of the downtown skyscape, pretending to be having a conversation with an anchor across the country. He'd get questions through an earpiece, which he would answer by speaking to a camera lens in front of him. He tried to remember the information officer's tip to look straight into the lens so he wouldn't seem shifty-eyed.

Goode wanted to tell the chief that his decision to use Stone for this purpose was hurting their investigation, but he didn't think that would be such a good idea. It might cost him his transfer.

About 2 P.M., Goode got a call from Byron on his cell phone that put a whole new perspective on things. The DNA tests had come back on the semen samples.

"They were definitely two different people, but you're not going to believe this," Byron said.

"Try me," Goode said.

"The first was Seth, obviously, but the second wasn't your other possible perp, Keith Warner," Byron said.

"No shit."

"That's right. We've got a third man out there."

"Wow," Goode said, pausing. "I wasn't expecting that."

He hung up feeling numb. Until he decided this was good news. The new DNA lead could very well point to Paul Walters as the third man. That said, he couldn't imagine how Paul would've gotten Tania into a sexual situation, let alone a threesome. It was also possible that the third man was someone else who'd inserted himself into the investigation, as killers often do, someone who had stayed under the radar so far. Maybe he lived in the apartment building and they'd overlooked him. Goode wracked his brain but he couldn't think of anyone who fit that description. There was always the bartender and Jake, but they seemed to be trying to distance themselves from the investigation, not insert themselves into it.

Then again, maybe he was trying too hard to eliminate Paul as a suspect. Even if he clearly wasn't a man on stimulants, could he be one of Seth's salesmen? Goode couldn't see any link between the two other than drugs.

Could they have murdered her together? The trouble
was, he saw no apparent motive for Seth other than
anger over getting blown off Saturday night. And that
was weak. Paul, on the other hand, seemed more like the
type to get upset at rejection and Goode knew of murders based on less than that, especially when drugs were
involved. From Alison's account, it wasn't clear how
hard Paul had tried to get Tania to go out with him. He
didn't seem like the violent type, but who knew? It certainly would be convenient to stalk your next-door
neighbor. But then where did Sharona Glass fit in?

Goode really wished he could go surfing to mentally
sort the new evidence, but he decided to settle for cruising by Windansea to look at the waves. That always
seemed to help. Part of the problem was that he couldn't
get Alison out of his head, which led to a train of unre-
lated thought he couldn't seem to derail. She was, after
all, the first woman in a long time that he'd allowed himself to kiss. He'd stuck to his resolve for the past few
years, but there was something about this case that was
causing him to come a little unglued. But what really
pissed him off was that kissing Alison had brought back
memories of his ex-wife, Miranda. Just when he thought
he was well on the way to recovery, the episode that
morning had put him back in line for the roller coaster.

He'd started dating Miranda their freshman year at
UCLA. She was like a drug to him. He couldn't stop
thinking about her and the way their bodies fit together
just so. It went well for the first year, but then she started
smoking cigarettes and hanging out in trendy bars in
Westwood, Hollywood, and Brentwood, and whatever
other -woods she could find. She said she was too young
to have a serious boyfriend, so she broke up with him
the summer after their sophomore year and he saw her
driving around town with some frat boy from Newport
Beach in his white Jaguar. The guy had the IQ of a poodle, and Goode hated poodles. She soon tired of him and

came back to Goode. All in all, she left Goode three times in college, but she always came back. "Ken," she'd say, "You're the best after all."

Post-graduation, he asked her to quit messing with his head and marry him, or take a walk. She said she wanted to think about it. She disappeared for a few weeks, came back with a tan and said yes.

So they got married. Goode had hoped she would soon be ready to settle down and have some little ones, but he obviously had blinders on. For five years she tried to find what she wanted to do with her life, and eventually got hired to read scripts at one of the big movie studios.

After that, they fell into the same arguments they'd had in college. Only instead of fraternity parties, it became hip Hollywood gatherings that she didn't feel comfortable bringing him to. Said a police officer would cramp everyone's style. There were a lot of illicit substances going around, not to mention high-priced escorts. So she went alone. At the time, Goode was working the three-to-midnight shift at the LAPD. But rather than deal with his troubled marriage, he simply worked more overtime. He finally came down with a virus that turned into pneumonia, which forced him to stay home and think. A couple weeks later, he suggested they separate. Smartest move he ever made.

Then he wussed out. Changed his mind. But she said, no, maybe he had a point. She wanted a divorce. Goode felt sad, but something inside told him it was the right thing to do. So he agreed. He only regretted that he hadn't been strong enough to do it first. At least he could've saved some face.

Then things started getting better. He did some good police work and applied to a few other departments, including San Diego. He started off in patrol and was soon able to transfer to a job in their Narcotics Unit. He'd been in San Diego for a couple of years when Miranda called from a resort in Borrego Springs. She said she'd gotten tired of running around with the Hollywood types and had settled down with a man she thought she could trust, but he'd disappointed her, blah, blah, blah, and she wanted to know if she could come down and see him. She'd been thinking, blah, blah, blah, that she'd made a big mistake letting him go. Goode thought something in her voice had changed. Or maybe he just wanted to. Anyway, he decided to give her one more chance. Dumbest move he ever made.

She filled his apartment with her stuff and was soon suggesting they get remarried. Stupidly, he allowed himself to be snowed. Again. As cynical as cops can be, it always amazed Goode how gullible they were in their personal lives. And he was no exception.

They decided to hold the ceremony at the St. James-by-the-Sea Episcopal Church, with the reception across the street at the La Jolla Contemporary Museum of Art. Their wedding day fell on a gloomy Sunday afternoon in June. The marine layer was starting to burn off as the church filled up with the fifty guests they'd invited. Miranda was ten minutes late, then twenty, then thirty. Goode developed a sick feeling of déjà vu. Finally, an hour after the scheduled start time, the minister pulled him aside. Said Miranda had just called to say she couldn't go through with it. She was at the airport on her way to the Caribbean.

Three women who worked with Miranda at a local television station overheard the conversation and took Goode to José's, a loud bar down the street that served Mexican food and pitchers of margaritas. They got him drunk and one of them spent the night with him. It certainly helped soften the impact. But more importantly, it taught him a lesson about Miranda. And any other woman like her.

"Never again," he said aloud as he drove down Nautilus Street toward Windan'sea. At the bottom of the hill, he could see an expanse of water so great that the horizon was almost a semicircle, as if he could see halfway around the globe. He parked his van in the lot overlooking the beach near the hut with the roof made of palm fronds. The sun was about to drop below the sea.

As usual, the locals were lined up for the daily ceremony known as Sunset, where they sipped wine or beer and waited for the big show. Some smoked cigarettes, their wet suits peeled half off, exposing deeply tanned backs that were freckled and leathery. Conversation stopped while the sun did a monologue center stage, its orange and gold reflection rippling. As the waves crashed onto the shore, Goode became hypnotized by the rhythm of the shoreline breathing. It was always a mystical experience for him. The ocean and Goode— they were connected somehow.

Then, as silently as it had risen that morning, the sun vanished under the horizon and he saw the green flash. That was the signal, like curtains closing, that everyone could leave, promising to come back tomorrow and watch the inevitable encore. Goode slowly returned to reality and flashed on the sensation of Alison's breasts pressing into his chest. He sighed and gunned the engine.

Fletcher hadn't turned up any kind of ties between Samantha Williams and Seth, Keith, or Tania. The escort service lead wasn't going anywhere, so Goode mentally shifted it to the back burner.

Despite Alison's remarks, however, Goode still thought his drug ring theory had merit. He was, after all, a narcotics detective. But he knew he had work to do to tie it to the murders, like talking to Clover about her drug source. Where was the woman, he wondered? In hiding? A saliva sample from Paul Walters was definitely in order, but he planned to try getting it the nice way first— ask him to give one voluntarily to rule him out as a suspect. He'd had his suspicions about the kid as soon as he'd laid eyes on him, but murder? Without more information, Goode didn't have enough for a court order to get the sample. Yet.

As Goode pulled up behind Paul's apartment complex, this time it was Maureen's body he imagined lying between the trash cans in the alley. He made his way up the staircase and imagined what hell it would be to carry groceries up to the third floor. His calves ached by the time he got there and was not surprised to see that Paul's curtains were still closed. Goode put his ear to the door and heard Jim Morrison of The Doors singing. Goode banged solidly three times with his fist. The music suddenly quieted, but Paul didn't open up.

"San Diego police," he said in his macho cop voice. "Open the door." Still no answer. "Come on, I know you're in there," he shouted. "I don't have time for hide and seek."

Goode jumped when he heard the woman's voice next to him. "What's going on, detective?" It was the manager, Mrs. Lacey, who had appeared at Goode's side as quietly as the night falls. "Is there a problem?"

"Well, ma'am, I'm trying to get Paul Walters here to open his door," he said. She moved to knock herself, but Goode held up his hand to stop her. "It would be better if you could go back to your apartment and let me handle this, Mrs. Lacey." He pounded again. "Walters, if you don't open this door, I'm going to break it down."

"If you do that, somebody's going to have to pay for it," Mrs. Lacey mumbled as she started down the stairs.

A disheveled Paul, his eyes red and glassy, opened up the door a crack. "What's going on?" he said, almost incoherently. "I'm sick and I was sleeping."

"Well, my friend, I need to talk to you. If you don't want to open up, then I'll need to take you downtown. *Comprendez?*"

"I told you everything I know about Tania Marcus," Paul said, sighing. "Can't we do this another time? I've got a temperature of a hundred and two. My head is killing me."

With one hand on the doorjamb, Goode leaned into

Paul's face. "I'm sorry you're not feeling well, but this can't wait any longer. Are you going to let me in, or do I have to make a scene and haul your ass out of here?"

Paul slithered around the door and stepped outside, pulling the door closed behind him. He stood with his arms crossed over his scrawny, hairless chest. His jeans hung beneath his navel, exposing a path of black curls and a strip of blue boxer shorts.

"Why don't we talk inside, Paul?"

"Okay," he grunted in a raspy voice, "but don't say I didn't warn you. I haven't had a chance to clean up in a while."

That was an understatement. A waft of nasty air that smelled like cooked peas hit Goode in the face. Glowing purple socks lay on the floor at random distances, as if a dog had been playing with them.

"You don't like doing laundry or what? And why are those socks glowing?"

"I told you, I'm sick."

Goode looked around the dismal living room. It was barely furnished and it was dark. The black walls didn't help. In the dim light, he saw a black light and understood why Paul's socks were glowing. "Mrs. Lacey know you did the walls like this?"

"No. I paid for the paint myself. Pretty cool with the black light, don't you think?"

"No comment."

Paul settled back into the sofa and pulled a worn red blanket over his bare chest.

"You ever ask Tania out?" Goode asked.

"I told you," he said. "I didn't even know the chick."

"Yeah, well, I think that's a lie. I know you knew her. I know you tried to get her to go out with you and when she wouldn't, you followed her around. There's a legal term for that. It's called stalking."

Paul looked at Goode with narrowed eyes and sighed. "So you're calling me a liar?"

"You tell me. If you look like a duck and walk like a duck, you're probably a duck."

"She didn't give me the time of day."

"Mind if I take a look around?"

"Yeah, just don't go in the bedroom. If you don't like the smell in here, you definitely don't want to go in there."

"I can take it. I've been in locker rooms before."

Goode heard a flick of a switchblade behind him. When he turned around, Paul was cutting the lip off a candle.

"You mind putting that away while I'm in here? I don't want to have to ask a doctor to pull it out of my back."

"Here. Want it?" Paul asked. He closed the knife and tossed it to Goode with a smile. It landed on the carpet at Goode's feet with a thud. When he went to pick it up, he could see pieces of cracker and other assorted crumbs embedded in the rug. They were glowing, too. Paul was right, the black light did make everything look pretty cool. But Goode wasn't about to compliment the little stalker.

"That's very funny, Paul. But you know what? I don't like your attitude. I don't care whether you're sick or not, we're going downtown as soon as I'm done looking in your bedroom."

"Fine, go ahead. I was just kidding. I can't help it if you can't catch."

"Stay right there," Goode ordered, pointing a finger at him. He headed into Paul's bedroom, past more dirty socks, record covers, and rock 'n' roll and porno magazines strewn all over the floor. A dog-eared copy of *Alice in Wonderland and Through the Looking Glass* lay open facedown on the bedside table, which actually was an orange plastic milk crate turned on its end. He turned on the bedroom light and that's when he saw that an entire wall was covered with Polaroid snapshots.

All of Tania.

"Oh, my God," he whispered. Tania was getting in and out of her car, wearing all sorts of different miniskirts, shorts, midriffs, her hair in a ponytail, her hair up in a knot, sunbathing. Getting the mail. Heading into her apartment with Seth.

Goode gasped. Asleep—or dead—there she was, lying on the same green and blue plaid blanket he saw on Paul's bed and wearing the same red pinstriped shirt he'd found her in. This was it, the break he'd been waiting for. As Goode was taking the incriminating photo off the wall for a closer look, he heard the front door open and Paul running away. Sick my ass, Goode thought.

He knew he couldn't take any of the photos without a warrant, so he dropped them on the floor, turned tail, and ran after Paul. The kid moved fast. Goode looked over the banister and saw that he was already in the parking lot running toward a beat-up brown pickup truck. Goode tried but couldn't quite make out the license plate number.

He stumbled and almost fell as he raced down the stairs after Paul, holding on to the railing to keep his balance. As Goode got closer to the parking lot, he was able to see the plate. Paul revved his engine and took off, turning west down the alley. The sticky lock in Goode's van held him up a few precious seconds, but he was soon in pursuit and calling for backup on the radio, which he kept in his cooler so as not to blow his cover. He gave the dispatcher Paul's full name, a description, the color of his truck, and the plate number. He put the portable red light on top of his van and took off after Paul.

Goode's tires squealed as he turned the corner, narrowly missing a kid on a skateboard. He kept meaning to get new tires, but he never seemed to have the time. Besides, he didn't chase all that many suspects in his van; his best weapon was his feet. He'd run track in high school and still managed to run a half marathon every once in a while. His adrenaline was pumping.

"Bond," he said. "James Bond." Too bad his headlights couldn't shoot missiles.

Paul's truck careened around the corner and headed east on Garnet toward the freeway. Paul was weaving in and out of cars and Goode almost lost him after he turned onto a side street. Suddenly, a red truck backed out of a driveway in front of Goode, who barely had enough time to swerve onto a neighbor's lawn.

"Asshole!"

By the time he maneuvered his van back into the street, Paul was long gone. "Shit!" Goode yelled, smacking the steering wheel with the heel of his hand.

Thankfully, a few minutes later he heard over the radio that a patrol car had stopped Paul a few blocks from the highway.

"Ask Goode what he wants us to do with him," Goode heard the patrolman say to the dispatcher. Goode recognized his voice. It was that idiot, Bennett. Goode was not a religious man, but he prayed that Bennett would pick up a brain somewhere between Garnet and the lockup.

"Tell him to arrest Walters for murder," Goode said into his radio. "I'll meet him down there. And tell him not to mess it up like he did that other one."

"Tell the detective, thanks for the advice, and he's a real honey pie," Bennett replied. "Next time he's pursuing a perpetrator, maybe he shouldn't lose him."

"Maybe he shouldn't lose him," Goode repeated to himself, mockingly.

By the time Goode got downtown, Paul had been given a T-shirt and some shoes to wear and they were taking his mugshot. Goode and another detective were discussing how they wished the Chargers would get to the Super Bowl again when Paul slid off the bench onto the concrete floor of the detention cage.

"He's not breathing. Get an ambulance," one of the officers screamed before he started performing CPR.

"Great," Goode muttered. "That's just great."

After working on him for a few minutes, Paul was breathing, but very shallowly, and his heartbeat was irregular. His face looked pretty sallow.

When the ambulance arrived, they shipped him over to UCSD Medical Center in Hillcrest to get checked out and do a drug screen. Goode made sure there was an officer stationed outside his door. Then he called Stone and they went to work getting a search warrant that would allow them to confiscate the photos and any drug evidence from Paul's apartment. The way Goode's luck was going, Paul would claim Goode beat him until he collapsed. Goode would get written up for using unnecessary force, not to mention sexually assaulting a witness. His promotion to Homicide would be derailed and Paul would go free for Tania's murder. If he did it, that is.

The Polaroids confirmed Alison's story about Paul stalking Tania, but they offered no link to Sharona Glass' murder nor to Goode's drug ring theory. When he went back to the apartment, he also intended to check for any link to his sister Maureen, who was still MIA.

Within a couple of hours, Paul was conscious and rehydrated. He shook his head at Goode from his bed and had the same stupid smirk on his face until Goode told him they wanted to take a saliva sample. The doctor also thought he had hepatitis, Goode told him, so they were waiting for those test results, too, before putting him into the jail population.

"No way, man. I can't believe this." Paul raised his chest off the bed, but not much since he was handcuffed to the bed railing. "I go out for a little jog while you're looking around my apartment without a warrant and the next thing I know, I'm thrown into a police car, punched in the kidneys, and poked by two cops. And not in a good way. Now you're here trying to test my saliva? I think you're way out of line."

"Calm down," Goode said. "It won't hurt a bit. Right, nurse?"

The nurse glared at Goode. Obviously she had no sense of humor.

"No way, man," Paul said.

"Fine. I'll be back with a court order," Goode said, using the movie voice of Arnold Schwarzenegger, California's governor.

Goode, who had obtained the warrant by then, called Stone and told him they needed a court order. Then he called the evidence tech to meet him at Paul's apartment so they could take down all the photos and log them in. Stone said this one was Goode's baby; Byron had his hands full. Luckily, none of the Polaroids featured Maureen. Goode searched through Paul's bedroom drawers and bathroom medicine cabinet. That's where he found some small oblong pills in a plastic bag. He'd seen these before: Flunitrazepam, otherwise known as Rohypnol, a date-rape drug.

He still hadn't found a trace of Sharona, which left him at a loss for tying Paul to her murder, but he still felt in his gut that the two murders were linked. Something else was troubling him, too. When he looked more closely at the Polaroid of Tania lying on the bed, there were no purple marks on her neck. He wondered if the shots had been taken right before her death, or if they just weren't clear enough to show what he was looking for. Perhaps Paul had knocked her out, carried her down to the alley and then strangled her. With that skinny body, it was hard to imagine that he was strong enough to carry anything but his own sorry ass down those stairs. Goode made a mental note to see if the nurse found any scratches on his body that could have resulted from the struggle that broke off Tania's fingernails.

When Goode found a pair of women's black nylon shorts crumpled up in a ball on the floor next to the closet, he stopped, took a deep breath and let it out slowly.

"That rat bastard," he said.

Chapter Twenty-eight

Norman

Norman sat ruminating in Denny's for forty-five minutes while he put away a bacon cheeseburger, fries, a chocolate shake, and two cups of coffee. He ordered a piece of lemon meringue pie so the waitress wouldn't give away his table, then walked outside to make a few calls on his cell phone. He tried the beauty school, but got an answering machine message saying they were temporarily closed.

Next, he called the toll-free number for the paper to try to get Tommy, one of the editorial assistants, to bring him some gas. But he kept getting his voice mail.

Finally, he called the auto club and the dispatcher said it should take about twenty-five minutes for the truck to arrive. Just enough time for him to eat the pie and walk back to meet the truck. He reached for his wallet, but couldn't find his keys. He must've locked them in the car. He was doomed. Doomed with a capital D.

As he walked back in the late afternoon sun, his belly was so full he had to undo the top button of his jeans. As he feared, his keys were sitting on the car seat in plain view. He climbed up on the hood and leaned against the windshield. He was starting to get woozy, lying there in the sun. Two hours later, the auto club driver roused him out of a sound sleep. He said the dispatcher had given him the wrong address.

It was too late in the day by then to follow through on his plan to crash the beauty school, so he headed back to the office. He wondered if this was a sign he wasn't supposed to be a reporter.

Norman sat dejectedly at his computer. He had the basic facts from the cops, but no good color. He'd tried to make some more calls, but that got him nowhere. He had nothing from the beauty school and no quotes from the Glass family. He didn't dare tell Al that this was all because he'd run out of gas.

With an hour to go until the early deadline, Norman broke through his writer's block and pecked away at the keyboard with his two index fingers. Don't back into the lead, Al's voice said in his head. His fourth try was good enough. Al could fiddle with it. It almost didn't matter what he turned in, he hardly recognized his stories in the next day's paper.

With ten minutes until deadline, an e-mail message from Al popped up at the top of his screen: "What's your ETA, Klein?"

When Norman didn't answer, Al gave up on the subtle approach and yelled at him from across the newsroom: "I need that story, Klein. I want to go home."

Most of the dayside reporters had already turned in their stories. Several from the government team were gossiping with Jerry, the city hall reporter, and trading dead-baby jokes. They smirked in Norman's direction.

"What's the matter, Klein?" Jerry said. "Too many cheeseburgers at lunch slowin' you down?"

Norman didn't even look up. Jerry would get his. What goes around comes around. "I'm almost done, chief," Norman yelled.

Who did they think they were, anyway? It wasn't like any of them had won a Pulitzer, for Christ's sake. Jerry was always telling people that it was only a matter of months before he'd get hired by the *Los Angeles Times*, yet there he was, still working at the same paper that had hired him right out of college.

Norman bore down and finished what turned out to be a twelve-inch story. He'd busted deadline by fifteen minutes, but it could've been worse. Then came the next stage of anxiety: editing by Al, who gave the story a cursory read, and then called him over.

"You're in past deadline and there isn't much of a story here, but I think it's salvageable, kid," he said. "Next time, take a company car if you're short on gas and don't miss deadline."

"Okay," Norman said as good-naturedly as he could, wondering how the hell Al found out what had happened. "See you at the Tavern later, Al?"

"Yeah, maybe," the editor snapped.

Al was forty-five going on sixty-five. A few greasy strands of a comb-over were all that was left of his hair. Marcy, the executive editor's secretary, said Al used to be a good-looking man, but he drank too much. Couldn't handle the stress. That got him a bleeding ulcer, a tire of flab that hung over his belt, and permanent bags under his eyes. Not to mention an off-and-on irritability that went unmatched in the newsroom. When it was on, reporters called him Al the Hun or Al's Evil Twin. Other times, he'd be perfectly charming. You never knew which one you were talking to until it was too late.

Norman headed over to the Tavern after the story had cleared the copy desk. He watched the door all night, waiting for Al to come in. He was nursing his fourth beer when he finally felt the weight of the day slide off his shoulders. The story was done and he still had his job. He'd tucked his cell phone into the waistband of his jeans, thankful he didn't have to remember to call the desk. But he spoke too soon. The damn thing rang at ten o'clock.

Al was still on the Metro desk when Norman called in. He'd ended up staying late to help out Big Ed because one of the city council members had a heart attack in the middle of the council meeting. Meanwhile, they'd heard about another murder in P.B. on the scanner.

"The shit never stops," Big Ed said. "You'd better get over there. Cops said it could be related to the beauty school killings."

Norman paused. His reaction time was a little slow.

"What's the matter?" Big Ed said. "We'll pay you OT."

That wasn't it, but Norman didn't want to tell him. Four beers do not a good reporter make. But who knew, maybe this would help his anxiety level, and solidify his concentration. The day wasn't turning out so bad after all. This time, he was determined nothing would go wrong. Norman tripped over the curb in the parking lot and fell on one knee, but he recovered quickly and shook it off. After all, the hole in his pant leg was pretty small.

Chapter Twenty-nine

Goode

Goode was still going through Paul Walters' stuff when his cell phone rang. Sergeant Stone was calling from home again, so he figured it must be serious.

"There's been another murder, right outside Pumphouse," Stone said. "Keith Warner."

"No shit," Goode said, remembering Keith's scared face in the van on the way back from the funeral.

"He was the guy whose chemistry didn't match, right?" Stone sounded a little irritated.

"Yup. That's him," Goode said. "What the hell happened?"

"Shot once in the back of the head. Not very clean either. I think it's safe to say he was dead on impact. Bartender called it in half an hour ago. Said he heard shots fired, then went outside and found the body in the parking lot. Saw nothing, knows nothing."

"How surprising." So if Paul was in the hospital, he wondered, who the hell was the shooter?

"Well, that puts my newest suspect out of the picture on this one," Goode said, tossing the Polaroids onto Paul's kitchen counter. "Seeing that he's been out of commission for the past few hours."

"Yeah, I know. You'd better meet me, Byron, Slausson, and Fletcher over at Pumphouse ASAP. I hope to God we can find an eyewitness. It sounded like you guys were making good progress, but the bodies keep piling up, so you'd better step it up a few notches. The chief just called again to say the mayor's office is involved now. They're getting a lot of pressure from the community for an end to this, not to mention all those damned media vultures, who have sharpened their focus on how we're handling these murders. . . Can you give me something to work with, here?"

"Well, we have Walters in custody, but as I mentioned, he can't be the do-er for all three and I'm still convinced they're related," Goode said.

"Yeah, well, maybe your theory is wrong."

Goode didn't like the edge in Stone's voice. "Do you know if Seth Kennedy was down at the bar?" he asked cautiously.

"Not that I know of. But who knows. Maybe we'll get lucky."

"Have you heard whether Tania's toxicology tests have come back yet? Or whether the lab has determined for sure what that white powder was in Sharona's apartment?"

"No, I haven't, but I'll see if I can shake some trees."

"Slausson and I each went separately to Clover Ziegler's house, but she wasn't home and she hasn't gotten back to me. We've got to find the source of all this white powder, among other things."

"I'm doing the best I can, Goode," Stone said, and abruptly hung up.

This wasn't good. Three dead bodies, two strangled and now one shot, in just a few days, all in the same neighborhood. The community was in an uproar and Stone was agitated, which wasn't like him. They were all feeling it.

Goode knew better than to ignore his instincts about the connection between the murders. Seth was looking like a good suspect again. It was too bad about Keith, though. He had seemed like such a nice kid. His death wasn't good news for the case either. Goode had figured he would turn out to be a good snitch once he'd had some time to think about his priorities.

Goode wondered if Seth had killed his buddy because he was worried Keith was about to rat him out about the murders, or because he'd learned that Keith had revealed his "recreational" drug use. Keith also could have been doing a deal himself in the parking lot, and it had gone bad. There were numerous possibilities. The Polaroids and the women's shorts in Paul's apartment proved he had to be involved in this whole mess. The question was how.

Goode tried calling Maureen from Paul's apartment one more time, but he got her machine again. So he drove to the bar, pushing his weak engine as hard as he could.

The Pumphouse parking lot was a mess of flashing red lights. Four cruisers were blocking the lookie-loos from getting past the yellow tape and mucking up the crime scene. He nodded at Slausson and Fletcher, who had split up to talk to neighbors and some kids with skateboards. He figured Byron was inside.

Goode approached one of the patrolmen, who was chatting up a young, tipsy blond woman—but not about the case, judging by the grin on her face. "Any sign of a dark-haired guy, late twenties?"

"Not that I've seen," the patrolman said.

That meant the bartender was first up for questioning. If Goode's drug ring theory was true, One-Eyed Jack had to be in on it. Goode walked into the empty bar, and there he was, sitting on a stool behind the counter, drinking a soda, surrounded by half-empty glasses of beer. Looked like everyone had left thirsty.

"We need to talk," Goode said, forgetting which eye to speak to.

"I already talked to that other detective," One-Eye said. "Brian or something."

Goode didn't have time for protocol. He had some questions for this joker. "What a coincidence. I'm a detective, and you get to talk to me, too. Any idea why Keith Warner got shot tonight?"

"No sir." He got off the stool, set down his glass and reached into the sink of soapy water for another one to wash. His hands were shaking.

Goode sat on a stool across from him. "How about you do that later? I'd like your full attention."

"Yeah, okay, whatever. This has been a pretty weird night. And not too great for business, if you know what I mean." He went under the sink, and Goode half-expected him to come back up pointing a gun. But when he surfaced, he was wiping his hands on a small white towel.

"What kind of business would that be, pal? A little cocaine action in the bathroom? Or maybe in the parking lot tonight?"

The bartender turned around and grabbed a cigarette from his pack of Camels on the counter behind him. He lit one and took a long, hard pull as he stared down at the sink. Then he looked straight up at Goode—as straight as he could with that eye. A stream of gray acrid smoke seeped out of his nose.

Goode stared right back, raising his eyebrows. "I'm not getting any younger here, and by the way, I already told you smoking in bars is against the law."

One-Eye shook his head. "Shit," he said, taking another puff, then stubbed it out on a plate. Goode planned to nab it when he wasn't looking.

"I take it that means yes," he said.

"No, not exactly," One-Eye said, letting out a long sigh and more smoke, which Goode batted away with his hand. "It's kind of complicated. After I caught Keith using it in the bathroom a couple times, I told him he had to take his party elsewhere. I thought he did. After that, there wasn't any 'business' here that I knew of."

It was too easy to pin the crime on a guy who couldn't defend himself. Goode was leaning even harder toward the theory that Seth was the brain of the operation and One-Eye was his lackey. "Let me be blunt, pal. I know Seth Kennedy was running a drug business out of here, so you have to be involved. If you don't start pointing me to your stockpile, I'm going to arrest you for distributing narcotics and three counts of conspiracy to commit murder." Goode pointed his finger at him for emphasis. "*Capisce?*"

"Now wait just a minute," One-Eye said, lowering his voice so only Goode could hear. "Just because drugs were being sold here doesn't mean I was involved. Seth paid me for the rental of a little storage space, and a little more to look the other way. That's all. I had nothing to do with any drug distribution or any murders. I didn't even know those girls."

"Well, I'm still finding it hard to believe that you're telling me the truth. Didn't you tell me two minutes ago that Keith Warner was the one selling drugs?"

"Yeah, well, my memory changed after you started telling me I was going to prison for murdering him and those girls," he said. "The poor kid's dead. He didn't do anything wrong but pick the wrong friends."

"That's for sure. Now, let's get back to basics. It seems like you'd want a bigger cut for all the risk you're taking by letting Seth work out of your bar."

"First of all, it's not my bar. I'm just the manager. And

second, I figured the less I knew about the drugs, the better off I'd be," One-Eye said.

"That's a pretty laissez-faire attitude, pal," Goode said.

"Whatever. That's how it is."

"Let's cut the crap and tell me where this storage space is. You know he'd sell you out in a minute if he was in your shoes right about now."

One-Eye shook his head with the sad realization that Goode was right. "Last I heard, he kept some stuff in the padlocked shed in the back parking lot. I also know he just got a shipment in from Mexico at his house. The stuff here is just for quick access and convenience."

"Now that's more like it," Goode said, smiling wryly. He turned to walk away, then thought of something. "Where's Jake tonight?"

"Damned if I know," One-Eye said. "He didn't show up for work."

By then, Stone had arrived and Byron had resurfaced. His wife had gone into labor and he had to run over to the hospital for a bit. The team huddled to come up with a game plan: Stone would handle getting the warrants, while Byron, Slausson, and Fletcher would go through every drawer and cabinet in the bar. Goode would head over to Seth's to conduct a surprise search.

Goode was feeling pretty good as he arrested Jack O'Mallory. His theory was in the process of revealing itself. He was sure that after a night in the tank, old One-Eye would be willing to connect some more dots for him. Before he forgot, he had the evidence tech grab the Camel butt from the plate.

One-Eye was right about one thing. Keith hadn't picked his friends well. Chances were, though, that he was somehow involved in this mess or he wouldn't be dead.

Goode felt a couple heavy wet drops fall on his head. Within a minute or two, the rain was falling harder and faster. Soon, the rain was hammering like gunfire at the canvas covering Keith's body. Goode watched as a pool of blood that had formed next to the body flowed into the gutter and down the street in pink rivulets. He felt a tap on his shoulder.

"I think there's something here you ought to see," Stone said, handing Goode Keith's open wallet. Inside was a row of four small photos featuring Keith and Maureen, kissing like lovebirds in one of those booths. Goode's heart started racing and he couldn't breathe for a minute. As he had feared, it looked like they'd been out on more than a date or two.

"Shit," he said, sitting down on the hood of a cruiser. "Shit, shit, shit." He jumped as the water began to seep through the seat of his jeans. But there was nothing he could do about the drops that were running down his neck and back.

"Want us to send another unit by her house, Goode?" Stone asked.

Goode couldn't answer for a moment. He pictured Maureen lying on her bathroom floor, her neck covered with purple marks from where this bastard had strangled her. "No thanks. I'm going to see for myself. I was just over there and no one answered the door. I could kick myself for not climbing in an open window."

Goode started for his van.

"I'll call the DA for the warrants right now," Stone yelled after him. "Call me in ten."

A few minutes later, Goode pulled up at Maureen's house and sprinted up the front path. He rang the bell five times in quick succession and hammered on the door. His mind was still playing tricks on him. He saw her dead on the closet floor. Drowned in the bathtub. Shot in the back of the head, execution-style, like Keith.

"Come on you guys, open up!" he yelled, banging again. His hand was aching but he hardly noticed.

Chris finally came to the door. "What the hell is going on?" he said, looking at his watch. "I've got to get up at five, dude."

"Where is she?" Goode demanded.

"How the hell should I know? I haven't seen her for three days. You have got to learn how to relax, man, I'm telling you."

"I don't have time to relax, you cretin," Goode said, grabbing him by the front of his rumpled T-shirt. "How do I know she's not lying dead in her bathroom and you haven't noticed? Don't you know that two women and one man have been killed this week in your neighborhood?"

"Dude, you are out of control," he said, prying Goode's hand off his shirt. "Listen. I don't know where she is. She's an adult. You're not her father and I'm not her keeper."

Goode couldn't think straight. He was so upset he wanted to rip the guy's lungs out. He tried to calm down, but he just couldn't.

"Mitch has been gone for three days too." Chris said. "Maybe they went to Vegas to get hitched."

Goode had no patience to deal with this smart-ass. "My sister isn't marrying a pool guy," he said. "Now get the hell of out of my way."

Chris stepped aside as Goode pushed past him. "Fine, whatever."

Goode headed directly for Maureen's room and whipped open her bedroom door. The bed was made and her clothes were all put away. She wasn't lying dead in the closet and she wasn't drowned in the bathtub. He felt like a fool, but for once, it was a good feeling.

He took a deep breath and walked back into the foyer, where Chris was sitting on the back of the couch, rubbing his eyes and yawning.

Goode put his hand on his shoulder. "I'm sorry I overreacted," he said. "There's a lot of shit going down and I'm just worried about my sister." He walked outside into the night and turned around. "Would you let her know I'm looking for her?"

Chris nodded wearily and closed the door.

From there, Goode headed back to the Pumphouse.

Chapter Thirty

Norman

By the time Norman arrived at the murder scene, the rain was coming down in torrents and a guy with a lazy eye was sitting handcuffed in the back of a cruiser behind the medical examiner's van. A virtual fleet of police cars was parked at various points around the Pumphouse parking lot, which was cordoned off with yellow tape. Norman looked around for Detective Goode again, but he wasn't there.

A man wearing a jacket and tie seemed to be in charge. Norman had figured out by now that cops without uniforms were generally detectives. He hoped this one wouldn't smell the beer on his breath.

"Lieutenant?" he ventured. "I'm with the *Sun-Dispatch*. You guys got a homicide, right?"

"It's sergeant. Can't talk to you right now," he said as he walked away, leaving Norman in one of the worst states for a reporter—on deadline with no one talking. Norman tried to act casual and stroll into the bar as if he'd been given permission. Several officers were opening drawers and cabinets, tossing paper napkins and bags of chips onto the floor next to two boxes containing plastic bags of a white powdery substance.

Norman felt a tug at the back of his collar as he was pulled out of the doorway from behind. "What's the matter with you? You can't go in there. We're in the middle of a search," a man's angry voice said. Norman was whipped around by his collar to face the sergeant.

"Sorry, I didn't know," Norman said, pausing before

he dove deeper into dangerous territory. "But I do have a deadline to meet. What's the white stuff?"

The sergeant gave him a pained expression. "What's it look like?"

Norman shrugged. "I don't know, cocaine?"

"Could be. Or meth. Or both. But you didn't hear it from me."

"Thanks!"

Norman used his cell phone to call Big Ed to warn him that he had a major story coming, but there was no way he would make the 11 P.M. deadline. It was five till.

"I don't know," Big Ed growled. "What do you got so far?"

Norman gulped and went ahead. "Cops won't tell me much, just that it's going to be a while before they can say anything on the record. There's a bunch of officers here and the medical examiner's van, too. The sergeant sort of told me that he had cocaine or meth in some boxes."

"What boxes?" Big Ed barked. "And what do you mean he sort of told you? Did he tell you, or didn't he?"

Norman was starting to sweat. "I peeked inside the bar and they're going through all the drawers and cabinets. The sergeant said I couldn't go inside because they were in the middle of a search. I saw some cardboard boxes full of white stuff, so I asked him if it was coke and he goes, 'Could be. Or meth. Or both. You didn't hear it from me.' Also, there's a guy sitting in one of the cruisers, handcuffed. He could be a murder suspect or a drug dealer or both. The police won't say anything official and they don't care that I'm on deadline."

"That's because they don't know you. So let's slow down and back up," Big Ed said. "Who's the dead guy?"

"I don't know yet, chief," he said. "I guess I got kind of sidetracked with the drug search."

"Well, listen kid, this is a daily newspaper, not a

weekly. You need to find out what's going on. Get the name of the dead guy and the suspect in the cruiser, and do it fast. We can stretch the deadline a little, but I've got to have something by eleven thirty at the latest. Maybe I ought to call another reporter in to help you out. This sounds pretty big."

"No, I can handle it," Norman said. "I swear. I'll call you back as soon as I've got something more. Okay?"

Big Ed paused. "Okay, but, don't screw this up. We need details, not broad-brush stuff. And this time, don't forget we don't print quotes from anonymous sources. Got that?"

"Got it, chief." Norman hung up the phone, muttering under his breath.

Norman knew he had to take charge of his destiny and push harder. He started writing down what he could see for himself. He didn't need a press release to say they were searching the bar or that they'd found boxes of white powder. A rap song with the lyrics "Fuck the police" was streaming out of the jukebox.

"You guys have interesting taste in music," Norman said to one of the other cops.

"Very funny," the cop said. "It was on when we got here and for some reason, it keeps repeating. Somebody's idea of a joke."

Norman stood under the overhang to stay dry, waiting to make another run at the sergeant for a statement. This was a big story and he couldn't afford to be shut out. Norman touched the arm of the guy with the tie and he whirled around. He looked relieved and a little annoyed to see it was only Norman.

"You again?" he said. "What do you want now?"

"I'm right up on deadline," Norman said matter-of-factly. "My editor is going to fire me if I don't give him something in the next few minutes before we put the paper to bed." Thankfully, the guy softened a little.

"Yeah, yeah, all right," the sergeant said, reaching inside his coat pocket and grabbing a handkerchief to wipe the water off his face. "Okay. What we've got here is a white male, late twenties, shot in the head. Pronounced dead at 10:35 P.M. The case is under investigation."

"What's his name?"

"Family hasn't been notified yet. You'll have to call the ME's office tomorrow." The cop turned and started to go inside.

"Wait. Wait," Norman said, grabbing his arm. The sergeant frowned at Norman until he removed his hand. "Who's the guy in the back of the cruiser out there? Is he the murder suspect?"

"No, that's the bartender, Jack O'Mallory. He called in the murder. For his trouble, we arrested him for possession and distribution of narcotics." The sergeant chuckled.

"What kind of narcotics? Meth and cocaine?"

"Could be either one or both. We'll have to test it to make sure."

Norman could feel his eyes getting bigger. He was living the dream. "Is this murder related to the two beauty school students?"

"Could be, but we don't know yet. You the one who's been covering the other murders?"

"Yes, sir. Don't you think they're related? They've all happened in this neighborhood."

The sergeant looked tense, almost a little angry. "I just told you, we don't know enough yet to say," he said testily.

"Okay. Can I get your name?" Norman asked, thanking God that he remembered since he had actually succeeded in getting some information on the record.

"Stone. Sergeant Stone."

"Great. Thanks, sergeant. You're the best."

Stone softened a little. "Let's hope so," he said wryly.

Norman looked at his watch and realized he had only

minutes to spare before deadline. It was cool being a reporter. Very cool.

As he dictated what he had over his cell phone to Big
Ed, he saw Detective Goode drive into the parking lot
and jog over to the sergeant. Judging by their expres-
sions, something else was up. Goode was gesturing excitedly. Norman thought it could be a break in the case,
so he tried to keep an eye on them while he finished dic-
tating. Goode and Stone talked, they both made calls on
their cell phones, then Goode took off.

The last time Norman had seen Goode, he'd been
pretty inscrutable and kept his cool. But not this time.
The detective was obviously hyped-up. If Norman
wanted to make it in the news business, he knew he'd
have to do a little late-night enterprise reporting. So he
jumped in the newsmobile and followed the detective.
Luckily, the beers were starting to wear off.

Chapter Thirty-one

Goode

Because Stone's patchwork homicide team was dealing
with a ridiculously unusual three murders in four days,
they all were being put to the test, both mentally and
physically. Keith's murder was obviously related to the
other two, and it confirmed that Goode's drug connection theory had merit. Once Goode got back to Pumphouse, he told Stone he wanted to call in Marshall
Rogers, his partner from Narcotics, to help with the
search at Seth's place. Stone was saying that sounded
like a fine idea when his cell phone started ringing.

It was the deputy district attorney and the judge on a
conference call to issue a telephonic search warrant for

Seth's house. Stone gave the thumbs-up sign to Goode and started scribbling on a form he kept in his car for such times. Goode took the opportunity to call Rogers, who wasn't so pleased. He was at a formal party with his wife and said she'd be pissed if he just took off. But Goode persuaded him that this was important and she'd get over it.

"At least you have a wife to piss off. And don't forget to bring Rocky," Goode said, referring to the department's best drug-sniffing dog.

Goode grabbed the warrant from Stone and took off. As he was driving down Mission Boulevard toward La Jolla, Goode thought about his little incident with his sister's roommate. He regretted being so hard on him, but the guy was such an idiot Goode just couldn't help himself. He'd never been able to figure out how Maureen could live with two pool guys who got up at the crack of dawn and played their guitars, knowing their roommate was still asleep.

Maureen sometimes complained about their weird habits, but said they didn't bother her enough to move. Goode was still worried about where she was, but he'd done all he could for the night, so he tried to let it go and concentrate on the case.

Seth lived a few blocks from the beach on Sea Lane, a street that crossed La Jolla Boulevard. His house was on the east side, where the houses were worth hundreds of thousands, if not millions, less than those across the boulevard. Maybe Daddy had bought him a fixer-upper, Goode thought. He hoped he hit the jackpot and found coke and meth there, and was betting that it matched the high-quality stuff found in Tania's apartment.

If Goode broke this case and made a big drug arrest in the process, he couldn't have asked for a better way to go out of Narcotics. Not that working Homicide would give him a normal life, but at least it would be different.

Goode noticed in his rearview mirror that a brown

Toyota behind him was changing lanes every time he did. He figured it was probably a drunk who couldn't drive without a pair of red lights to follow. He knew he should probably head straight to Seth's, but he figured a quick drive by Windansea wouldn't add any significant delay. He needed to psych himself up for what could be a nasty, if not dangerous, confrontation. Besides, Rogers would need a little time to placate his wife before coming to meet him, and it was against procedure to go into this type of situation alone. Although that hadn't stopped him in the past.

Through his open window, Goode could see that the tide was high and a good swell was coming in. The ocean worked on his nerves better than any Elmore Leonard novel ever could. He watched the waves crest, fall, and pull away like a lacey negligee of suds, revealing the sandy skin of the only woman that seemed safe to love these days.

The sound of the water brought back the dream he'd had the night before. He was standing on the muddy bank of a river, watching it flow past him, like threads of a self-weaving fabric. The movement of the water was so quick it seemed almost still. He was mesmerized by it. Slowly, a few feet in front of him, a woman's face emerged from the river, facing toward the sky, her eyes closed, her mouth open and her long dark hair hanging straight back to expose a neck mottled with purple blotches. It was Tania Marcus.

Even in the dream, Goode found it uncanny that Tania could stand in one place when the current would have swept anyone else down the river to the craggy rocks below. She opened her eyes and smiled at him, slowly raising her hand in a Miss America wave, one of those with the cupped palm rotating side to side. Then, she beckoned to him and her smile turned a little wicked, conveying a promise of pleasure if he joined her.

"Come join me on the riverbank, you'll be safe here," Goode yelled.

Tania's smile faded as she shook her head. He realized how stupid it was to be discussing safety with a dead woman. And even more stupid that she would refuse. Then Tania started to sink back under the surface.

"Who did this to you?" Goode blurted out. But it was too late. She was gone.

Between the dreams, the diary entries, and the interlude with Alison, he'd been sexually aroused for four days. It had been a few years since he remembered feeling like this, but he hadn't realized how dead inside he'd been until the last few days. Joining the living was a scary prospect.

But something about this renewed awareness felt wrong. Wasn't it a little pathetic that he was infatuated with a damaged woman who'd been molested, not to mention a woman whose death he was investigating? Goode tried to think of something that would bring him back to center. He conjured up an image of Alison in her bathrobe, kissing him. He remembered how her breath felt on his neck and he suddenly felt flushed all over again. What was happening to him? His emotions were all over the map. He was acting like a teenager, for Christ's sake.

"Enough," he said to himself. "It's showtime."

Goode looked in the rearview mirror again and saw that the brown Toyota was creeping along behind him.

"Who the hell is that?" he barked out loud. Whoever it was, he was going to lose the bastard. Goode drove up Nautilus toward the stoplight at La Jolla Boulevard and flicked on his left turn signal. The Toyota did the same. Goode pulled into the intersection and started to turn left, but then went straight instead so that the Toyota had to veer suddenly to follow him. Goode swerved again, this time to the right, and lurched into a mini-strip mall where they sold gas, roast chicken, and bikinis. The Toyota's tires screeched as it straightened out and kept going. Goode sped out of the driveway in front of him, turned the corner and headed up Nautilus after the Toyota. He put on his flashing red light and motioned the driver to pull over. He walked up from the rear of the car and pointed his flashlight through the driver's-side window. The light reflected off the driver's wire-rimmed glasses and Goode recognized his tail.

It was that damn cub reporter from the *Sun-Dispatch*, Norman Klein, the kid with ink on his face who didn't know what "off the record" meant. He sure looked frightened. And well he should. Goode needed to teach him a little lesson about anonymous sources and the inherent problem with trailing a detective on the job.

"Roll down the window," Goode ordered. Norman promptly complied. "What the hell do you think you're doing?"

"I was just, umm, hoping to get some more information on what's going on," Norman said, his voice a high-pitched squeak.

"Yeah, well, I've already seen how you don't know the meaning of 'off-the-record' and Sergeant Stone told me you just casually strolled into our crime scene at Pumphouse tonight. You know, you're putting your life in danger following me and I am not particularly impressed that you've chosen to take up such aggressive reporting tactics, Mr. Klein. I strongly suggest that you turn this little trash-heap of yours around and head home."

Norman's mouth hung open slightly, his fingers white from gripping the steering wheel so tightly. "I'm really sorry if I upset you," he said. "I didn't think you'd mind some credit for finding the body. . . . Can I call you tomorrow for an update?"

"No, you can't. From now on, you go through the sergeant for quotes."

Goode took no small satisfaction in scaring the kid,

but he decided to have mercy and lighten up on him. "Besides, I'm just heading over to my girlfriend's house, so you can rest easy. You're not missing any story here, Scoop."

Norman looked relieved. If he only knew what he was going to miss, Goode thought. Ha.

Goode got back into his van and waited until he was sure Norman was gone before he rolled to Seth's house and parked down the street. As the minutes ticked by, he could feel his blood pressure creeping up. His testosterone levels were so high he was starting to feel like a time bomb with a faulty trigger. Where the hell was Rogers? The man knew how much Goode hated to wait when he was fired up and ready to make a bust. Goode was worried if he took much longer that Seth would have already flushed his stash down the toilet.

Rogers once told Goode that he had a bad case of the lone wolf syndrome, daring death to touch him when he had no backup. Rogers was right. Seth Kennedy was a murder suspect, but Goode was too impatient to wait any longer. He had the address. Rogers would be there soon enough and he could join him inside. Goode was going in, lone wolf or not.

Seth lived in a squat white house with dark blue shutters and a very small but well-kept lawn. The garden was lined with red, white, yellow, and pink rosebushes, interspersed with purple, yellow, and raspberry pansies. White track lights lined the brick walkway, casting an almost fluorescent sheen over the pansies.

Inside, Goode could hear a man and a woman arguing. He put his ear to the door. The woman was sobbing.

"Look, Clover, I told you, it's over between us," Seth said. "I have no time for your hysterical outbursts anymore. We were never dating. This was always a sexual thing. You knew that. I've moved on and so should you."

Goode heard high heels clattering across what sounded like a wooden floor, so he dashed around the side of the house. He took a deep breath in and let it out slowly so no one would hear him panting.

"Jake was right about you," Clover screamed. "You're just a narcissistic asshole."

She flung open the front door and ran toward the street. Goode ducked down behind the rosebushes, hoping she wouldn't see him as she got into a red Mercedes convertible and sped off into the night. Just what he would have expected from the Clover he had heard so much about. Nice car, he thought. Very upset driver. Not a good combination.

Goode was pissed. There he was, finally close enough to talk to her, and he had to pass up the opportunity. But first things first.

Goode rapped the brass knocker on the front door three times. When he got no answer, he did it again. "Police. Open the door," he ordered. "Kennedy, I know you're in there."

When Seth finally opened up, he looked highly annoyed. "Detective Goode, it's almost midnight," he said sharply, looking at his watch for emphasis. "What's so important it can't wait until morning?"

Seth was on the offensive. He almost had Goode believing that he didn't know his best friend had just been murdered.

"Do you mind if I come in?" Goode asked. When Seth didn't move, he held up the search warrant as he pushed past Seth into the living room, saying, "Well, like it or not, I'm coming in anyway. I have a warrant." Goode loved that part of the job.

"I really don't know why you couldn't do this at a civilized hour," Seth snapped. "I've got to work tomorrow morning."

"Sorry," Goode said with complete insincerity. "No can do."

Closing the door behind them, Seth said, "You're just wasting your time and mine. I've told you everything."

Goode knew better.

Seth was wearing a white pinstriped shirt like the one Tania was wearing when Goode found her, only this one had thin black stripes. Seth's suit jacket and a red tie were strewn across the back of a maroon leather chair that looked like it belonged in a lawyer's office.

"Nice place you've got here," Goode said. He walked along the wall, admiring the artwork, and inspected each piece. He leaned closer to read the signature on a small sketch.

"Is that a real Picasso?" Goode asked incredulously. The frame was a big, deep, fancy gold one that didn't really fit with the drawing.

"Sure is. My parents gave it to me for my twenty-first birthday. It's just a sketch, but it's quite valuable. Someday, I'm going to line the walls of my mansion with Impressionist paintings. I really like flowers."

How sweet, Goode thought. "Yeah, I noticed your garden. You have a mansion?"

"No. I meant someday when I have a mansion," Seth said, pausing as he leaned against the door frame to the bedroom. "So what's this bad news? And what's up with the search warrant?"

The boy certainly seemed a little more jumpy than the last time Goode had seen him. Could it be that he had just killed his best friend, or that he had massive amounts of drugs on the property? Or both? Goode had no doubt about the drugs. They had to be there somewhere. And if Seth didn't commit the murders, he probably knew who did.

"Let's get down to business," Goode said matter-of-factly. He sat on the matching maroon leather couch. Seth's expression remained unchanged. Was he some kind of sociopath or did he really not know about Keith?

"Your friend Keith Warner is dead. Shot in the back of the head tonight at Pumphouse." He paused, watching Seth closely for his reaction.

Impressively, Seth's face fell as he stared at Goode. "Wait, whaat? Say that again."

"Your friend is dead."

Seth started pacing across the hardwood floor in his black Italian dress shoes. "You're lying. You're just trying to get me to say something you want to hear," he said.

Seth's footsteps sounded hollow, as if there was some space under the house, perfect for storing wine—or drugs.

"No, Mr. Kennedy, I'm dead serious."

"When did this happen?" Seth asked, turning around to face him.

Goode wondered if Seth was scrambling for an alibi. "We got the call a couple of hours ago," he said. "Where were you at that time?"

"Give me a break," Seth said, shaking his head. "You can't be serious. Keith was my best friend. I can't believe you would talk to me in this kind of tone. Besides, why would anyone kill Keith? He never did anything to hurt anybody."

Typical answer. "Well, I'm sorry for your loss, but everyone is a suspect right now," Goode said. "That said, my eye is on you for the moment, so why don't you answer the question? Where were you?"

"I was showing a property on Whale Watch Drive in the Shores," Seth said, running his hand through his hair. "To Dr. and Mrs. George Sherman. It's a four-million-dollar property. I'm this close to closing the deal," he said, pinching his fingers almost together. "Make myself a bundle."

Seth threw himself into a chair. "I can't believe Keith is dead," he said, rubbing his temples and focusing on a point in front of him. Goode followed Seth's line of sight and saw he was looking at a snapshot of Tania taken at night on the beach next to a fire ring. He wondered if it was one of Paul Walters' Polaroids.

"Where'd you get the photo?" Goode asked.

"I asked her for one of herself before I left her apartment Saturday afternoon. It was taken in Malibu."

"By whom?"

Seth shook his head and frowned. "How the hell should I know? What does that have to do with Keith's murder? She got it out of a shoebox in the closet. Jesus." Seth breathed out a long sigh. He shook his head and looked up at Goode, squinting. "He was my best friend, man, my best friend. How could you possibly think I could kill him?"

Goode thought Seth was either a really good actor or he didn't kill his friend. And since Paul was in the hospital when Keith was shot, he couldn't have done it either. Goode wondered if the bartender could be as innocent as he claimed. So far, no one had found a gun at the bar.

"Seth, why don't you just answer my questions? No one is accusing you of anything. Yet. If you have an alibi, there's no problem. What time did you get home?"

"Time. Whatever. I got back about ten thirty and this girl I was seeing for a while was sitting outside in her car, waiting for me. She insisted on coming in. I told her to leave, and she threw one of her usual hysterical fits. Then, she tried to seduce me. As you can see, it didn't work."

"I assume you mean Clover Ziegler," Goode said.

"That's the one."

"Do you know Maureen Goode?"

"Why, she your wife or something?"

Goode felt his hackles rise again. "I'm the one asking questions here. Do you know her?"

Seth raised his eyebrows nonchalantly. "Vaguely. She dated Keith for a while. You guys must not be that close, huh? You divorced?"

Goode really wanted to belt the guy. "She's my sister, all right? Have you seen her at all this week?"

"Oh . . . No, I haven't. Why, you think I killed her,

too?" Seth said sarcastically as he got up and started pacing again. "Look. This is all just too fucking weird."

Goode didn't like the way this conversation was going. "I never said Maureen was dead. You know something I don't?"

Seth scratched the back of his head. "Don't put words in my mouth. I'm going to have a drink . . . if that's all right with you."

Goode didn't like Seth's tone, but it proved his questions were getting to him. He hoped the alcohol would loosen him up so he would slip up. "You going to answer my question, or what?"

"No, I don't know something you don't," Seth said, opening a cabinet door in the living room. Inside, several rows of crystal decanters and bottles of expensive liquors stood at attention like soldiers at a party. "I only met your sister once. She's a little on the wild side."

"That's enough of that kind of talk," Goode said.

Seth poured some amber liquid into a tumbler of ice. Whiskey was Goode's guess. The noise of the ice crackling rang out like a shot. Without carpets, the room was an echo chamber.

"Want some?" Seth asked.

"No, thanks. I'll just take a look around." Goode slapped the warrant on the coffee table, but Seth barely glanced at it.

"You won't find any gun here," Seth said, taking a healthy sip of his drink.

"Actually, I'm looking for drugs. Large quantities of coke and meth. But now that you mention a weapon, I'll look for that, too. Why don't you make it easy and tell me where everything is and maybe I'll ask the DA not to go as hard on you. Maybe conspiracy to commit murder instead of murder one. Unless, of course, it was a solo job, and then I can't help you."

Seth's face went tight. "You can't pin the murders on me and you won't find any drugs here," he said.

"So you're telling me you weren't selling drugs with Jack O'Mallory at the Pumphouse?"

Seth grimaced. "Who told you that?"

"O'Mallory is down at the station right now, giving his statement about your little drug operation. No wonder you have so many nice things. I understand business is booming."

Seth stared at him blankly. He was good. "Yeah, well, he's lying," Seth said. "My business is growing, but it's real estate. Look around as much as you want. You won't find any drugs here. I'm clean. That bartender has more than one screw loose. Why don't ask him about his record? I wouldn't be surprised if he and Keith had something going. Maybe they had a fight and that's why my best friend is dead."

Seth sat in the chair again, his legs spread wide apart. He sipped from the glass and avoided Goode's eyes. Goode wondered if Seth was strategizing how to kill him and get away with it.

Goode stood directly in front of Seth, which gave him a perfect view of the perfect part in Seth's perfect hair. "Well, since we have him in custody, it'll be pretty easy to ask him about that," he said, walking casually over to the Picasso so he could stand behind Seth and make him uncomfortable, throw him off balance. "So, tell me, how do I get under your house?"

"Under the house?" snarled Seth, who had to crane around to respond. "What do you want under there? Nothing there but some pipes, mildew, and probably a whole lot of mud. The sump pump doesn't work very well and it rained last week."

Goode turned around and counted to ten. "So, I repeat," he said, enunciating every word, "how do I get under your house?"

Seth was saved by the doorbell, but not for long. "I'll get it. Don't move," Goode said, pointing at him.

His hand on the gun, Goode peered through the peephole. It was Rogers. Goode opened the door. "Thanks for stopping by," he said under his breath, motioning a clearly unhappy Rogers into the foyer.

"What the hell are you doing, going in without me again?" Rogers hissed.

Rogers was a stickler for procedure. But this was not the time for that conversation. "Just relax, everything is going according to plan," Goode whispered. "Did you bring Rocky?"

Rogers nodded toward his car. Rocky was not only good at sniffing out drugs, he was also renowned for biting perps on the run.

"So, here's the deal," Goode told him. "I bet you ten bucks we find coke and meth somewhere here, like maybe under the house. I hear there's a little mud down there. Glad you're dressed for it."

Rogers was wearing a camel hair coat with a shirt and tie. "Ver-ry funny. You're the one in jeans. Why can't you go under?"

"'Cause Rocky knows you better, and I'm in the middle of an interrogation. I don't want to lose my momentum. See what you can find and if you hear me stomp on the floor, get up here quick."

Goode could talk to Rogers like that because they went way back, all the way to La Jolla Elementary School. When Goode was in sixth grade and Rogers was in fourth, Goode kicked his ass in dodgeball and after the game he kicked it some more. They'd been friends ever since.

"All right. I've got some other clothes in the car. I can't believe I finally have a night off with my wife and you call me to go mud wrestling. Then you don't even wait for me to go in."

"Save it, Rogers." Goode watched Seth try to slither into the bedroom without him noticing. "Go to work. I've got to run."

Seth was rifling through his drawers when Goode strolled in.

"Looking for something I should know about?" Goode asked. He had to hand it to Seth for keeping such a straight face.

"You know, you're always wondering if I know something you don't," Seth said. "You must not be a very good detective. If you must know, I was just going to put these out of sight in the laundry hamper." He held up a black negligee and a pair of handcuffs.

Goode was laughing inside, but he didn't want Seth to know it. "I can assure you that I'm not here to investigate your bizarre sexual practices. So why don't you let me do my business? Here, why don't you sit on the bed where I can see you while Detective Rogers inspects your pipes, mildew, and mud?"

Seth wore his best poker face, but his body gave him away. Big wet spots had formed on his shirt under his arms and his forehead was practically dripping. Goode couldn't help but enjoy scrounging around in Seth's drawers. He found silver and gold cufflinks engraved with his initials, a zillion neatly folded pairs of underwear in different colors, and a dozen pairs of cashmere socks. The contents were so far out of his price range he couldn't even guess how much they cost.

The walk-in closet was the size of a small bedroom. Seth's shirts were arranged from white to pastels to bright colors to black. On the floor, he had lined up his shoes from black to navy to oxblood to beige, all in Italian leather or suede. Everything smelled fresh and clean. Not like Goode's mildewed closet.

"So, what's this about Jake calling you a narcissistic asshole?" Goode asked, just to taunt him.

"I have no idea where that came from. I hardly know the guy, and Clover, as you've probably heard, is highly emotional. She probably made it up. Besides, even if she didn't, what does he know, anyway? He's like a dish-washer or something."

After searching the bedroom, Goode went through the kitchen, bathroom, and living room cabinets. By then, his patience was wearing thin. Seth was still pacing.

"Okay, pal," Goode said. "Why don't you make this easy for me and tell me where to find the stuff? Other-wise, you and I will be up all night while I tear this place apart."

The front door opened and Rogers came in holding nothing in his hands but Rocky's leash. The dog, covered with mud, followed close behind, put his snout in the air, and looked around.

Seth's face went white when he saw Rocky. "You didn't say anything about bringing a dog in here. He's filthy."

"Sorry about that. Guess you'll have to pay the maid a little overtime this week. If you're still living here, that is."

Seth frowned and shook his head. "What do you mean?"

"I mean, if you're not in jail."

Before Seth could say anything more, Rocky shook himself, sending globs of mud and drops of brown water all over the floor.

"Goddamn it," Seth said. "Is this really necessary? I'd call this harassment."

"Rocky," Rogers said in a low voice, "go find the drugs."

The dog immediately headed over to the Picasso and started jumping up on the wall, leaving a trail of muddy streaks. Seth went nuts.

"Get that dog away from my Picasso!" he screamed. "That thing cost a fortune." He started moving toward Rocky, but stopped short when the dog turned and growled at him.

"Rocky, sit," Rogers ordered. The dog looked at him quizzically but remained doggedly in front of the Picasso, looking back and forth between the sketch and his master.

"You want to do the honors, Detective Goode?" Rogers said.

Goode nodded and smiled as he walked over and patted the dog on the head. "Good boy," he said. "Let's see what we've got here."

"If you cause any damage to that artwork, so help me God, my lawyer will have your ass in court," Seth said, pointing his finger accusatorily at Goode—and with such impressive bravado.

"Didn't your mother teach you it's not polite to point?" Goode said, smiling. "If you don't get out of my face, I'm going to arrest you for obstructing justice. Now sit down and shut the hell up."

Seth backed away and slowly lowered himself to the couch, his eyes moving between the dog and the Picasso. "Maybe the dog is smelling the steak I cooked earlier." Seth said. "There are no drugs in this house. I told you."

"Rocky doesn't lie," Rogers said flatly.

Goode pulled the Picasso off its hooks, brought the frame to the chair and sat down. He unhooked the metal levers holding the wooden back in place and pulled out a rectangular block wrapped in foil.

"What a surprise," Goode said. Inside the foil was a black sticky slab. "Gee, Seth, whatever would you be doing with Mexican heroin in your Picasso? Expanding into the heavier stuff, I see. No wonder you said your business is growing."

"It's not mine. I've never seen that before," Seth said. "I want a lawyer. Right now."

Goode turned to Rogers. "You know, I have the funniest feeling. Like there's some cocaine lying around the house somewhere. And some meth, too. What do you think, Detective Rogers?"

Seth was seething.

"I think you might be right, partner." Rogers liked to needle people like Seth as much as Goode did.

"Why don't we let Rocky nose around the rest of the house?" Goode said.

"Good idea," Rogers said, nodding his head with mock seriousness. "Find the drugs," he said to Rocky, who scampered off into the bedroom, his nails scratching across the floor. Rogers went after him but stopped in the doorway. He placed his hands on either side of the frame as he watched the dog go to work.

Goode put Seth's arms behind him and was clicking the handcuffs around his wrists when Rocky started tearing something apart in the bedroom. It sounded like plastic ripping.

"Good boy!" Rogers said loudly. "Goode! Get in here!"

Seth's face was whiter than white. "Let's go see what they found, huh, big guy?" Goode said, pulling Seth toward the bedroom.

Rogers was grinning from ear to ear. In each hand, he held several rocks of coke, the perfect size to fit in the toe of a shoe. On the floor, several more rocks had fallen into smaller chunks around several pairs of dress shoes that were lying askew. Chewed-up pieces of clear plastic were scattered around like goose feathers after a pillowfight. Goode kicked himself for not looking inside the shoes, which had been stored in a hanging case with rows of see-through plastic pockets.

"You're lucky Rocky didn't chew up your Italian shoes," Goode said mockingly, raising his eyebrows at Seth. He was not amused.

Goode cocked his head toward the door in a signal to Rogers that it was time to go downtown. "Seth Kennedy, you're under arrest for possession of narcotics, possession for sale, distribution of narcotics, and trafficking of narcotics. You have the right to remain silent. Anything you say can and will be used against you."

Chapter Thirty-two

Goode

While Goode was booking Seth, Sergeant Stone and Lieutenant Wilson each called to congratulate him. That meant a lot, given the late hour. Stone told him to keep following his instincts until he could show how the drug operation was linked to the murders. The lieutenant congratulated Goode for walking into a homicide investigation and making two major drug busts in the process. But he made sure to remind him that the mayor, the chief, and he, as the lieutenant who would decide whether Goode got the soon-to-be-vacant Homicide slot, wanted these murders solved ASAP. All the news networks had been camped outside police headquarters around the clock, and they were also swarming P.B. The series of murders had become quite the national story.

Goode knew he needed to get at least a few hours of sleep or he wouldn't be able to function. But when he reached his cottage, he was wide awake. Stress was funny that way. What he really needed was some serious shut-eye. He saw Gary Bentwood's DVD beckoning to him from the kitchen table and decided it could be the perfect stress reliever.

During his brief meeting with Gary B., he could tell the guy was nothing more than a pathetic pervert. His kinky leanings may have creeped out Tania Marcus, but Goode saw no motive for his wanting her dead.

Goode kneeled on his living room carpet and slipped the DVD into the player. As the opening credits began to roll, he felt the same excitement and nervousness that he did on a first date with a very attractive woman. He'd pictured Tania as he read her diary, and he couldn't believe he was finally going to watch her move, hear her talk, and look into her eyes. Well, sort of.

The scene started with the shot of a sidewalk and the sound of heels clicking on cement. The clicking grew louder as a pair of red suede pumps approached. *Tap, tap, tap, tap.* The camera panned up from a young woman's thin ankles to her slim but shapely legs, to a black mini skirt cinched at a tiny waist, up to a stretchy red top that hugged her breasts. God, he thought. She was perfect.

The camera moved up her long neck to her chin and chiseled crimson lips, which filled the screen as they spread slowly and warmly into a grin, causing a mole just left of her mouth to disappear into a dimple. Then the shot locked onto her eyes. They were bedroom eyes, with black liner across the top lid, which set off the turquoise of her irises. Next, the camera backed away to an overall shot of her kicking off her heels, exposing her red toenails. She lay down on a blanket in the grass and extended her hand to a man who was drinking beer from a bottle. He gave her the beer and, as she reached out to take it, her red fingernails caressed his thigh.

Then, just like in his dream, she tilted her head back, revealing her exquisite neck. She poured the ochre liquid down her throat, and when she was finished, her entire face lit up with a smile. A wicked, sexy smile.

"It's summertime again," said a sultry woman's voice, which may or may not have been Tania's. "The best time for Buck's."

Goode watched it again. Four more times, in fact. It seemed that the more he played it, the more he got to know her. She was amazing. No wonder so many men wanted her. You'd have to be comatose not to.

Chapter Thirty-three

Norman
Thursday

The next morning, Norman got a call from Al to come in and work some more overtime. Charlie was still sick and Al wanted him to do another follow-up story on the murders. Norman was reticent after the humiliating experience with Detective Goode, but he assumed he must have done a competent enough job of dictation from the Pumphouse bust or Al wouldn't have asked.

When Norman arrived at his desk, he found a press release that had been faxed over by the San Diego PD, presumably after Al had called him that morning. A note was scrawled in red pen across the top.

"You totally missed this, Klein. See me ASAP. Al."

Norman's outrage grew as he read the release, which said police had made *two* big busts the night before. One involved a stash of cocaine and meth from Pumphouse worth $500,000, and the other $750,000 worth of rock cocaine and Mexican heroin from a house in La Jolla owned by real estate agent Seth Kennedy. The release credited Ken Goode and Marshall Rogers with making the second bust around midnight.

"Lying scum," Norman sputtered. "Going to his girlfriend's house, no scoop, my ass."

Norman marched over to Al's desk to tell him how Goode had lied to his face, bitten off his head, and spat it out. But Al was busy listening to Jerry sell a story idea, so Norman had to wait until Jerry sauntered back to his desk, his chest puffed out like a cockatoo. What an asshole, Norman thought. Al sipped his coffee and paused, taking his time before meeting the young reporter's eyes. He was visibly disappointed in him. Norman decided to go on the offensive.

"So, look at this, Al," he said, holding out the release. "The police lied to me last night. Can you believe it? I followed one of these detectives to La Jolla. He was obviously on his way to the drug bust, but he pulled me over, with the whole flashing red light thing, and told me to go home because he was just going to his girlfriend's house. Swear to God."

Al still looked pissed, but Norman obviously had a good excuse. "I'll have to talk to Big Ed when he comes in, but in the meantime, go chase this down and clean up your mess," Al said before he whirled around in his swivel chair and knocked over a cup of coffee on his desk.

"Goddamn it! Look what you made me do. Get me some paper towels," Al shouted. "Not tomorrow. *Now*."

Norman ran across the newsroom, swerving to avoid Jerry and several women who were clustered around the coffee machine, laughing. By the time he got back to the city editor's desk with a wad of brown paper towels, the coffee had already been mopped up. Jerry handed a sopping mess to Norman.

"Here you go, buddy. Do something with this, will you?"

Norman glared at Jerry and dumped the dripping towels into a trash can. He tried to reach Sergeant Stone, but he kept getting voice mail. It was going to be another long day.

Chapter Thirty-four

Goode

Goode slept only a few hours before heading over to the Pannikin, an outdoor café in La Jolla where birds are known to clamp their beaks onto innocent croissants and fly away with them. After downing a double cappuccino, he headed downtown to the county jail.

Goode tried to organize his thoughts as he cruised down Interstate 5, listening to a CD of a local blues guitarist. He hoped a night behind bars had improved the memories of Seth Kennedy and One-Eyed Jack. Someone was going to tell him who was doing all this killing.

While he was questioning the two suspects, Slausson and Fletcher were taking care of some loose ends and Byron was attending Keith's autopsy. How could they not break this case with three suspects in custody?

Goode saw three possible scenarios. One, that Seth Kennedy or One-Eyed Jack had murdered one or more of the victims. Two, that Paul had killed Tania, but not the other two. Goode didn't even want to consider the third, that the murders weren't related to the drug operation and he would fail to prove he was Homicide-worthy.

Still lacking a motive, he decided to start with One-Eye to see if he could put a hole in Seth's alibi for the night of Tania's death. He knew the two men were working the drug angle together, but with Keith dead, he might never learn any more than that.

Seth was right about One Eye's priors. He had a long record of petty theft, possession of unlicensed firearms, and several DUIs, not to mention nonpayment of child support, fifteen unpaid parking tickets, and several out-standing warrants for failure to appear in court. Goode wondered how he had managed to get a job, let alone avoid arrest for violating parole.

Downtown, the streets were crawling with men in suits, walking briskly as they carried briefcases and large cups of designer coffee. He figured most were lawyers on their way to the courthouse, bureaucrats going to city hall to overspend his tax dollars, and commercial real es-tate brokers trying to sell office space in one of the tall glass buildings. The planes flew so low as they came into Lindbergh Field he wondered how they never crashed into one.

Goode ended up waiting in the interview room for half an hour because the sheriff's deputy took his sweet time bringing One-Eye down from his cell. With its fresh paint and new carpets, the refurbished room was quite a contrast to its predecessor, where the rug was so worn the cement showed through and the walls were the same sickly, pale blue as the bathroom in the house where Goode grew up. After his mother died, his father acci-dentally painted the window closed so no one could open it, and it wasn't long before the mildew and the smell of wet dog took over. So whenever Goode used to sit in this room, memories of that bathroom and its dank odor came back to him. He felt a twinge of nostalgia for the old days.

Turned out the delay in bringing Jack down wasn't the deputy's fault. Apparently, One-Eye had been taken to the infirmary, so the deputy had to wait while a nurse bandaged a nasty wound on the brow over his bad eye. When he was finally brought in, Goode couldn't help himself.

"So, how are we this morning, Mr. O'Mallory?" he asked. "Did you sleep well in our luxurious Gaslamp District hotel?"

One-Eye glared at him, if that was possible with

mono-vision, and Goode was silently amused at how fitting his moniker turned out to be.

"I could use a cigarette," One-Eye mumbled. Slumped in the orange vinyl chair, he touched the tape around his eye and winced. "And some coffee too. With cream."

"What do you think this is, the Hyatt?"

"You just called it a luxurious hotel," One-Eye retorted. "I'm only trying to get a couple of amenities here. I called room service, but they never showed up."

"Ahhh, I see," Goode said. He had to give it to the guy. At least he had a sense of humor. Goode stuck his head into the hallway and passed the request on to the officer.

"Do I look like your bitch?" the deputy said under his breath.

Goode sat facing his prisoner across a long table with a faux wood-grain finish, his hands folded in front of him. They stared at each other until One-Eye leaned over and rapped on the table with his knuckle. "So, do I need a lawyer, or what?"

"That's up to you, pal," Goode, said. "I say, why don't we just talk for a while?"

One-Eye folded his arms across his chest. "Well, I didn't do nothing, so I don't really want to hire one, but since this drug charge you got me on is all trumped up, I might need one."

Until One-Eye actually demanded a lawyer, Goode intended to press on. "We don't trump up charges here, so listen up," Goode said, reading him his rights. "You can't deny that we found large quantities of cocaine and methamphetamine in your bar. Also, you've admitted to knowing there was a drug ring operating out of that fine establishment, correct?"

One-Eye shrugged and nodded. "I thought it was just coke, and there's no ring. It's just Seth. But go on."

"So," Goode said, "if you come clean and tell us how the drugs are related to these murders, I could see some reduction in the conspiracy to murder charges. Of course, I'll have to get the DA to agree, but I can be pretty persuasive."

"Okay, wait a minute," he said, leaning toward Goode. "What conspiracy charges? And who the hell is part of this conspiracy?"

"You tell me," Goode said. "Seems to me that if you were involved in the drug operation and the murders were somehow related to that operation, then you're involved in the murders, right?"

One-Eye frowned and shook his head. "No, that's not right. I told you I don't know nothing about no murders. I talked to that Tania girl about the taxi, and that was it. I don't even really remember that other chick you showed me. And the Warner kid, well, let's just say he was in the wrong place at the wrong time."

"No argument there. But I'm guessing there's more to it than that. I'm thinking maybe you set him up because he wanted you out of the business. What, did he want in, or was he already in and he just wanted a bigger cut?"

One-Eye grimaced.

"No? Well, he seemed like a pretty good kid, and you, my friend, seem shady. So, maybe he threatened to rat you out? Or maybe Keith wasn't involved at all, and you killed him for jollies, and then went back to serving drinks like nothing ever happened."

One-Eye banged his fist on the table. "I don't like where this is going, man. I was behind the bar the whole night until I heard that shot outside. What about Seth? Where's he? He's the guy who left with Tania. He's the guy selling drugs. He's the guy you should be talking to. Not me."

As the prisoner grew increasingly jumpy, Goode felt all the more calm. "Well, as a matter of fact, Seth spent the night in one of our deluxe suites. I've got him booked on serious drug charges with some murder charges on tap, too. Now, if you don't want to join him in prison, you need to tell me now, not next week, how the drugs and the murders are tied together."

"I told you. I. Don't. Know," One-Eye said, enunciating every word.

"Okay. If that's how you want to play it," Goode said. "Did you see Seth the night Tania was murdered?"

One-Eye sighed. "Yeah. He was in the bar most of the night. I saw him talking to that redhead who was in the papers this week. Warner was there, too."

Ah, Goode thought. Now they were getting somewhere. "Sharona Glass?"

"Yeah, I think that's her name. She's a regular. Used to come in with that Clover chick Seth was seeing for a while."

"See anything funny going on between them?"

"Who?"

"Seth and the redhead."

"No, they were just talking. They went in and out of the bathroom a few times to do some lines, I guess. Then she took off and Warner and Kennedy went to some party."

Goode took down the chronology in his pocket notebook. "What time did they leave?"

"I don't remember," One-Eye said. "It was pretty busy."

Goode rapped his pen several times on the table. "Try harder."

One-Eye rubbed his eyes for a while and sighed again. "Maybe around ten or so."

Goode nodded, calculating in his head. That left thirty minutes before the end of the window the ME set for Tania's time of death. And estimates, by definition, were never precise. Just to cover his bases, he though he'd better ask about his body-finder. "Where was Jake that night?"

Goode noticed that the bartender's hands had started shaking. "He had the night off. Where's my coffee and smokes?" One-Eye asked. "This is cruel and unusual punishment."

"It's coming," Goode said. "So if it wasn't you, then who wanted Keith dead?" Goode stared at him, waiting for the truth.

"What do you want me to say? Look, Warner never gave me no problems. And I already gave you enough info to bust Seth last night."

"Did you see any friction between Seth and Keith?"

"No. Come to think of it, I've never seen them fight."

Goode couldn't shake the suspicion that One-Eye knew more than he was telling. "What was Keith's relationship with Clover? He sure had a few choice words to say about her, but he never even mentioned Sharona."

"I know he didn't like Clover much. He thought Seth should tell her to get lost once and for all, but Seth kept doing her. She's pretty wild, I guess."

Goode cocked his head. "What do you mean, wild?"

"In bed, you know. Seth would tell me about her. Got me all hot and bothered more than once."

Clover's "narcissistic asshole" comment popped into Goode's mind. "Did Jake know Sharona Glass?" he asked.

"Hell if I know," One-Eye said. "What he does in his off time is his business."

Goode closed his notebook and stood up. He was wasting his time with this guy. He'd just gotten a whole lot of nothing. "We're done here, for now at least. I'm going to have a few words with Mr. Kennedy. I'm sure he'll sell you out in a heartbeat. Sure beats the death penalty."

At the very least, Seth Kennedy would never own a gun or hold public office with all the felony convictions he planned to put on the guy's record, the murders not withstanding. Goode hoped he would be able to pin at least one of them on him. It would do him some good to be behind bars for a while. Teach him some humility. But then again, Goode thought, Seth might learn from his prison pals how to do even dirtier deeds and not get caught.

Goode was surprised Seth's daddy hadn't bailed him out already. Perhaps he was trying to show his son the consequences of his bad behavior. Goode was all for that.

By the looks of it, Seth didn't have a much better night in jail than his partner. "Good morning, Mr. Kennedy," Goode said as he walked into the interview room next door.

Seth sat slouched in his chair. His face was gray, probably from lack of sleep. He didn't look so good unshaven. "Not really," Seth snorted.

"So, let's talk," Goode said.

Seth refused to look at him. "What if I want my lawyer present? My dad's hired one of the best. He's going to get me off."

"Oh, who might that be?"

Seth looked pleased with himself. "Milton Biggs," he said matter-of-factly. "He's a power broker from L.A. who represents all the high-profile celebrities when they're targeted by false accusations and drug plants by police. He's flying back from his vacation in Hawaii just to represent me."

"Really?" Goode said, settling back into his chair as much one could with jail furniture. Form follows function and all that. He wasn't going to let the kid play him. "If you don't want to talk to me, that's okay. You can just listen to what I have to say, and then once your lawyer gets here, you can answer some questions."

Seth shrugged, his expression blank. "Whatever."

"I was just talking to your bartender friend, Jack O'-Mallory, and he told me everything I needed to know to get those drug charges to stick. I'm also thinking your alibis for the nights of the murders are a little on the loose side, so you're looking good for three murder charges, too."

"You have absolutely no evidence that connects me to these murders," Seth declared, keeping his composure.

Damn, Goode thought, he is really good. "We'll just

see about that," he said. "In answer to your 'drug plant' reference, why would anyone on a jury believe the San Diego Police Department would ever want or need to plant drugs in a bar and in your house, all in the same night, just to pin murder charges on you? This is not L.A., my friend, and you are not O. J. Simpson."

Seth shook his head with a snide look, his mouth a straight line. Goode pressed on. "So, let's talk about your alibis. 'Your honor, I was selling drugs in a bar at the time of the murder.' Or how about this one: 'I was selling a house when my drug-dealing partner was shot, and I was with him at a party the night I didn't kill Tania Marcus.' "

Seth was clearly not amused. But he remained silent.

"Frankly, I don't think it looks too good for you, my friend," Goode said. "What do you think?"

Goode was still fishing for a connection between all of these events, hoping Seth would say something, anything, to make some sense out of this mess.

"No offense, detective, but I think you're full of shit," Seth said. "We're done here. I want my lawyer present."

"That is your prerogative. But your bodily fluids, your fingerprints, and oh, yeah, your drugs, are all over this case," Goode snapped. "Get your counsel down here tomorrow morning and we'll get down to business. We have plenty to talk about."

Chapter Thirty-five

Norman

Norman stared into space while he waited for people to return the half dozen calls he'd put out. His head was throbbing and he wondered if maybe he just wasn't cut out for all this stress. But he wasn't going to give up. He was going to prove to Al and Big Ed, and to himself, that he could do this.

Somehow, other reporters got their sources to talk. Why was he having such a hard time? He'd called the cop-shop several times looking for Sergeant Stone and Detective Goode, but the secretary kept saying they were out. He got his hopes up when she said she'd fax him a press release, but it turned out to be the same one as before.

Norman went to the bathroom and doused his face with water, hoping it would help ease the pain behind his eyes. When he returned to his desk, he found a letter sitting on his keyboard, addressed to him. He flipped it over and saw a waxy red imprint of two lips across the back flap of the envelope. He took a ruler and ripped it open along the edge so as not to disturb the lip print and pulled out a letter written on white, blue-lined notebook paper:

> *To Norman Klein:*
> *I am writing to tell you that Seth Kennedy murdered Tania Marcus, Sharona Glass, and Keith Warner. I'm scared I'm going to be next.*

Norman's heart was beating wildly. "Wow," he whispered, recognizing Kennedy's name from the press release.

> *Seth was my boyfriend, so I've seen his violent side. I read your story about the marks on the necks of those two girls and I knew immediately that Seth was the one who did it to them. He grabbed me by the throat one time and I think he would have strangled me to death if Keith hadn't knocked on the front door. If anything happens to me, don't let him get away with saying it was a suicide. I'm scared he's going to get to me when he figures out that I know about the murders. After reading your stories, I feel I can trust you. I have to stay anonymous for now.*

Norman read the letter one more time to make sure he wasn't hallucinating. He could barely contain his excitement. This could be his big break. He made a beeline for Al's desk and shoved the letter under his nose. Al was making small talk with Sabrina, the very shapely, but not too bright, obits clerk. Al tried to wave Norman away, but Norman would not be denied. Not this time.

"Al, you've got to check this out," he said. "It's huge."

Al glared at him as if to say, "Not now."

"It's important. It's about the guy who was arrested in that drug bust last night. This letter says he's the P.B. killer."

"I'll catch you later, Al," Sabrina said.

"This better be good, kid," Al said in a low voice. "Couldn't you see I was busy?" His eyebrows went up as he read the letter. Then he frowned. Always the skeptic. "Where'd this come from? You didn't write it, did you?"

"Of course not. I found it on my keyboard just now. It must've come in the mail this morning," Norman said as calmly as he could muster, nearly paralyzed with anger and disbelief at the implication of Al's questions. He showed him the envelope flap. "Here, look at these lips. They obviously aren't mine, right? You think it could be worth A-1?"

Al took the envelope and examined the lip imprint more closely. "Just hold your horses, kid. I'll take it into the morning editor's meeting and we'll talk about what we want to do. It's not even signed, for Christ's sake. You don't want us to get sued, do you?"

There went the lawsuit argument again. The other reporters were always complaining about the paper not having any guts. "Well, no, but geez, it seems like a good story, don't you think?"

"Look," Al said. "We don't know where it came from, or who wrote it, or what their intentions were. There could be some legal problems if we run it. In the meantime, see if you can figure out who Seth Kennedy has been dating lately. Maybe we can track down whoever wrote this letter."

Norman could barely maintain his composure. He'd gotten the nod. "They'd better print it," he mumbled as he walked back to his desk. "They've got to."

Chapter Thirty-six

Goode

Goode told the jail deputy that he was done with One-Eyed Jack. He could do nothing more with the bartender until he'd questioned Seth Kennedy. In the meantime, Goode planned to head over to Keith Warner's house in La Jolla, where he had lived with his parents, and see if they'd let Goode poke around his room for drugs. He thought the Warners also might know if Keith and Seth had been at odds recently.

Their small cream-colored house needed a new coat of paint and the lawn was unevenly mowed and mottled with white patches, signaling that they either had brown thumbs or couldn't afford to hire a gardener. With Keith still living at home, Goode figured it was the latter.

Martha Warner invited Goode into the living room, where her husband, George, was sitting on a green and blue paisley couch. The room was sparsely decorated, with only a few pieces of furniture, one of those clichéd paintings of a roiling ocean at sunset, and crocheted white doilies on practically every tabletop and chair arm. Martha sat next to her husband and directed Goode to sit in a stiff wooden armchair with a cushion that matched the couch. They both stared numbly at the detective.

A silver antique teapot and four cups sat on a matching tray on the coffee table between him and the Warners, almost as if they'd been expecting company.

"I'm very sorry for your loss," Goode said. "You must be in shock."

"Would you like some tea?" Martha asked, holding the pot over one of the cups.

"No, thank you," Goode said.

She proceeded to fill the cup and set it in front of him. "Just in case you change your mind," she said.

"Keith always liked tea," she said, her voice breaking. She set down the pot and dabbed her wet eyes with a tissue she pulled from inside her sleeve. "He was such a good boy. Studied very hard in school. He said his goal was to buy us a bigger house. We've owned this one since the seventies."

"I read in the paper that you've arrested Seth Kennedy and put him in jail," George said.

"Yes, sir, we have."

"Good," George said, nodding. "We always thought he was a bad influence on our boy."

"Were Keith and Seth getting along lately?"

"Oh, my, yes. They'd been friends since elementary school," Martha said.

Martha poured cups of tea for herself and then George, who looked like he was approaching eighty. Doing the math in his head, Goode calculated that George must've fathered Keith in his late fifties. George slurped his tea and set the cup in its saucer with a clatter. Martha promptly refilled George's cup. She looked at least twenty years younger than him.

"You don't think he had anything to do with Keith's death, do you?" Martha asked.

"That's what we're trying to determine, Mrs. Warner," Goode replied. "Do you know if Seth or any of Keith's other friends own a gun?"

Martha frowned and shook her head. "Oh, my, no."

She twirled her salt-and-pepper curls around her index finger as she rocked back and forth slightly on the sofa. "We miss him so, don't we George?"

George didn't answer. He was busy counting out sugar cubes from the bowl, placing them on the tray with a pair of silver tongs. He moved them one at a time from the tray to a wall he was building on the table.

The Warners seemed a bit out of touch with their son's life, the way older parents or grandparents can be. But Keith was their son. Goode hoped to have children before he was like George and too old to relate to them.

"Sugar, sweetheart?" George asked Martha as she poured another cup for herself.

"Yes, thanks, honey," she said. Then, smiling sadly at Goode, she said, "He takes such good care of me."

Funny, but it seemed to be the other way around to him. Goode smiled back at her. They were a bit eccentric, but quite sweet, really. Goode's cell phone went off. He didn't recognize the number and decided to finish talking with the couple and have a look around before calling back. He stood up. "You mind if I take a quick look in Keith's room?"

"No, go ahead," Martha said, sipping her tea.

Goode found nothing unusual in Keith's closet or under his bed, other than how it was fastidiously neat and clean. He saw a ginger tabby cat run out of the room and his nose and eyes started to itch. It was time to go.

He walked toward the living room, but stopped just before he reached the doorway so he didn't intrude on an intimate moment. Martha was stroking George's head, which was resting on her chest, and saying, "Remember that time he brought home that poor sick bird and wanted to nurse him back to health?" Her lips were pursed, as if she were about to cry again.

"I've got to run to an emergency," Goode said gently. "I'll see myself out."

Chapter Thirty-seven

Alison

Alison woke from a nap feeling that something bad had happened, but she was so groggy she didn't even know where she was. Her eyes roamed the room, which was cast in the shadows of the gloaming. She was startled by the figure of a man standing by the window, but she soon realized it was the silhouette of the hat stand she'd bought on an antique-shopping trip with Tania. Slowly at first, then in a flood, the events of the last few days came back to her.

She wrapped her arms around herself, closed her eyes and rubbed her cheek against the pillowcase, trying to simulate the feeling of someone stroking her face. But it didn't work. As hard as she tried to push the sad thoughts away, they kept coming back. Finally, she gave up and threw off the covers. She padded into the bathroom, but didn't much like the puffy and depressed face in the mirror.

The phone rang in the living room. She picked it up and heard static, followed by a man's voice going in and out. Someone was obviously calling her on a cell phone with bad reception.

"Alison?"

A current rushed through her body at the sound of the man's voice. It was Tony.

"Alison? Can you hear me?"

"Yes," she said softly, barely able to breathe.

"How are you?"

She felt scared, shocked, and alone. But she wasn't going to tell him that. "Why are you calling me?" she asked in the harshest tone she could manage.

"What do you mean? I thought you'd be happy to hear from me."

She didn't even know where to start. "It's just really weird, after the funeral and everything," she said. "How did you find me?"

"You're listed."

"No, I mean, how did you know I was in San Diego?"

"It's a long story. Tania had mentioned you to her mother, who then gave the police your name after we got the bad news. I called information and there you were."

Alison couldn't answer right away. She felt uneasy talking to Tony. Violated. As if he'd burst into her apartment uninvited.

"What do you want, Tony?" she said finally, hoping to keep the conversation brief.

"I just wanted to hear your voice. Why, you don't want to talk to me?"

Alison heard a sad, vulnerable note in his voice. "Well, all right. But only for a couple minutes."

"Okay, good. I mostly wanted to tell you it was good seeing you at the funeral. It's been pretty rough for me at home lately. I still can't believe you left L.A. like that. No phone number. Not even a good-bye."

"I'm sorry," she said, not meaning it. "About Tania, I mean. You know, I almost died when I saw your photo on that display at the funeral."

"I've missed you."

Alison paused again. Tony wasn't listening to a word she was saying. She felt confused. "I wanted to start over down here. You know, go somewhere and be a whole new person, where no one knew me."

It was Tony's turn to be silent. Something about this conversation seemed ominous to her. She told herself she was just being paranoid.

"How come you never told me about Tania?" she said. "She turned out to be the best friend I had here."

Tony sighed. "I guess I figured that if I didn't tell you about her that she would never know you existed. Some twisted logic, huh?" There was that pain in his voice again.

"Yeah. I'll say."

"So you met Tania at the beauty school?" he asked.

"Yeah."

"Alison." There was another long pause. When Tony started talking, his voice broke. "I can't believe . . . she's dead. Who . . . would do something like that?"

He sounded so pathetic. Alison felt sorry for him and a little guilty for leaving him the way she did. "I have no idea, Tony. I wish I knew."

"I need to see you," he said abruptly.

"Tony, I already told you—"

He cut her off. "Things are different now. I told you I was sorry about that night at the hotel. I had a very stressful afternoon and you made me angry, and then something inside me just snapped. I've never done that before. It won't happen again. I promise."

"I don't know, Tony."

"Alison, don't you care about me at all? What about all the things I've done for you?"

There it was, the "You owe me" part. She knew it would come sooner or later. She tried to choose her words carefully, but they came tumbling out. "I did care. But you hit me. Why should I believe that you wouldn't do it again?"

"I drove down to San Diego to see you. I'm coming over," he said.

"No, Tony, don't."

"You'll see. It'll be good for both of us."

The line went dead and she started to panic. How did he know where she lived? Her hand slipped off the phone, leaving a wet sheen where her palm had been.

She looked at the measly little lock on her front door and pictured Tony bursting through it, sending shards of cheap wood flying. She paced across her living room carpet. *What to do, what to do, what to do?* She grabbed her purse and tossed its contents on the rug, searching frantically for Ken Goode's card. She called his number and got voice mail.

"Shit." she said. She tried his cell phone next. "What if he doesn't have it turned on?" she whispered. "Please Ken, answer the phone."

Alison again got voice mail, punched in her number, and hung up. She gripped the cordless phone, as if holding it tightly would cause it to ring. *Answer the page. Answer the page.*

She took a diet soda out of the fridge and placed the phone on the counter. Something in the garbage smelled rank. She knew she should've taken the bag out the night before, but she couldn't face going down to that alley, not after what had happened to Tania. She wondered if she should buy some of those stick-up pine scent deodorizers Grandma Abigail used to hide in the bathroom. They never seemed to work, though.

She poured her diet soda too full and let out a squeal as it foamed onto the counter, creeping dangerously close to the phone. She was mopping up the mess when the phone rang.

"Hello?" she said frantically into the receiver.

"Alison? Is that you?"

Alison collapsed onto the couch with relief, setting her drink on the coffee table. "God, I'm so glad you called back."

"What's up? You sound upset."

Alison could hear voices and street noise in the background. "Yeah, I am. 'Member I told you about Tony, the guy I used to date who turned out to be Tania's father?"

"Uh-huh."

"Well, he just called and said he's coming right over. I told him not to, but it was like he didn't even hear me He sounded really weird. I'm scared."

"How does he know where you live? I thought you said you left L.A. and didn't tell him where you were going."

Alison drew a heart in the moisture on her glass "Well, he said he got my number from information and I guess my address, too. Can you come over?"

Goode paused. "Um, yeah, sure. Hang tight and I'll be there as soon as I can."

Alison took a long gulp of her drink and was so startled by a noise in the room that she nearly dropped the glass. The wind coming through the window had knocked down a poster she'd taped to the wall. It was a black-and-white photograph—the famous one of the two French lovers kissing after news hit the streets that World War Two had ended.

Chapter Thirty-eight

Norman

Norman called everyone he could think of in his search for the author of the red-lipped letter. He also tried every Warner in La Jolla and Pacific Beach, hoping to find Keith's parents. He got a few wrong numbers and left a bunch of messages on answering machines. Still, he refused to lose touch with the feeling he'd woken up with—that this was going to be his lucky day.

Norman was determined to call every person named Glass in San Diego County, which was no small feat. If he kept calling—leaving periodic messages for Detective Goode and Sergeant Stone in between—he figured he eventually had to hit pay dirt. Norman checked off the names in the phone book as he went. His next call was to Glass number eighteen in Lemon Grove. A woman with a nasal voice answered the phone, sniffling.

"Hi there," he said. "This is Norman Klein with the *Sun-Dispatch*."

"We already get the paper," she said wearily.

She was about to hang up when Norman interrupted. "No, wait. I'm a reporter. I'm not trying to sell you a subscription."

"Oh, well, if it's about Sharona, we've already been interviewed by the TV station. Why don't you call them and get a copy of the interview?" she said, trying to hang up again.

He pushed on. "Mrs. Glass, I know this a hard time for you and I'm very sorry for your loss, but I was hoping to ask you a couple of questions. My story might prompt the police to move faster on this case, or maybe it will generate some new leads for them." Getting this woman on the phone had been half the battle. Now all he needed was to hook his fish on the line, reel it in, and snag that baby. But Mrs. Glass wasn't biting.

"Listen, can't you call back another time?" she asked. "I was just lying down. You know, I've hardly slept the last two days."

"I know and I'm really sorry, but I'll make this quick, ma'am, I promise. Do you know a Seth Kennedy?"

Mrs. Glass paused. "Seth Kennedy. No, that name doesn't ring any bells. Seth Kennedy. Wait a minute, now that you mention it, that name does sound familiar."

She seemed to be waking up now. "That's right. He knew my daughter's friend Clover, I believe. I remember him now. He may have called here once or twice for Sharona. Why?"

The fish was biting, Norman could feel it. "I think he might be involved in all of this somehow," he said. "Do you know if Clover was romantically involved with him?"

"Well, yes, I think she was."

"And what did you say her last name was?"

"Ziegler. Clover Ziegler," she said. "Sharona always said Clover could do better than that boy. I guess he didn't treat her very well. Clover is a very striking girl, you know, but she isn't well. Never has been, really. What does this have to do with Sharona? Are you going to put what I'm saying in the newspaper?"

"I was hoping to. I think our readers are very interested in these murders. Most people think of San Diego County as a safe place. Didn't you before this happened?"

"Well, yes, I suppose I did. That's why we moved here from Los Angeles when Sharona was little."

"Uh-huh," he said, trying to encourage her to keep talking. "Doesn't it seem like the police are taking a long time to get the investigation off the ground?"

"Well, yes, yes, it does. They won't tell me anything and I can't sleep, waiting, wondering if they're going to call. I want to know what happened to my daughter. She'd never hurt anyone. I'm just sick about it."

Norman had caught his fish. He stopped asking questions and scribbled furiously. *Let them fill in the silence.* That's what Al told him.

Mrs. Glass sighed and paused. "You know, the police came around here right after she was killed and they haven't been back since. Do you have any news you could share with me? I've been watching the TV, but they keep saying the same thing over and over again."

"That's TV for you," Norman said. It was hard to talk and write at the same time. He needed practice. "They don't have as much time as we newspaper reporters do to investigate stories. And as a matter of fact, I have some information I could share with you, and maybe you could help me understand what it means."

"Yes, all right."

Norman read the letter to her and she gasped right after the mention of Seth. Then he heard her sniffling. "Are you all right, Mrs. Glass?"

She sniffled some more and then let out a long, loud

sigh. "Yes, I'm all right. What did you say your name was again?"

"Norman Klein."

"Well, Mr. Klein. Do you think it's true? What do the police say?"

"I'm not sure if it's true and the police don't know anything about it yet. I wanted to do some investigating on my own first."

"Well, I hope that poor girl isn't in any danger. What I want to know is if Seth Kennedy killed my daughter, why isn't he in jail?"

"He is in jail, but only on drug charges. . . . I think I'm all set here. Thank you very much for your time. I hope things get better for you and your family."

"Thank you. I hope they do, too."

Norman was having such luck, he decided to shoot for the moon. "Oh, and Mrs. Glass, I need your first name. And would you happen to have Clover's phone number?"

"It's Patricia. And yes, I think I have her parents' number. Let me go see."

Norman scribbled the number down and hung up. "Yes!" he yelled so loudly the other reporters turned around and glared at him. He smiled and waved.

By noon, Norman was feeling *mucho grande*. He had a second donut with coffee so his brain would keep clicking along at top speed. Al walked over to Norman's desk after the eleven o'clock news meeting.

"So, what have you got?" Al said.

"I think I know who wrote the letter, chief," Norman replied.

Al looked skeptical. "And who would that be?"

"Her name is Clover Ziegler."

"Have you talked to her?"

"Not yet, I was waiting for you to get out of the meeting. What's the decision on running the letter?"

"Well, we'll run it if you can back it up with responses

from the families and reactions on how the police investigation is going. We want our readers to know that this newspaper is taking a strong interest in seeing these murders solved. After you talk to this Ziegler girl, I want you to get back over to the cop-shop and hold the chief's feet to the fire on this letter. Ask him why he hasn't made any significant progress on the investigation. If he says he has, then ask him why he hasn't told the public about it. They'll probably seize the letter as evidence, so be sure to make a few copies before you go. Got all that?"

"Yes. Thanks, chief," Norman said, scribbling down Al's instructions.

Norman was excited that Al had changed his tune. But he was feeling the pressure. Big time. That load of crap about the newspaper "taking a strong interest" sounded like it came straight from the mouth of the executive editor, the one he saw feeling up the woman in the parking lot. These people talked just like the politicians they ripped every day on the editorial pages.

Norman called the number he'd just gotten for Clover Ziegler. A woman answered and said she was Clover's mother. Clover wasn't home.

"Yes, she dated Seth Kennedy for a while, but she hasn't seen him lately. What does that have to do with anything?"

Norman tried to explain about the letter, and when that didn't work, he decided to read it to her. She wasn't impressed.

"Well, who knows if she really wrote that letter? Have they arrested that Kennedy boy for murder?" she asked. "I never liked him."

"Not that I know of," Norman said. "We're still trying to get some straight answers out of the police. What would be a good time to call back to reach your daughter?"

"I'm not sure," she said. "I don't know where she is. Sharona Glass was her best friend, you know, and she's been very depressed since she died. They closed the beauty school for the week because of all this, so she's been spending a lot of time at the mall."

Norman left his number with her and hung up. He was starting to drag from the sugar high and subsequent drop. Stopping outside the Coffee Hovel, as reporters fondly called it, he overheard Al talking to another editor.

"That kid, I don't know how he manages to keep pulling himself out of the messes he gets into. That letter was a gift from heaven. But I'm telling you, if he blows it on this one, I'm going to talk to the powers-that-be around here."

That was all Norman needed to hear. "Gift from heaven, my ass," he muttered. "I'll show them."

At the cop-shop, Norman looked for Ken Goode's van, but didn't see it anywhere. Too bad, he thought. He was in the mood for a good confrontation. On the other hand, he figured it might be better to ambush one of the sergeants he'd just met. Or better yet, the chief himself.

He approached the front counter, where a hard-edged brunette in her late forties was working a large phone console. She had so little hair where her eyebrows were supposed to be that she'd drawn them in. When she looked up at him for a split second, she pursed her thin lips, like he was moldy cheese or something.

"I'm Norman Klein from the *Sun-Dispatch*," he said glancing quickly at her name tag, which read DIANA SCOTTSDALE.

"I've been to Scottsdale," he said, smiling. "Is the chief in? I need to interview him about the P.B. killer case."

She was unfazed by his attempt at charm. "You have an appointment?"

"No," he said.

"Then why don't you sit over there and I'll page the Homicide sergeant," she said, nodding over at the ratty plaid armchairs that stood against the wall like prisoners in a lineup at a thrift store. The seats were ripped and torn, with yellow foam padding hanging out.

After twenty-five minutes went by, Norman was feeling ignored and none too pleased about it. He got up, marched back over to Ms. Scottsdale and leaned into her face. "Have you reached him yet?" he asked.

"Oh, yeah. I'll page him now," she said, giving him a nasty half smile.

"Thank you," Norman said curtly and returned to his seat.

Her voice came out over the speakers in the ceiling: "Sergeant Stone, Sergeant Stone, there's a reporter here to see you."

It was another ten minutes before Sergeant Stone came through one of the doors, holding it open with his body. Norman stayed where he was, assuming the sergeant would come over and talk to him.

"Mr. Klein, I don't have all day to hold this door open for you," Stone said.

"Oh," Norman said, jumping to his feet.

As they entered the detective bureau, Stone sat behind a wide metal desk in his office and motioned for Norman to sit in a chair across from him. "So what can we do for you today?" he said.

"Well—"

Stone pulled out a drawer and put his feet up on it. "I've been reading your stories. A little on the light side, but hey, that's the way we like them around here."

Norman decided to let that one pass and pulled out the letter. "This letter was sent to my attention this morning." He placed it on the desk between them. "So, what do you think?"

"I think it's very interesting," Stone said, raising his eyebrows. "We'll have to keep this as evidence, of course."

The sergeant reached for the phone and pressed a buzzer. A man in a jacket and tie came in, took the letter from Stone's outstretched hand and read it silently, expressionless. When he was finished, Stone jerked his head toward the door and the two of them went into the hall. "Back in a minute," Stone said over his shoulder.

Norman figured the letter was a big break in the case for them. He wondered if maybe he should apply for a job as a police officer and forget the reporting thing altogether.

It was fifteen minutes before the sergeant came back. "So, listen. Thanks for bringing that in," Stone said. "I've got a meeting I've got to get to."

"Well, wait a minute," Norman said. "I've been here for almost an hour, waiting to talk to the chief about the letter."

Stone sat back down at his desk. He scowled as he leaned back in his chair, the springs squeaking, and intertwined his fingers behind his head. He paused. "Listen, Mr. Klein. This is a very sensitive case. I don't want to screw up our investigation by releasing too much information, so we're not going to be able to comment on the letter. Off the record—"

"Sergeant," Norman interrupted, "I came to talk to the chief. And I've really got to ask you to stay on the record on this one." He suddenly felt brave. He'd given them the letter. He was the guy in the know, the guy who worked for the company that bought ink by the barrel. He would not be rebuffed. "Is he available?"

Stone's expression said Norman was an annoying but potentially dangerous predator. "No, he's not," the sergeant said. "He's over at City Hall in a budget meeting. He's asked me to handle all press inquiries on this matter."

If Norman couldn't get to the chief, at least he had to get a comment from the sergeant about how the investigation was going. "Look. I'm writing a story about the case, sort of an update," Norman said, "and I've got some general questions about the investigation."

"Such as," Stone said.

"Such as, do you have any good leads you're working?"

Stone answered in a very measured tone. "We've got many good leads. The community has been calling in anything and everything they think is suspicious in the Pacific Beach area, and we are very encouraged by that. We're hoping to catch this murderer as soon as humanly possible."

Norman pressed on. "Some of the victims' families say the investigation is going at a snail's pace and they're criticizing police for being too slow in releasing information. What's your response to that?"

"I haven't heard that from anyone but you, Mr. Klein. The calls we've been getting are all very much in the way of thanking us for working around the clock trying to catch this killer, whoever he may be."

"So, have you recovered any murder weapons?"

"I'm not going to comment on that."

"Do you have any suspects in custody?"

"Suspects?"

"Yes, you know, the people you think committed these crimes?" Norman was feeling a little cocky. Maybe a little too cocky.

Stone lunged forward in his seat and spoke soft and low. "Don't get smart with me young man, or I'll throw you out of my office."

Despite the sergeant's tone, Norman could see he was squirming. Still, Norman figured he ought to back off a bit. "Sorry, I was just kidding."

Stone paused. "Well, this is no laughing matter. All I can say is that we are questioning several people at the moment."

"So you have arrested more than one person in the murders?"

"I didn't say that."

"So what do you mean?"

"Off the record—"

"Sergeant."

"Listen, I can't really explain anything further on the record right now. Don't you people understand how much damage you can cause with one story? It screws up our investigation—tips off suspects, lets them know what we have so they can be ready with good lies."

Norman wasn't going to let him off the hook this time. "But the public has a right to know what's going on with this investigation, sergeant," he said, following his editor's advice. "Now, who do you have in custody?"

"Look, kid, I'm not trying to be evasive here. You are welcome to look at our arrest log. That's all I have to say. Now, is that all? I've got to get back to work solving this case."

"What about the letter? Can I get a statement on that?"

The sergeant took another long, deep breath before he spoke. "You don't give up, do you? Okay. Here's what I can say. You ready?"

Norman nodded.

"A letter has come to our attention that may help point us in a certain direction in the investigation, but it's too early to comment on exactly what direction that will be," he said.

Norman rolled his eyes and kept his pen in midair. He didn't write a word of it down. "Sergeant."

"What?" Stone said.

"That's a total nonresponsive statement. I can't use any of it."

The sergeant kept on as if Norman hadn't said a thing. "The letter has been passed on to our handwriting expert and will be checked for fingerprints. Other than that, we'll just have to wait and see."

Norman knew that wasn't going to be good enough to satisfy his editors. "What about the contents of the letter? Do you have any idea who may have written it?"

"No, we do not."

Ha, Norman thought, letting out a silent whoop of victory, reveling in the fact that he had more than the cops did on this one. Unless, of course, the sergeant was lying.

"Have you questioned Seth Kennedy about the murder?" Norman asked.

"I can't speak to that right now," Stone replied.

Norman groaned. "So what's the deal?"

"What deal is that?"

"C'mon sergeant. This is ridiculous."

Stone looked exasperated. "Kennedy is in custody on drug charges. You know that. It's in the press release. We arrested him for possession, distribution, and trafficking of narcotics last night. We found cocaine and heroin at his house, plus you know about the bust at Pumphouse. So, that's it and that's all. I'm afraid your time is up, Mr. Klein," he said, rising to his feet.

"What about the chief?" Norman asked.

"As I said, he'll be tied up in meetings all day." Stone stood with his hand on the doorknob, waiting for Norman to get out of his chair.

"So the chief is refusing to comment?" Norman said, refusing to move.

"I'll see you out," Stone snapped. "And I'm asking you not to put any of the contents of that letter in the paper. It could really interfere with our investigation."

"I'll take that under advisement," Norman said sarcastically.

One thing was clear: if it were his ass or the sergeant's, Norman would have no problem choosing between them.

Chapter Thirty-nine

Goode

Goode was walking up to Alison's apartment door when he heard her cry out, but he couldn't make out the words. Goode banged his fist against the door four times. "Alison? Are you all right in there?"

Silence.

"Alison?"

There was still no answer, but Goode could've sworn he heard a man's low voice through the door. He pictured Tony holding her down with his hand over her mouth. Maybe he was even choking her. Alison's call was all the probable cause Goode needed to enter the premises by force. Especially after being invited.

He kicked open the door, his gun drawn, and he was right. Tony was straddling Alison on the floor, his hand placed squarely over her mouth. Goode saw fear in Tony's eyes as he quickly rolled off Alison.

"It's not what you think," Tony said. "I was just trying to talk to her but she wouldn't stop screaming. All I wanted to do was talk."

A tear rolled down Tony's cheek. But Goode found it difficult to feel any empathy after what he'd witnessed. Alison seemed physically unharmed as she lay there, but her blank eyes told him she'd gone deep inside herself.

"You must be Tony Marcus," Goode said. "We talked on the phone the night your daughter was murdered. I'm Detective Ken Goode."

Tony nodded.

"Listen," Goode said. "We've been working hard to solve your daughter's murder, but you have no right to take out your frustrations on Alison. She's been going through a rough time as well and I don't think she needs you harassing her. You want to press charges, Alison?"

She shook her head.

"Well, that's lucky for you, Mr. Marcus, but I still have a few questions."

Tony looked at Goode with a mix of fear, confusion, and sadness.

"Where were you the night your daughter was murdered?"

Tony's expression turned to disbelief. "What are you talking about?"

"I'm talking about your temper, and maybe you took it

out on your daughter just like you did a minute ago with Alison."

Tony shook his head and dug his fingers deep into his eye sockets. Goode could hear the squeak of Tony's eyelids as he rubbed them.

"Well, Mr. Marcus?" Goode asked.

Tony didn't answer. He just kept rubbing his eyes. When he finally looked up, it was with such hopelessness that Goode almost felt sorry for him.

"I don't even know how to answer you except to say that I would never hurt my daughter," Tony said. "But if you must know, I was at home watching TV with my wife."

He sounded sincere to Goode, who stood at the ready, his legs apart, one hand free at his side, the other on the gun under his Windbreaker. Tony was not going to mess any more with Alison if Goode had anything to say about it.

"Well, I certainly hope that proves to be true," Goode said.

Tony heaved himself to his feet and lumbered toward the open door, turning so his face was in shadow.

"Can I call you, Alison?" he asked weakly. "I promise I won't upset you again."

But Alison was unreachable. She lay on her back, staring blankly at the ceiling. Even after Tony left the apartment, she didn't move. Goode kneeled down beside her and touched her shoulder. "Are you okay?"

She wouldn't meet his eyes. "I wonder if he could have done it," she said after a minute or so.

"I doubt it," Goode said, relieved that she'd come out of it. "But if it's him, my drug-dealing motive is definitely out the window."

Goode paused to give Alison a chance to say something more. She didn't, so he continued. "Besides, what would his motive be to kill his own daughter? And why would he want to kill Sharona and Keith?"

"My head hurts," Alison moaned, covering her face with her hands.

"Did he hit you again?" If he had, Goode would run outside, grab him, and throw him to the cement.

"No," she said, rising to a seated position on the floor, leaning against the couch. "You got here in time."

Alison didn't appear to be hurt physically, but he could tell the incident had caused some emotional damage. He wanted to help if she would let him.

"What are you thinking?" he asked gently, touching her arm.

"Nothing," she said in a monotone.

"You can tell me."

"No, maybe another time." She turned and gave him a weak smile. Her voice was barely audible. "Tell me about the investigation. What have you been up to?"

Goode smiled back, relieved to have been given a safe topic of discussion. "I just came from Keith's parents' house. Let's just say they seemed, well, out of touch."

"How are they taking it?" Alison asked.

"They seemed pretty shaken up."

"What if Tony comes back?"

This time, he could see the fear in her eyes. Good question, he thought, especially with what he'd done to the doorframe by crashing through it. He hated to see her so scared, but he didn't really know what to do about it. "Is there a friend you can stay with for a couple days?"

"No," she said, shaking her head. "Not really."

"How about going back to L.A. to your grandmother's?"

That must have stirred something in her because she got off the floor and sat on the sofa. "No, I haven't talked to her much since I got here," she said, "and I'm not up to going back up there."

"You could stay at my house for a night or two," he blurted out, wondering why in the hell he couldn't keep his mouth shut. "I have a sofa bed."

Alison's face lit up like a child grabbing at a helium balloon at a birthday party. "Really? That would be great. Are you sure?"

He couldn't back out now. "Um, yeah."

"That would be really great," she said. "Let me get some stuff together."

Alison disappeared into the bedroom and returned a few minutes later with a small overnight bag. "I won't get in the way, I promise. And I'm a heavy sleeper, so I won't even hear you come in late or anything. . . ."

He knew the sergeant wouldn't like this, so the sergeant wasn't going to learn anything about it. Goode wondered what he was getting himself into.

"You aren't going to get in trouble for this, are you?" she asked. What was she, a mind reader?

"What the sergeant doesn't know won't hurt him," Goode said. He half-hoped that saying it out loud would make it true.

Just then, a loud crunching sound erupted from the parking lot, like metal on metal, and they both jumped. Goode ran outside and peered over the railing into the parking lot below. A white BMW had crashed into the stairs, its front end crushed as if it were made of cardboard.

Tony was yelling something as he ran up the stairwell, but Goode couldn't make it out until Tony was almost on top of him. "My cell phone is dead. Call an ambulance!" he said, gasping for breath after the sprint up the stairs. "My wife crashed her car into the stairwell."

Goode pulled out his cell phone and called for an ambulance and a patrol unit right away. Then he ran down the stairs to check on the driver. Tony was right behind him.

Helen was unconscious, her face pressed into the airbag. The sweet smell of gin filled the car. He couldn't tell whether Tony's wife had passed out because of the impact or from drinking. Maybe both.

"God, she reeks," Goode said to Tony, who nodded in agreement. "What happened?"

"She must have followed me here. She just tried to run me over," Tony mumbled, shaking his head in disbelief.

Nice marriage, Goode thought. "Why would she do that?"

"I didn't even see her until the car was coming right at me. Luckily, I was able to jump up the stairs and out of the way."

When the paramedics arrived, they agreed with Goode's suggestion to take Helen over to the nearest hospital with a detox unit.

"You need to make sure she gets into treatment," he told Tony. "She a daily drinker?"

Tony shrugged. "Yeah, I guess."

"Looks to me like she has a problem. Don't you think?"

Tony nodded, his eyes cast down.

"Well, I would suggest you leave Alison alone and concentrate on salvaging what's left of your family," Goode said.

Tony nodded again.

By then, the patrol unit had arrived and Goode gave the officer a quick report. After he'd finished, he went upstairs to give Alison his address, and told her to wait a while before she came over. Said he wanted to clean up a little first. The truth was, he needed some time to clear his head.

Chapter Forty

Goode

Alison arrived at Goode's cottage about an hour later. He gave her a quick tour, steering her quickly through the bedroom without calling attention to the queen-sized bed, and told her she could sleep on the foldout couch in the living room. Letting her stay there was bad enough, but he was determined not to let anything more happen, at least until the case died down a bit. Still, given how long it had been since he'd been intimate with a woman, he couldn't be sure whether he could stick to his resolve.

The two of them were chitchatting about getting Alison's apartment door repaired when his cell went off again. It was the sergeant calling. Goode feared that somehow Stone found out that Alison was in his living room. He excused himself, closed the door to the bedroom, and took the call.

"It's your lucky day," Stone said, a note of triumph in his voice.

Goode thanked God it was just his paranoia acting up again. He sat on the bed, which he'd quickly made before Alison arrived. "Yeah, why's that?"

"Goode, listen. With all these photos, we've got plenty of evidence to charge Paul Walters for Tania Marcus' murder, so that's what we're going to do. I'm sure his DNA will match the stuff on her stomach. We're going to make sure his health is A-OK, and then we're going to transport him over to the county jail. We'll parade him in front of all the television cameras and pat you on the back."

"Well, this is all good news," Goode said. "But I've got to tell you, I think something is still wrong with this picture. None of the suspects seems like he could be responsible for all three murders. But my gut says—in fact, I would sacrifice my firstborn child on it—that there was only one doer."

"Okay, well, if it turns out he isn't the guy who did all three, maybe the doer will think he got off scot-free, start bragging to his buddies and implicate himself. Criminals are stupid. That's why they get caught."

"Yeah," Goode said, kicking off his shoes. He needed a shower. "Maybe you're right."

"Besides, you're on a roll," Stone said. "Multitalented narcotics detective with a penchant for homicides hits it big, first time out. Pulls in three suspects *and* makes two big drug busts. You'd like to taste some glory, wouldn't you? We'll make the charges stick. Don't worry your pretty little head about it."

"You think?" Goode still wasn't all that comfortable with the scenario. He rubbed the lint off his feet.

"There is one thing that happened today that kind of struck me as odd, though," Stone said.

"Yeah?"

"That cub reporter from the *Sun-Dispatch* came in this morning with a letter from someone claiming that Seth Kennedy killed all three people. It was supposedly written by one of his ex-girlfriends, but it wasn't signed." Stone read it to Goode.

"Sounds like Clover Ziegler wrote that," Goode said.

"You're probably right. But it might just be a prank."

"Could be, but worth checking out, don't you think?"

"Yeah, I'm having the crime lab take a look at it."

"Why send a letter like that to the newspaper and not to us? You know, until we check this out some more, I'd feel better if we held off making any big announcement about Paul Walters. Seth still looks like he's involved in this somehow. The bartender, too. Can we wait just one more day?"

Stone paused for a minute. "Well, this Walters arrest looks pretty good to me, plus, if Kennedy is involved, maybe Walters will turn on him. But if you feel that strongly about it, I'll see if I can buy you some more time. Trouble is the chief has been in my face to get charges filed first and ask questions later. He wants the mayor off his ass."

"He said that?"

"Yeah. I need a confession from Kennedy or that Walters character or whatever other wild card you can pull out of your ass by tomorrow afternoon at the latest. Use the letter if you have to. Get it?"

"Got it."

"Good."

Goode hung up and went back into the living room, where Alison was sitting on the couch with that feminine look of concern on her face. It was a nice change, not having to reassure her for once. She gave him a half-hearted grin, which he took as a positive sign after the scene in her apartment earlier.

"What's wrong, Ken? You look sick. Got a virus or something?"

Goode appreciated her attempt at humor. And come to think of it, he was feeling a little under the weather. But he figured it was a case of his mental, not physical, health. The pressure was starting to get to him. "I'm fine, really, it's just that . . ." he trailed off. She had enough on her mind without being burdened with his problems.

"What? You can tell me. It's okay." Alison patted the sofa next to her.

"No, I don't want to bother you with my stuff."

"Hey, you were there for me. Now let me return the favor. Maybe I can help. What is it?"

Goode sat beside her. He really wanted to help her, let her stay at his place, but he didn't want to get too close. Not yet, anyway. "That was the sergeant. He says we've got enough evidence to ask the DA to file charges against Paul Walters."

"That's great, Ken," she said, excitedly. "But you don't look happy. What's up with that?"

"I'm not so sure that he killed Tania, let alone the two other victims."

Alison's mouth fell open. "What do you mean? What about the photos and the shorts you found? You know he had a motive—rejection and all that."

"Yeah, I know. But something isn't right. I don't know. I see no motive or connection with him killing Sharona Glass or Keith Warner, and I have a gut feeling that the same person did all three murders. I told the sergeant, and he said I'm doing a great job, blah, blah, blah. Even so, the last thing I want to do is put the wrong guy in jail."

Alison gave him one of those "I'm proud of you" looks. "It's great that you're so conscientious," she said. "I mean, you took me into your place and, well, it's not all that big. I'm sure you'll figure this whole thing out."

Alison offered to make dinner, but Goode said he really needed to get back to work. After she described the menu, however, he decided he could squeeze in a quick bite before trying again to interview Clover at her house. They'd tried mornings and afternoons, so maybe they'd have better luck at night. He gave Alison a couple of twenties and directions to the supermarket so she could pick up fixings to liven up his bottled pasta sauce.

"One more thing, Alison," he said. "I would feel better, and I think you would, too, if you got a restraining order against Tony first thing in the morning, just in case he decides to come back."

"He won't find me here," she said.

Despite her earlier insistence that she would stay with Goode for only a day or two, he sensed it might be tough to get her to go home. "No, but this is temporary and he knows where you live."

"I guess you're right," she said.

After showering, Goode was getting dressed when his cell rang again. "Yeah, it's Goode," he answered.

The night watch commander, a real snotty guy and a perfect example of the Peter Principle, gave him a short retort: "Paul Walters says he wants to talk to you right away. He's still in the hospital and his fever has spiked to one-oh-four. They're not sure what's going on with him. He may have caught one of those hospital bacteria deals."

Goode scribbled a note to Alison, telling her to go ahead with dinner, that he'd be back in a while. He grabbed his tape recorder and wondered whether his feverish murder suspect was about to confess.

Chapter Forty-one

Paul

Paul's head was pounding. His thoughts were so loud, he was sure everyone else in the hospital could hear them. He wanted God to hear him, but no one else.

I didn't want to do it. I didn't mean to do it. It was an accident, I swear. I loved her.

Another voice in his head was mocking his thoughts, repeating them. He couldn't tell whether it was real, whether God was punishing him, or if it was just the fever. He didn't mind being punished, though. In fact, he reveled in it. He would just endure it until he saw a sign that God had forgiven him.

Paul pictured Tania's face as she lay on his bed on Saturday night. Lifeless. Her eyes closed. He'd finally gotten her, naked, in his bed, and she'd fallen asleep. Damn her. She was the queen of his temple. He'd partially covered one wall with Polaroid shots he'd taken of her going to school, buying food at the supermarket, picking up her mail. Paul was convinced that he was in love with her. He'd never felt such a deep, all-encompassing feeling of desire before. He wanted her and he wanted her to love him back.

Even before the fever hit, he had been feeling empty and depressed since she died. He missed her.

A woman was poking him in the arm again. Another damn nurse. She smelled like cigarettes. It made him want to puke. She could go to hell along with him.

So, it had all come to this. All because Tania had betrayed him.

He'd been forced to listen to her moaning next door with

that pretty boy on Friday night and again the next day. Then he saw her kissing the loser outside the apartment, wearing each other's clothes, no less. Tania had on his red and white striped shirt and he was wearing her oversized UCLA sweatshirt. Paul felt sick at the sight of them.

He knew he'd been a little on edge Saturday because he hadn't been sleeping well. He'd been drinking double espressos from the coffeehouse down the street and then pacing across his living room floor, late into the night, blasting Pink Floyd on his headphones. He often lay on the couch with a pillow and imagined it was Tania in his arms. He would close his eyes and run his fingertips over her perfect breasts, steeped in the warm glow of candlelight. Then he would take her thin, delicate wrists, taste her soft neck, and stroke her long hair. He was in the midst of one of these interludes when he first heard her through the wall. That's when he shaped his plan. He wasn't going to let that loser complicate matters.

Paul waited a couple hours after the pretty boy had left, figuring Tania would be too tired to refuse the invitation this time. Before he knocked on her door, he lit the fifty-two white candles he'd stuck into wine bottles that lined his bedroom. He loved that freshly burnt match smell.

Tania opened her door with wet hair and a comb in her hand. He could see the black nylon shorts underneath the loser's pinstriped shirt. "Hi. What's up?" she said.

As he predicted, she seemed tired and her defenses were down. "Can you come over for a minute?" he asked. "I want to show you something." Just looking at her heightened his senses. She was so beautiful it almost hurt.

"You know, I'm kind of busy. I've got a bunch of stuff to do before I go out tonight. Anyway, you don't look so good. What's the matter, are you sick?"

"No, I'm fine," he said. "Just for a few minutes? I made something for you."

"I really don't have time," she said.

He could tell she was trying to dismiss him, but he

wouldn't have it. Paul's whole body tensed up. He could feel the excitement building. She was going to bend. He just had to try a little harder. "It's a surprise. Please?"

Tania twisted her mouth to one side as she contemplated his request. "Well, all right. Just for a few minutes. Seriously, though. I'm running late as it is."

Paul felt a burst of euphoria. He took her by the hand and led her into his apartment, closing the door behind them. There, he thought. I'm in. He took her comb and laid it on his kitchen table. She pulled away a little when he tried to lead her into his bedroom, so he had to take her arm.

"Ow," she said.

"Sorry."

Tania wrinkled up her nose as she walked into the doorway and then stopped. "God, it smells like something died in here."

Paul had made a lot of effort that morning to prepare the temple for her, but he hadn't had time to do laundry.

"This is really weird," she said, trying to move back into the living room.

"Where are you going?" he said, holding her firmly by the arm. "It's in here."

Tania tried to tug away again. "I've really got to go. Ow. Cut it out. You're hurting me."

"You can't go. I won't let you."

"What do you mean, you won't let me?" she said, turning toward him and glaring. "Let go of my arm."

This was not going the way it was supposed to. Paul had to use force to pull her into the bedroom. He let go of her for a minute so he could reach for the chopping knife he'd placed on the bookshelf just in case things didn't go well. With the knife in one hand, he held her tightly with the other. He didn't really want to hurt her, he just wanted to let her know he meant business.

Paul had sharpened the knife earlier that afternoon.

He'd tried to cut through a roast beef sandwich, but ended up pulling the red, wet slab off the bread and onto the counter. He spent a good half hour scraping the blade across a long metal sharpening rod until the knife was able to slice cleanly through the meat.

Tania's arm went rigid as soon as she saw the knife. He felt her trembling and heard her breathing speed up. She must know what's coming, he thought. They were finally going to make love. He smiled as he watched the reflection of the candle flames dancing along the blade. Tania didn't seem quite so smug by then. Not so smug at all. He lowered her into the wooden chair he'd placed in the middle of the bedroom so she was facing a vertical mirror mounted on the wall.

"Paul, you're scaring me. I want to go ho . . ." Tania's voice trailed off as she saw his collection of Polaroids on the wall.

Things were finally becoming clear to her. Good, he thought. Now all she needed to do was get in the mood. Paul reached for the tumbler of scotch on the rocks he'd prepared for her, containing a Rohypnol he'd purchased in Tijuana in anticipation of this event. He often stole drugs from the La Jolla pharmacy where he worked, delivering drugs to the homebound, the rich, and the lazy. But they didn't sell sedatives categorized as date-rape drugs in the United States. He wanted to make sure Tania felt comfortable with him before they made love, so he only used a portion of one pill.

"Here, drink this," he ordered.

She shook her head no, her long, wet hair swinging back and forth. It was beautiful, silky, and smooth when it was dry, but when wet, she looked like she had a head of rat tails. Funny, the things you learned when you got to know someone intimately. Her hair reminded him of a poem from *Alice in Wonderland* that he'd memorized in high school for a speech class assignment. He decided to impress her with his knowledge, and at the same time, show her that she must do as he instructed. He recited the poem:

"Fury said to a mouse, That he met in the house, 'Let us both go to law: I will prosecute you—Come, I'll take no denial: We must have a trial; For really this morning I've nothing to do.' Said the mouse to the cur, 'Such a trial, dear sir, With no jury or judge, would be wasting our breath.' 'I'll be judge, I'll be jury,' said cunning old Fury: 'I'll try the whole cause and condemn you to death.' "

"That's from *Alice in Wonderland*, Lewis Carroll," he finished proudly, pausing to let the message sink in. What was the matter with her anyway, not wanting to take a sip of his love potion? He leaned into her face. "Drink it, I said."

But Tania didn't move. She sat stiffly in the chair, pulling on her fingers. Why wouldn't she do as she was told? Paul held the knife against her wrist. "You need to drink this, just like Alice did before she became Queen Alice. Because, after all, you are my queen."

Tania's lips parted and he could feel her warm breath on his face. "Paul, why are you doing this?" she asked in a small voice that certainly was not fit for a queen. "This is crazy. Why don't you let me call someone to come and help you? A therapist or something."

"Quiet!" he barked.

He'd had more than enough of her deliberate insubordination. "If you don't do what I say, I'll have to help you cut your own wrists," he said through clenched teeth. "They'll just think you killed yourself."

Then he softened and smiled tenderly. He couldn't help it. She was so beautiful. "I really don't want to do that. I love you, you know." Paul dropped to a sitting position on the carpet at her feet and gazed up at her. He noticed how her hair made the shirt wet around her breasts. He wanted to caress them, but it still wasn't the right time. Not yet.

Finally, she took a sip of the potion. He was pleased to see she was no longer acting so righteous, so indignant. Still, he needed to show her that he was in charge.

"That's it. Now drink all of it," he said forcefully.

Tania looked at him and then at the knife he was pressing into her flesh. Closing her eyes tightly, she drank the rest and then went into a coughing spasm. When she opened her eyes, they were all watery. Good, he thought, I've broken her will.

Paul had recently reread *Through the Looking Glass*. He'd remarked to himself how oddly parallel the characters were to people in his own life, always changing the rules. He often felt he was on the other side of the mirror, so that his entire world was reversed. He wanted to explain this to Tania so she would see things the way he did. And now that she'd calmed down, he could begin.

Unfortunately, he saw that her eyelids had grown so heavy she could hardly keep them open. He hadn't gotten a chance to say anything he'd wanted to. He got her to stand up and guided her over to lie down on the bed. He sat beside her, touching her shoulder, her cheek, and even her breast, but she did not respond. She was out.

Paul pounded the bed with the flat of his hand. "What are you doing? I wanted to explain some very important concepts here."

Tania was a smart woman and he knew she'd appreciate his mind. That's why he'd chosen her. How dare she cut the intellectual foreplay short. Paul decided he'd better begin the next phase of his plan. Tania was sure to wake up in the middle and moan like she did for that pretty boy. He unbuttoned her shirt, pulling back each side to unveil her magnificence. Each nipple was the lightest shade of pink he'd ever seen. They felt like velvet. He pulled off her little black shorts and threw them on the floor in the corner.

Touching himself until he was hard took no time at all. He pushed himself against her, trying to get inside. Only he couldn't seem to get in. And she didn't moan. She just breathed, and shallowly at that. This was not the way it was supposed to be. Still, he was overcome by the sensation. It was overwhelming. He couldn't hold it in another second. He lost control. His body shuddered as he left a small white pool in and around her navel. Then he lay down next to her.

This was quite a letdown after all the fantasizing he'd done. He'd thought he would feel happy and close to her after they made love. But the whole experience had left him feeling like a failure, disappointed and ashamed. A hot flush crossed his face and he broke out in a sweat. This wasn't your fault, he told himself. She was a terrible lover. She had just lain there.

His nerves felt raw. He resented her mere presence in his bedroom. Even her breathing made him feel agitated. He paced around the room for a few minutes, trying to decide what to do. He wanted her out of his bed and out of his apartment. Truth be told, he wanted her dead.

Paul grabbed a tie out of the closet, the funky green one he'd bought at the thrift store. He lifted her head off the pillow, circled the tie around her neck, and pulled it tight until he couldn't hear her breathing anymore. Good riddance, he thought.

He carried her into the living room and dropped her on the couch. He would deal with her later. For the moment, he needed to calm down. He couldn't remember ever being this angry. Paul wandered around the living room in the dark until he tripped over a bottle on the floor. His ankle twisted over on itself.

"Shit!" he cried out as a shot of excruciating pain ran up his leg, causing him to lose his balance. He fell to the floor. The pain lessened, but only to a sharp throbbing. He scrambled over the floor on his butt to the couch, feeling with his hands as he went. He reached under the sofa and pulled out his stash of pot, the stuff with the little red hairs that made him see his alter ego in the mirror.

Lighting up a bowl, he inhaled deeply, holding in each mouthful of smoke. By the fifth puff, he finally felt the pain diminish. He went from feeling calm to light-headed and dizzy. He must have fallen asleep soon after that because when he looked at the clock on the VCR, it was just before midnight. And when he turned on the light, Tania was gone. The police found her body in the alley the next day, dead as a dormouse. He certainly hadn't meant to kill her, and try as he might, he simply could not remember carrying her body down those stairs.

Chapter Forty-two

Goode

As usual on a Friday night, the emergency room at the UCSD Medical Center was a maelstrom of activity. Two homeless men wearing dirty oversized clothes were talking to themselves. A nurse told Goode that Paul Walters was in Room 314, on the third floor. He nodded at the officer who was parked outside, engrossed in a Michael Connelly detective novel.

Paul wasn't faring too well. His face, covered with sweat, glistened even in the dim light of the room. A nurse, who was mopping his brow, put her finger to her lips. "Shhhh. He's sleeping. He's got a raging fever, hepatitis, and he might have some bacterial infection, too. We're testing to make sure we give him the right medication."

Goode sat in the chair next to the bed, waiting for her to leave so he could hear what was so damned important. Actually, he almost hoped Paul would finger Seth Kennedy so he could nail the slime bag. He also wanted to show that his instincts had been right about Paul. He definitely was a deviant, but logistically speaking, he couldn't have killed all three people. The nurse shook her head in disapproval at Goode. She obviously felt he was disturbing her sick patient. She finally took her wide hips and piano legs out the door.

Goode pulled a small tape recorder out of his pocket, pushed the RECORD button and laid it next to the pillow.

"Paul," Goode said quietly, touching his arm. "Hey, Paul. You awake?"

Paul was breathing in short, shallow spurts.

"Paul, you awake?" Goode repeated a little louder, shaking his shoulder. The patient opened his eyes into slits. "You wanted to talk to me?"

Paul nodded.

"Well, I'll have to read you your rights first," Goode said, and then did so.

Paul's words came in short gasps, so Goode had to bend over, bringing his ear just inches from Paul's mouth. He lifted the recorder up so he could capture every word.

"She was in my apartment that night. . . . I gave her a sedative to relax her, but then things went wrong and I lost it on her stomach. I wanted her out of there, so . . . I tied a tie around her neck. . . . But I don't know how I could have killed her. I loved her. I don't remember taking her down to the alley either, but she was gone from my apartment. . . . If I hurt her . . . I don't want to live anymore." Goode stepped back and Paul turned his head toward him. "Do you think I did it?" he whispered.

"I don't know," Goode said quietly. "I'll come back tomorrow and we'll talk some more once your fever goes down. Get some sleep."

Goode's head was reeling. Say Paul did kill Tania. Why would he then do in Sharona? And that still left no link to Keith's death. Goode hoped Paul could answer some of these questions once he was in better shape and perhaps Seth or One-Eyed Jack could fill in the rest of the puzzle. With one quick call, Goode arranged for a county psychiatrist to evaluate Paul the next morning to determine whether it was his fever talking. A defense attorney would probably get the judge to throw out a statement given under these conditions anyway.

From the hospital Goode went straight to Clover's. He really wanted to ask her about the letter and find out what she could tell him to make a case stick against Seth, or Paul, or anyone else, frankly. But this was not to be. The house was dark and the driveway was empty. He wondered if the family had left town, and if it would do any good to stick Slausson or Fletcher outside the house until she showed up.

Goode went home, looking forward to a home-cooked meal. Even if he had to microwave it.

Chapter Forty-three

Goode

Alison was curled up under a blanket on the couch when Goode got home. The place smelled of a tantalizing mix of garlic, tomatoes, and sausage that had simmered for hours. He opened the fridge to get a beer and saw a plate of spaghetti and sauce, covered in plastic wrap. He stuck it in the microwave, grabbed a beer, and went to his room to eat.

Lacking the energy to brush his teeth, he finished his beer and shut off the light. But he couldn't stop the frenzy of evidence running through his head or the evolving list of interview questions for Seth Kennedy that his brain was compiling. So, he rolled over and switched on the light so he could empty his mind onto a piece of paper. After that, the cerebral noise quieted enough for him to drift off to a serene place.

He was bicycling on a dirt road that ran along an isolated beach, the air heavy with humidity, when he came to a cove where the turquoise water was calm and inviting. Sweaty, he stopped and leaned his bike against the seawall, tossing his backpack onto the sand. He climbed over the wall and walked out a few feet. The sand burned his feet, so he tore off his T-shirt and took a running dive into the sea. It was warm but still refreshing. He could see his hands against the coral pink backdrop of the ocean floor as clearly as if they were under glass. He floated on his back, watching the palm fronds flutter in the breeze. When he grew tired of floating, he waded out and lay facedown in a cool crevice he dug out in the hot sand. Soon the sun had dried his back and he put his T-shirt over his head to block out its rays.

A few minutes later he felt a woman straddle his back. He could tell it was a woman from the way she touched him as she seated herself, her hair brushing lightly against his shoulder blades and her bottom pressing into his lower back. She rubbed hot coconut oil into his skin in circular motions, her legs, soft and smooth, hugging him firmly on either side. The massage was so good he started to feel woozy. Her soft hands slid their way down his spine to his lower back, probing and pushing the tension out, pouring more oil on his back as she went. At first it felt relaxing, but when her hands started creeping lower by degrees under his swim trunks, he felt himself getting excited. He tried to turn over, but she wouldn't let him. She held his wrists above his head, a little rougher but still playful. She didn't mean him any harm. This was a game for her.

She teased him by rubbing herself over him, pressing herself into him, riding him. He was hers. She had taken him. She stopped moving for a moment and he waited with anticipation, wanting more as he listened to his own blood rushing through his head. Why was she stopping? As if she could read his thoughts, she started caressing his back with her fingertips, and then her nails. She leaned over and licked around his ear, teasing him, taking the lobe into her mouth. He could feel her full breasts, still covered by a tight shirt, pushing into his back. She squeezed him harder with her legs. Then she took her shirt off, allowing just her nipples to tickle him. He thought he was going to explode. Finally, he couldn't stand it anymore. If she wouldn't let him turn over, he had to break the silence.

"Tania, let me turn over," he whispered, his words slurred with sleep. "I want to touch you."

She got off him and was gone. Goode heard his bedroom door close and sat up with a start.

Chapter Forty-four

Goode
Friday

Goode left early the next morning before Alison was awake, careful to close the front door as quietly as possible. He couldn't face her after what had happened in the middle of the night. He was so embarrassed, he didn't know how he could undo what he'd said to her. He'd been so sure he was having another dream about Tania. The beach scene, with those hands rubbing his back, kept repeating itself in his mind. He was still all charged up.

Once he got to Harry's Coffee Shop, he bought a newspaper from the machine outside and tried to focus on work. That turned out to be easy. Norman Klein's story was on the front page and it was all about the letter Stone had mentioned. It also included an interview with Stone that he hadn't mentioned.

EX-GIRLFRIEND FINGERS DRUG-DEALER LOVER IN
PB MURDERS
Victims' families accuse police of dragging their feet

By Norman Klein
Staff Writer

A 27-year-old La Jolla man jailed on suspicion of selling cocaine and methamphetamine is the target of a letter accusing him of being the Pacific Beach beauty-school killer, the San Diego Sun-Dispatch has learned.

The letter, sent anonymously to the Sun-Dispatch yesterday, claims that real estate agent Seth Kennedy murdered two beauty school students and his best friend, Keith Warner. However, the letter did not offer an explanation or any possible motive.

Police officials ordered the newspaper to turn over the letter as evidence in the multiple-homicide investigation.

The author claims to be Kennedy's ex-girlfriend.

Kennedy was being held at the downtown jail on $200,000 bail on felony drug charges last night and was unavailable for comment.

Clover Ziegler, 23, dated Kennedy until very recently, according to her mother, Rosemary Stratton. However, it could not be confirmed yesterday whether Ziegler had authored the letter. Ziegler was a close friend of the second murder victim, Sharona Glass, 23.

The first cosmetology student victim was Tania Marcus, 24, whose body was found in an alley outside her apartment on Sunday.

Ziegler, who lives with her mother in La Jolla, did not respond to a phone message left at her home.

Police refused to comment on whom they think wrote the letter, saying it could interfere with their homicide investigation.

"A letter has come to our attention that may lead our

investigation in a certain direction, but it's too early to comment on exactly what direction that will be," Sgt. Rusty Stone said.

Glass, Ziegler, and Marcus were students at a new beauty school in Bird Rock, aimed at training cosmetology entrepreneurs to open their own salons. Glass had injuries consistent with strangulation and Warner died from a fatal shot to the back of the head, county Medical Examiner's officials said. Marcus' cause of death is still under investigation.

Goode stopped reading at that point, gaining a new respect for the cub reporter. He'd done his homework on Clover Ziegler. It looked like now, more than ever, that she was key to solving this case. He wondered for a fleeting moment whether she could have killed Tania out of jealousy and framed Seth for it. But he dismissed that as unlikely since it wouldn't explain the death of Sharona or Keith.

After breakfast, Goode stopped by the station to check in with Sergeant Stone, who said the *Sun-Dispatch* story had caused a big ruckus with the brass over his failure to squelch the cub reporter. Most of the rank and file cops were speculating why anyone would send a novice reporter like Norman such a letter in the first place. The detectives joked about Sergeant Stone's completely meaningless statement, but the ribbing was meant as praise, not criticism. That's why he got paid the big bucks.

Goode found the sergeant in the men's room. He didn't look so good.

"Hey, buddy, what's up?" Goode asked.

"You're questioning Kennedy again this morning, right?" Stone said, his tone charged with anxiety.

"Yes, sir."

"Well, we got the tests back on those busts. The cocaine and meth from Pumphouse came from the same batches as the high-quality stuff we found on Tania's table and in Sharona's apartment. That Kennedy kid must have some connection. And by the way, the mayor skipped calling the chief and ran directly all over my ass this morning, asking why we haven't talked to Clover Ziegler yet. I almost told him he should take over the investigation if he wants to be involved. . . . Why it is again that we haven't taken her statement?"

"We've been trying, chief. Slausson's gone over there, I've been there twice and left a card, but she's never home and she isn't calling back. I was wondering if we should stick Slausson or Fletcher outside the house until she shows up. She might have left town. I was planning to go over there again after I interviewed Kennedy."

"Let's hold off on the surveillance idea for the moment," Stone said. "With practically a murder a day here on this case, we don't have enough manpower to do that."

The sergeant let out a long sigh and headed back to his office. Given his mood, Goode didn't want to tell Stone about Paul's pseudo-confession until he could figure out what connection Paul had to Seth, if any.

Goode pictured Alison as he had last seen her that morning, her hair all messed up and her mascara smudged under her eyes, apparently from crying, a contrast with the erotic creature who had straddled him in the middle of the night. Maybe he'd only thought he'd heard the door close. Maybe it really had been a dream. He could only hope. But he didn't have time to think about that. He jumped back in his van and went over to the county jail for his appointment with the Little Prince Kennedy and his high-priced lawyer.

When Goode got there, the kid was as smug as ever, despite not having shaved or showered for thirty-six hours. Seth's attorney wore the expected uniform of a dark gray suit, crisp white shirt, royal blue Hermes tie, and black loafers with tassels. Goode could only hope a man in blue would catch him driving drunk someday. The guy needed a humility check, big-time.

"So you must be Mr. Kennedy's attorney," Goode said as he sat facing them across the rectangular table in the interview room.

"Milton Biggs," the lawyer said, offering his hand to Goode.

"Yes, Mr. Biggs. We've heard a lot about you around here. Always representing the nice rich folks who get into trouble."

Biggs was not amused, but he kept his cool. "Let's get down to business, shall we? I interrupted my vacation for this."

"All righty then," Goode said. He spread out the newspaper and Clover's letter on the table. "Take a gander at this incriminating evidence, gentlemen."

They read the story and letter intently as Seth grimaced and Biggs turned pale under his Hawaiian sunburn. "Could I have a moment alone with my client?" Biggs said, his face tight.

"Sure, I'll go get myself another cup of coffee," Goode said, thinking he could never be too alert.

Goode was beginning to enjoy himself. He still didn't know whether Paul had killed Tania, and Seth had some explaining to do. But the turn of events made him happy to be a detective. He enjoyed making two men of privilege squirm. By the time he returned with a tepid cup of coffee from the vending machine, Seth and his attorney had recovered their collective composure. The coffee was barely drinkable, but it served its purpose. Goode was tired.

"Gentlemen? Are we ready?"

Biggs nodded. His brow was furrowed and his eyes serious. Goode sipped from his cup, glanced back and forth at the two of them, and let the silence sink in. He wanted them to feel uncomfortable.

"So, Seth," he said finally. "You told me you had nothing to do with the murders of Tania Marcus and Keith Warner. Does that go for Sharona Glass, too?"

"Yes, it does." Seth looked as if he'd had another rough night in the pokey. His eyes were droopy and his left cheek was bruised, a little scuffle on the cell block, perhaps. But Goode was not a ruffian. He would do his work on Seth with words, not fists.

"Then how do you explain this letter?"

Biggs straightened his tie. "First of all, my client doesn't answer any more questions about the murders unless you agree not to seek charges on the drugs found in his house or at Pumphouse. He says they aren't his. Someone planted them in his house and he has no idea who has been selling drugs at the bar, other than Jack O'Mallory. This letter was obviously written by Clover Ziegler, one of my client's former acquaintances who has spent time in a mental institution."

So Biggs was starting big, Goode thought. "Well, I don't know anything about that," Goode said, "but I assure you, we will be seeking to gather any corroboration this witness can offer. Now, you know I have no power or authority to offer you a deal. That's up to the DA. But what I can say is that we believe these killings are the work of one person and whatever you can tell us to prove you are not that person can only help you. I have to tell you, Mr. Kennedy, it doesn't look good for you. The same drugs were found at Pumphouse, your house, and in Tania's and Sharona's apartments."

"You didn't find any meth at my house," Seth said quietly. "And I don't know how you make the leap from drugs to murder in the first place."

"Okay. So what I'd like to know is this: Who do you think might be interested in planting these drugs and pinning these murders on you?"

"We were just discussing that," Biggs interjected.

Seth licked his lips and ran his fingers through his tousled hair. Goode saw some white strands he hadn't noticed before. Seth was only twenty-seven, but Goode had heard of some people going white as early as eighteen. Could it be the night in jail had been a little harder on Seth than he was letting on?

Seth shifted in his chair. "Well, Clover Ziegler for one. She's a psycho. She got all obsessive and possessive with me over the summer. She was at Pumphouse the night I met Tania and she was outside in the parking lot, waiting for me when I left. On the day Keith was killed, he told me she'd followed us that first night to Tania's house, and he'd gone after her. When he followed me to Tania's apartment, he saw Clover sitting in her car in the alley after Tania and I went upstairs. So she knew where Tania lived. Keith wasn't sure whether she saw him or not, but—"

Goode interrupted him. "So, you're saying that maybe Clover killed Tania and then went after Keith because he saw her parked outside Tania's apartment?"

"Exactly," Seth said. "When I first met her, I would never have believed she could do anything like this. She was so affectionate and sweet. But she got all weird later on, and violent, too. Last week, Sharona and I had lunch and things got a little intimate. But that's not important. What's important is that she told me something you might be interested in."

"Yeah, what's that?"

Seth had Goode's full attention now. "She's the one who told me that Clover spent the spring in a private hospital," Seth said. "The doctors initially said she'd had a psychotic episode set off by cocaine use. But after they kept her there for a while, they diagnosed her with drug-induced schizophrenia. I didn't know any of this until last week."

"So if your theory is correct," Goode said, "why would Clover kill her best friend? Just because she's mentally ill doesn't mean she's a killer. People with mental illness of-

ten hurt themselves, not others." Goode knew that only
too well.

"I have no idea," Seth said. "Maybe she found out that
Sharona and I had sex last week. Maybe there's a history
there we don't know about."

Goode decided to shift into a higher gear. It was confrontation time. "Seth, we found rock cocaine in your
house, not to mention that slab of heroin. Your business
associate, Jack O'Mallory, assures us that you were selling drugs at his bar. He has also admitted that some of
the beauty school students bought and did drugs at
Pumphouse and he specifically mentioned Clover and
Sharona."

"He's just trying to save his own ass. With a record
like his, he'll say whatever you want him to say. Maybe
he's the one who planted that stuff in my house."

"Look. We've got plenty of evidence to make all the
drug charges stick. We know you have to have a big
enough bank account to buy these kinds of quantities
from your source in Mexico, while the bartender has few
if any assets to his name. This letter names you as a serial
killer, so as soon as we can prove how these murders are
related to this drug importing business, you will be facing
the death penalty. That is, unless you start cooperating."

Seth whispered with his lawyer before answering.
"Okay," Seth said, sighing. "So I bought small amounts
of blow and did it with my friends at the bar. But I'm not
a drug lord for Christ's sake."

"And why do that with Clover if you knew she had a
problem?"

Seth shrugged again. "I didn't know she had a problem. I mean I noticed she acted a little crazy sometimes,
but only lately. Besides, the coke made her wild, if you
know what I mean. Is having good sex a crime?"

It is when he wasn't getting any, Goode thought. "No,"
he said. "Not unless it's with a prostitute."

"Well, Clover wasn't a prostitute. She just liked co-caine. It was like a love potion for that girl."

"It's also an illegal drug, and it's a serious crime to sell it. So you said Clover got violent with you. How?"

Seth paused for a minute and stared at the wall. "She broke the head off a champagne bottle and threatened me with it. . . ."

"Did Sharona mention anything about Clover being violent with her?"

"She said Clover trashed some of her stuff. When we had lunch, she said, 'Clover would kill me if she knew we were here together.' I didn't think she was serious at the time. But maybe she was."

"So tell me again why Clover would want to kill Sharona if they've been best friends for years?"

"I don't know, maybe she found out about our lunch last week and thought we'd been sleeping together be-hind her back for months. Who knows? Maybe she was worried Sharona would tell me about her having been in a mental hospital."

"Seems thin to me. Isn't it true that Keith Warner tried to get you to stop seeing Clover because she was getting to be a drag?" Goode asked. "He told me she was neu-rotic as hell and a pain in the ass. Was that just to throw me off or was he involved in this little scheme you have going down at the Pumphouse?"

Seth huddled with his attorney for a moment. "Yes, Keith also sold to our friends. And so did Jack. Just as of-ten as I did. But Keith cut Clover off, and I should have, too. Come to think of it, Keith asked me to loan him a big chunk of money a month or so ago, but he wouldn't tell me what it was for. He told me not to ask any ques-tions, and to just trust that he needed it. He was my best friend, but I don't know what he was up to."

Goode had heard just about enough out of this guy, throwing blame around like rice at a wedding. "That's funny, because according to Keith, he was trying to convince you to get out of the operation, not push you into it. I can't believe you would try to finger a dead man who can't speak for himself. Frankly, I think you killed him to shut him up."

Biggs banged his fist on the table and stood up. "That's enough of that kind of talk, detective. If you're not going to arrest my client for murder, this meeting is over."

Goode glared at him, speaking low and calmly. "I don't think that would be in your client's best interests. Why don't we all take a minute."

Seth trained his eyes around the room, anywhere but on Goode's face. His attorney pulled out the newspaper and read the story again. Goode could see both of them were trying to keep their cool, but having a very difficult time of it.

"Detective, are you really intending to pursue murder charges against my client on the basis of a slanderous newspaper article and an anonymous letter? It's no better than pulp fiction." For all the big talk, though, Biggs looked even more drained than before. Seth, slumped in his chair, looked as if defeat was finally sinking in.

Goode, on the other hand, was feeling pretty upbeat. "Well, it depends on whether Mr. Kennedy gives a full confession about the drug operation. If his alibis check out and we learn he wasn't involved in these killings, then there will be no murder charges. But that seems unlikely.

"One more thing, Mr. Kennedy. We've tried to talk with Clover Ziegler several times this week with no luck. Why don't you make things easier for us to prove your story and tell me how and where she spends her time?"

"She goes shopping a lot. Sometimes, at night, she goes skinny dipping by Scripps pier. She also likes to watch the hang gliders above Black's Beach."

"How long were you two together?"

"Off and on for a few months."

"When did you stop seeing her?"

"I cut it off a few weeks ago, but she wouldn't let go."

Goode threw him a slow pitch to see if he would swing. "Sounds to me like it all went to hell when you danced cheek to cheek with Tania Marcus."

"What's that supposed to mean?" Seth snapped.

Goode smiled and nodded at Seth and his attorney, then motioned for the deputy to let him out. "I guess we'll see about that," he said. "Now you two gentlemen have a good day."

Chapter Forty-five

Norman

Norman slept in until ten thirty or so. He tripped as he pulled on some sweats and staggered to open the front door of his apartment to grab the paper. His story was above the fold on Page One. Cool. Very cool.

Al had done some polishing, but Norman's original work still shone through. He had even received a glimmer of a compliment from the guy as he was leaving the newsroom for a few celebratory beers at the Tavern.

"Good hustle today," Al said. "But remember. You're only as good as your last story."

Norman sat down at the kitchen table with a mug of coffee and read his story several times. He was living the dream, as the veteran reporters liked to say. Only he wasn't kidding.

Based on his conversations with Sharona's and Clover's mothers, Norman was sure Clover had written the letter. His plan was to pay her a visit and confront her about the claims involving Seth Kennedy. This would be a very important interview for him.

Norman felt a little intimidated driving up Nautilus Street, where the houses were three times larger than the one in Jersey where he'd grown up. On La Jolla Rancho, he saw a Mexican gardener blowing fallen leaves with a long tube connected to a jet pack that was strapped to his back.

Clover and her parents lived at the top of Mount Soledad, where you felt like you could see to Hawaii. Unless it was one of those mornings when the fog hadn't burned off yet, and the sky was so white you couldn't see the ocean only two miles away. On his way to Clover's house, Norman stopped at the cross on top of the hill, where he could see all of San Diego spread out below him. The sky was a striking azure and he swore the gray blobs on the horizon were islands.

Norman pulled into Clover's driveway and checked out the cars lined up on the asphalt: a Lamborghini and a BMW. Hopefully, one of them was Clover's. He knocked on the heavy oak door and tried to peer through the small windowpane in the middle of it, but the beveled glass was etched with a floral pattern, so he couldn't see inside. When no one answered, he pressed the doorbell. He heard chimes ringing inside and a dog yapping. He put his ear against the door to see if he could hear anyone moving about. The cold, smooth varnish felt good against his damp skin. The door opened suddenly and Norman lurched forward, almost falling into a woman in the foyer he presumed was Clover's mother.

"Sorry, I was trying to see if anyone was home," he sputtered.

The woman did not look pleased as she stood with her arms crossed. "Well, as you can see, here I am. And who are you? I hope you aren't selling the *Sun-Dispatch*. It's not worth the paper it's printed on."

Norman tried to ignore the jab and pressed on. "As a matter of fact, I'm Norman Klein, a reporter with the *Sun-Dispatch*. We talked on the phone yesterday. Remember?"

Her face softened a bit, but not much. "Sure, I do." Then she smiled mischievously. "Maybe you can move on to a better paper once you get some more experience."

Norman didn't quite know how to respond to that. "Is Clover home?"

"No, she isn't."

"Any idea when you expect her?"

The woman shook her head. "No, not a clue. She's old enough to take care of herself."

"Do you mind if I wait inside for her, Mrs. Stratton? It's awfully hot out here."

The woman, her hair in a neat chignon at the nape of her neck, looked up at the tallest eucalyptus tree in the front yard and watched a flock of starlings fly out of it. "No, I don't think that would be a good idea. I've got to go out in a few minutes, and I'm not going to let a strange young man camp out in my living room." She stepped backward and started to close the door.

"Well, I'll wait in my car then," he said. "Sorry to bother you, Mrs. Stratton."

This wasn't going the way he'd envisioned. But he wasn't going to give up. "Wait," he called while the door was still open a crack. "Can I ask you a few questions?"

"No," she said, her voice creeping around the door. "I'm already late for a lunch date. Sorry." With that, the door thudded shut.

"No, you're not," Norman whispered, slapping his notebook against his hand.

Norman could smell Rosemary Stratton's rose perfume all the way to the oleander bushes. He sat in his car with the door open, hoping the breeze would cool the black vinyl interior.

About forty-five minutes later, Mrs. Stratton came out of the house in a short tennis skirt, exposing jiggly legs that would be better off in pants, and climbed into the Lamborghini. She peeled out of the horseshoe driveway and took off down the street with a roar. Norman wondered if the woman's heart was like the door to the house, shiny and cold with a core that would shatter on impact. Norman hoped it wasn't genetic.

His legs were getting stiff, so he got out of the car and strolled down the sidewalk a ways. He was about a block from Clover's house when he saw Detective Goode's van pull into her driveway. Norman hid behind a eucalyptus tree and watched the detective walk purposefully up to the door and ring the bell.

Goode shifted his weight from side to side as he waited for someone to answer. He, too, tried to look through the opaque window. He gave up after a few minutes, got back into his van and left. Some of us have more patience and fortitude than others, Norman thought, as he stood knee-deep in ivy. After waiting a few minutes to be sure Goode wasn't coming back, Norman climbed back into his car and flipped on the radio.

Half an hour later, he saw a twenty-something blonde woman drive up in a little red Mercedes convertible. Clover, he presumed. She got out of the car, carrying several shopping bags with looped handles, then tripped and spilled one bag's contents on her way up the front walk. She bent over and picked up what looked like red lingerie, mumbling something he couldn't hear. He felt a sneeze coming on, and before he could do anything to squelch it, he let one out. Clover spun around, but he pulled his head in quickly, hoping she didn't see him. She went into the house, and after giving her a few minutes to put down the bags, maybe get a diet soda, he slunk out of his hiding place.

Norman tamed his hair with the plastic comb-brush that folded up into his back pocket, wiped the sweat off his face with his sleeve and strolled up to the house, whistling, like it was no big deal. But inside, his stomach was churning. He pushed his index finger squarely into the gold doorbell.

The dog yapped again as the chimes echoed throughout the foyer. Only this time, no one came to the door. "C'mon, I know you're in there," he whispered.

Norman wondered if Clover was swimming in a pool in the backyard and couldn't hear him. He sat on the front step, feeling frustrated and glum. He was not going to get this close and then come back with nothing. He decided to wait a while, and then try again. He was so close to glory he could smell it.

Chapter Forty-six

Clover

Clover Ziegler thought she heard someone sneeze as she was coming up the walk, and once she was in her bedroom, she could've sworn she heard something rustling around in the front yard. But when she looked down from her second-story window, all she could see were her mother's rosebushes, pristine as usual. Clover was relieved that the gardener had finally cut back the eucalyptus trees. She'd asked her mother to have that done a couple of weeks earlier after the voices started again. She didn't say why.

Lately, it had been hard to sleep over the din of the leaves scratching against the windowpane. The voices in the wind mocked the way she dressed, the way she wore her hair, and the pooch in her belly that stuck out even in a tight skirt. They'd been at it again the night before.

"You might as well stop trying to get Seth back," a high-pitched woman's voice whined. "He doesn't want a girl with cellulite on the backs of her thighs."

"Stop it!" she said.

Clover took the pillow and put it over her face, hoping that muffling her own breathing would squelch the sounds. But it didn't work. Sometimes she heard her mother's voice or a twisted version of her own, like a record playing too fast or too slow. The voices said horrible things to her, told her what a bad and worthless person she was, that she couldn't do anything right.

It was all true, what they said. She skimmed her index finger over the scars on her wrists. The redness had paled to a dark pink. She remembered slicing into the bluish-white skin and watching her crimson inner-self flow into the bath water. She'd hoped the bloodletting would ease the pain and dispel the confusion that fogged her head. But instead, she woke up in the hospital with her wrists bandaged and an overwhelming sense of disappointment and failure.

Clover jumped up from the bed and opened the window. Maybe some fresh air would help clear the static. She took a deep breath and smelled the jasmine, comingled with the oleander and the roses. The scent was so sweet and so pure that her eyes brimmed with tears. She breathed in, deeper this time, yearning to cleanse some of the dirtiness she felt inside. She wished she could be as good as that smell.

She'd never really found a way to be happy, at least not since she was a little girl, when she played with dolls and had them talk to each other in different voices. But ever since she was in junior high school the voices seemed so much more real to her, as if they came from somewhere outside herself.

Clover would never forget the parent-teacher conference at Muirlands Middle School, where, for the first time, the voices started causing her real problems. With a smile frozen on her lips, the principal talked to Clover's parents about her as if she weren't sitting right there listening.

"It's not that she's stupid," Mrs. Quincy said. "Quite the opposite. She has a rather high IQ. It's more that she has no concentration and she talks to herself, which distracts the other students. But the most serious problem is that she fights with her classmates, even the boys. I think you should send her to that residential school in Santa Barbara we talked about the last time. We just can't deal with her here anymore."

Her parents took the principal's advice without asking Clover for her input. Clover was almost relieved, really. They'd think she was crazy if she told them whom she was talking to.

Once she got to the new school, the staff there didn't know what to do with her either, so they experimented with different drugs. But regardless of their shape or pastel hue, the pills shut off the vibrancy of the sounds and colors around her, and filled her mind with gray. She was better able to do her schoolwork, which pleased her parents, but the pills never made Clover happy. So one day she started tucking them under her tongue and spitting them out when the nurse wasn't looking.

She hated the doctors, too. All they cared about was declaring some new diagnosis. But they were never really sure what was wrong because she didn't respond well to any particular medication. How could she if she never took any of it consistently? Besides, Clover found a potion she liked better: a combination of Wild Turkey and marijuana. She smoked it with some of the other students and, for the first time in her life, she felt like she fit in.

Then things started going bad. The kids stopped inviting her to their little get-togethers. They gave her strange looks and said she was weird. Then, one Friday night when she was feeling edgy, she knocked on the door of a boy down the hall. But the boy closed the door in her face and laughed. She felt that familiar rage rise up inside her and banged on the door until he opened up, then pummeled him with her fists until his face was bloody.

She broke his nose, but didn't do him any permanent

damage. They placed her in the locked ward for two weeks so they could monitor her medications more closely. She finally decided to give in and take the stupid pills every day so she could graduate and get out of there.

She did all right for a few years after graduation, taking a few classes at the community college. But she eventually tired of the grayness again and stopped taking the pills. Cocaine helped her feel more like herself and enjoy the world. The sky was so blue it made her feel clean. The oranges and pinks of the setting sun were so painfully beautiful they made her cry. That's how she got the idea for the bloodletting and ended up in another hospital, this one specifically for psychiatric patients.

The doctors told her to stay away from cocaine. They also sent her to Narcotics Anonymous meetings at the hospital. But she didn't relate to the people there. They didn't know what it was like to be her. There was only one person she liked, a gay orderly named Fred, whom she affectionately called "Better Dead than Fred."

"It'll fry your brain, honey, bring on a psychotic episode faster than you can say 'Pass me another line,'" he told her. He gave her a book to read, which she kept next to her bed, called *Postcards from The Edge*, by Carrie Fisher, the *Star Wars* actress, about her time in rehab. Carrie was bipolar.

Clover could still conjure up the sterile smells of that hospital. She preferred to smell the jasmine, even if it meant living with her mother and stepfather, Steven. She wondered where her mother was. It was already three o'clock. Steven was the one who'd heard about the new beauty school in La Jolla and thought it would be good for Clover. He put her mother in charge of monitoring Clover's intake of medication, entrusting her to pass out pills from one of those little plastic organizers with a slot for each day. But Clover had gone back to her old ways when she felt Seth pulling away from her. She was sure it because she was becoming dull and boring. So she put the pills under her tongue, swallowed the orange juice, and then spat them out when her mother wasn't looking. She never knew the difference. Clover enjoyed feeling like herself again, even if the voices had come back. Trouble was, they were often louder, angrier, and more frightening than ever before.

Just then, the doorbell chimed downstairs, and Pepe, her mother's terrier, went crazy. She could hear him barking and clawing at the door with his nails. She was in no mood to talk to anyone, so she didn't go downstairs. She wanted to escape the voices, but she didn't know how. She peeled off her jeans and blouse, dropped her bra on the bedroom floor, and got in bed. She closed her eyes, but she couldn't relax.

Seth smiled at her from the pewter frame on her bedside table. She stroked his face through the glass. She loved him so much. All she'd wanted was for him to feel the same way about her. Was that too much to ask? She couldn't believe that Seth didn't love her a little during those nights they spent tumbling over the sheepskin rug on his living room floor. Or when they made love on the red, cold, and slippery satin sheets that soothed her sunburn and made her feel like she was on a Hollywood movie set.

Seth helped act out her fantasies. He let her be in charge, get on top of him and tease him. He told her how soft her skin was, how much he loved her legs wrapped around him, and that kissing her was like being on vacation from the rest of his life. He talked sexy to her while they were making love, touching a place in her that no one else had. He made her feel wanted in a way she never had before. But then he used his possession of that special place inside her to take advantage, to get her to do what he wanted. He used it to hurt her.

She clutched the baby blue blanket she'd had since her seventh birthday, the one her mother gave her when the emotional troubles started coming on.

"This blanket will protect you from the monsters," her

mother said. "At night, it will take you flying over magic kingdoms with gold temples and neon flowers. And when you take a nap in the afternoon, it will skim over fields of yellow daffodils, red tulips, and four-leaf clovers. That's why we named you Clover, sweetie, because we knew you'd be lucky in life."

Of course, the blanket never took her anywhere and it never protected her from anything. It grew thin and worn and became covered with little balls she would pull off when she had to grasp onto something, so she wouldn't go over the edge.

Seth used to tell her he liked that about her. "Clover," he'd say, "you're so on the edge. You're different from any girl I've ever met. We have this, I don't know, special chemistry."

But there had been no more teetering on the edge for the past couple of weeks. She'd finally fallen into that lonely, dark vortex and couldn't find her way out.

She pulled the covers more snugly around her neck. The thought that she shouldn't do any coke only made her want it more. She had to think. But she was so tired. Going shopping hadn't helped at all. She'd spread her new clothes over the bedspread so she could look at them, but she didn't feel like hanging them up. They could just lie there for all she cared. No one slept on that side of the bed anyway.

Clover sat up abruptly, reached for her purse and retrieved her little glass vial. Dumping a pile of coke onto the hand-held mirror she kept in her nightstand, she drew the white powder into a thick arc and inhaled a noseful through a rolled-up dollar bill. That comforting rush surged through her body. She wanted the high to last forever.

But as usual, it wasn't long before the high faded and she started plummeting down. She went over to the shelf where she kept her collection of figurines from *The Simpsons* cartoon and picked up the Bart and Marge dolls.

Marge was quieter than usual and her plastic face showed only a blank expression. Clover tried to find some life in Marge's eyes.

"Oh, now you have nothing to say," she said.

Clover threw the dolls against the wall. "No one understands!" she yelled. One of the figurines chipped a small piece of paint from the wall before landing with a dull thud on the carpet, but she still didn't feel any better. So she picked up the dolls, opened the window, and threw them into her mother's vermilion rosebushes.

Clover slammed the window shut and just stood there, staring at those roses again as images from the past few days swirled through her mind: arguing with Sharona about her afternoon tryst with Seth, then driving around La Jolla with a tuft of red hair on the passenger seat, but not remembering how it got there. Climbing into bed, sleeping fitfully, then waking up the next day to read in the paper that Sharona had been murdered. Running into the bathroom and throwing up.

Clover pulled on some jeans and a T-shirt and walked as fast as she could down the stairs, trying to leave the voices and the images behind. She paced around the living room and felt a pull toward her stepfather's study, which he called the Head Room. Steven owned two collections—guns and stuffed animal heads—which were displayed on two walls, facing each other.

Some of the guns were bulky and black with polished wooden handles. One was light and thin as a pen, like a spy would use. Her stepfather had warned her many times that no matter what the size or shape, these guns were designed to kill, through and through. He taught her how to hold a hunting rifle one afternoon while her mother was baking chocolate chip cookies. He took great delight in describing how bullets could enter human skin, how they'd dance around inside, tearing through tissue like a wooden spoon mixing cookie dough, ripping through bones as if they were walnuts.

Clover gazed at her reflection in the glass display case. The rifles cut across her face like the stripes of a wild animal. Steven was right about one thing: Guns were definitely one way to solve problems.

Her eyes looked back at her, black and ghoulish, as if she'd already left her body. Her head started to throb. Jakira, the head of a tiger Steven pretended he'd killed, was looking at her with that condescending way he had. "Oh, get over yourself," Clover told him.

She had to get out of the house. She thought maybe if she walked along the cliffs over Black's Beach and watched the hang gliders, she could find some peace. She opened the desk drawer where Stephen kept the keys to the gun cases, unlocked the latch, and took out a small revolver with a mother-of-pearl handle. She put it in her purse, hopped in her car and headed for the beach. She didn't notice Norman following her at a safe distance.

Chapter Forty-seven

Goode

Goode went straight from the jail to Clover Ziegler's house, and rang her doorbell, but he got no answer. He was getting so close to solving the case but he couldn't finish the job if she wouldn't answer the damn doorbell.

He decided to run down to the Village to grab a sandwich and then come back in an hour or so, checking in with Slausson and Fletcher to catch up on where they were.

The second time he came to Clover's house, he had better luck. He had just pulled into the driveway when he heard the sound of tires crunching on asphalt behind him, and turned to watch an older blond woman pull up in a Lamborghini. Clover's mother, he assumed. She got out, holding a tennis racquet, and walked angrily to the front door, which she slammed shut.

Goode had to admit he was a bit cynical about La Jolla matrons. He'd be at the beach, pretending to relax in the sun while he waited for a drug deal to go down and inevitably a woman in her midforties would lay her towel near his, produce a tube of suntan lotion from a straw bag and coyly glance his way.

"Beautiful day, isn't it?" she'd say when what she really meant was, "Why don't you come over here and spread this all over me?"

But he wasn't interested in these women. Not their flashy cars or unnaturally preserved faces, their lips puffy with collagen and the skin around their eyes stretched up like a cat's, their loneliness as loud as cheap perfume.

Clover's mother still seemed annoyed when she opened the door and saw Goode standing there. She took one look at him and dismissed him as unimportant.

"Hello, are you Mrs. Ziegler, Clover Ziegler's mother?" he asked cautiously.

"Yes, I'm Rosemary Stratton. And you are?" When her eyebrows went up, her forehead didn't even wrinkle. Botox, he thought.

"I'm Detective Ken Goode, ma'am, San Diego PD, Homicide," he said, flashing his badge and extending his hand. That sure had a nice ring to it. She took his fingers and gave them a perfunctory loose squeeze.

"Is your daughter home?" he asked.

"No, I'm afraid she's not," she said, glancing around him at the driveway.

"Would you mind if I came in and asked you a few questions?"

"Well, I suppose so. My damn tennis game got cancelled, so I have a few hours to kill before dinner," she said, barely able to move her face it was so tight. Botox, indeed.

She led him over to an ivory couch, spotless and stitched with satin thread in a floral pattern. Her tennis racket, purse, and sweater were sitting on a table next to a tall blue vase of flawless long-stemmed red roses. As she sat on the white sofa, she eyed Goode's faded black jeans with an expression of concern, as if perhaps they weren't clean enough to sit there. He ignored the look. They had just come out of the wash. She pointed him toward a chair next to her.

"Special occasion?" he said, pointing at the flowers.

"Why, yes," she said, her mood brightening. "You must be a good detective. Today is my wedding anniversary. It's been four years. We're going to spend the weekend at La-Vee. You know where that is, don't you?"

Goode smiled and nodded, choosing to ignore her patronizing tone. She was referring to La Valencia, a historical landmark and the most expensive hotel in La Jolla. "Yes, I grew up in La Jolla," he replied. "I'm sure that will be very nice."

Her voice took on a warmer tone now that she thought he was one of them. "Oh, really? Interesting . . . You're the third person looking to talk to my daughter today, you know," she said.

Goode felt his stomach lurch. "Oh?"

"Lucia, our maid, said there was a young man here this morning and a second one came by when I was home. It was that reporter who's been writing about all these murders."

Goode felt the acid rising in the back of his throat. "Really? What did he look like?"

"Young. Kind of disheveled. Newspaper ink on his face. He was very persistent."

Damn that Klein, he thought. It irked him that a cub reporter could manage to keep up with him, let alone get one step ahead.

"What about the other one?"

"Oh, I don't know. I'd have to ask Lucia. Her English

isn't very good, though. She described him as a nice young man who said he was a friend of Clover's and wanted to leave a gift for her up in her room. When I asked what it was, she was embarrassed to say that he wasn't actually carrying anything. I told her not to let strange people wander around the house in the future."

Goode was antsy to move on to the business at hand. "I'll get right to the point," he said. "What is Clover's relationship with Seth Kennedy?"

"He's the son of some friends of mine," she said. "They're very nice. Well-connected. Give fabulous parties. But frankly, I don't like their son much. He treated my daughter with no respect, like she was some sort of trailer trash."

"Did you know he's in jail for selling drugs in the bar where your daughter hangs out? And that he's been selling drugs to her?"

"No, I didn't." Her mouth went tight as she tried to hide her emotions.

"So, how long were they dating?" he asked.

Rosemary shook her head and sniffed, then cleared her throat. "I don't know that you could call it dating. They didn't go out to dinner or anything like that as far as I know. I kept trying to tell Clover that she deserved better, but it didn't do any good. Recently, he hasn't been calling and she's been very depressed about it. Then she lost a childhood friend. But you must know that already. She's a very emotional girl, you know."

He nodded, letting the conversation stall so that Rosemary would feel the need to talk. "It's just that Clover has been through a lot. She's not all that . . . stable, I guess."

"How's that?"

"I shouldn't have said anything. It's not relevant to your investigation," she said.

Goode pulled the anonymous letter out of his shirt pocket and handed it to her. "Well, actually, it might be. Tell me if you recognize this handwriting."

She pored over the note and she looked puzzled. "What is this?"

"Please, Mrs. Stratton, the handwriting?"

She placed it matter-of-factly on the table. "The reporter already read this to me, and, no, detective, I don't recognize the handwriting. What's this all about?"

"The author says she is Seth Kennedy's ex-girlfriend and accuses him of murdering three people. I think your daughter wrote this note."

She waved at the air with her hand. "Well, that's not her handwriting. And, why, might I ask, aren't you at the jail right now, asking Seth about it?"

"I was there this morning, as a matter of fact. The man says he didn't kill anyone and says he has alibis. We're holding him on the drug charges for now, but without more evidence, we can't charge him with murder."

She shook her head. "I thought La Jolla was so safe. I just can't believe this."

"There are bad people everywhere, doing bad things to each other," he said, standing up. "Do you mind if I have a look around Clover's room?"

"Whatever for?"

Because, he thought, he didn't have a search warrant and he wanted to look around. "I thought I might find another note in there," he said, "maybe something to confirm that Seth Kennedy really did commit these murders."

Rosemary looked worried. "Clover isn't in any trouble, is she?"

Goode almost felt sorry for the woman now. He needed to choose his words carefully. Suspicions were all he had at the moment, but he didn't want any evidence he found to be ruled out later. "No, not that I know of," he said.

The tension in her eyes eased a little and the color crept back into her cheeks as she pulled herself off the couch. "Well, since the maid just cleaned up in there, I guess it would be all right. Follow me."

She led him up the carpeted stairwell, her hips swaying side to side provocatively as she walked. She obviously had no clue as to his feelings about La Jolla matrons. The door to Clover's room was closed, but Rosemary walked right in. He wasn't about to stop her.

"Well, go ahead and look around," she said, guiding him along with her hand on his lower back.

Once she'd flounced out of the room, Goode sighed with relief to be alone, finally, in the palatial bedroom of Clover Ziegler. Like Tania's, Clover's walls were covered with framed art prints; but these pictures reflected fear, dark dreams and twisted perceptions.

He saw a mound of clothes on the bed and a pile of empty shopping bags on the floor. When he opened the mirrored double doors of the closet, he saw more of the same. She either had a voracious appetite for clothes or she was a compulsive spender. Because price tags were still attached to many of the items, he figured it was more likely the latter. He'd never seen so many shoes. Imelda Marcos would be jealous.

He crossed the room to get some air and clear his sinuses at the open window. From above, the garden was quite striking. He wondered how many times Clover had stood there, waiting for Seth to drive up.

On the bedside table, there were a couple of prescription drug vials, the names of which he didn't immediately recognize. He pulled open the top drawer and found a small mirror with traces of white powder and a rolled-up dollar bill. He turned around and caught a glimpse of himself in the mirror over the antique dressing table, with a backdrop of Munch's *The Scream*. He sat on the velvet-covered stool at the vanity, picked up a hand-painted Chinese box with thronelike legs and opened the hinged lid. Inside, displayed on the purple felt liner, were a collection of red fingernail tips, a lock of auburn hair and a signet ring with the initials KTW. His body shook.

"Oh my God," he whispered.

He couldn't believe what he was seeing. He'd merely been planning to come over and talk to Clover. He'd thought she might be able to corroborate the note, make some sense of this mess. But other than that fleeting thought, he never thought of her as the murderer. He closed the lid and prayed the box would still be there when he came back with a warrant.

"Mrs. Stratton?" he called as he jogged down the carpeted stairs. She was sitting on the couch, holding her martini and munching on one of her three olives.

"Ready for some coffee, handsome?"

"No, I'm sorry, I've really got to run. Can you tell me where I might be able to find your daughter? It's very important."

"Only if you come here first," she said, patting the couch next to her. "I went to the trouble of making a cappuccino for you."

This woman just wouldn't quit. "I'm really sorry, but I've been called out on an emergency. Please, Mrs. Stratton, do you know where she is?"

She sighed and looked out the window toward the pool. "She could be shopping over at University Towne Center. She might be at the Glider Port. Or she might be down at José's, drinking a margarita, for all I know."

"Okay, great, thanks. And sorry about the cappuccino, Mrs. Stratton."

She turned back to look at him, a sadness in her eyes. "You think I'm old enough to be your mother, don't you? That's why you're running out."

Not this. Not now, he thought. "No, Mrs. Stratton—"

"Rosemary, please."

"Listen, I've got a job to do. Really. It's nothing personal. I promise." He took her hand and gave it a squeeze. Her face brightened a little.

His heart was racing madly now. He thanked the woman and felt a slight twinge of regret. It wasn't going to be pretty the next time he saw her, after her daughter was arrested for murdering three people. As soon as he stepped outside, he got Stone on the phone and told him what he'd found. They agreed that Slausson and Fletcher should run over to Clover's to keep her from destroying the evidence while Stone got a telephonic warrant for the items in her bedroom and Goode made sure she didn't kill anybody else.

Goode drove as fast as he could over Mount Soledad and down through La Jolla Shores, the most direct route to Black's Beach. As he was looking for a parking spot in the dirt lot at the Glider Port above the beach, he saw a red Honda CRV out of the corner of his eye. He knew it was a popular vehicle, but he put his car in reverse to take a quick look for Maureen's decal that featured the Christian fish symbol with legs, a political statement favoring evolution over the creation theory. And there it was.

"Oh, shit," he said, emphasizing the t.

All he could do was pray she was down at Black's, surfing. If not, he hoped to God that he had gotten there in time.

Chapter Forty-eight

Norman

Norman followed Clover to the Glider Port and watched her stride over to the cliffs with purpose, her purse bouncing off her hip and her long hair catching the wind behind her. As he got closer, he noticed the muscular definition in her arms.

"Clover," he said. She didn't turn around, so he said it a little louder. "Clover."

She whipped her taut body around with a frantic expression as she tried to place him. She clutched her purse as if it contained something precious.

With his notebook tucked in his back pocket, he reached his hand toward her. "Hi. I'm Norman Klein."

When she didn't move to take it, he was confused. He'd been so sure that she had authored the letter. "With the *Sun-Dispatch*," he prompted her. "You wrote me that letter?"

Her eyes were strange and glassy and all pupils. "Letter? What letter?" she asked, frowning.

This wasn't the answer he was expecting. "Well, let's forget that for now. I was wondering if we could talk for a minute. I'm writing a story about Sharona Glass and the other murder victims. I know you two were friends."

Clover paused and then started pacing back and forth. "I'm not really in the mood to talk," she said, her voice tense. She stopped and stared out at the ocean. "What do you want to know?"

Norman could tell he was going to have to do a real sales job. She was so jumpy, he thought she must be on something. He could see her grinding her teeth together. "You know, what kind of person Sharona was, how you'd like people to remember her. And then we can talk about Seth."

Clover frowned. "I don't know," she said in a faraway voice. "I don't feel very well."

"I can understand that, losing your friend and all."

"It's more complicated than that," Clover snapped. She walked toward the bluff, her eyes following a speedboat as it cruised along the shore and continued south. Norman could see her lips moving, like she was talking to herself.

"Quiet," she hissed. "Stop it."

"What?" he said.

"Nothing."

He stepped a little closer and tried again. "You come up here a lot?"

She nodded, glancing at him briefly. "I came up here to be alone. I've got a lot on my mind."

Norman felt sorry for her. He wished he didn't have a job to do so he could just talk to her, try to make her feel better. He could tell she'd been through a lot. She seemed so lost. She intrigued him.

"So, how old are you, Clover?"

"Twenty-three."

"This week must've been pretty tough for you, huh?"

The speedboat was a tiny white spot now.

"More than you know," she said.

She turned to look at him again, her blue eyes suddenly blazing into his. They were so intense it startled him. "What did you say your name was?"

"Uh, Norman. Klein."

"Well, Norman, I lost a couple of friends this week," she said, her voice turning sharp again. "And you know what? I'm not really sure how I feel about it."

Norman nodded to encourage her to continue. "Did you see my story in this morning's paper?"

"No," she said.

"Well, I wrote about the letter I was talking about, the letter that blames your boyfriend, Seth Kennedy, for killing three people in P.B."

Norman watched for Clover's reaction, but there was none. They say the eyes are windows to the soul, but hers seemed so empty. Clover started talking fast in a kind of singsong voice, as if he hadn't mentioned the letter.

"Sharona and I have been friends for a long time, but we've definitely had our ups and downs," she said.

Norman hadn't gotten the knack yet for writing fast while standing. He needed to rest his notebook on his knee. "How about we go back and sit on the bench?"

Clover ignored him and kept talking. "Sharona had an affair with my dad while I was away at boarding school. My mom found them having sex on our couch one afternoon. Sharona tried to be my friend again when I was in the hospital. Then I just found out she slept with Seth a week ago. Then he slept with Tania, who I was just starting to get to know. I loved him, but nobody cares about my feelings." She turned to Norman and frowned again. "You're writing this down?"

He tried to respond calmly, but it was hard. "Yes, I'm writing a story for the newspaper."

Clover shook her head. "I don't want this in the paper. It's personal."

Norman felt that panic again. Why did this keep happening to him? "Well, there's no guarantee I'll use it. I won't know until I hear the rest of the story."

Clover turned to leave. "I've got to go."

Norman reached out and touched her arm. "No, wait. Don't go. I want to talk to you."

She batted his hand away. "Don't touch me."

Why was she so upset? "Sorry. I didn't mean to offend you." She seemed highly agitated.

"Just leave me alone," she said.

He had to get her to stay. He had to. "C'mon. People will be interested in this. If you know who killed those girls, you have to tell me. Please."

She turned around and crossed her arms, her purse still clutched in one hand. "I don't know who killed those girls. And besides, people who read the newspaper don't care who betrayed me."

"I care," he said, "and I think other people will, too. Is that how you felt about Seth? And Sharona? That they betrayed you?"

"Yes," she said.

They stood in silence for a minute, facing the ocean. He wondered what she saw out there. Norman had so many questions, but he had to try to get her to focus. "Why were you in the hospital?" he asked.

Clover spoke in a low tone, conspiratorially, as she watched another boat zigzag across the water. "They thought I was crazy, but I'm not. I just feel things a lot sometimes."

"Uh-huh." Norman felt even more sorry for this pretty blond woman. Her moods were so up and down. But she was opening up to him, and that was all that mattered.

"Promise you won't print what I'm telling you," she said.

He decided he would try to talk her into letting him use the stuff she was saying after she was done telling her story. "Sure, whatever you want."

"Okay. So, I did cocaine. It made me feel good, not like the pills they were always giving me. My mom wanted me to go to rehab, but I told her I didn't need that."

Norman wondered if she was coked up now. "Really?"

"Yeah, well, I don't know. My parents and I talked about the drugs and the whole Sharona thing in family group therapy. It never did any good, though. I hate doctors."

"How did you and Sharona end up at the beauty school together?"

"When I was in the hospital, Sharona told my stepdad she was going, so he decided I should go, too. Things were going pretty well with Seth and I thought maybe we might get married someday. Then things changed."

Now they were getting to the good stuff, Norman thought. "So what happened between you?"

"He screwed Tania. They were all over each other in the bar that night, right in front of me," she said. Her voice broke as she started to cry, and the words came streaming out. "I followed them back to her apartment that night and then when he didn't come out, I knew what they were doing in there, so . . ."

Clover stopped talking. Her makeup was running

down her face in streaks and Norman didn't really know quite what to do. He was so new at this. He just wanted her to keep talking. "Go on," he said, cautiously. "It's okay. I'm glad you decided to confide in me. I think if we put all this in the paper, then maybe everyone will understand better what happened."

"Well, it's all Seth's fault," she said. "He's the devil and he really messed with my head." She turned abruptly. "I've got to go."

"Miss Ziegler," a man said from behind them. "I'm glad I've found you."

Norman swiveled around. It was Detective Goode. "What's up, Detective?" Norman said.

Goode's tone was short. "Listen, have either of you seen a tall, pretty young woman with long brown hair?"

"Nope," Norman said. He thought he saw Goode's face relax a bit.

"Good," the detective said. "So, how about you go back to your car, Mr. Klein. I need to talk to the young lady alone. Police business."

"But I'm right in the middle of an important interview," Norman said, hoping the detective would understand from his tone and the look on his face just how important it was.

Goode looked serious and a little high-strung. He wasn't getting it. "Well, I'm sure my interview is more important than yours, and I don't think Miss Ziegler and I need any company."

That's when Norman felt Clover's arm come around his neck from behind and the pressure of a cold, metal object poking into his temple.

"I'm not going anywhere with you," Clover told Goode in a thick, hard-edged voice.

Norman didn't really want to think about what the cold object was. "Clover, what are you doing?" Norman asked, hoping she or the detective would answer him.

"Everything's going to be okay, Norman," she said,

"You and I are going to get in my car and this cop is going to leave us alone."

Goode's voice went soft. "Clover, why don't you put the gun down and we can talk about this."

"I've already told Norman everything I have to say. You can ask him."

Norman felt faint. "I can't breathe," he managed to choke out.

Goode took a step toward them and held out his hands. "Why don't you let Norman go? Then you and I can talk."

"No," she said firmly.

Clover moved her arm down to Norman's chest, crushing his left arm against his side. She was pointing the gun at Goode now. The fingers on Norman's left hand, which were gripping his notebook, were starting to cramp up. He couldn't lose those notes. Not now. Clover started backing away from the detective, pulling Norman along with her. His feet shuffled back, matching her steps as they made their way down a grassy slope, moving in the opposite direction from the parking lot. They seemed to be heading toward the edge of the cliff, where the hang glider pilots jumped off. He wished he had eyes in the back of his head. The drop down to the beach had to be two hundred feet.

Norman started thinking about his short-lived journalism career and all the things he'd never get to do. Like work his way up to a job at the *Los Angeles Times*, see a stripper, and go on a date with Lulu. Have a family. Make enough money to buy a new car, a new house. Or tell Al and Big Ed what he really thought of them. His body started to go limp.

"Stand up. You're too heavy that way," Clover ordered.

Norman wished he knew how close they were to the edge. Why was this happening to him? Clover jerked him back and down a sharper slope, hard. His legs slipped out from under him and he fell backward, head-first, into the dirt. Then everything went black.

He wasn't sure how long he was out, but when he

came to, he was on the ground, looking up at the sky, and pain was shooting through his head, neck, and back. Clover was standing over him, pointing the gun at his face. She was going to kill him. He almost peed his pants.

"Get up," she said.

Norman felt dizzy as he slowly rose to his feet. His vision had gone all blurry. He wondered if he'd gotten a concussion. They were on a ledge about five feet lower than where they'd been and Norman couldn't see Goode anywhere. A few moments later, the detective appeared at the top of the slope, pointing his gun at them. Norman hoped he was a good shot.

Clover didn't budge. "I told you to leave us alone," she shouted up at Goode. "And you'd better stop pointing that gun at us or I'll shoot him."

Before Norman had time to react, Clover grabbed him by the wrist, jerked him up, and turned him around so she was behind him again, using his body as a shield. He felt her gun jabbing into his side as she closed her elbow around his neck once more.

"Okay, Clover, I'll put the gun down, but there's no way out for you now," the detective called down to them. "I saw your collection of souvenirs in your bedroom, the ones you took when you killed Tania Marcus, Sharona Glass, and Keith Warner."

"Whaat?" Norman said in disbelief. So, Clover was the killer? This woman holding a gun to his head? He wouldn't have believed it fifteen minutes ago. He felt like a total idiot.

"I didn't kill anyone," Clover said in a low voice, directly into Norman's ear. "I went to her apartment complex Saturday night to tell her I was hurt that she'd slept with Seth, but when I was in the parking lot I saw some guy wearing a backward baseball cap go into her apartment. I figured she was probably doing him, too, so I left."

Norman wasn't sure what to think. He could hear her breathing harder and faster. She was strong, crazy, and high on who knows what. He didn't want to do anything to piss her off. As he saw it, this could go one of two ways. She would either throw him over the cliffs or Goode would save him and he would write the best story of his life. He tried to think positive thoughts.

"I know you're not well, Clover," Goode yelled over the wind. "Maybe we can find a sympathetic judge and get you some help, send you to a hospital instead of a prison. But there's no chance if you don't let Norman go."

"I'm never going back to a hospital," she told Norman.

"Prison would be worse," he said.

Goode made a move like he was going to come down the bluff, but Clover started shuffling backward again, forcing Norman to come with her, so Goode stopped. Norman felt so powerless. He hated not being able to see where she was taking him.

"So, if you didn't kill anyone, why are you holding a gun to my head?"

"Because I was in the middle of doing something private here and the two of you interrupted," she hissed at him.

"Don't come any closer," Clover shouted up at Goode, "or I'll push him over."

Out the corner of his eye, Norman could see they were only a foot or two from the edge. One false step and he was a dead man. He started shaking and couldn't stop. Clover let up a little on her grip around his neck as she moved them along the ledge. He was going to lose it if he didn't come up with a plan. She may be serious that she wasn't going to hurt him, but they were awfully close to the edge.

"Clover?" he asked, tentatively.

"Not now," she said.

But Norman knew he had to do something. He was fighting for his life. "If you let me go I'll get your story out. People will understand that. If I tell it right, maybe they'll let you off with an insanity plea."

"I'm not insane," she said. "And I told you I didn't kill anyone."

"Well, temporary insanity then. You know, a crime of passion."

Clover stopped moving. He wondered if she was considering his suggestion.

"They'll believe you," he said. "I know they will."

"Be quiet," she said, tightening her grip before she pulled him down a dirt slope with her.

Still dizzy, he let his mind go blank. This is the end, he thought. Norman felt a rush of relief as they stumbled a few feet down onto another ledge that he hadn't realized was there. That said, they were that much farther from Goode and not close enough to yell up at him anymore. He could see Goode, staring down at them and then up the coast.

That's when Norman heard a beating noise, a low thunder. As it got louder, Norman realized it was the low roar of an aircraft approaching. Maybe the sheriff's air rescue helicopter or the Marines were coming to save him. Goode or someone else must've called for help.

"You hear that?" Clover asked. She whirled them both around to see a helicopter about a half mile to the north, heading right for them. Her fingers were still gripping his arm and he had no idea what she was going to do. As the chopper got closer, a man leaned out of the window with a bullhorn and said: "Drop your weapon and let the hostage go."

Norman's toes were only a few inches from the edge. He could see nude men sprawled out on towels below, their faces turned up toward the helicopter. There were no more ledges, only the final drop.

Norman felt Clover let go of his neck and step away, but he stood still, not wanting to move for fear she was still pointing the gun at the back of his head. She stepped forward so that she was standing next to him and took his hand. The gun was still in her other hand, but she wasn't aiming it at anyone. She was going to try and take him with her.

"Look at those people down there. They seem so free," she said softly. "I want to be free."

"Drop your weapon and let the hostage go," the man with the bullhorn repeated.

The wind whistled in Norman's ears and blew the hair into his eyes. "Clover, it doesn't have to end this way," he said. "I don't want to die. You don't have to either."

"I was never planning to hurt you or anyone else," Clover said, dropping his hand and the gun, too. She leaned into his face and kissed him on the cheek. "Bye, Norman."

Then, in one swift motion, she stepped off the cliff. Partway down, as her body sliced through the air, she spread her arms like an angel, a strange grin on her face. Oddly, it seemed to slow her fall a bit.

"Oh, my God," Norman whispered.

She hit the sand a couple seconds later, a crumpled mess of bones. He stepped back from the ledge and stared out at the ocean, shaking. He heard footsteps behind him and felt a hand on his shoulder.

"Hey, kid. You okay?" It was Goode, who kneeled down and put Clover's gun in his pocket.

Norman nodded. He just felt numb. In shock, really. "Yeah, I'm all right, I guess. You?"

Goode nodded back. "Yeah, I just wish I could've stopped her from jumping."

"I know," Norman said. "But you can't blame yourself. . . . I guess some people just don't want to be saved."

They looked down at the beach, where a crowd of naked men and a few surfers in their wet suits had gathered around the body and were craning their necks to watch the helicopter descend.

"Please move away from the body," the bullhorn voice said.

The people scattered like insects, grabbing their towels and running, their flesh jiggling. The sand blew every which way as the helicopter set down on the shore.

As Norman stood there next to the detective, he felt happy to be alive. But at the same time, he felt slightly ashamed that he'd ended up with a story out of this.

"That poor girl," Norman said. "She was so mixed-up, I don't know what to think. . . . Did she really kill those people?"

"It sure looks that way, kid," Goode said. "I searched her room an hour ago and I found a box with the tips of red fingernails, a lock of red hair, and a ring with Keith Warner's initials. And you can print that this time."

"Maybe not," Norman said.

"What do you mean?" Goode asked.

"Well, right before she jumped, she told me she didn't kill anyone, and that she never planned to hurt me or anyone else, whatever that means. She said she was about to go talk to Tania on Saturday night, but some guy wearing a backward baseball cap got to Tania's apartment ahead of her, so she never went in."

"Really?" Goode asked, growing silent. "No shit."

"Then she said she wanted to be free, and she just jumped, almost like she thought she could fly."

The two stood there for a minute before Goode blurted out, "You all right, kid? I've got to go."

Chapter Forty-nine

Goode

Goode jogged back to his van in the parking lot, his mind racing with what had just happened. Now he wasn't sure what was going on. Why would Clover deny being the killer if she was about to kill herself? She had nothing to gain by lying.

Goode was sure Stone would have the telephonic warrant for Clover's bedroom by then, and he wanted to go back and secure the gilded box before it disappeared. He also felt a moral obligation to be the one to personally notify Mrs. Stratton about her daughter's suicide, a duty he did not relish on her wedding anniversary. He took some solace in the fact that she had come on to him that afternoon—on said wedding anniversary.

He ran through the suspects and witnesses in his head, scanning his memory, and the only guy he could think of wearing a backward baseball cap was Jake. The problem was, Jake had no apparent motive. That said, if he had murdered Tania, it would make sense for him to return to the alley to see if she was still there, maybe wait until the cops arrived so he could tell them he had just happened upon her. Then he could touch the body, accidentally on purpose, so he'd have an excuse in case they found his DNA on her. If that's the way it played out, Goode would feel like a sap.

He punched Stone's number into his cell phone so they could come up with a game plan. While he was waiting for the sergeant to answer, he riffled through his little notebook for the scribblings he'd made about the men in the diary entries.

There it was. The notation about J. the guy Tania had made out with at the strip club. Jake didn't seem like her type, but then again, she had definitely been into experimentation.

Stone sounded a little harried. He said he was right in the middle of setting up a press conference at headquarters so the chief could reassure the public that the residents of La Jolla and Pacific Beach were officially safe now that Clover Ziegler was dead.

"I'd tell him to hold off if I were you," Goode said.

"What now?" Stone groaned.

Goode filled him in and Stone was just as befuddled as

he was about the new lead. They agreed to hold off on the press conference for a few hours while they pursued the Jake angle further, starting with a quick call to Goode's buddy, Artie, who happened to be the ME investigator assigned to this series of murders. Byron was over at the hospital with his wife and new baby, so Stone dubbed Goode the lead detective for the moment.

Goode called Artie as he drove to Clover's house. Now, more than ever, he was chomping at the bit for Tania's toxicology results and a definitive cause of death. With all these mixed clues, he felt in his gut that the results held the key. What the hell had Jake been doing in her apartment? And furthermore, why would he have killed her?

"Artie, dude. Please tell me all those test results are in," he pleaded. "I'm dying here."

"Hey, Goode. You're in luck. I was just getting ready to call you guys," Artie said. "You know how you said you found coke and meth at either end of Tania's table? Well, she's got some alcohol, an extremely high level of methamphetamine, a small amount of amphetamine, a barely detectable level of ephedrine, and a small amount of Rohypnol in her blood. But there was no cocaine."

"What's that mean in English?"

"Based on the autopsy report, I'd say it means that someone knocked her out with a date-rape drug, got all excited, but then lost it on her stomach, if you know what I mean. Then I'd say she did some meth, sometime after the Rohypnol had worn off. Only it looks like it was such incredibly pure meth that she died from a heart attack or arrhythmia. Then someone tied something around her neck, really tight, to make it look like she died of strangulation."

Before Goode could absorb all that information, Artie went on. "But wait, listen to this. In Sharona Glass' body, we found coke but no meth, and this time, she was strangled *before* she died. What do you think?"

Goode paused for a minute, and then ventured a guess. "Well, given the sexual nature of this case, I suppose she could've allowed someone to tie off her air passage, possibly as foreplay, cutting off oxygen to the brain to try to get even higher."

"Could be."

"Or maybe the killer pretended to be playing around, but had planned to kill her all along."

"That also could be."

"Or the third option is that she was doing some coke and someone she knew came up and choked her from behind. Her body's position on the floor looked like she had been pulled backward."

"Right. By the way, there were no signs of struggle on Tania's body other than her broken nails. And, oh yeah. I meant to tell you—I took a closer look at them and they weren't broken off. They were torn off. Like the killer wanted souvenirs."

Goode sat in silence for a minute, as he tried to process it all.

"Goode, you there?" Artie asked.

"Yeah, sorry. That was a lot to take in all at once. Thanks."

Goode tried calling Stone back, but the line was busy. He didn't want to waste any time, so he called the crime lab and asked to speak to George. They called him G-man because his lifelong—yet unfulfilled—dream was to join the FBI.

"Hey, G-man, I don't know if you've already sent these results on to Sergeant Stone, but I'm following a train of thought here. Did we ever hear what caliber gun shot Keith Warner?"

"Yeah, the ballistics tests came back last night. It was a nine millimeter," George said.

Goode pulled Clover's gun out of his pocket. It looked like a 9mm, but they'd have to run a test on the bullet and see if it matched the one that shot Keith.

"How about the crusty splooge on her stomach? Was there a match with Paul Walters?"

"The DNA tests aren't back yet."

"How 'bout those cigarette butts?"

"The two in Tania's trash were Camels, but they were the only ones that were the Turkish Gold brand. The other two you guys gave me, from Alison Winslow and Jack O'Mallory, were Camel Lights and regular Camels."

"Please tell me you have a match with the ones in the trash."

"You bet."

Goode's heart was practically beating out of his chest. "The suspense is killing me," he said.

"The butt you got from that Jake kid, the one who found the body, was Turkish Gold brand, too. You pulled it out of his planter, right?"

"Righto."

"And guess what?"

"What?" Goode was feeling the kind of euphoria he'd heard about from drug users, but this was the real thing.

"Well, the guy had taken only a few puffs, so there was plenty of paper left to pick up traces of the high-purity methamphetamine he must have had on his fingers. And just in case you're still wondering, his DNA tests match, too. We not only have his cigarette butts from the first victim's trash, but his DNA matches a hair we found embedded in the second victim's neck wound."

"You are kidding me."

"No, I'm not."

"So the meth on the Camel butt must have been on his fingers, right?"

"Yeah, like he'd been swimming in it. More than likely, he'd been cooking it."

Goode's brain was spinning. A biochemistry master's program indeed. Free access to a lab was more like it—a particular bonus if it was full of graduate student geeks who didn't notice that weird chemical smell.

He still didn't have a motive for Jake, but he couldn't argue with the forensic evidence. If Jake was cooking meth, he had to be selling it, too, and that would explain why Goode found no stash at Seth's house. So why hadn't One-Eye mentioned Jake during the interview? Maybe because the two of them had a side deal, and if Seth took all the heat, One-Eye and Jake could lie low until the cops stopped coming by. Theoretically, anyway.

So if Paul gave Tania the date-rape drug late Saturday afternoon, Goode figured that Jake must have come over while she was still groggy, they did the meth, and it gave her a heart attack. But then why the strangulation wounds? Maybe Jake freaked out, and wanted it to look like someone else did it. Seth was an easy target because he and Tania had been seen dancing in public on Friday night and had a date planned for Saturday. But where did Sharona and Keith fit in?

"Hello?"

"Yeah, sorry. My mind was going in a million different directions," Goode said. "You done good, G-man. You're all right."

Goode still had a lot of dots to connect, but he felt like he was very, very close. At least he could now tie Jake to the crime scene and to Tania's and Sharona's bodies.

"Hey, one other thing," G-Man said. "Seth Kennedy's fingerprints were all over the plastic wrap on the heroin. Stone was telling me all of his stories—'I was framed,' 'Someone planted this stuff,' and 'My dead best friend did it'—and I'm here to tell you that they are all unadulterated bullshit."

"I figured, but I am still so glad to hear you say that. I can't wait to watch his face when I tell him. You've made my day twice in five minutes."

Goode called Stone back and this time he answered

right away. Goode filled him in on everything that Artie
and G-Man had just told him, along with his list of theories. Stone was just as excited as he was. They agreed
that Stone should get back on the horn to the DA to get
telephonic warrants to search Jake's house and his lab at
UCSD. Stone said he would meet Goode at the house so
Slausson and Fletcher could go up and hold the lab until
the warrant came through, just in case he and Goode
missed Jake in P.B.

If they moved fast enough, they could stop the kid
from dumping his most recent batch of meth even if the
warrants were still being processed. They both were convinced that Jake wouldn't have set up a lab off campus.
Why bother when the state was paying the rent?

Goode said he'd drive down the other side of Mount
Soledad to P.B. to meet Stone as soon as he finished taking care of business at Clover's house.

As predicted, Goode did, in fact, feel like a sap. Plus,
he felt stupid for not connecting Jake's UCSD biochemistry master's program and the high-quality meth angle
sooner. But then again, it hadn't occurred to Stone either.
And it had been there the whole time, right in front of
their faces.

He was grinning as he pulled into Clover's driveway,
but his good humor faded as soon as he started thinking about the task at hand—notifying Rosemary Stratton of her only daughter's death. Goode told Slausson
and Fletcher what was going on, and sent them off to
UCSD. Then he stuffed a pair of latex gloves and a couple evidence bags into his jacket pocket, tried to calm
down for a minute, and walked up to the front door to
do the deed.

Rosemary Stratton cried fitfully in Clover's room,
where she clutched her daughter's nubby blanket as
Goode packed the gilded box and its contents carefully
in the evidence bags. She stopped for a moment to tell
him she'd asked the maid for the name of the young

man who had come over earlier that day to put something in Clover's room. The maid didn't remember his name, but she did recall that he had been wearing his baseball cap backward.

Chapter Fifty

Goode

As Goode was driving up to Jake's house, he saw the kid get into his Saab. He quickly called Stone, who luckily was parked down the street a ways. Stone said not to worry, he was already on it and would follow the suspect to his destination, which, as they both suspected, was his lab at UCSD. Stone told him he had already gotten the telelphonic warrant for Jake's house and to go ahead inside.

Fletcher and Slausson were waiting for Jake in the UCSD parking lot, where they surprised him as he was getting out of his car. Stone was right behind them. Jake tried to play innocent, but it didn't take them long to find his latest meth cocktail in the lab. He'd stored the raw stuff in the refrigerator in an opaque plastic orange juice jug. It was all ready to be cooked up, just as soon as the nerds left for the night to play video games.

Meanwhile, Goode picked the lock on Jake's front door and started his own search. In a trash bag in the garage, he found a hoard of empty boxes of generic Sudafed, which contained pseudoephedrine, the main ingredient used by meth cookers. Since the law limited consumers to buying cold medicine containing no more than nine grams of the stuff, Goode figured Jake must have driven all over town to collect enough to make just one batch. Jake obviously knew what he was doing.

But the coup de grace, the king of all dot connectors, came when Goode opened the lid on Jake's toilet tank and found a 9mm pistol in a plastic Ziploc bag. That clinched it. Jake's fingerprints would surely be on the gilded box, on Tania's coffee table, and, in case there was any doubt, on the gun that shot the bullet into Keith's head. Plus his hair in the neck wound and the cigarette butts. His ass was Goode's.

Slausson and Fletcher took Jake down to the station to book him, and Stone came back to join Goode at Jake's house so that they could hold the long-awaited news conference. It was always good to show the public that the law was cracking down on serial murderers, especially when they were also meth manufacturers. The local patrol officers helped them out by keeping the media from going inside the house.

A throng of reporters, including Ready Rhona, huddled together with their cameramen on the sidewalk and front lawn at Jake's, while Goode and Stone waited inside for the mayor, Chief Thompson, and Lieutenant Wilson to arrive. There were so many of them, they spilled out into the street and were joined by curious neighbors. When the natives started getting restless, Stone told them it would be just a little while longer.

"What's taking so long?" one of the reporters called out. "Justice delayed is justice denied."

"Not tonight," Goode retorted. "Be patient. We promise it will be worth the wait."

Once everyone arrived, the chief told the press about Jake's lab bust and said he would also be charged with the recent series of murders, which would make him eligible for the death penalty. The crowd cheered.

Some arrogant reporter named Jerry from the *Sun-Dispatch* was there, looking very put out. Goode wondered where Norman was. Probably still giving TV interviews at the Glider Port, he chuckled to himself. He figured Jerry was jealous that Norman, the cub reporter, was getting so much attention. But hell, he deserved it after what he'd been through.

As the press conference was breaking up, Goode saw Maureen standing behind all the cameras. Her house was right around the corner, after all.

"Hey bro, what's up?" she said as she approached. She smiled with a trace of the trademark Goode family sarcasm.

"Where have you been the past three days?" he asked, and not all that nicely. "And why haven't you returned any of my calls? Obviously you heard what's been going on?"

Maureen rolled her eyes. "Hey, hey, calm down and I'll tell you. I saw the helicopter at Black's, but I didn't know you were involved until I was driving home and saw you standing up there in front of all these cameras. My famous big brother. What a scene," she said, moving in to hug him.

"Yeah, pretty much," he said, still waiting for an explanation on her whereabouts.

She pulled back but kept her hand on his shoulder. "Listen, I didn't tell you because I knew you wouldn't approve, but Mitch and I hooked up last weekend. We decided to fly to Tahoe for a little love excursion, so I've been out of town. I was listening to what you guys said at the press conference and I could not believe this all happened in my neighborhood while I was gone. Did you know I dated that Keith guy a few times? I knew all those girls from the Pumphouse, too. Talk about freaky."

Goode nodded and sighed. "Yes, as a matter of fact, I did know. So now you can understand why I was so worried. You really scared me," he said quietly. It was just like her to do that—run away from him when she knew he wouldn't like something she was doing.

"Well, I hate to admit it, but I guess you had a right to

worry this time," she said, pausing. "Look, why don't we have dinner in the next couple of days and you can tell me all about it. I'll call you," she said, turning to give him a little wave.

Goode was still reeling with all the adrenaline flowing through his body as he drove back to the station to take care of some loose ends. Jake was in custody and they were going to get all their ducks in a row before interviewing him in jail the next morning. They had him cold, so it was really just to fill in some holes. After running around with very little sleep for five days, he needed to try to come down slowly. Once he got home and had a beer or two, he knew he'd crash with exhaustion. Then he remembered Alison was at his place. He wasn't looking forward to dealing with that situation.

Goode went home after filling out about ten million reports to find Alison sitting on the couch, reading one of his crime novels.

"Hey, I saw you on the news," she said, grinning

"Yeah," he said, heading into the kitchen to grab a beer. He didn't feel much like talking.

Alison must've picked up on his mood because she said she was going to take a shower. Goode settled back into the couch and tried to settle down. There he'd been, following the escort service, the gang-bang, the drug-ring and the frame-up theories, thinking it was a male murderer because of the sperm, then a female, then a male again, but not for the reasons he'd originally assumed. He had to give himself a little credit, though. He'd figured it out in only five days.

Nonetheless, he'd been chasing the wrong suspects, ignoring the basic rule that the guy who finds the body always remains a suspect, and for some reason, he hadn't seen all he should have in the evidence. The chief and the lieutenant made a big deal out of his work at the press conference, but he still couldn't help feel the praise rang empty somehow. Of course he'd played it to the media like he'd known the truth all along. But inside, he knew he'd been on the wrong track for days. And it bothered him.

It was also disappointing he hadn't been able to save Clover Ziegler from herself. Three people, well, actually four now, were dead, and Goode had been as successful in preventing her from taking a dive off that cliff as he had in stopping his own mother from jumping. History kept repeating itself and there was nothing he could do to stop it. But at least Clover hadn't taken Norman with her and Maureen had come out of all this unscathed.

Goode had worked for years to get to Homicide, and now that he'd proven himself, the transfer was just a matter of paperwork. Still, he felt confused. You know what they say: Be careful of what you ask for, you might get it. He'd expected to be more excited. Maybe he was just tired. He'd probably feel better after he took a few days off.

When Alison emerged from the bathroom, her curly hair was wet, her cheeks were pink, and her eyes were bright. She was wearing one of his flannel shirts and a pair of his running shorts. At any other time, she would've been a welcome sight. She put a hand on his shoulder, and said, "I can see it on your face. You're being too hard on yourself."

Goode thought she was sweet for trying to make him feel better, but she didn't understand. He wanted to wallow for a while in his mistakes. He got up and went to the kitchen to get another beer, and then sat in the chair so she couldn't sit next to him. He was too tired to deal with their limbo-land situation.

Norman's words echoed in his head: *Some people just don't want to be saved.*

Goode wavered over whether he should try to talk to Alison about what was really bugging him, even though he wasn't exactly sure himself.

"You know, even if Seth didn't kill anyone, I still think

this was largely his fault—him and his bad behavior," she said. "He got everyone killed with his arrogance and his libido. I sure hope he gets what he deserves."

"Yeah," Goode said. "Me too. Unfortunately, his rich dad has hired him a big fancy lawyer who probably plays golf with most of the judges. I'll do my best to make sure he doesn't get off easy, though, that's for sure."

"That's good."

Goode had made up his mind. He would tell her at least part of what was going through his head. "You know, when I was standing on that cliff at Black's, watching Clover drag that poor reporter around with a gun to his head, all the training in the world couldn't have helped me. Situations like that, I mean, they're all different, and when you're dealing with someone who has mental problems you have no idea what they're going to do."

Alison gave him a sympathetic smile. But pity was not what he wanted. "I'm sure you did the best you could," she said. "I've seen you think fast on your feet. Look how you saved me from Tony."

"Well, that was different. He didn't have a gun."

She shook her head. "You didn't know that. I told you he could get physical. And come on, you even told me you wondered whether he could've killed Tania."

"Yeah, that's true. I did."

"So, stop being so hard on yourself."

Goode looked at Alison smiling at him and wondered how he really felt about her. He had developed a strange obsession with a dead woman because it was safe. Alison was very sweet, but he didn't know whether he was the best person for her to get attached to. He didn't want her or anybody else depending too much on him. He suddenly felt claustrophobic. "Alison? You know what?"

"What?" She must have guessed his thoughts because her face fell. "What's wrong?"

"Nothing. I don't know. Maybe there is. It's just that, well, I was thinking you should go back to your apartment. Now that this case is all wrapped up, you aren't in any danger. I've got a lot of unwinding to do and I don't think I'm going to be very good company."

Alison looked hurt. "Was it something I said?"

"No, no." He tried to sound calm, but it was hard when his nerves were so raw. "I think you're terrific, but I'm really tired and I need to be alone right now. I hope you can understand."

"Sure," she said. Still, he could hear the hurt in her voice. She got up from the couch and started gathering her things from the living room floor.

"Now don't go away mad," he said, reaching for her.

She pulled away. "Don't."

Alison picked up her clothes, magazines, and tennis shoes and stuffed them into her backpack. "Thanks for letting me stay here," she said as made a beeline for the door. "I guess I'll see you around."

"Alison," he called to her.

She stopped for a minute, her hand on the doorknob. "What?"

He tried to give her an encouraging smile, but he wasn't sure he succeeded. All he could think about was lying down and sleeping for two days. "I'll talk to you soon."

"Yeah, sure, whatever," she said.

Her departure left a leaden silence hanging in the air, thick with her pain and his guilt.

Goode decided to take a bath, one of those relaxation techniques they taught in stress management class. A sergeant had strongly suggested that he take one a few years back after he lost his temper. As the tub was filling with water, he went into the cabinet under the sink to find a new bar of soap. In the back corner, he saw the bottle of bubble bath Miranda had left behind. He'd been unable to bring himself to throw it away for the past six years, using it periodically to test his reaction when he smelled her scent again. The label was so faded he couldn't even tell what kind it was anymore. He undid the top, took a sniff, and smiled. He'd finally reached the point where he truly felt nothing. So he tossed it soundly into the small plastic trash bin next to the toilet.

"You are dead to me," he said triumphantly.

After cooling the bath with a little cold water, he got in. The temperature was just right, a tad hotter than he could stand.

Goode leaned his head back, held his nose and submerged his face under the water. As his mind replayed the images of his mother and then Clover stepping into the nothingness, he wished again that he hadn't been so helpless to stop them. Then the words of the Camus essay he'd been reading came back to him: "It is . . . hard to be satisfied with a single way of seeing, to go without contradiction, perhaps the most subtle of all spiritual forces. The preceding merely defines a way of thinking. But the point is to live."

People defined life, thinking, and spirituality so very differently. Often, they didn't even agree on whether life was worth living. Norman Klein was no Albert Camus, but at that moment, his words held a significance for Goode that was just as weighty.

Some people just don't want to be saved.

Goode scooted up and back so that his head rested against the wall, the words echoing in his head. He inhaled deeply, listening to his own breathing, and let it all out. Finally, as he visualized the guilt flowing out of his ears and into the sudsy water, his mind began to loosen and the tension slowly drifted away.

Chapter Fifty-one

Norman

It was early evening by the time Norman got back to the office. He knew the editors would be upset he hadn't called to warn them he had a huge story coming, but he'd lost his cell phone somewhere on the cliffs. His upper body was sticky with sweat from the ordeal and his hair was stuck to his forehead in curly wisps. His appearance merely reflected what he had been through: a near-death experience, perfect for page one.

Norman saw Al and Big Ed sitting at their computers, sharing a big bag of chips as they both were reading Jerry's story about the press conference. At first, Al refused to acknowledge his presence. Norman stood patiently, waiting for him to look up, but Al was playing his usual power game. He was going to make Norman wait until he was good and ready to stop what he was doing. Big Ed, too.

"So glad you decided to join us," Al said, finally looking up from the screen. "We saw you being interviewed on the news and we've only been calling you for the past two hours. Why the hell didn't you call in? Don't you know it's our story before it's theirs?"

"I lost my cell when that woman tried to kill me, chief, but I've got tons of stuff they won't have on TV. It's an amazing story," Norman said, trying to restrain his enthusiasm. Dammit. He deserved to gush. But the editors didn't seem to care that he had almost been pulled over a cliff to his death.

"Yeah?" Big Ed said. "I'll believe it when I see it."

"Clover Ziegler jumped off a cliff. And she almost took me with her," he said in desperation.

"Yeah, we know," Al said. "But even so, you're going to have to pull yourself together. It's getting close to deadline and we need a story. Are you up to writing it? Or do we need to have Jerry interview you and insert it in the story he's already turned in?"

"No, I'm fine," he said. "This is my story and I'm going to write it. We can insert the stuff that Jerry got from the press conference and give him a tagline."

"Fine," Big Ed said. "Then get the hell to it. Since it happened to you, you won't need to worry about getting yourself to go on the record. Ha."

Norman felt relieved that they were finally joking with him. "I've got it all right here," he said, tapping on the side of his head.

"Well, I should hope so," Al said. He paused for a moment. "So, what's your lead?"

"Maybe we can work one out together," Norman said, hoping to make Al feel a part of the story and draw him in. Big Ed gave him a salute, as if to say, "You two go for it."

Norman made a few more calls to check some facts, then Al shooed everyone away so the two of them could sit together at the computer and craft the story. Norman told his tale, and for the first time ever, he captured the city editor's attention. It was better than sex, no question about it. Al even blew off Jerry, who came over at one point to see if he could help. Al told him to go home; they had it under control. When they were done, Norman had to admit that he couldn't have written it as well without Al.

Afterward, Norman invited Tommy to celebrate at an Italian place next door to the Tavern. He could hardly hold in his ego, it had expanded so much. He was looking forward to a late dinner of antipasto salad, spaghetti bolognaise, and at least one bottle of Chianti. They arrived just after nine thirty and were seated right away.

"Do you know if Lulu is working at the Tavern tonight?" Norman asked the waiter.

"Lulu? She quit today. Something about a baby on the way."

Norman felt a sinking feeling in his stomach. "You're kidding," he said as calmly as he could manage. "Who's the father?"

"You know that guy she's been seeing, the prison guard?" The waiter, who knew Norman from his many meals there, leaned over and whispered, "Well, from what I hear, it's not his."

Norman gulped, a difficult task given the huge lump in the back of his throat. "Give us a minute, will you?"

"Sure."

Norman turned to Tommy. "Can you believe that? He's got to be lying. She's not that kind of girl."

Tommy put his hand on Norman's shoulder and said, "Buddy, I didn't want to burst the bubble you've been blowing for months, but yes, she is."

Norman shook off Tommy's hand. "Yeah, whatever. We're supposed to be celebrating, here. Forget the Chianti. Let's get something serious, like some Jack Daniels. Where's that waiter?"

Chapter Fifty-two

Goode

Once Jake's attorney realized that the police had his client cold, he tried to make a deal with the DA to try to save Jake from death by lethal injection at San Quentin. The DA said he wasn't making any promises, but he might be more lenient if Jake gave a full confession and held back no details. The nation wanted to know why he'd killed those people. Goode didn't see how the DA could withhold the death penalty and still get reelected, but he did what he was told. Only Jake didn't really want to confess to cold-blooded murder.

"It was an accident," he told Goode in the jailhouse interview room. "Tania and I had this hot night at a strip club a couple of weeks back, and then to see her from the kitchen, dancing with that asshole, Friday night . . . It just ate me up inside. So, on Saturday night, I decided to go over to her apartment and warn her about what a womanizer and a prick Seth was."

Goode nodded, thinking how familiar Jake's reaction sounded. He had experienced similar feelings as he'd read Tania's diary. Why had she picked such jerks?

"We were talking in her living room and she didn't look well, so I asked her what was wrong. She said she felt groggy, but all she could remember was going next door with her neighbor and then waking up sometime later in his dark apartment. I told her I had just what she needed, and offered her some meth to perk her up. I was thinking I had a few other things to offer her, too," he said, acting like this was a big joke. Nudge, nudge, wink, wink. Smart man to smart man.

Goode couldn't take his tone. "Don't you have any conscience, you little freak?" he said, lunging at him across the table. He grabbed Jake by the collar of his orange jumpsuit and yanked.

"Dude! Calm down," Jake said, startled, as he tried to pull back in the chair. He couldn't move much, though, because his hands were cuffed behind him.

Goode let go of him and sat back down. "Show a little respect," he said curtly.

"Okay, okay," Jake said, taking a deep breath before he went on. "So at first she wasn't sure she wanted to do it. She said she'd never tried meth before and didn't really want to be high when she met up with Seth that night. Well, it was my plan for her to hang out with me all night. So I told her about the incredible euphoria—not to mention the intense sexual energy—she would feel if she snorted some. And that's how I got her to try it."

Goode nodded. Sounded true so far.

"But then, after doing like three lines, she stopped breathing all of a sudden. I freaked out, but then I got a hold of myself and started doing CPR. Only she just lay there. All I could think was that I couldn't let my life end like this. I had big plans. I was going to medical school to become a surgeon. But I got scared that no one would believe she died on her own, and they'd blame me for overdosing her or something. So my first impulse was to make it look like someone else killed her. Everyone had seen her with Seth on Friday night and she was supposed to go out with him that night, too, so I decided he was my best bet. I yanked the lamp cord out of the wall and pulled it around her neck to make it look like she was strangled to death. Then I also thought I should make it look like a sexual crime, so I ripped off her panties and put them in the trash. Then I carried her down to the alley. I figured the coke on her table was leftover from the night before, that you'd find out Seth was selling coke at Pumphouse, and that would be that. I remembered later that I'd left some meth on the table, but I figured coke is often cut with meth, and Seth would get blamed for it all anyway.

"So I went back to the alley on Sunday to see what was going on and there you were. But I thought that all went pretty cool, so I wasn't worried. Then on Monday night, I was taking a break at Pumphouse, when Clover came in and poured out this big sob story, that Seth did her, then he did Sharona and then he did Tania, right in front of her. I'd been hanging out some with Sharona, too, so that didn't sit too well with me either. So I went over to Sharona's apartment to shoot the shit and get high with her. I was coming down hard from the night before and was feeling a little strung out. We were talking about what had happened and she was defending Seth, saying he wouldn't do this because he was actually a good guy if you got to know him. She had just done a couple lines of coke on the counter and I tried to kiss her, but she pushed me away, and I guess that just set me off. Things were so fucked-up already and they just kept escalating. The next thing I knew I was strangling her and she wasn't breathing anymore."

"Why Sharona? What did she ever do to you?"

"It was the meth, man. I didn't even know what I was doing. . . . So then I started wracking my brain what to do next."

Goode tried to remain expressionless, but it was extremely difficult. Despite his claim of accidental death, and blaming his plight on methamphetamine, Jake did not sound even remotely remorseful. "Go on," he snapped.

"I knew Jack wouldn't snitch me out to the police about selling meth at Pumphouse because we talked about it, and he said he thought this would all blow over once Seth was sent away and we could get back to the business at hand."

"Good thinking," Goode said wryly.

"Yeah, well, I thought I was in the clear. But then Keith comes to me in the Pumphouse parking lot the night after Tania's funeral as I was about to go into work and says he wants to talk to me. He says he had it all figured out, and the sucky thing—for him, anyway—is that he did. So I had no choice. I shot him. He said he was on his way to tell you all about it."

So Keith was smarter than Goode had given his credit for, the poor schmuck.

"That's when I decided to send a letter to Norman Klein at the *Sun-Dispatch*, and make it sound like Clover wrote it. I figured since Sharona was Clover's friend and Seth had just slept with her, you guys would have your hands full figuring out who did what to who and why, but you'd focus on Seth and then Clover, and not on me. So then I turned on the charm for Clover's maid and went upstairs to put Keith's ring, Sharona's hair, and Tania's fingernails in that box. Dude, I thought I was golden."

Goode shook his head. The guy was clearly not thinking rationally, and being a meth-addled sociopath did not a defense make.

"So, seriously. What was it?" Jake asked earnestly. He really did want to know. As if it were an academic test he wanted to improve on the next time. "How did I blow this whole thing?"

Goode paused long and hard, for effect as much as anything else. "You thought you were smarter than everybody else. And that mistake, my friend, is worth at least a life sentence. But I've got to tell you, a lethal injection is more likely."

Chapter Fifty-three

Goode

The moon was just shy of being full as Goode walked the length of Crystal Pier. The water glistened as the two-foot waves gently broke against the pilings underneath. It felt very peaceful there.

When he got to the end of the pier, he kneeled and set his cappuccino—decaf—on the ground in front of him. Then he pulled his wallet from his back pocket and slipped the photos out of their slot. They were warm in his hand as he opened up the two folded ones and laid them out in a row next to the faded shot of his mother. She really did have a bizarre resemblance to Tania. It was almost surreal. He put his mom back into her resting place, and then, after a few moments, also replaced the photo of Alison. As he stared at Tania's smiling face in the moonlight, he could feel her presence there with him. He also swore he could detect the fleeting sweet scent of gardenias.

"I hope you've found some peace, Tania," he said. Almost as if on cue, he felt a warmth come over him and a sense of serenity.

"Good," he said. "I'm glad. Then my work is done."

Goode wished he'd brought a gardenia in her memory, but all he had was the photo. So he slowly ripped it up into a handful of little pieces and then tossed them over the side. He watched them flutter down to the water and then sink, forming sequined bubbles that reflected the light of the moon.

As the water swallowed the shreds of photo, Goode felt his obsession with her go down with them. Tania had died young, but she seemed to have lived more than most. Even in death, she'd taught him that life was about taking chances. He also felt the guilt in not being able to save Clover recede as well. She wanted to be free and now, hopefully, she was.

He pictured Alison's cute, lopsided smile, her curly golden hair and the scared-deer look in her eyes that had begun to dissipate as he gained her trust. He wanted to see her happy, but he wasn't going to let her draw him into her problems and he wasn't going to try and save her from them. Not this time. He figured it would be best for both of them if they took it slow and hung out as friends for a while, at least until they knew if there was a chance for something real. He didn't want to be another man who hurt her.

He never thought it would happen, but the dead feeling inside him had gone. All this real-life stuff still made him want to sprint home and hide. But he'd already decided he wasn't going to run anymore. He was going to sit right there and watch the sequined lady dance.

AUTHOR'S NOTE AND ACKNOWLEDGMENTS

Before I get into the meat of what I want to say here, I should caution readers that they probably ought to wait to read this note until after they finish the novel or it may give away parts of the story. Your choice.

This book started off as a short story inspired by a news article I wrote when I was a staff writer for the *Springfield Union-News* and living in Northampton, Mass. After writing more than 2,000 news stories during my twenty-year career as a daily newspaper reporter, I barely remember the details now. But I do remember this: a young woman, who happened to be an old friend of my then-boyfriend, was murdered in New York City and my boyfriend took me to her wake. That true-crime story worked as a creative catalyst that led me to create the character of Tania and the plot built from there. (Tania, by the way, is not based on the young woman I wrote about in the newspaper, whom I never met. For that matter, no character in this book is modeled on a real person.)

Even though I've spent much of my journalism career covering government and politics, I've always been interested in stories about bizarre deaths, the psychology of the criminal mind, murders, and suicide in particular. I've been drawn to stories involving addiction not only because I've dealt with those issues in my own family, but also because it's such a devastating problem in our society. Ironically, I conceived of this plot far before I met my late husband, who turned out to be an alcoholic and ultimately committed suicide. Sometimes, it seems as though I have this strange power to foresee the future as I craft my fictional tales. A good friend of mine often jokes that the next time I write about some lottery numbers, I should share them with him.

Before I crafted the final version of this novel, I gained a good deal of new insight into my pet themes—addiction, suicide and murder—by covering the fascinating Kristin Rossum murder case at the *San Diego Union-Tribune*, where I was an investigative reporter until September 2006. The Rossum case led me to pursue my first non-fiction book, *Poisoned Love*, which came out in July 2005. Rossum was convicted of poisoning her husband with the powerful narcotic painkiller fentanyl after staging his death to look like a suicide scene while high on methamphetamine. The jury didn't believe her story that he sprinkled red rose petals over himself in bed before taking a fatal dose of fentanyl.

As I continued to write and rewrite *Naked Addiction*, I took courses in fiction writing and screenwriting, participated in writing workshops, and attended numerous writing conferences. At the same time, I was also honing my investigative reporting skills and learning to craft stories that read like fiction but were factually-based, a narrative style that proved to be symbiotic with my creative writing. These skills have now coalesced and grown to support each other; however, I am still very conscious of the line that separates fact and fiction.

Of course, I've read hundreds and hundreds of books over the years, but I was most inspired to write in this genre by reading thrillers, particularly those by Michael Connelly and Patricia Cornwell, and most recently by Jess Walter. As my writing worlds have been intersecting, it just so happens that Cornwell has come up in both of my nonfiction books, the second of which will be released in 2008. It is the story of two married FBI agents, Margo and Gene Bennett, a lesbian love triangle with Cornwell, a kidnapping and an attempted murder. And yes, it's all true.

Now I'd like to thank the many people who have provided professional and emotional support and feedback over all the years that this novel has been in the making. Because I started writing it so long ago, I cannot possibly list everyone, and I hope no one will be offended if I've left him or her out inadvertently. This book has changed significantly and has passed through many readers since I finished the first draft at least a dozen years ago.

Michael Connelly deserves special thanks not only for agreeing to read this book before I even had a publisher, but also for giving me a most helpful critique, which I then used to redraft and modify this book into the version you are now reading. I also used his sage and gracious advice as I crafted a sequel to this book, which I was still writing when I wrote this note.

Susan White, my favorite editor and a dear friend, has been a great help and source of support, teaching me how to write in the narrative form and for reading I don't know how many drafts of *Naked Addiction* over the years.

Samuel Autman has provided me with the emotional, professional and spiritual support that has been unmatched to date. Samuel, you have been a godsend, an angel and an inspiration.

My mother, Carole Scott, a voracious reader of this genre, with whom I was long scared to share my fiction (per the advice of my first writing workshop leader), recently has proven to be an astute reader who makes insightful comments and offers constructive criticism, in addition to being my favorite mother. Thanks also to my stepfather Chris Scott for his support and comments as a reader.

I'd also like to thank the following people:

Bob Koven, for listening to me read and tell my stories by phone and in person since time began, and for his many years of generosity and friendship.

Laurie Agnew of the San Diego Police Department, a real-life homicide detective whom I met while writing *Poisoned Love*, who helped me by providing police procedural and other investigative feedback.

My agent, Gary Heidt, for agreeing to take on a first-time novelist and to Stephany Evans, for making that possible by taking me on as a first-time author.

Jon Sidener, for his friendship, support, Web site and computer help, as well as his reader's comments.

Anne Dierickx, my friend and legal adviser, another voracious reader, for always being the first to finish and for giving me helpful tips.

Ted Ladd, Seth Taylor, Arthur Salm, Anna Cearley, Tony Manolatos, George Varga, and Jeanne Freeman-Brooks, for their reader's comments on the earlier versions.

Dr. Harry Bonnell, for his help with the forensics and toxicology of the drugs involved in this story.

Detective Randy Aldridge, also of the SDPD, for answering my questions about homicide relief teams, narcotics detectives who want to move into homicide, and methamphetamine manufacturing.

Authors Alan Russell and Jennifer Egan, for sharing their knowledge, encouragement and suggestions at UCSD and the Bread Loaf writing conference, respectively.

Don D'Auria and the other folks at Dorchester, for publishing my first novel, which, if all goes well, will be just the beginning of a long series of books.

Robert Rother, for his patience and perennial computer support.

Finally, thanks to the rest of my family and close friends for listening to the ups and downs of breaking into publishing all these years, with special appreciation to Kathy Glass, Kathy Brunet Eagan, Maureen Magee, Jeff McDonald, John McCutchen, Michael Stetz, Ron Powell and Alexa Capeloto.

Michael Siverling

The Sterling Inheritance

Private investigator Jason Wilder has the toughest boss in town: his mother. Working in the detective agency his mother founded is always exciting, but sometimes it can be downright dangerous. Like the case he's on now. All he was supposed to do was locate a missing businessman. But when he found the guy in a run-down motel, Jason never expected him to start shooting. He also didn't know the man was wanted for homicide. Now it's too late. Jason is right in the middle of the case, and the only way out is to see it through to the end. His search for answers will lead him down some deadly, twisting roads…and to a dilapidated movie house that people seem willing to fight—and maybe even kill—for.

ISBN 13: 978-0-8439-6002-0

THE
WATER
CLOCK

JIM KELLY

A mutilated body found frozen in a block of ice. A second body perched high in a cathedral, riding a gargoyle—hidden for more than thirty years. When forensic evidence links both victims to one crime, reporter Philip Dryden knows he's on to a terrific story. What he doesn't know is that his search for the truth will involve a mystery from his own past. As his investigation gets increasingly urgent, he will come face-to-face with his deepest fears…and a cold-blooded killer.

ISBN 13: 978-0-8439-6000-6

SIMON WOOD

PAYING THE PIPER

He was known as the Piper—a coldhearted kidnapper who terrified the city. Crime reporter Scott Fleetwood built his career on the Piper. The kidnapper even taunted the FBI through Scott's column. But Scott had been duped. The person he'd been speaking to wasn't really the Piper. By the time the FBI exposed the hoaxer, time ran out...and the real Piper killed the child. Then he vanished. But now he's back, with very specific targets in mind—Scott's children.

ISBN 10: 0-8439-5980-0
ISBN 13: 978-0-8439-5980-2

To order a book or to request a catalog call:
1-800-481-9191
This book is also available at your local bookstore, or you can check out our Web site **www.dorchesterpub.com** where you can look up your favorite authors, read excerpts, or glance at our discussion forum to see what people have to say about your favorite books.

THE WHITE TOWER

DOROTHY JOHNSTON

It's a mother's nightmare come true. Moira Howley's son, Niall, has been found dead at the base of a communications tower. While the authorities are content to consider it a suicide, Moira won't accept that. She knows only another mother could understand....

Crime consultant Sandra Mahoney is Moira's only hope. While juggling her own daughter, a lover, and an annoying ex-husband, Sandra will travel halfway around the world in search of the truth—a truth hidden by a web of deceit, manipulation...and murder.

ISBN 13: 978-0-8439-5936-9

SWEETIE'S DIAMONDS

RAYMOND BENSON

Diane Boston is a suburban mom with a secret. As her son discovered when he found an unmarked videotape, Diane had a former life as Lucy Luv, star of hardcore adult films. Somehow word of Diane's past has hit the streets, and now all hell has broken loose. Sure, the high school where Diane teaches is upset, but that's the least of her worries. It seems that when Lucy Luv mysteriously disappeared, she took a cache of stolen diamonds with her. And a West Coast porn czar with strong mob ties wants them back. With interest.

ISBN 13: 978-0-8439-5859-1

GATES OF HADES

GREGG LOOMIS

Jason Peters works for Narcom, a company that handles jobs too dangerous or politically risky for U.S. intelligence agencies. But when his house is attacked and he barely escapes the smok-ing wreckage, he knows this new case is out of the ordinary, even for him.

Jason will travel the globe—from Washington, D.C., to the Dominican Republic, to the volcanoes of Sicily—in a desperate race to uncover the ancient secret that lies at the heart of an unimaginable—and very deadly—plot.

ISBN 13: 978-0-8439-5894-2

COVET

TARA MOSS

Makedde Vanderwall has done something few women can claim—she survived a terrifying ordeal at the hands of the sadistic Stiletto Murderer. Eighteen months later, she has steeled her nerve to confront him again at his trial. But her worst nightmare comes to life when the killer escapes, aided by an accomplice no one could have suspected. The Stiletto Murderer has only one goal now…to find Mak and finish what he started.

WILLIAM P. WOOD

STAY OF EXECUTION

Bobby Carnes was just a small-time crook until he walked out of a drug deal carrying a .44 and leaving four dead bodies behind him. Now Carnes is up for trial, and LA County District Attorney George Keegan is handling the prosecution personally.

For Keegan, there's a lot more on the line than just winning another case. A high-profile trial like this will be sure to gain him wide-spread media coverage right in the middle of a tough reelection campaign. But it could all blow up in his face if he loses his star witness. If Keegan doesn't play this perfectly, his career will be finished—and a vicious killer will go free.

ISBN 13: 978-0-8439-5704-4
